I0562206

MICHAEL ATAMANOV

GAME
CHANGER

*Wishing you safe travels on
your fantasy journey,*

Michael Atamanov

REALITY BENDERS
BOOK THREE

MAGIC DOME BOOKS

All books
by Michael Atamanov:

TABLE OF CONTENTS:

Introduction

The Enemy's Plans

"CONSEQUENTLY, honorable Coruler Thumor-Anhu La-Fin, our strategists deemed that plan unsatisfactory as well. Our troops would get bogged down in the enemy defenses and be unable to achieve their objectives in anything resembling a reasonable timeframe. We would completely lose the element of surprise. Then, the enemy would reinforce, and it would all be over."

With a wave of his hand, the young Mage Diviner Mac-Peu Un-Roi dismissed the hovering helper drone that had been giving him cues for his speech. He then

1

gave a respectful bow to his leader and rejoined the dozens of other advisors, allowing the Coruler to see the map and think things over at his leisure. The great mage Thumor-Anhu La-Fin, one of humanity's three Corulers, was feeling peevish today and, with each subsequent report, his face went gloomier and gloomier. But this time, he had no criticism. Despite Un-Roi's young age, he was considered one of the most talented soothsayers of modern times. He was so renowned for his deep multilayered analysis of the lines of fate that his predictions were simply taken at face value.

The Coruler didn't take long to consider the information on the tactical screen and soon swiped it away with a wave of his hand, returning the map to its initial state. With obvious strain, bracing his trembling arms on his magic staff, the aged Thumor-Anhu stood from his chairman's seat and walked on his stiff legs up to the glowing screen on the wall. The ghoulish old mage spent three minutes looking from the tactical map back to his ever more flustered advisors as they crumbled in fear. Finally, the great mage spoke, not even trying to hide his dismay:

"So am I to understand that, even with a three-fold advantage in manpower, a rapid-response air force and a battalion of nearly indestructible armored vehicles, my advisors still cannot find a single path to victory? Do you really think I will simply accept that?! You know, it might be time for me to really shake things up around here! After all, it seems none of my advisors are fit for the task at hand!"

The all-powerful mage furrowed his brows severely and, turning his gaze from one advisor to the next, read their emotions with ease: terror, indignation at unjust criticism (that was Mac-Peu Un-Roi), exhaustion and annoyance with his fickle manner, even some hate. No matter, fear of one's superiors was the natural order of things, utterly normal. It was even acceptable for underlings to hate their lord and think him a despot unless that enmity became strong enough to serve as a limiting factor. Most importantly, Thumor-Anhu did not sense any treason or intentional sabotage. His advisors had not deceived him. They really did not see a route to speedy victory over the Human-3 Faction.

After calming down a bit, Coruler Thumor-Anhu returned to his seat and asked his advisors to review the scenarios he had criticized the least. The First Advisor approached the glowing screen, leaning on a crooked knotty staff. The once fearsome combat mage Avir-Syn La-Pirez was far past his prime but he was still the right hand of the Coruler both in the real world and the game that bends reality.

The great Mage fully trusted his First Advisor, who he considered his closest friend and basically a relative. Thumor-Anhu La-Fin's only daughter, the unearthly beauty Princess Onessa-Rati had been married to Avir-Syn's grandson, but they both perished in a terror attack orchestrated by enemy mages. However, the couple were survived by a daughter, Princess Minn-O La-Fin. Though not wealthy or too influential, the La-Pirez dynasty was ancient and proud and if Thumor-Anhu were to pass unexpectedly, they would be Princess Minn-O's only source of protection and support. The Coruler always bore that in mind and so tried to maintain good relations with the First Advisor and his kin.

Meanwhile, the doddering old Mage Avir-Syn slurped down two magical strength elixirs, not ashamed to consume them in full public view. After that, he set his heavy staff aside. The old man was not accustomed to new-fangled antigrav helper drones so, as in days of yore, he picked up a remote control and a laser pointer.

"Of the plans elaborated by my colleagues, just two warrant further consideration. The first: try another blitz through the muck of the swamp hexagon. That proved quite ineffective ten days ago, but we could consider our errors and, instead of spreading our forces out along the whole front, concentrate on destroying the enemy citadel. Our three and a half thousand soldiers will surely be enough to overcome the enemy's staggered defenses and occupy the oil-rich territory."

"Stop right there!" said the great mage, interrupting his ancient friend and advisor. "As I already said, I will not allow all our troops to all be used in one attack! It is unthinkable and crosses all bounds of reasonable risk, giving our enemy a chance to score cheap points! I can hardly believe that the militarily erudite H3 Faction, will just stand calmly by and watch us devastate their hexagon. More likely, they will take advantage of our unguarded borders and mount a counterattack!"

"Exactly!" came an invited military expert, supporting the leader's objection. "As soon as we start trying to erect pontoons, the enemy will rain fire on us. Our armor will be destroyed or get stuck in the mud like last time. And while thousands of our players trudge from landmark to landmark through waist-deep muck, struggling to keep their weapons clean, the enemy will burst into the grain or capital hexagon and destroy infrastructure we cannot afford to lose! Last time, they were able to do just as much damage with one lone raiding party as we did with our whole assault. But this time, the enemy has hundreds of galloping centaurs at their beck and call and many raiding groups. Sure, we may capture the swamp hexagon, but it will come at the cost of our most productive and developed lands! And then our faction's position will be truly hopeless!"

"The most we can allocate to any assault without risking disaster is two thousand three hundred soldiers," said Thumor-Anhu La-Fin, setting a concrete limit. The advisors then got back to thinking.

For a long time, no one said anything. They were

all too immersed in calculations and studying the lines of fate. Finally, the prolonged silence was broken by the youngest advisor, Mage Diviner Mac-Peu Un-Roi:

"With an assault force of that size, the likelihood of capturing the grain hexagon is just eighteen percent. Given that is the most promising vector of attack, the enemy will be expecting us there. So, I'm sure that not only will their previous fortifications be rebuilt, they will also have new lines of defense, firing points and mine fields. There is more than an eighty percent chance that our first attack wave will be entirely wiped out... but then, I must admit, there is something in the lines of fate I cannot read... My guess is that the enemy will set some kind of trap. In any case, the probability of our faction holding the swamp hexagon for more than three days is exactly zero. It is unfeasible to supply a garrison there, and that hexagon is too near the enemy capital. I'm afraid nothing can be done about that."

After such an unambiguous statement, continuing to discuss the clearly hopeless plan was no use, and Thumor-Anhu ordered the alternative brought up on screen. The First Advisor eagerly switched scenarios, and the colored markers and arrows on the map changed position.

"A more promising plan is to launch a concentrated mass attack on the unfinished enemy fortress in the Rocky Shores. Then, without losing speed, we could push toward the enemy capital and try to penetrate as deep as possible before they come to their senses and stop our advance. This plan does have certain downsides, though. Above all, after our recent unsuccessful attempts to use NPC's against the enemy fort in the Rocky Shores, they beefed up their garrison and are still on high alert. And we shouldn't expect the element of surprise either, so our losses in the first stage of battle will be extreme. What's more, the dreaded Second Legion is in charge of defense there..."

"Gerd Tamara..." Thumor-Anhu said with vexation, spitting out the hated name.

"Yes, precisely. The enemy Paladin will be there, and the new Priests will be with her. That means their soldiers will have mental protection, so magic attacks will be of precious little use. Everything will be decided by brute force and firepower, but at least we have..."

The speaker sharply fell silent and gave a low bow because the door suddenly flew open and Princess Minn-O La-Fin strode quickly into the chamber. The Coruler's granddaughter usually preferred not to wear official dress, which was a bright and loud proclamation of membership in a ruling mage dynasty. She had to wear it for official functions, but she generally changed into something less gaudy at the first opportunity. Her personal style placed more emphasis on comfort and beauty. But today she was wearing a dress of the proper cut in her own home with all the regalia befitting a Princess of her stature.

Everyone was struck by the change, and the

great mage Thumor-Anhu no less so. He watched with satisfaction as all members of the council bowed respectfully and even obsequiously to his beloved granddaughter, even though she had no magical gift and thus could not claim a high position in society. That deference was new. Well to be fair, they had always treated Minn-O with elementary politeness, but this was the first time there was anything even close to true esteem. That meant there must have been a leak. Everyone clearly knew the beautiful Princess now had a husband with magical abilities and, consequently, expected that Minn-O would soon give birth to a mage of the great regnant house La-Fin. Or perhaps — the old mage gave a sad sigh, remembering his one hundred and eighty years of age — she would even be regent if her child were to be elevated to the throne before coming of age.

"Honorable mages, your suggestions for the upcoming battle have been taken into consideration, but now I need time to think them over and come to a decision. And I know just the person to help. Extend an invitation to General Ui-Taka, self-proclaimed monarch of the Second Directory! I want to find out if he really is as good a strategist and commander as they say."

"Hrmm..." Thumor-Anhu's last order baffled his advisors. They started exchanging glances, not hiding their incomprehension. "But General Ui-Taka is an illegitimate pretender, not acknowledged by the council of rulers. Would the honorable Coruler Thumor-Anhu like the rebellious General dragged here by force?"

Minn-O couldn't hold back and snickered, imagining an attempt to arrest a commander surrounded by hundreds of unwaveringly loyal soldiers. Coruler Thumor-Anhu turned to his granddaughter, furrowed his brow severely and she immediately stopped giggling.

"No, we mustn't be rude. The General is popular in the armed forces, and we would like to keep our soldiers happy. I would like to invite him to my palace as a guest and military expert. I'm quite sure the first non-mage to rule in eight hundred years will be eager to pay me a visit. He is desperate for recognition from other rulers, so I'm sure Ui-Taka will not only show up, he will be on his best behavior and do whatever I ask. But now, honorable mages, please forgive me, I must speak with Princess Minn-O."

A minute later, only the old mage and his beloved granddaughter were left in the chamber. Thumor-Anhu even got up from his seat and went over to close the doors a bit tighter to make sure no one was eavesdropping.

"So, Minn-O, I see that you have news. Tell me! The enemy Gerd Gnat has visited your prison cell again. Did I guess right? Has he made any specific promises on when you are to be freed?"

"Prison cell?!" the Princess feigned surprise. "Thumor-Anhu, for the last hour and a half, I have been flying into deep space on a Geckho vessel!"

The expression of surprise and confusion on the wise mage's wrinkled face was so unnatural and silly looking that the Princess couldn't help it and broke down laughing. He was used to knowing the future, so this caught him off guard. But the old man quickly came to his senses and connected the dots:

"So, Gnat's Geckho friends came to get him, and your husband has taken you with him into space!"

"Yes! Grandpa, you told me a number of times that Gnat is exceptional, and the Geckho bring only him into the cosmos. But that is only partially true. The Geckho do adore Gnat, and practically wait on him hand and foot. If only you knew how happy the crew was to see him! The Geckho bared their teeth and rumbled so loud that, if I hadn't studied their body language, I'd have thought they were going to devour my husband! But Gerd Gnat is not the only one! There's a whole band of enemies there. I counted at least four! Gnat himself, then a Pilot, a Space Commando, and a Gladiator you said was Gnat's friend. And that is if I don't count the two little Miyelonians Gnat keeps around for some reason. With them, it's a whole squadron! In fact, I found it strange he didn't bring his lover."

"Well, Anna the Medic would never have gone..." the old mage suddenly stumbled midsentence, having reconsidered explaining some finer points and sharply changed topic. No, that was beyond the mind of a mere mortal. "And actually, that leaves Anna in an interesting position. For the first time, we found a person the wary Gnat let get close. We'll see what comes of that. You shouldn't be counting the Miyelonians out either. Do you know what that modest looking Translator did yesterday?"

Minn-O shook her head. She had spent the last two days in a prison cell and had no way of knowing what happened on the outside.

"That bushy-tailed stinker led a combat training session for the First and Second Legions! I don't know how she did it, but my informants all say she significantly improved the elite troops. Even their highest-level player Gerd Tarasov leveled up twice! It's simply unbelievable! And here I am crawling out of my skin trying to train an army before the battle and at least somewhat narrow the level and skill gap. Now that little Translator has brought it all to naught!"

The old man could barely contain his burbling emotions. The top of his magical staff even started to glow with seething energy. Just in case, the Princess took a step back. That way, if some death spell spilled out, at least it wouldn't hit her. Her loving grandpa would never hurt her on purpose, but the dread old man was known to accidentally burn holes in walls or splash random servants and robots with his rage.

In order to distract her grandfather from the burdensome thoughts, Minn-O started to tell him about her space voyage so far. She was not staying in the same bunk as Gnat as she assumed, but in a bunk with some Geckho merchant whose thick black fur was mottled with unnatural white spots. After the prison cell, Minn-O's only clothing had been a track suit and pair of slippers.

"Gnat noticed that and brought me a ladies' spacesuit before takeoff. But when he held it up to me, he shook his head, called me a giraffe and said that he would give the spacesuit to the ship Mechanic to have it brought out. And Gnat gave me weapons, one of our common laser pistols, maybe even my old one and some antiquated hunting rifle. And believe it or not, it still shoots bullets not lasers! But it does have an ornately carved stock, a bunch of modifications, and its own name: Krechet! Oh yeah, I almost forgot, Gnat changed class from Prospector to Listener!"

The great mage, previously listening with measured interest to his granddaughter's chirping, sharply straightened up and raised his eyes:

"You're such a blockhead! You should have started with that, not the slippers and other crap! Tell me right away, what is this class? What bonuses does it give? And why did he change? Also, find out where the ship is going, why and what you should be doing. Definitely try and sniff out some info on the Miyelonians, too. Why are they with Gnat, are their services for hire and how much might that cost?"

Minn-O put on an unhappy grimace and, lifting the hem of the uncomfortable skirt, took a seat on the

12

edge of the high table and crossed her long legs.

"And why should I do that? I'm Gnat's wayedda now, so he's no longer my enemy... And that's at the very least! I'm legally married now, and I'll probably make friends with the Geckho and Gnat's pals soon enough. It was you that pushed me into his arms, so don't be surprised if my attitude toward this whole war starts to change! I will not be your spy!"

This came as an unpleasant surprise for the old mage. However, the Coruler Thumor-Anhu La-Fin knew the Princess very well, so he quickly found the right words:

"In that world, you are a sponger, dependent on a poor student. And he will treat you with apprehension his whole life. You will never truly belong there, and no one will ever trust you. Here, you are a proud Princess, a member of a ruling house and respected by all! If you play your cards right, you can climb the ranks higher and become much more important in our society. You may even be Coruler of humanity one day! Can you see the difference in your position between here and there? And you'd be making the same choice for your future children. They can either be Crown Princes and Princesses, the future rulers of mankind, or spend their lives as outcasts and pariahs, strange freaks on the margin of society!"

He probably could have stopped there. The experienced Psionic Thumor-Anhu could sense that he'd already hit his mark. But this issue was too serious to just let go, so he figured he needed to use a bit of mind control. The Princess wrinkled her nose, jumped off the table and, just like in early childhood, fell into the arms of her powerful grandpa, begging for consolation.

"I'm sorry, Thumor-Anhu, I was wrong! Of course, I will always remain loyal to house La-Fin and will do everything I can to bring victory to our faction and world! But Gnat is no longer a stranger to me. I think about him all the time and cannot do anything about that!!! Don't make me spy on him! You are a powerful and wise mage, so think up some way of getting Gnat over to our world. That's the best way to solve all this!"

The old man embraced his beloved granddaughter and reassured her, but his mind was on something else. Princess Minn-O was growing distant from him. A larger and larger part of her heart was occupied by this other man. Sure, today he could use mind control on her, but that would only get harder and harder. One day, Minn-O would break with him once and for all. The little pink bundle of joy bound with flowery ribbons he had taken from the arms of his mortally wounded daughter Onessa-Rati, the little girl he'd raised since birth, who he'd always thought of as small and unintelligent, had suddenly become adult...

At the same time, the experienced psionic only needed a small spurt of trust and openness to read all the information he needed from the Princess's mind.

Minn-O really did not know where the ship was heading and did not understand one iota of the Geckho-language conversations. The only curious information was a conversation she had overheard when four people from the H3 Faction had been quarreling in the next room over.

As it turned out, Gnat and his companions were not exactly burning with desire to fly off into space, and instead wanted to fight in the next day's big battle with the Dark Faction, which they now considered inevitable. His faction was respected by the enemies and even somewhat feared, but they were prepared to fight to the last drop of blood, then respawn and go back into battle. Anything but retreat. Hrm... Victory would not come easily...

On the one hand, what did the Mage Diviner say earlier...? The chance of success was just eighteen percent, and winning would mean just a temporary change of borders, not a serious shift in the war with the H3 Faction? This was proving a hard nut to crack. What was more, the enemy was expecting an attack, had even made allies and was more prepared for battle than ever. It was not the best time to go on the offensive, to put it lightly.

On the other hand, not attacking would mean showing a lack of confidence and that might work against the defeatist propaganda he'd been trying so hard to instill. What to do? They needed time to train their troops. And Thumor-Anhu needed long consultations with General Ui-Taka, the most experienced and fortunate strategist of the magical world. Hopefully, the two of them could find the key to the enemy's defenses. But how to achieve that without damaging his own authority?

The great mage gave his dear granddaughter another warm embrace and, smiling, looked the Princess right in her teary eyes:

"Minn-O, go back into the game and tell Gerd Gnat that I give your union my blessing! If your husband were here in our world, I would bequeath him the ancient palace of House La-Fin and two hundred servants at his beck and call. But Gnat is only in the game for now so, in honor of my daughter's wedding, I grant his pitiful faction an additional five days of cease-fire!"

Chapter One

Technical
Difficulties

FOR THE LAST FEW HOURS, I had been seeing messages on the inside of my helmet in the ancient Relict language. I couldn't read it, but it was all written in an alarming shade of red. Some of the symbols blinked, while some were particularly bright and others a bit dim. And now, another block of text had just shown up. The mysterious syntactic brambles weren't so much blocking my view as they were annoying me with the mere fact of their presence. And that was breaking my concentration. Earlier I had somehow managed to dismiss them, but every time was a big headache. I hadn't yet noticed any logic or pattern to how I made them go away, either. Maybe it was nothing I was doing, and the messages were just expiring. Or maybe, which would be much worse, the system was just automatically making important decisions for me because I had reached the time limit.

I tried to give all kinds of commands in every language I knew although, to be honest, I was trying to be quiet so my Miyelonian bunk mates wouldn't wake up. Well, actually just Ayni because Tini was now in the real world. I also tried using mental commands and even moving my pupils to dismiss the bothersome red symbols. For a minute nothing happened, then I saw something I could read:

The Break-in skill has been marked for deletion. Confirm? (Yes/No)

Just what I needed! I hurriedly removed the helmet of my Listener suit and just held it in my hands. I noticed before that the words would turn off if I wasn't wearing the helmet, just dissolving in the matte-black glass. And this time as well, without power from the nuclear battery in my backpack, the screen on the face shield started flickering and quickly went dim. With a sigh, I set the helmet aside.

Ugh, what a day I was having. Everything was topsy-turvy... First, I fought with Anya. Then I set off on a voyage with a Geckho crew to a war that had nothing to do with humanity. And I had no choice in the matter. It was "an offer you can't refuse," just like *The Godfather*. Even my closest and most loyal friends were not too delighted to be heading into space, as it meant we were deserting our friends right before a massively important battle. Just imagine what the rest of the faction would think... I suspected that was what caused the stinging three-point drop in my Authority.

Even our new leader Ivan Lozovsky couldn't hold back some unflattering comments, despite the fact he had promised me complete freedom. That said, I suspected the newly-minted Gerd was not so much upset I would miss the battle with the Dark Faction as he was that I had taken the high-level Morphian with me. Lozovsky was counting on it to kill enemy leaders. Yes, things had turned out poorly... Everyone was mad at me.

And what was more, my traveling mistress Minn-O was acting haughty and weird, not only avoiding conversations with Geckho and Humans but even shying away from me. Everything in her appearance betrayed that she felt alien and uncomfortable on this ship. Also, the light spacesuit I had asked Uraz Tukhsh to lend Minn-O La-Fin was too small. I had to spend all my remaining crystals and even go slightly into debt, asking my friend Uline for spare change so I could pay the ship Mechanic to have it refit for her lanky frame.

Captain Uraz Tukhsh was acting strange, too. Either he was embarrassed or admired me, but he never once came to talk to me in the many hours the Shiamiru spent on Earth, preferring to communicate through Uline. And on the starship, when I walked up to him to ask about the spacesuit, the captain clearly felt out of his comfort zone and agreed to everything quickly just to get me out of his cabin. It was unusual behavior for the haughty Aristocrat, to put it lightly. And I couldn't find an explanation.

And now my space suit was acting up... What a disaster... How could I play or do anything useful with all this ancient claptrap blocking my view? And I never knew when more might come! As if the class change was worth all this! With a certain trepidation, I glanced down at my troublesome helmet. I wondered if I had stopped it from deleting Break-in. Unfortunately, my game information was no help. It was strange too. Some of my skills were missing, as were Hitpoints and Magic Points. And it showed my game class as "changing:"

Gerd Gnat. Human. H3 Faction.	
Level-61 ??? class changing ???	
Statistics:	
Strength	13
Agility	17
Intelligence	23 ↓ 3
Perception	26
Constitution	15
Luck modifier	+3

Parameters:	
Hitpoints	1704 of ???
Endurance points	861 of 958
Magic points	237 of ???
Carrying capacity	58 lbs.
Fame	49
Skills:	
Electronics	41
&6%%##@@!	49
Cartography	52
Astrolinguistics	67
Break-in [inactive]	0 of 23
Rifles	45
Mineralogy [confirmation pending]	???
Medium Armor	44
Eagle Eye	59
Sharpshooter	28
Targeting	18
Danger Sense	28
Psionic [inactive, critically low value not compatible with class]	36
Mental Fortitude [inactive, critically low value not compatible with class]	27
Machine Control [inactive, critically low value not	12

compatible with class]	
Attention!!! You have nine unused skill points	

Ugh, my character was chopped to bits... The first thing that caught my eye was that the Scanning skill had been replaced with a collection of symbols. And the scanning symbol I had been using since my very first moments in the game was just gone, which made me queasy. Who had I become? Or who was I supposed to become? What were the features of my new class?

The once unavailable information on the Listener class could now be read, but only as columns of incomprehensible symbols, as if tech support (if such a thing even existed) had neglected to have it translated since the times of the Relicts. I had no one to complain to, so apparently I would have to figure it all out by trial and error. And that included class abilities, how to use my suit, reactivate missing skills, and read the Relict language. But I had to start from the beginning and fix whatever I could.

"Critically low value not compatible with game class." Maybe I could figure out what value would not be "critically low." And that was exactly what I decided to do, adding points one by one to the inactive Psionic skill. One, two, three... I had already started to worry that it was all for naught, and I wouldn't have enough points, but when the skill reached forty, the line changed from grayed-out back to normal:

Psionic	40

That's better, one problem down. Now it would be nice to pull Mental Fortitude and Machine Control out of inactivity as well. I looked at my five remaining points with sorrow. If I assumed that forty was what the other skills also needed, I wouldn't have enough. And that proved to be the case. I placed all five remaining points into Mental Fortitude, raising it to thirty-two, but nothing changed.

Alright, I was out of points so I'd need to work on another problem. For example, what did "Break-in [inactive]" mean? Probably it was because the skill was in the process of deletion. But how could I delete a skill? I basically thought that was theoretically impossible, and every skill a player took was forever. I knew for sure the game menu had no option for wiping a skill. I had combed through all the settings very carefully and never seen anything like that.

By the way, what was the difference between Break-in and Medium Armor? Why was the game system fine with the latter, but found fault with the former? Maybe a Listener was not supposed to break into things, because that went against their purpose. I already knew some professions couldn't use certain skills. The Prospector, for example was not allowed to do any piloting, and a Space Commando couldn't use any guns except Heavy Weapons. So, following that line of thought, if I approached the issue from a purely technical standpoint, was the game trying to delete a now incompatible skill from my repertoire? But there was no option in the settings for that...

I looked glumly at my black helmet. I only saw the system messages when I had on the full Listener suit. Clearly, the Relicts had a way to duplicate the game menu on helmet screens. Perhaps, when their ancient race still existed, there was no other way to access the game menu. Seemingly, like it or not, I'd have to put the helmet back on and navigate the confusing array of incomprehensible symbols and look for a way to delete the now inactive skill.

Ugh, it was a shame, of course, Break-in gave me such interesting perspectives. But here I remembered an old Russian gamer joke: "If you're playing a mage and you get a quest to find a two-handed war hammer with bonuses for pickpocket, must have been leveling your character wrong." This was exactly such a case.

Listener, decision accepted. Break-in skill deleted.

Half the points in that skill may be reallocated.
You have received eleven skill points!

What, just like that? I just put on the helmet but couldn't do anything else before everything was decided for me. And again I didn't understand if I had made a conscious choice or just run out of time.

Listener, your new class requires the Scanning skill.

You have taken the skill Scanning level 1.

Son of a bitch! What was that then? What did the game system not like about my already level-49 Scanning ability, or as it was now called, "&6%%##@@!"? I was enraged that it needed to be replaced with that very same skill at level one!

As if hearing my annoyed thoughts, the game algorithms realized I had two Scanning skills, and a new message came before my eyes:

The &6%%##@@! skill has been marked for deletion. Confirm? (Yes/No)

I just waved a hand. A headless man doesn't have to worry about going bald, per the Russian saying. What else could I do? I had to delete this obviously glitched skill. I didn't even manage to think my agreement before the decision was accepted:

Listener, decision accepted. &6%%##@@! skill deleted.

Half the points in that skill may be reallocated.

You have received twenty-five skill points! (total points accumulated: thirty-six)

Thirty-six points... Alright, settle down... I needed eight points to bring Mental Fortitude up to forty, and twenty-eight for Machine Control, giving a total of no more and no less than thirty-six... Was that just a coincidence? Should I give it a go? I started putting the points into one skill, then the other:

Mental Fortitude	40
Machine Control	40

Both skills activated, and the lines lit back up. Right after that, another bedsheet of incomprehensible symbols ran before my eyes, then the bothersome text suddenly disappeared, replaced with legible system messages. What a relief!

Congratulations! Class change to Listener complete!

Hitpoints reduced from 1704 to 1278.

Magic Points increased from 237 to 555.

ATTENTION!!! At present, you are the only Listener in the game that bends reality!

Fame increased to 50.

Fame increased to 51.

I removed the helmet and wiped the condensation from the glass. I pulled it off! I managed to smooth over almost all the problems with the class change, too. Although I did have to delete one and reset another to level one. And to be honest, the system still said my Mineralogy level was unknown, but I was hoping to handle that soon enough as well.

By the way, with the reappearance of Scanning, the button was also back though it had changed color to green. What was the difference between it and the old violet one? Naturally, I tested it out.

My mana bar dropped a good bit, and my mini-map just showed a schematic rendering of the nearest walls and characters. As I might have known, my scanning radius was tiny again, and my abilities were weak, so not much was being shown. Although... now this was interesting... I zoomed in and saw some unfamiliar markings. When I read the text, I was elated:

Airlock control unit. Interface chance: 17%. Total control chance: 2%.

Right maneuver thruster control system. Interface chance: 4%. Total control chance: 0%.

Laser cannon control unit. Interface chance: 1%. Total control chance: 0%.

Navigation system. Interface chance: 0%. Total control chance: 0%.

Tini Wi-Gnat. Level-48 Miyelonian. (inactive)

Level-279 Morphian. Interface chance: 12%. Total control chance: 0%.

When I saw that I could take control of a living creature, I was bemused. But I was much more interested in the fact that I now had a different type of Scanning. First of all, it required me to spend mana, and quite a bit of it. Second, a scan showed me computer systems and creatures I could attempt to interface with or even control. What was more, even at level one, it was showing me the Morphian's true nature, not its guise as a Miyelonian Translator. Now that was better than the old Scanning!

Seemingly, I was beginning to gradually understand the Listener profession. This class had a noticeable inclination toward magic, and was specialized in Scanning, but also Machine Control. It could even control living creatures. That made it something of a hybrid between a Prospector and Psionic Mage. Sure, I wasn't quite as good at mind-control magic, but I also wasn't so narrowly specialized. I now had quite a lot more Magic Points, too and that was very nice. But as for Hitpoints, I had a fair amount less, which of course was not great. But everything came at a price, including changing to a unique class.

By the way, was I even able to use the Prospector equipment now? That crucial question needed to be answered right away, so I took out the Prospector Scanner and a geological analyzer. I could still handle the "laptop" and metal tripods and set them in the requisite slots, but I was not able to use them. Fortunately, I just didn't have enough skill points:

Your character's Scanning level is insufficient to use this item. Minimum level: 19.

On the one hand, that was very strange. An item I had used before was now beyond me. On the other hand, I couldn't be too upset by how things came together. It would be much worse if the system didn't recognize it as compatible with my new skill and required the type of Scanning now called "&6%%##@@!."

After I thought I'd handled all the changes, I saw another set of incomprehensible red symbols, which thankfully transformed into a readable message:

Listener, access confirmed.

Searching for available units...

I froze, rereading the lines again and again and not understanding what was happening, or what the algorithms of the game that bends reality were searching for. A minute passed, then another... And after I'd made up my mind that the system had simply frozen, my patience was generously rewarded:

Appropriate unit found.

You have received a Small Relict Guard Drone.

Chapter Two

Going to a Comet

A SMALL COMBAT DRONE of an ancient race! Just like the deadly lightning-fast drone that took down the Shiamiru's whole guard team at the Relict base! Cool!!! That would make a great addition to my team! However, my joy was short-lived. All the rest of the text was illegible, so I couldn't figure out how to control this drone, nor where it was located. Furthermore, based on how long the algorithms spent searching, it must have been very, very far away. I would be lucky if it was even in the known part of the Universe.

In order to find answers to these questions, I would have to learn the ancient Relict language. Without that knowledge, I might as well have been stumbling in the dark, just swaying chaotically from side to side, hitting random objects and never really knowing what they were. But where to begin studying a long dead language? There were no dictionaries, and certainly no teachers. Not that I could access anyway.

The obvious answer was to start studying the Listener class description. From what I'd seen, such texts followed a formula: first the name, then a brief description, required skills and finally limitations. I could also be sure that the text would contain the word Listener, probably more than once. I would most likely also be seeing the word Scanning, given the skill was required for the profession. I brought up the syntactic bramble and started trying to decode it.

It was hard to figure out where to start reading. Was it left to right, right to left, or maybe even vertical? I mentally thanked the heavens that the Relicts actually used separate symbols or letters, not jerky continuous lines like the Geckho.

Oh! A familiar symbol. Interlaid circles like ripples in calm water. It was also used in the Scanning button. I thus suspected it meant "Scanning." One symbol per word. So, the Relicts didn't have a proper alphabet, these were logograms.

Astrolinguistics skill increased to level sixty-eight!

The Scanning symbol was used a few times, and that got me somewhere. Apparently, it read vertically top to bottom, in columns going right to left.

Lines of text ran across the visor again, and I wanted to dismiss them as usual, but suddenly found some familiar symbols, and it dawned on me! This mysterious text was just the class information in Relict!!!

Then that complex doubled sign must be my status and name: Gerd Gnat! Here it would of course have been interesting to know what the Gnat glyph meant: were there bothersome little bloodsucking flies on the ancient race's homeworld, or was this symbol a phonetic representation? I had no way of knowing. However, I did pick out the word Listener in the information. It was similar to the Scanning symbol but wrinkled as if flattened out. I managed to move the new text with mental commands and placed it next to the class information for convenient comparison. The Listener glyph was also used a few times in both texts, as I supposed. But then, if this description was formed by the same pattern as usual, the next segment of text should have been: Level-61 Listener. And this one meant my race: Human.

Astrolinguistics skill increased to level sixty-nine!
Electronics skill increased to level forty-two!
You have reached level sixty-two!
You have received three skill points!

That came just in time! Before my very eyes, my character info shifted, allowing me to identify the numbers 1, 2, 4, 6, 8, 9 and 3, which was in a new line that must have meant: "Attention!!! You have three unspent skill points." My vocabulary snowballed, allowing me to decipher more and more symbols. I was definitely on the right track, so I found myself very excited and overcome with well-deserved pride.

But then I got distracted. Minn-O La-Fin was back in the game. The Dark Faction Princess knocked politely at my open doorframe. She didn't enter and just stopped in the doorway, staring at Ayni and Tini as they slept on the upper bunk opposite me. I scooted over on my bench, making room for her, but the proud Princess didn't want to sit:

"Gnat, I am like to know why you is put I alone in room with big black-fur trader? You no want living with me, and talking kitties is take I place?"

I could read slight offense and near envy in Minn-O's voice. I couldn't hold back and laughed good-heartedly, trying to quickly reassure the upset Princess:

"That scary black-haired trader is actually a Geckho woman by the name Uline Tar, and she is considered very pretty by their standards. And just so you know, never let it slip that you didn't know she was a woman. Uline will get very offended. Trust me, I've made that mistake before. In fact, you were given a great honor. Despite the cramped conditions on the Shiamiru, they put you in a less crowded women's cabin."

The Dark Faction lady thought for a second, then gave a silent nod toward Ayni, clearly wanting to know why this Miyelonian was not also placed with the women. I understood that the keen and curious Morphian had probably already woken up and was just pretending to sleep and listening to our conversation. I extended a hand and gave the fluffy creature a friendly ruffle of her well-groomed neck scruff.

"Ayni is a special case. She is a surprising and very loyal creature, who I trust with my life. She has lightning-fast reflexes and moves so fast you can barely see it. Her intuition is great, and she has a wealth of experience with the most unbelievable races. She has saved my life three times in dire battles, and I am very grateful to her."

Without opening an eye, the fluffy Translator gave a satisfied purr, just like a house cat, then turned her head, exposing her neck and whiskered cheeks for petting. I'm not sure that a real Miyelonian, a race known for their subdued emotions, would have behaved that way. The Morphian was probably more reading my expectations and playing up to them. Minn-O then, with a heavy sigh, said unexpectedly:

"Gnat, I have to admit, I come for other reason than this. I only now is talk with ruling grandpa Thumor-Anhu La-Fin. He to be very glad for us together and offer in honor of celebration five more days ceasefire you faction. He also ask about Miyelonians, especially Ayni. My Leng is very impress with Miyelonian capable Translator fast-fast teaching you soldier. He even ask me figure out how much is cost her service."

At that very moment, Ayni sharply opened an eye, confirming my guess that she hadn't been sleeping for some time, and started smiling with a mouth full of sharp teeth:

"My services cost very dearly. Your faction doesn't have enough crystals."

"But..." Minn-O tossed a quick gaze at me and fell silent, however I understood her unvoiced objection. If the H3 Faction had the funds, the rich Dark Faction had more.

"I did that just for Gnat's sake. He's my only friend in the Universe. And as you're Gnat's wayedda, I am willing to train you as well. And you too, Gerd Gnat. You could stand some training, along with your friends. We've got an ummi and a half before we get to the Geckho base, and I suggest we use it intelligently."

"Do you know where we're going?" I asked in surprise, because I was still in the dark.

In response, Ayni gave a nod of confirmation just like a person, smiled and, tossing a quick gaze over Minn-O, switched to Miyelonian:

"It isn't hard to guess. The Geckho have only one military base in this sector of the galaxy, on the Un-Tesh comet. Around here, there are only Meleyephatian and Miyelonian stations. It's actually strange that the Geckho were the ones who found your home planet first."

I immediately latched onto the rare chance to

speak about grand-scale galactic politics and asked the Morphian what would have happened had the Meleyephatians found our Earth first. Ayni considered it and answered honestly that she didn't know:

"For my race, as you know, being subjugated by the Meleyephatian Horde ended in tragedy. It is possible that your kind would meet just such a horrible fate. On the other hand, the Horde contains dozens of races, including some similar to yours but from other stars. So it's hard to say. The Meleyephatians are harsh and have no patience for other ways of thinking, but subject races somehow learn to live with them and even grow in a manner of speaking... Yes, they lose their freedom, pay a heavy tribute, are subject to total control over birth rates, science and production, and must provide troop levies at a moment's notice... But some races choose that path consciously and are even proud that they managed to join such a powerful union as the Meleyephatian Horde, whose heavy footsteps make the whole Universe tremble."

"Are the Geckho a better master for humanity? And overall who is stronger, the Meleyephatians or the Geckho?" I asked, knowing my questions could be extremely important, maybe even vitally so.

"Gnat, never confuse vassalization with enslavement!" Ayni's voice rang out in agitation. Her pupils shrank into tiny dots. I'd seen this before when a Miyelonian got angry or concentrated. "You and your people must pray to all higher powers that the Geckho will win, otherwise your situation will grow drastically worse! But I am not taking a side in this war. Meleyephatian-Geckho relations have been a powder keg for a long time, and this is not my war! I know the Un-Tesh comet well. I have been there a few times in various forms and I know the layout well. Gnat, I'll be leaving you there. It was nice knowing you. Ah yes... the Priest Leng Amiru U-Mayaoo's tail. I know you're hiding it in your inventory. You can keep it as a gift. Let it serve as compensation for all the stress I put you through!"

OTHER THAN ME, Minn-O, and other people from the H3 Faction, three Geckho wanted to train combat and fitness: the twin brothers Basha and Vasha Tushihh and, much to my surprise, Uline Tar. It was impossible for such a large group to practice in the narrow corridor and even more so in the tiny cabins, so Uline asked the captain to open the cargo hold.

After converting the Shiamiru from a peaceful cargo and passenger shuttle into a combat spaceship, the size of the cargo hold had been severely reduced. Half of it was now occupied by additional forcefield generators, but there was still enough room for our purposes. Uraz Tukhsh agreed with unexpected ease, which surprised me even more. The captain was unusually agreeable, which struck me and even put me on guard. Something was wrong with our loser aristocrat, but I never found a good time to ask Uline why he was acting so strange.

Earlier, I told Eduard Boyko to go into the real world and inform Lozovsky of Leng Thumor-Anhu's offer of a five-day ceasefire extension, so we waited for him to return before we got started. On my very first day in game, Svetlana the Assassin led us in fitness training. And the session Ayni conducted was distantly reminiscent of that, but only because she put us all into a big group to track our Endurance and Hitpoints. In every other way it was different. Ayni told us the main idea of her training style was that skills grew more actively when a player was on the verge of death, when one well-timed shot or successful dodge was all it would take to, at the very least, send health into the red and possibly force a respawn.

"But we're on a starship!" I noted reasonably, inferring that all our respawn points were very, very far away. After all, such extreme training could end in us having to sweep back through the galaxy to pick up our crew!

"Well, then you have that much more motivation to survive!" the Miyelonian said with a predatory smile, once again demonstrating her small sharp teeth. "Or, if you're not sure you'll survive, you can change your respawn points onto the Shiamiru, although that carries a huge risk. Then, if the ship blows up, you die once and for all, both in the game and real life."

No way! It only took me one time to learn that ghastly lesson for the rest of my days. When the Shiamiru just barely escaped the explosion of the Relict base, it was a miracle I made it out alive! I categorically refused to move my respawn point onto the shuttle and forbid my friends from doing so either.

"Then let's begin!" the trainer proclaimed and started an endless series of sparring sessions with combat weapons, ending only when each of us had taken a severe beating and even some gunshots. It very painful and unpleasant, but it allowed us to level our armor, dodge and other skills at an advanced rate.

Over the next few hours, I was frequently reminded of Anya. She would have been delighted to be here. We got knocked out or lost lots of blood regularly, and our Medic could have gained a decent number of levels reviving us if she weren't stubborn as an ass. Without Anya though, we still had the ship Medic. I saw and even felt him using healing magic.

But I wasn't bothered by that. Before Ayni even got started, we had an audience, and that was annoying. Three large high-level Geckho from the Waideh-Tukhsh clan, the captain's bodyguards, had come into the hold to watch us. They were talking at high volume, hectoring us, and not even hiding their mockery of the small peaceable Translator, saying she'd taken on a job that was bigger than her britches. Honestly, I was distracted by some new message on my helmet at the time, so I didn't hear what Ayni said when she finally responded. Maybe she was challenging them to a fight, but I'm not sure.

But I did tune in eventually, and I clearly heard the Miyelonian ask those jerks where they had their respawn points. They said the Un-Tesh military base. Ayni apparently deemed that acceptable and disemboweled all three in the space of fifteen seconds. And she disemboweled them in the literal sense of the word — their rib cages were cut open, their innards fell out and their large arteries were severed. Their skulls were even trepanned to show us a living Geckho brain. And the Translator explained everything she was doing in real time. In fact, in a calm businesslike manner, she taught us three different methods of quickly and effectively neutralizing a Geckho using nothing but a knife and set of sharp claws.

Even I was struck, although I had seen the Morphian perform such lightning-fast refined butchery before when Fox sliced up the Great Priestess of the Miyelonian race in front of the thousands of worshippers. Just imagine my companions. For them, the devastating and bloody slaughter of three high-level Geckho enforcers came as a big surprise. Uline just passed out, while Minn-O nearly turned inside out. The noble Princess's eyes rolled back, then she turned green and strained to hold back vomit. But the killing also had its positives. Our training session could now continue in peace, and our trainer's Authority took off to unthinkable heights.

There is no sense in recounting the whole session, so I'll just go over the most memorable parts. First of all, there was an intense sparring session between Imran and Eduard. Both opponents took off their shirts, revealing fit bodies, made of solid rippling muscle. The Dagestani athlete was somewhat taller and more flexible than his opponent, but the Space Commando was an indestructible mountain of a man. All the sambo expert's punches and attempts to grapple just bounced off him. Eduard's meat hook hands whistled as they sailed through the air and could have knocked the wind out of the Gladiator if he had been reckless enough to let him get near even once. They were like a mongoose and cobra... Everyone watched their match. Even actively sparring partners couldn't resist. And although the Gladiator was using his Fast Jump ability, getting out of dangerous situations and landing behind his opponent time and again, brute force won the day. After backing Imran into a corner for the umpteenth time, the Space Commando caught his nimble opponent and brutally knocked Imran out with a series of dastardly strong blows.

After the ship Medic brought Imran back to his senses and restored his hitpoints, Ayni commented on the battle, telling each of them their mistakes. The Gladiator had started off almost perfectly but, after taking half of Eduard's hitpoints, he became predictable and relied too much on his class ability. Fast Jump, she said, wasted too many Endurance Points and had too long a cooldown time.

"If I had my blades, I'd have won!" the hot-blooded Dagestani disagreed, having taken the defeat too close to heart. But Ayni reasonably noted that if both soldiers were fully equipped, the Space Commando heavy exoskeleton would have rendered his blade ineffective.

And of course, how could I avoid my own part... I'll do my best to be honest. At first, I looked pathetic compared to these fast, muscular warriors. Eduard, Imran, or even Dmitry, who'd graduated from a military academy, all put me to shame. And that was to say nothing of the beefy Geckho, who surpassed me in every way and didn't leave me a single chance. I only beat the Princess twice. The first time was stupid and because of armor advantage. My suit's forcefield allowed me to absorb all the cartographer's blows and get right up to her, then I used my superior strength and crushed her like a bug. But as for our second fight, we were on even footing. I was wearing just a track suit, and that made the duel critically important to both of us.

For the first time, Minn-O and I were squaring off on equal footing, so we were both very invested in the outcome. I decided to play fair and refused to use my psionic abilities, although I didn't say that out loud. It was hard without magic. The nimble girl moved unpredictably and with blazing speed, attacking with her hands and feet. She was also not at all ashamed to take cheap and crippling shots. I was helped only by intuition and luck. Over the course of our duel I raised my Danger Sense skill by four points and Minn-O, I suspect, did as well. Probably, if my wayedda wasn't afraid to look me in the eyes, she could have won. But she was constantly expecting me to use magic, so she kept her eyes averted and missed a simple leg sweep. That was no easy trick to pull off, though. You try doing one without thinking about it. And so I won again, having broken the Princess's arm in a submission lock, immobilizing her and forcing her to admit defeat.

But near the end of the training session, Ayni said I was allowed to use magic... After that, everything turned on a dime. I suddenly knew how to fight! It really was a feeling of omnipotence. And I got payback for all my defeat and humiliation! None of my opponents could touch me. As soon as the matches started I took control of my opponent and forced them to make mistakes, stop fighting or even surrender. In the end, I managed not only to restore but even to slightly raise my Authority, which had fallen in the first half of the session. Repeatedly losing and waking up unconscious in the capable hands of the ship Medic tended to do that.

After six hours of practice, I had leveled up twice, increased Strength and Constitution by one each, and seriously improved a bunch of skills! I simply couldn't get enough of my delightful new stat table:

Gerd Gnat. Human. H3 Faction.	
Level-64 Listener	
Statistics:	
Strength	14
Agility	17
Intelligence	23 +3
Perception	26 + 2
Constitution	16
Luck modifier	+3
Parameters:	
Hitpoints	317 of 1420
Endurance points	61 of 1050
Magic points	7 of 582
Carrying capacity	62 lbs.
Fame	51
Skills:	
Electronics	44
Scanning	7
Cartography	52
Astrolinguistics	69
Rifles	48
Mineralogy [confirmation pending]	???
Medium Armor	49
Eagle Eye	60
Sharpshooter	32

Targeting	19
Danger Sense	38
Psionic	47
Mental Strength	45
Mechanism Control	41
Attention!!! No skill chosen	
Attention!!! You have nine unspent skill points	

Sure, Mineralogy was still up in the air, but I was hoping to solve that by using geological analyzers for their intended purpose, not just as a skeleton key to break locks or fry electronics. First though, my Scanning would have to be brought up to 19. But that was all on track. The first skill levels always went very fast, then I would hit ten and start spending free points.

I didn't think long over what to choose as a fifteenth skill. After the recent class change, my character was now extremely mana dependent. Even Scanning now took Magic Points, which was to say nothing about Psionic and its huge expenditures. And so, my mana reserves and restore speed had become critically important.

You have taken the skill Mysticism level 1.

As the skill description said, each level of Mysticism increased my Magic Points by one percent and boosted their regen speed by just as much. Yes, it wasn't much yet, almost unnoticeable, but Mysticism would become more significant as it grew.

Chapter
Three

Seeing a
Comet

I RETURNED TO MY BUNK and discovered Tini sitting on a bench, now back in the game. The kitten was clearly spooked and, just after seeing me, he hurried to say why:

"Master Gnat, in the real world I was contacted by the Miyelonian lady who plays Ayni! Well, she is just baffled, because her Fame keeps shooting up. She's also mad at us for leaving the Medu-Ro IV station without her! But master, that means that our Ayni... well, the one who is here on the ship... is not who she's pretending to be! I think she might even be..."

Here the kitten took a pause and gave a heavy sigh, clearly afraid to continue, so I finished his sentence:

"A Morphian. And not just any Morphian, this is the one that killed the Great Priest Leng Amiru U-Mayaoo."

After confirming his most ghastly suppositions, the Miyelonian youth melted in fear and pressed his ears to his head, so I hurried to reassure him:

"Don't worry, Tini, your rulers have known this for some time, and they have no problem with it. Or do you think your authorities are so foolish that they would let an assassin get near their sacred Priestess?! Personally, I doubt it. Let's say her bodyguards were simply yawning and missed the assassination. Seems unbelievable to me, but who knows? If that was so, would they not increase security measures after the attack? But they didn't. They allowed the Morphian to walk around freely in the form of a First Pride warrior! Those elite soldiers know one another very well, they've probably been working together for a long time, and you think that a new one just showing up wouldn't arouse suspicion? Unthinkable! Your rulers allowed the Morphian to do its work, paid in full and let it leave the station unimpeded."

"But... how can you be so sure, Gerd Gnat?" Tini asked, still dubious.

"Come on, even at my low Psionic level I could tell that thing wasn't Ayni by its thoughts. Heck, I noticed a few times! But the Truth Seekers are professionals. They read me like an open book! They could tell a fake guard from a real one in a second! That wasn't when I noticed, though. After the Truth Seeker interrogation, we needed to walk through an inspection corridor between the main station and space port zone. Well, the First Pride, clearly acting on orders from the Truth Seekers and in violation of every safety protocol in the book, led Ayni and I around the checkpoint without being scanned or searched at all! Why? Because they didn't want the Morphian to be discovered! I didn't notice at first, but eventually all the pieces of the puzzle came together and I realized what happened. You want me to tell you what really took place on the Medu-Ro IV station?"

Tini, still scared and pressing his ears back, slowly closed and opened his eyes, which for a Miyelonian was equivalent to a nod of approval. I started explaining with gusto:

"Leng Amiru, or another no-less-important Miyelonian hired the Morphian to kill her. With thousands of pilgrims watching, the wicked Morphian was supposed to gruesomely murder the priestess and provoke righteous furor in Miyelonian society. After all, that was a live broadcast to the whole galaxy! The completely predictable rage of billions was supposed to lash out at the masterminds of the crime, who would soon be revealed by Truth Seekers investigating the murder. The murder of the incarnation of the Great First Female would be a legal and indisputable reason for war, and the target of this secret operation was none other than the Meleyephatian Horde."

"Ah, that's right!" Tini said, now lighting up. "I noticed all the news channels showing anti-Meleyephatian propaganda before the murder of the incarnation of the Great First Female. You're right, master! It all adds up!"

"Yes. The Morphian was supposed to take the appearance of a Meleyephatian, meet with some random members of that race on the station and, in full view of many security cameras, spend some time with them before committing a vile murder. And there was a backup option in case the Meleyephatians who spoke with the Morphian were somehow able to prove their innocence. After all, maybe they could provide a recording of their interaction and show their whole vapid conversation. That most likely could not stop the war now, but it would put the Union of Miyelonian Prides in a very unfavorable light before the Geckho, Trillians and so on..."

Here I was forced to take a short pause, because Minn-O came into the cabin, now wearing the refit spacesuit. She was clearly expecting some comments on her new look, and I expressed all the anticipated words of praise. And it wasn't just white lies. Minn-O looked impressive and even stylish, a true space Amazon! Satisfied with my reaction, she didn't return to her bunk, just plopped down on a bench. But she didn't know Miyelonian, so I continued the story for Tini:

"So, I'll finish up about the backup option. As you know, there are many races in the Meleyephatian Horde, including a few human groups. And the Miyelonians found some people on Medu-Ro IV who fit that role perfectly. They were from Tailax, and the Morphian was told to spend some time with them as well. But there was a cock-up. The Morphian met me instead and left plenty of clues leading back to Gnat and my humanity. But eventually it became clear that my faction was a Geckho vassal, not Meleyephatian! The Miyelonians had no quarrel with the Geckho, so the Truth Seekers had to make some adjustments, urgently wipe the camera footage and put on that whole circus with thought reading and whatnot. But the mission was nevertheless accomplished. They pinned the blame on the Meleyephatians, then the Morphian received its reward and calmly flew off aboard the Tiopeo-Myhh II. And so Tini, don't you worry about this false Ayni. In fact, take advantage of the unique chance to be trained by an excellent warrior and teacher! Don't be ashamed, go into the cargo hold while Ayni is still with us! And don't come back until you hit level fifty!"

AS SOON AS my ward left, the noble Princess stood up and closed the metal curtain into the corridor.

"Gerd Gnat, I wanting talk with you. First of, is praise. You be amazing! When you not surrender, but use all abilities, the difference between simple muscular warrior and true mage-ruler is obvious!"

After a second of hesitation, Minn-O sat down on the bench next to me and placed her arms modestly on her knees. She was clearly trying to get near me in her bashful way. And I didn't get antsy, or try to feel her up, afraid to spook the already shy Princess. She spent half a minute in silence, then decisively turned to me and looked me right in the eyes:

"Gnat, according to all traditions and customs of my world, you already have been me legal husband for whole day, but I still no affection. I am your wayedda, supposed to be you most closest person. But still, I don't know lots about you, your past and present, your goals and wishes. And, what makes me bitter and even somewhat afraid, I do not have slightest idea of your plans about me."

I noticed Minn-O's grasp of my language had improved. She still wasn't perfect, but she was speaking quite fluently. This learning speed spoke not only to leveling Astrolinguistics, but also high Intelligence. And so, not knowing where to start, I praised her progress with my language and asked about her character's stats in the game that bends reality.

To me it seemed a simple and even banal question. But Minn-O unexpectedly turned away and refused to answer, saying that every lady had her secrets. She wanted to stay mysterious and revealing her character sheet was the same as standing naked before me. Here I couldn't agree:

"Ladies' secrets are little tricks like inserts that make your boobs look bigger, or strapless bras that push them together. Those are the kinds of details men better not delve into. But I am not asking you to reveal ladies' secrets. I just want basic game information. It would allow me as a commander to understand just how much I can rely on your level-55 Cartographer in a serious fight, and what use you might be in times of peace."

Minn-O lowered her eyes and looked embarrassed, her ashen-gray cheeks even flooded with red blush. I realized that I had accidentally broken some moral taboo of her world and had said things that were utterly beyond the pale. Her next words confirmed my guesses:

"Talking about that is consider uncultured. Also, the 'ladies' secrets' you described are not need in the game... As for stats and skills of Cartographer... no, I can't, too personal. I'll have to explain why I chose this or that, what guided this choice. If really is necessary, read them from my thoughts, you can use Psionic magic, after all."

Minn-O then looked me in the eyes, as if inviting me to mental conversation. I had to admit, I was intrigued with this mysteriousness and stubbornness.

So, I met eyes with her and... drowned in the stream of the Princess's thoughts.

"How can I communicate to Gnat that I care about him? I'm crawling out of my skin to attract his attention. And he looks at me so distantly, I don't even know if he likes me or not. I even took the Lover skill for him. After all, I didn't want to disappoint such a sophisticated and cute boy with so many past girlfriends. But the most important is how to bring my husband into my world. Grandpa said it was possible. His backwards H3 Faction is doomed. And its days will be all the more numbered after the legendary General Ui-Taka takes up the fight. I need to save Gnat and bring him to our world before his faction gets wiped out. After all, doesn't Gnat understand that a mage like him will live better in our world?"

I averted my gaze, breaking the mental contact. No, that wasn't how it would go. I needed real information, not this poorly masked propaganda!

Psionic skill increased to level forty-eight!

Mysticism skill increased to level two!

Mysticism skill increased to level three!

I didn't get mad at her, despite the flagrant attempt to lure me to her side. Instead, I gave a good-hearted smile and suggested we just talk like normal people and get to know one another better. I even suggested we combine a free conversation with language lessons. I could teach Minn-O the language of my people and the Geckho race, and she could act as my teacher of the Dark Faction language.

It was a good idea. Minn-O grew visibly calmer and, generously peppering her speech with words from her world, she began to tell me about the mageocracy, the ruling families and the twelve directories. I listened carefully, not interrupting, just occasionally clarifying the meaning of a certain word or asking for more information when I didn't understand. At a certain point, Minn-O scooted closer, and I gathered the courage to tenderly hug the Princess. She didn't object one bit. In fact it was the opposite. She pressed up close to me and put her head on my shoulder.

The ice of distance between us quickly melted. I was no longer so constrained and, when telling her about my world and past life I joked around a lot, acted silly, and the Princess laughed infectiously. As it turned out, Minn-O had a nice sonorous laugh reminiscent of the peal of silver bells. I didn't even know who initiated it, but at a certain point, our lips met in a kiss.

"I'd already stopped hoping you'd work up the courage," Minn-O smiled, and naughty little devils started dancing in her eyes. "You sold me a whole song and dance when I was naked and tied up on the Geckho ferry. You said that if I ended up your prisoner one more time, I wouldn't get by with just kisses. I'll admit, I was worried, but you actually turned out pretty timid. I had to wait a whole two days just for a kiss..."

I understood perfectly that the Princess was just

joking, and that if I pushed too hard, I might scare her and demolish the shaky trust we had established. But in one way or another, our relationship was fated in the stars and, at some point, it would reach the point of "leveling the Lover skill." By the way, what did that do? I tried to open the description, and received only the following message:

Information unavailable. This skill is incompatible with your character.

Then I just asked Minn-O and my wayedda didn't hide anything, reading aloud:

Lover. This skill is available only to female characters and allows its bearer to better attract the opposite sex* (both NPC's and living players). It also helps women please and keep their men. Leveling this skill gives new conversation and behavior options, improves the relationship modifier, and increases Endurance Points. This is the main skill for the classes Prostitute, Favorite, and Matriarch.

* For races with variable gender, the Lover skill may temporarily become inactive.

** For races with more than two gender options (for example, Meleyephatians or Cleopians) the Lover skill is only active between partners capable of conceiving young.

"Well then..." I couldn't hold back the surprised exclamation. "It looks like I seriously underestimated your feminine wiles. Are you already using the skill on me?"

"I took that skill back on the Geckho ferry and even tried to use it on you then," Minn-O admitted with a satisfied smile. "But I didn't notice any effect. In the prison block either. You're just impossible to get through to!"

We kissed again, this time bolder and with less restraint. I even started thinking about taking it further and letting my hands wander a bit, given that my companion was in a playful mood. However our placid cooing was interrupted by a heavy knock at the door, and I hurried to raise the curtain before it got broken down by the strong and impatient visitor. In the doorway was Geckho Trader Uline Tar:

"Gnat, there you are! We're almost there. We can already see Un-Tesh. But that wasn't why I came looking for you. We got a message from the base that our shuttle will be boarded and inspected by a group of Geckho soldiers, and you and the Miyelonian Ayni are to be placed under arrest by order of Kung Waid Shishish himself. Tell me, Gnat. What did you do this time?!"

The shocking news made my jaw drop. Kung Waid Shishish was a fearsome and unrestrained Geckho military leader, who had massive territorial holdings throughout the galaxy, including my very own Earth. And he had ordered me arrested? But why?! I mean, Gnat was not some innocent little lamb, and my gameplay might have upset the Geckho on several occasions. I could remember at least ten reasons for our suzerains to be mad at me. Just inviting the Miyelonian smugglers into the exclusive zone of the Geckho was enough. But that was all in the past now and I had already made a report to Geckho Diplomat Kosta Dykhsh about it. I couldn't really think of any transgressions since that time.

Uline didn't understand why Kung Shishish would be mad either, and neither did Captain Tukhsh, who had passed this alarming information along to the Trader. By the way... although this wasn't the best moment, I asked the furry lady if she knew why the captain was treating me with such strange agreeability.

"Are you implying I might not know!" Uline frowned as if my lack of faith insulted her. "Our young handsome Aristocrat got it into his head to marry! And not just any old Geckho, but a respectable and pretty Geckho lady from a rich clan that controls a network of Galactic highways and a whole flotilla of trade ships. It was a marriage borne of pure calculation. The groom is a famous aristocrat from a now destitute family, and the bride is from a family of rich traders with no title. But the obstinate lady gave our captain a clear and unambiguous condition: he had to achieve glory and become a Gerd, then put all his free stat points into luck and thus rid himself of the curse. As it is, everyone knows about his bad luck. It's practically broadcast on the galactic news."

I thought for a bit and put some things together. Based on the words "pretty Geckho lady," "rich traders" "ships," and "curse," I came to a firm conclusion:

"That obstinate pretty bride must be you, Uline!"

"Gnat, you're as good a guesser as ever," my huge furry friend rumbled out in satisfaction. "My fiancée, not least of all at my behest, sees you as a talisman of luck and his best chance for a happy marriage. And that's why he's so nervous around you. He's afraid of losing you. And I share his conviction, so I'll try to help you with this weird arrest even though I don't know what has upset the head of clan Waideh-Tukhsh."

Chapter Four

Master of Earth

I'D BEEN ON ASTEROIDS before. Several in fact, so I wasn't exactly a space greenhorn. I'd seen plenty of astral vistas before, too. But still, the view I got from the surface of Un-Tesh surprised and delighted me. There were so many ships here both on the spaceport landing field and just drifting in space nearby! Interceptors, assault frigates, heavy cruisers, landing ships... There were hundreds! And although we were on the dark side of the comet, opposite the local sun, the spaceport's huge field of ice glimmered like a million stars, reflecting the many ship lights and emphasizing all the military might of the great Geckho race. What a pretty sight!

And what was more, this comet had an

atmosphere. Not a very thick one, but still! Through it, the black starry sky looked washed out and almost dirty. A huge combat starship hovering a few miles over the surface looked very indistinct. It was so blurry I couldn't even read its class or make out any details. Most likely, this was the gigantic battleship Dmitry Zheltov told me about, but I had no way of confirming that. I couldn't see further than half a mile, and there was no distinct horizon here either. Nothing but a swirling ash-gray haze, like wisps of steam mixing into the dark sky and bright blue ground of the icy space port.

The barometer in my suit sleeve confirmed my observations about the atmosphere, showing a pressure of nine thousand pascals, which was pretty significant. In fact, one twelfth of the average on earth. For a celestial body that was not a planet and didn't seem all that massive, the pressure was very significant. But the composition of the atmosphere meant it would not be breathable.

Apparently, the substance underfoot was not exactly ice in the normal sense of the word, either. The ground was just too crumbly and light to be normal frozen water. To be more accurate, there probably was some water in it, but it was not the main component. I looked closer at the dark violet frozen ground and thought. It didn't look like frozen oxygen or nitrogen, and they weren't commonly found on comets. What was more, the temperature was just negative one hundred thirty Fahrenheit, which would not be enough to maintain nitrogen or oxygen in a solid state.

I came to the conclusion that this soil was primarily frozen ammonium, billions or probably even trillions of tons of it. Logically, the side of this comet pointed toward the sun would be hot enough for it to sublimate. There were probably a large number of ammonium geysers over there. The surface on that side may even have been liquid, with whole seas of toxic boiling ammonium. The mass of this heavenly body allowed it to retain most of the sublimated gas, which is what made up the local atmosphere. Although not all the ammonium stayed, some of the gas escaped into space, which is what made the comet's tail.

Eagle Eye skill increased to level sixty-one!

Mineralogy skill confirmed. Detected level: forty-nine.

You have reached level sixty-five!

You have received three skill points! (total points accumulated: twelve).

Oh! Mineralogy not only "turned on," but sharply jumped from twenty-three to forty-nine. Seemingly that was the game algorithms' evaluation of my prior education in the field. Ugh, if I'd only known this would happen, I'd have never left the library and studied geology and the composition of astronomical bodies for days on end...

I had enough free points to raise scanning to nineteen and give me back my ability to use the

Prospector tool. But I was in no hurry. I could do that any time. At this early stage, though, Scanning was leveling quick, so I could afford to save them.

But where was the landing party? Where was the division that was going to board our shuttle and arrest me and Ayni? Would I have to stand here at the gangway for long?

Ayni took the news of her upcoming arrest with surprising calm and told me and everyone on the shuttle that she had no desire to speak with the Geckho military leader, so she'd rather commit suicide and respawn somewhere safe. None of the crew members dared contradict the fearsome Miyelonian, much less try and stop her. Ayni bid us all farewell, went into the cargo hold, and no one saw her again.

But I'm certain the Morphian was fibbing. At the very least, after the Shiamiru landed on the surface of the comet, the Morphian was still on board. I saw its marker when I ran a scan. I guessed Fox was hiding in some utility room, planning to blend in with the locals when the chance presented itself. It could easily pretend to be from one of the many starship crews or working a service job on the base. I could not imagine how it was technically possible, even with a change of appearance, to go into such a toxic and sparse atmosphere as this comet with no armor. But my friend had been to this base a few times before, which meant she knew the local conditions and was prepared for them.

"Gnat, don't leave the ship! The antigrav with Kung Waid Shishish's soldiers is on its way and will land near our ship soon."

The voice in my headphones belonged to Captain Uraz Tukhsh. I just shook my head in reproach. I didn't know about Fame (it sometimes went up due to ill repute and obvious foolishness), but the young Aristocrat could never achieve positive Authority. After all, it seemed to me that any more-or-less accountable captain would at least try to figure out why their crew member had been called to speak with their commander. A good one might even feel the call to personally go and defend his subject. That would be the logical and proper move. After all, who would want to serve a captain that didn't give a damn about his crew?! But Uraz Tukhsh just threw up his hands and, not wanting to fight his vaunted relative, just stepped aside, letting me go to the hands of fate.

The only one to express a desire to support and protect me was Uline Tar. The Trader even tried to come to the meeting with Kung Waid Shishish herself to figure it all out and "restore justice," but I talked her out of it. I needed Uline on the ship. She was the only one I could trust with my most valuable objects: the Annihilator, the Priestess's tail and my wallet with a large number of crypto.

Finally, I saw a small quickly moving antigrav in the sky up above. It nearly jumped past our Shiamiru, which must have been nearly invisible compared to the other starships but, at the last second, it made an abrupt maneuver and started landing. The side hatches opened, and ten Geckho soldiers came out of the antigrav in identical heavy red armor. Their weapons at the ready, they surrounded the Shiamiru and froze stock still. Only when they were all in position did their commander emerge, slowly and with dignity:

Gerd Ost Rekh. Geckho. Clan Waideh-Rekh. Level-156 Shocktroop.

One hundred fifty-six?! A real badass. I should not joke around with him. But just then, I got distracted because an airlock hissed open behind me and, covering her face with a hand to block the bright spotlight, Minn-O came down the gangway in her new spacesuit. What the hell was she doing??? Or... I activated the Scanning icon, but discovered this was the real Minn-O La-Fin.

I took a step toward the Princess and first checked the air in her tanks, then made sure they were all hooked up right, and her batteries were charged. The last thing I needed was for my wayedda to lose consciousness in this corrosive ammonium atmosphere. While I tightened and readjusted the straps of her space suit, then cinched down her rifle strap, the Princess explained why she was here:

"Gnat, the pilot man told me that my husband was in trouble, and they even want to arrest you. Well, I decided to be by your side in this difficult moment and share your fate!"

Well, well! An unexpected move from my traveling mistress. But still I couldn't hide that it was very pleasing. I had just finished adjusting Minn-O's spacesuit, when a bulky Shocktroop walked up to the gangway and stopped a step away:

"Kento duho, Gerd Gnat! Uh, I was told the second would be a Miyelonian..."

If only you knew the relief I experienced when I heard that fearsome Geckho's first words! The weight of a mountain fell off my shoulders! The "kento duho" greeting meant he was friendly. It definitely could not be used to address a criminal or arrestee. I greeted the squadron head and explained with all possible politeness that the Miyelonian Ayni had killed herself as soon as she found out our shuttle was going to a Geckho military base. She said that it wasn't on her way and it was better for her to respawn on Medu-Ro IV. That was exactly what Ayni told the crew, so I just recounted it word for word.

"Too bad... Kung Waid Shishish REALLY wanted to speak with that Miyelonian," the Shocktroop said, putting special emphasis on the word "really." I couldn't make out what he meant by that intonation, though. Either he wanted to emphasize how mad his leader was, or he just had a sincere interest. And maybe he was also expecting problems now that he hadn't carried out the Kung's full order.

In one way or another, I needed to figure out my status in all this, and I directly asked the Shocktroop what the military leader wanted from me.

"Kung Waid Shishish is angry and would like to see you personally. He has a lot of questions for you, Gerd Gnat. In your place, I wouldn't make the Kung wait. He is not known for his patience."

I guess it wasn't all good... I had apparently pissed off the great and powerful Geckho Kung. This was of course not an arrest, but there was still little to be happy about. I needed to go at once to mitigate the master of Earth's dismay as much as possible. Hopefully I could at least somewhat smooth over the sharpness and turn this from a hostile interrogation into an official visit. So I pointed Gerd Ost Rekh to my companion:

"Minn-O is my spouse and a Princess of my race, the granddaughter of a Coruler of mankind. It would be proper to have her come with us in order to express her respect to Kung Waid Shishish."

The Geckho did not object, and soon we were in the antigrav racing off toward a distant ice massif barely visible in the cloudy mist. It was a true mountain ridge made of frozen ammonium. From closer up, I was able to see the whole chain of icy peaks, which were over half a mile in height. Then I noticed that our flying machine was flying straight into a vertical ice wall at enormous speed. I felt Minn-O shudder in fear as I grasped her hand. I was not worried one bit, though. My Danger Sense was quiet, which meant there was nothing risky in this maneuver. And in fact, our antigrav passed through the seemingly solid wall without resistance. For a second, colorful sparks and flashes of electricity blasted out around us. However, I had seen this before, when we discovered the illicit platinum mine on an asteroid. It was a cloaking screen, hiding something behind it.

Fame increased to 52.

Authority increased to 31!

"You're not easily scared, Gerd Gnat!" the leader of the Geckho group called out respectfully, removing his helmet and showing his yellowed tusks. "Not many react so calmly the first time. Some have even passed out or tried to jump out a window."

By then, the antigrav had passed through a second defensive shield and into a spherical room, which I imagined was an airlock. After that, the walls of the tunnel were no longer ice but some kind of gray ceramic-metal composite. The air here was now breathable, so I followed the Geckhos' example and took off my helmet, holding it in my hands.

When Gerd Ost complimented my bravery, I didn't tell him what I was thinking or feeling. I just said I trusted the pilot, so I wasn't concerned.

"Well reasoned," the Shocktroop rumbled in satisfaction. "My division has the best of the best, and their skill is beyond doubt. What's more, Kung Waid Shishish would skin us each thrice if we didn't bring you to him in one piece. Alright, we're there! From here, go straight down the corridor. In the farthest room, there will be a small test of your luck! Try not to disappoint our fearsome boss!"

AFTER MINN-O AND I got a bit further from the antigrav and Geckho I found the chance to thank her for her courage, which bordered on self-sacrifice. But the Princess clearly did not understand the reason for my gratitude. By the harsh laws of her world, a wayedda was expected to follow her spouse into war or exile, and even up the gallows. And that, by the way, was one of the main differences between a "junior, traveling wife" and a "senior" one. A senior wife was considered the keeper of the domestic hearth and child-raiser, who generally stayed out of dangerous ventures.

"Not in my world. Wives, as a rule, never follow their husbands into war. Exceptions are very rare. Same goes for exile. There were of course the Decembrists' wives, who followed their husbands to Siberia..." here I was forced to make a pause, because my companion had clearly lost the thread. So I quickly summarized that historic episode. "Two hundred years ago, there was a rebellion of a large group of aristocrats against... how to explain... one of the Corulers of my world, the head of the largest directory. The uprising was harshly suppressed, five of the leaders were executed, and around four hundred thousand were deprived of title and exiled to far-away lands."

"That's what they call 'harsh' in you world???" Minn-O couldn't hold back and laughed uncontrollably. "Gerd Gnat, a year ago while suppressing of a hunger riot in the Ninth Directory, my grandfather ordered the execution of more than six million rebels just so there wouldn't be so many mouths to feed. And Thumor-Anhu is not an outlier. Every Coruler has conducted themselves that way since time immemorial! And as for threatening the life of the Coruler, anyone crazy enough to try something like that would be executed as harshly as possible along with three generations of their family... Yikes! Gnat look!!!"

Her last sentence was about a colossal hall now visible through an oval window. In it there were rows of thousands of Geckho soldiers in exoskeleton armor. I abruptly forgot my acrid commentary on Minn-O's severe world and her grandfather's harshness. I was struck by this amazing spectacle.

There were many ideally even rows of stock-still soldiers, primarily in identical black and silver armor suits just like I had bought for Eduard. Mixed into the main mass of infantry, I could clearly make out commanders in more advanced and expensive orange shock armor, and also... My jaw dropped in astonishment when I saw the very depths of the room... There was a group of thirty titanic figures armed to the teeth, each the size of a nine-story-building!

Eagle Eye skill increased to level sixty-two!

Greiss Ukhkh-Tor. Heavy Geckho Shock Mech.

Now that's power!!! Yes, there were sufficient forces here to capture not only a space station, but a whole planet the size of my Earth! Humanity, even all together, didn't stand a chance against such an army... And this probably wasn't even close to our suzerains' total forces because, while Kung Waid Shishish was an influential "leader of many divisions," responsible for a certain sector of the galaxy, he was just one of many such Geckho commanders.

Sure, I knew the Geckho were a great and powerful space race, but it was one thing to understand that based on abstract data, and it was quite another to see that with my own eyes. I walked in thoughtful silence to the next room, where Kung Waid Shishish had apparently set up some kind of test.

Ho-ly crap... There was a meeting underway. Fifteen furry Geckho wearing identical red armor were sitting in a semicircle on small pillows before a larger Geckho in a glimmering pure white suit of armor sprawled out on a throne in a stately manner. And there was no other way to call this gem-encrusted carved armchair. It was the throne to end all thrones. I would have assumed the white-armored individual was the Kung, but it was unmistakably an, albeit large, Geckho female! She was just huge for a lady... for a man too, actually... She didn't have female markings on her fur or any jewelry, but I had spent enough time in the company of Uline Tar to learn the seemingly insignificant anatomical differences between Geckho genders. The arms were somewhat different proportion to the body, the ears were turned back and the eyes were lemon-yellow unlike the males... Yeah this was definitely a female! What was going on here? Where was Kung Waid Shishish? Or was I confused, and my captain's famed relative was a woman? It seemed unlikely. Uraz Tukhsh always referred to him with male pronouns...

Extremely confused, I stopped at the entrance and looked around. I couldn't read character info about any of the Geckho. However, according to etiquette rules and diplomatic protocol, I was supposed to approach Kung Waid Shishish first, get down on one knee and give a low bow to express my respect for the Master of Earth. But who to approach? Clearly, this was the test Gerd Ost Rekh was referring to.

The lady on the throne must have been a trap. If I couldn't tell her apart from the real Kung, I would shame myself in the most serious fashion. I'd never wash off that stain, even in a hundred years. But who of these fifteen was the Kung? I had one guess. One of the warriors was intentionally looking away from me and trying to blend into the crowd. Also, I could play with Danger Sense to find the right move. But I didn't risk it and just used scanning.

Scanning skill increased to level eight!

Everything became clear at once. My suspicion proved correct. A comparatively modest Geckho was shown on the mini-map as:

Kung Waid Shishish. Geckho. Clan Waideh-Tukhsh. Level-279 Space Commando.

I didn't hesitate for more than a second. I took a precise step toward the respected leader of my planet and bowed in a proper greeting. Minn-O did the same and fell down next to me on one knee. But the Kung's reaction was one of clear dismay. Seemingly, he was hoping to play us jackass outworlders for fools and have a little fun.

"Hey, no fair! Did someone tell you? No? Ah! You've probably seen me on signs! Or was that just your luck?"

"No, my Kung, luck had nothing to do with it. A blind person could tell a Geckho man from a woman, even one so awe-inspiring and strong. And from there it was easy. Everyone else was clearly afraid they might be confused with the great and legendary Geckho commander. Only Kung Waid Shishish was acting casual and enjoying the game."

Yes, I told him a story that had little to do with reality, but it seemed like the right move. After all, flattering one's superiors a bit never hurt. But Kung Waid Shishish gave a rumble of dismay and raised his voice to a shout:

"Gnat, do you mean to say I might sour on an

advisor just because they could be confused with me?! Do you think me some ghastly despot?"

My heart ran off on its heels. Seemingly, I was not on the right track... I didn't manage to think through the potential danger before the end of the military leader's next sentence threw everything topsy-turvy:

"Well, you are completely right, Gerd Gnat!!! If you bowed to any of these other Geckho, I would have shot them at once and forbid them from ever appearing before me again. What need do I have for an advisor who can eclipse me with their presence?! Well, Gnat, you've confirmed your reputation and earned the right to speak with me."

Psionic skill increased to level forty-eight!

Fame increased to 53.

Chapter Five

Audience

THE "CONVERSATION" if that term can be used to describe the stream of trick questions the Kung poured onto me, began with a complaint that I had smuggled his property off the Relict base. Clearly, my fancy Listener suit had gotten under the fearsome military leader's skin. After all, he had invested significant funds buying the rights to the ancient race's base and had nothing to show for it. I had to remind the Geckho leader as delicately as possible, that myself and three other Shiamiru crew members had entered the base ourselves without anyone's help. I also said we had no idea the rights to base had been sold until the (at that time) Leng showed up, at which point we immediately left the ancient base. I went on to tell him about my contract with Captain Uraz Tukhsh and the absolute legality of my keeping whatever I could carry out.

In order for it not to look like a one-sided and banal attempt at self-justification, I also told the Kung I'd since had the armor refit for a human and added some accessories:

"Installing a bracelet in this special slot helped activate the ancient device's electronics. And that caused a spontaneous change in class and other problems of a technical nature. But overall it showed I was on the right path. Like here," I said, pointing to a ring-shaped cavity in the chest of my Listener suit, "there's clearly a slot for something else: either a dome-shaped disk or a ring. I seem to remember seeing such disks on the base, but I didn't take any, because I had already received Leng Waid Shishish's command to leave the outpost. And I did not dare disobey an order from my overlord. The artifacts my Geckho friends took, and there were definitely some disks among them, were stolen by space pirates."

Kung Waid Shishish listened attentively and didn't have any response. No matter how badly the fearsome Geckho wanted to claim my trophies, he had to admit I was right. The next question was a fully expected one about the Listener class. Carefully choosing my words, I answered that I myself didn't understand yet:

"All the information the game has given me so far is in Relict logograms, so for now I have to learn the bonuses and restrictions by trial and error. Although I already know that a Listener is very similar to a

Prospector, and that may have been why the change was relatively smooth. The class also prioritizes Perception and Intelligence, and uses Scanning, but not so much for finding ore deposits and anomalies as for finding hidden devices and living creatures. My hitpoints fell, but I got more Magic Points, which are now used on Scanning. Overall, I'm gradually figuring out my new class and I'll be sure to tell my Kung more as that information becomes available."

The hotheaded commander, already having shooed the huge lady off the throne and taken his spot, gave a happy rumble, content with my answer. I already thought the hardest part of the conversation was behind me, when suddenly another accusation was added:

"Alright, we'll set aside the topic of the artifacts and your new class. That's all behind us and has little bearing on the present. But because of your recent poorly considered actions, my Authority fell by two whole points! How am I to understand that, Gnat?! I've killed my closest advisors and friends for less, you know!"

Here I froze with my mouth agape, not able to find an explanation. On the one hand, I couldn't really cast aspersions on the words of the great commander. But on the other, what did I have to do with the Kung's fall in Authority??? And so, without questioning the facts or my possible complicity, ask him to clarify when it happened and under what circumstances.

"Just an ummi ago, three reasonably good soldiers of the Waideh-Tukhsh clan, who I personally selected as bodyguards for my relative Uraz Tukhsh, got smacked around and killed by a noncombat character of a very middling level. The story has spread far and wide here on the base and put Clan Waideh-Tukhsh, and me as its leader, in a very unflattering light. After all, how can you speak of a clan having any true power if warriors selected personally by its head can be taken down by some Cook or Translator of a much lower level?!"

Danger Sense skill increased to level thirty-nine!

Near the end of his speech, Waid Shishish was fully roaring and shaking his huge furry head in rage, spraying spittle in every direction. Minn-O was staring at me in alarm, not fully understanding what was happening, just seeing a huge enraged Geckho verbally assaulting her husband. I then, despite the warning message and the Kung's aggressive demeanor, waved off the problems with exaggerated calm:

"Ah that... Well the Authority of the honorable Clan Waideh-Tukhsh would have suffered in any case, and I had nothing to do with it. Your Authority fell at the very moment three of your warriors disputed the professionalism of a hand-to-hand combat trainer, selected by a captain of your clan to train his crew. In fact, I suspect that the Authority of Clan Waideh-Tukhsh would have fallen even more if the respected trainer had lost a fight with some two-bit ruffians."

"Ruffians??? You forget yourself, Gnat!!! The three who were killed were not some mere ruffians or bandits, they were Waideh-Tukhsh Bodyguards at over level ninety!"

Danger Sense skill increased to level forty!

The Kung was about to explode in rage, and the second system message in a row bore witness to that. Nevertheless, I stuck to my guns and portrayed absolute calm. Then I expressed an extremely scornful, almost insulting opinion of the "professional" Bodyguards' combat skills:

"They didn't seem much like honorable Bodyguards to me. They acted boorishly, itching for a fight and damaging the Authority of Clan Waideh-Tukhsh, which I respect immeasurably. Although I don't know what they were hoping for. Who could stand up against a Morphian warrior with combat experience measured in centuries, whose level is the same as that of the respected Kung, two-hundred seventy-nine?!"

The Geckho in the room all gasped at once. The hot-headed commander himself seemed ready to answer very aggressively and even took in some more air to do so but, after my last sentence, he sharply rethought and even visually deflated. Sitting back down in his throne, which he'd jumped up from in the heat of the dispute, Kung Waid Shishish gave an inquisitive nod at the Princess behind me. Seemingly, he thought she was the Morphian. Unfortunately I had to correct my vaunted boss:

"No, this is my spouse Minn-O, the granddaughter of a Coruler of humanity. She doesn't understand a word of Geckho, but I thought it was my duty to bring her to my great leader and discoverer of our race, so Minn-O could pledge her fealty to the most-powerful master of our planet. The Morphian didn't want to come to this comet and committed suicide. Much to my dismay, I had no way of stopping the powerful creature."

Minn-O, having heard her name, found her place and gave a graceful bow to the most important Geckho. Kung Waid Shishish greeted my companion in return with a careless nod and a wave of his clawed paw, after which he lost all interest:

"Too bad... I'd love to speak with a Morphian... Just think of all the ways we could work together..." Waid Shishish cooled down remarkably quickly. There was not a trace remaining of his former aggression and hot-headedness. Now the Geckho before me was a wise military strategist of a great spacefaring race.

Psionic skill increased to level forty-nine!
Psionic skill increased to level fifty!
Mysticism skill increased to level four!

Now that was interesting! So I wasn't able to get by without a bit of psionic manipulation after all. And my strange confidence even at the most worrying moments was explained by, among other things, the fact that I was somewhat influencing his behavior. By the way, I barely had any mana left, just 83 of 615

Magic Points...

"Gerd Gnat, tell me everything you know about the Morphian's assassination of Leng Amiru U-Mayaoo and the beginning of the war between the Miyelonians and Meleyephatians," the Kung asked in a calm tone, leaving all his grievances in the past.

I breathed a sigh of relief and told the Geckho leader exactly what I'd told Tini earlier. Kung Waid Shishish listened carefully and, when I'd finished the story, spent some time in contemplative silence. Finally, the huge Geckho shuddered:

"That is a different story than the one the Great Miyelonian Priestess told me. But yours is more plausible. The Miyelonians have been sitting on the sidelines for a long time, gathering forces and preparing to expand their presence in the galaxy. And when the Union of Miyelonian Prides thought it was ready for war, all that remained was for them to think up a reason to start one. By the way, Leng Amiru U-Mayaoo had a lot of praise for you, calling you a clever and helpful Human."

Fame increased to 54.

Kung Waid Shishish kept silent and spent a long time boring into me with his attentive black eyes, thinking deeply. Then he continued:

"I don't really know what you did to make such an impression on the Miyelonian Priestess, but I have to admit I don't much like adventuresome chaps who intrude where they're not invited and don't have respect for common order. Although I will agree with Leng Amiru that such troublemakers sometimes are useful. But mostly they bring harm. But one of my subjects considers you a good luck charm. He thinks the whole operation is doomed without you. And as that's so, what are you doing nested up in the little Shiamiru? Get your friends and go to *Grokh-Uvachch*, the largest and most fearsome ship at the military base. It is the powerful Ashdeh-Wayn Clan's contribution to our common cause." With these words the severe military leader pointed at the giant Geckho lady in glimmering white armor and her marker on the mini-map told me who she was:

Leng Amothy Yore. Geckho. Clan Ashdeh-Wayn. Level-221 Starship Pilot.

He must have been talking about that gigantic battleship floating in space near the comet. Of course, it would be interesting to spend some time on it and see a real Geckho military starship in person. However, before the military leader finished his sentence, I already knew it was another trap. Kung Waid Shishish spoke so often with his relative Uraz Tukhsh that he'd even heard of his "good luck charm," so he had to know I had a contract for one more voyage. Was I being tempted into breaking it? I had to imagine that there were serious fines and sanctions for that, the most obvious of which would be confiscation of everything of any value. Nope, no thanks!

I had to carefully choose my words to refuse the

"great honor," making the excuse that I still hadn't finished a contract with Clan Waideh-Tukhsh. And I guessed right. The Kung gave a happy rumble, clearly content with my decision, then said:

"Well Gerd Gnat, I have to praise your devotion to principle! Uraz Tukhsh could stand a good luck charm.' Although I don't think this campaign will bring my relative or his crew many trophies or much glory. Noncombat starships will be in the third attack wave, when the space battle will already have long been over, and the landing troops will have taken everything of value from the combat ships. Nevertheless, I am very glad you're helping my family. And if you, Gerd Gnat, have any requests, now is the time to voice them."

I got back down on one knee and told him a problem I'd been wracking my brains over:

"Due to the unexpected coming of the Shiamiru and the extreme rush to pack, I not only forgot to prepare a gift worthy of my great Kung, which makes me immeasurably anxious, I also didn't manage to provide my whole team with spacesuits. I'm missing just one, for a Gladiator. And if there are any I could take here on the base, or ones that could be refit for a large person, I humbly beg Kung Waid Shishish to have one issued. But the problem is that I cannot pay for it right now except in Miyelonian crypto... or I need a money changer, even though I know how illegal that is."

Fame increased to 55.

Fame increased to 56.

For some reason, that request seemed very funny to the Geckho leader. The fearsome Kung Waid Shishish bared his teeth into an unthinkable grimace, rumbled and even lost control and slid off his throne onto the floor. His advisors were laughing too, or more like rumbling loudly, baring their fangs and furrowing their furry brows. Finally, the military leader had laughed it off and said:

"Even if we don't have a spacesuit for him on the base, I'll order one brought in at once. It wouldn't be right to leave such an unusual request unattended, or a great warrior unable to even leave the ship and take part in battle. And I'll try to get by without your money, Human. Yes, it will be hard," here the Geckho once again lost control and started rumbling in laughter, "but I think I can survive without your crypto. Let it be a gift to you and your companion for the good humor. And your gift to me, Gerd Gnat, shall be our common victory in the great war! Prove to us all that you truly do bring luck!"

And with that, the audience was over. One of the Kung's advisors called me and said the attack was beginning in one and a half ummi. Captain Uraz Tukhsh's Shiamiru had been transferred to the eighteenth, reserve flotilla and would be in the third wave of ships, and for secrecy reasons, everyone on the shuttle was strictly forbidden from leaving the game until the battle. Also by order of the Kung himself, everyone who would take part in the attack was supposed to move their respawn to a safe place here on the base, where new teams would be formed and sent to the front in a centralized manner.

I confirmed that I understood and accepted all the security rules, and that my companions would not be committing any violations. After that, Minn-O and I headed back to the antigrav. When we got far enough away from the council chamber, my companion asked an unexpected question:

"If it's no secret, who was that clown? I mean, the one who made the warrior in the stylish white armor get off the throne. He was constantly fuming, baring his teeth, roaring at you and stamping his feet in such a funny way."

I stopped sharply and prepared to die, because Minn-O had said these words into a functioning microphone, which meant her seditious question would not go overlooked. And there were probably recordings being made here as well. It was a top-secret military base after all. Later, I realized she was using an earthbound language and, most likely was not understood by the local security goons. In any case, my wayedda had to be taught a lesson for her loose tongue:

"I'll have you know that was Kung Waid Shishish, master of huge territories in space and the all-powerful ruler of our shared planet Earth. Didn't your grandpa ever tell you about our suzerains?"

Minn-O tripped and almost fell. I caught her at

the last moment. In just a few seconds, my companion's skin changed color from ashen-gray to white, her lips quivering in horror. Maybe, what I said next was too much, and I shouldn't have scared Minn-O so much, but I couldn't help myself:

"I tried to ask for five of those big robots." We had just come back into view of the hall full of Geckho troops and I pointed Minn-O to the immobile titans in the distance. "Not for long, just for a couple of days. I think that will be enough to settle the issue of your grandpa's faction and leave it completely in the past. What do you think?"

"And... and what did the Kung say?" My wayedda started to hiccup nervously, so I took pity on her and admitted that it was just a stupid joke. After all, the Geckho never interfered in disputes between their vassals.

"Every joke has a measure of truth," said the Dark Faction lady, showing plainly that her world had sayings similar to my own.

Minn-O, still not having fully escaped that fear, smiled in embarrassment, looked at me and begged forgiveness for her mistake. I looked the Princess in the eyes, and I read her mind despite myself. Although I didn't break the mental contact either.

"Just think, my ruling grandpa Leng Thumor-Anhu La-Fin is making grand plans, inviting the best strategists and conducting meeting after meeting. He thinks he has the situation fully under control and his

enemy's days are numbered. But in fact, the Leng isn't even close to understanding the power he's tussling with! 'Poor student...' We'll see about that! Just think, this 'poor student' was well received by a great ruler of the Geckho race! With one well-timed phrase, my husband can steer the Kung wherever he likes. And he just has to wave a claw, and all that will remain of my faction is memories... What a brainless idiot I am! As soon as I open my mouth, I talk my way into a death sentence. Good thing my husband is kind-hearted and lets me get away with little mistakes..."

Then, instead of a whole long-winded diatribe, my wayedda said a very short sentence:

"Gnat, I can't hide it, I'm in shock!!!"

Chapter Six

To war!

"EIGHT OF CLUBS!"[1]

"Pass!"

"I have an eight too, trump suit! Still pass!"

"No fair! You three are all team up against me one girl! And kitten is cheat again!"

"Meee not is cheeeating! Just move the deck no playing card! Uline fat ass move and dump all."

"Yooou is call fat who, shitt-mouth?!"

"Don't fight! What are you playing the bitch for?! You picked up a ten in the last round, get rid of it!"

These spats had been going on for quite some time, disturbing my sleep. First, I took the many bullshitting voices as just a part of my delirious dream.

---

[1] Translator's note: in this scene, the crew is playing the Russian card game Durak (literally meaning "fool"). Comparable to the American card game President, the objective is to get rid of all your cards.

In it, Gnat was walking through an endless gloomy desert, the black stony surface of which was filled with blinking red broken lines to the very horizon. And they formed all kinds of sentences in Geckho. I walked along these blinking lines, jumping from sentence to sentence, sometimes finding myself on Miyelonian inlaid geometric shapes. All the while I tried to line up the text with the languages of my Earth, the Dark Faction, Relict glyphs and for some reason the language of the Precursors. Very few knew anything about that. And at that, I saw the odd message about improving Astrolinguistics, after which I saw some previously unapparent connections between the various languages of the Universe.

It was an interesting dream and probably had some kind of deep meaning, but the black desert of symbols gradually lit up and seemingly dissolved. And my friends' agitated shouting only grew stronger and took over everything else. It became harder and harder to ignore their voices and, at a certain point, I finally fell asleep. I batted open my eyes with difficulty and... didn't immediately realize what was happening. My dream was continuing in real life! So that's what the hell this was. I guess I fell asleep with the Listener helmet on, and there had been glowing and blinking red symbols in front of my eyes the whole time. Clearly, that is what gave root to my strange delirious dream. Dazed, I led an unhurried gaze over the system message:

Astrolinguistics skill increased to level seventy-eight!

Seventy-eight??? Wait just a second! What did I have before I went to sleep? Sixty-nine I thought... Or was it seventy? I couldn't say for sure but, in any case, it was much less than the system was currently telling me. Had I been studying languages in my sleep? Was that even possible? I hurried to open my stat sheet and made sure that it hadn't just been my imagination. Astrolinguistics really had grown significantly!

And at that, the main progress was apparently from decoding a large number of Relict glyphs. The process I had initiated yesterday of studying and learning glyphs in the unfamiliar language had continued in my sleep. My knowledge of the mysterious ancient race's language had expanded at a simply explosive pace, and every new logogram I could read served as a catalyst and sped up my learning even more. In fact, I could almost read my class description in its entirety now:

Listener. On the second rung of the Relict Pyramid, this class specializes in detecting and understanding computerized systems of any type using mental faculties or scanning systems. As level and skills grow, discovery chance, volume of data transmitted [unknown logogram], interface distance and total control chance are all increased. After reaching a high enough level, class may be changed from Listener to [unknown logogram], Thinker or Administrator.

Primary skills: Scanning, Machine Control, Psionic.

Class limitations: May not equip light or power armor. May not use mental boosters to improve reflexes and statistics. May not change gender at this stage of development, reduced Regeneration and loss of wings.

Loss of wings didn't worry me all that much as I had never had them, and I was quite happy to see I couldn't change my gender. The last thing I needed was another surprise change like had happened with my class!

I didn't understand every word in the description, and I was especially confused by the part about the Relict Pyramid and further progress. But all the same, it was quite interesting, and the Listener was just an intermediate stage in my evolution. Distracted by thinking, I didn't notice right away but the ship had started slightly vibrating and the main thrusters had started giving a monotonous hum. Apparently, the Shiamiru was in motion. What a trick! I guess I had contrived a way to sleep through a takeoff! Although I suppose we were taking off from the small Un-Tesh comet with minimal gravitation, so there shouldn't have been too much turbulence.

"This is for you, Tini. The sixes are coming out!" Minn-O exclaimed joyfully, after which my friends all laughed and rumbled happily together.

I lowered my feet from my bed to the floor and glanced out into the hallway. The picture I saw was not much less surreal than my recent delirious dream: in the opposite cabin, my friends were all enthusiastically playing durak. The huge furry Uline in her short colorful robe was taking up almost a whole bench by herself. Opposite the Geckho lady was the little Tini with rumpled cards in his clawed hand, and the happily laughing Imran, Eduard and Minn-O, all squeezed in together. Only Dmitry Zheltov was missing, but our pilot was probably on the bridge.

"Ah, Gnat is awake!" said my friends, welcoming my appearance with glee. I greeted them all and asked how they had all learned to talk together, in what language.

They exchanged confused glances, seemingly considering this for the first time themselves. Uline Tar answered for everyone in Geckho:

"I mean, what's to understand? This isn't quantum physics or some scientific tract in a dead language, it's just a simple little game. You only need twenty or so words. Dmmmitry sat down first and helped us translate, then he went to prepare the Shiamiru for take-off. We had already figured it all out by then. But Tini keeps cheating, making the excuse that he doesn't know the rules. Anyway, with his class that seems about right."

"Uline is lying! It was just mistakes, not on purpose!" although my kitten was objecting in his native Miyelonian tongue, he was demonstrating an unexpected ability to understand Geckho.

Seemingly, Tini had taken my advice to take Astrolinguistics at level fifty, and his currently level of 52 had been earned from, among other things, improving that. Just then, Imran called for my attention and, asking Uline to step aside, slipped into the corridor of the shuttle. There he changed his usual clothes for a raspberry-red Geckho officer's suit, which had been refit for a human.

"Look at this! I got it right before takeoff!" the Dagestani athlete demonstrated the flexibility of the articulated armor suit, crouching, jumping, waving his arms and legs and not hiding his excitement. "It's fully sealed, comfortable and strong! It has enough air for a whole four hours! There's a slot on both shoulders to attach extra equipment, but my class is incompatible with the Avashi Shock plasma-grenade launching system that came with it, so I sold it to those guys," Imran said, pointing at the twin brothers Vasha and Basha Tushihh. "But Dmitry Zheltov said I could attach something else there: a jet or gravity booster pack, distance measurer or even a mobile interstellar communication system!"

"Better brag to Gnat about what's written on the armor," Eduard Boyko interrupted the elated cries of the Gladiator, and Imran turned, demonstrating the complex jerky line engraved on his right shoulder plate:

"*This armor is my gift to a great warrior of the human race. Let this armor serve him long and faithfully, defending its bearer in the most furious scraps, and let the warrior himself live up to this gift! Kung Waid Shishish, commander of the Geckho Third Strike Army."*

"We already got it translated," Imran started smiling happily, then grew serious. "It is an impossible rarity, but also quite a responsibility. Wearing this armor, I'm obliged to be an example of honor and bravery, so I don't bring shame on the great Kung! My Fame grew by two points to five as soon as I got this amazing suit!"

"And Gnat, they tried to poison me!" Minn-O cut into the conversation, seemingly envious I was talking with my friends and not paying her any attention. "They gave me this food that had something in it, and now my throat won't stop burning!"

"Come on, it was just soup," Imran did not agree with the Princess, "In fact, I'd add a bit more garlic and pepper. It tasted almost like lamb shurpa, just like they eat back home!"

I was saved from discussing the gastronomic preferences of various cultures by a loudspeaker announcement. It was Uraz Tukhsh asking me to come to the bridge. And he asked politely, not the drawn-out "Gnnnat!" I was used to hearing when something bad happened on the starship.

On the bridge, beyond of course Uraz Tukhsh in his luxurious pearl- and gem-encrusted outfit, were all three of the captain's bodyguards, Dmitry Zheltov at the helm, the old navigator Ayukh and the leader of the boarding group. I had not yet had the chance to get to know the last one. A large severe Geckho, he had only come aboard the Shiamiru recently, and had practically not left his cabin, speaking only with his ten underlings.

"Gerd Gnat, please sit down," the captain pointed me to a chair slowly levitating around the room, and I hurried to take it. "Look what a wonder has joined us!"

I didn't understand right away what it was or where to look, then I realized I should look at the large monitor before the Navigator, which was showing an image from our external cameras. Apparently, there was some kind of swift disk-shaped object corkscrewing around the Shiamiru. It was going so fast it was hard to measure its linear dimensions, but still it was much smaller than our shuttle. A drone? Some external module? I turned to captain for an explanation.

"Quite the rare and mysterious appearance. No one knows for sure what it is, but such objects sometimes appear out of nowhere and accompany ships for a time. Perhaps they are automatic recon drones from some as-of-yet-unknown highly developed civilization. And maybe it is the technology of a long extinct race that is still in working condition. For example, it could be from the Precursors, Relicts or Mechanoids. At any rate, they don't like attention and they immediately disappear when anyone attempts to study them. They are commonly referred to as satellites or symbiotes."

"Symbiotes?" I caught on the familiar biology term. "So do they help ships out?"

The captain went silent, and the question was instead answered by the old navigator Ayukh:

"When I was young, I heard from old space veterans that they do. Like they can somehow connect to a ship's systems and interact with it — to power up the energy shield, repair the armor and external modules, or even attack enemies. Though I haven't ever encountered verifiable information, only old wives' tales. It might all be bullshit. But in any case, the arrival of a satellite is considered a very good omen, presaging interesting events and great fortune!"

"Yes, I've also heard that symbiotes bring luck!" Uraz Tukhsh generously splashed an alcoholic cocktail into his glass, at the same time filling another and extending it to me.

I refused, because I understood perfectly that the captain would not have called me over just to show me the symbiote. I could sense that Uraz Tukhsh was jittery. Apparently, this conversation would be serious, so I needed a clear head.

"As you like," Uraz Tukhsh didn't insist, set the glass aside and leaned toward me. "You see, Gerd Gnat, I have taken the decision not to extend your contract."

Ah, fu... Good thing I was sitting... I was prepared for a lot of possibilities when the captain called me for a serious conversation, but I was definitely not expecting it to turn that direction. Thousands of alarming thoughts were sloshing around in my head. What to do now? How to return to earth? How would my friends take the news? What would my faction heads say? But most important, of course, was why had he made such a strange decision? What had changed in the last few hours. After all it wasn't all that long ago that Uraz Tukhsh had come all the way to Earth just to pick me up!

From the corner of my eye, I saw that Dmitry Zheltov was no less shocked, even taking off his headphones to eavesdrop. I was also expecting an explanation. But Uraz Tukhsh was clearly embarrassed and stumbling as he looked to the powerful Geckho behind him for moral support. Then he started to explain:

"You see, Gnat, you're a good Prospector... well you aren't really a Prospector now, but a Listener. That doesn't matter, though... We don't need anyone to find minerals now, so the job I hired you on for... we don't need any more... And in the war... I mean what kind of war will it be for the Shiamiru, staying back in the third wave?! I doubt we'll even see any Meleyephatians today!"

And what of it? I could not see the connection between the auxiliary role of his Shiamiru cargo shuttle and the end of my contract. Had the captain just not guessed before that his hastily rejiggered cargo ship would not be allowed to fight on the front lines against fearsome enemy cruisers and battleships? He probably knew, and yet he had hurriedly flown off to get me.

So I understood perfectly that he was not telling me the truth. And he knew I knew it. So a second explanation followed that was no less stupid than the first:

"The whole Geckho Third Strike Fleet only has members of other races on a few ships. One has a very talented Trillian Gunner, who cannot be replaced by any Geckho. Another has a legendary Cleopian Navigator. Waid Shishish himself on his *Tinakuro* cruiser has two Crystallide Engineers, both indispensable defensive experts. But on my ship, there are Humans of all stripes, a Miyelonian thief, and apparently even a Morphian... The other captains point their claws at me and say I command nothing but a band of space gypsies..."

Mysticism skill increased to level five!

I noticed the skill bump then raised my gaze. For some reason, Uraz Tukhsh was just feeding me a line instead of giving an honest answer. After all, he knew perfectly well about the Miyelonian and my human companions when he picked me up from Earth! But it didn't bother him then!

With a heavy sigh, the captain continued his speech, and I could sense we were reaching his true motives:

"The presence of such a notable player on my little ship shifts the center of power and authority, weakening the position of the captain. I can see that half of my crew looks to you with admiration and awe, they hang on your every word! To them, you are in charge here. They listen to you more than their captain! And many authoritative Geckho in this fleet, including the commander himself, refer to the Shiamiru shuttle from the eighteenth flotilla as 'the one with the human Gerd Gnat,' not 'the one with Captain Uraz Tukhsh!' I simply cannot have that! I wavered for a long time, practically expecting a sign from on high, and here it is," the captain said, pointing to the symbiote flickering about on the screen. "That is the signal that it is time for me to make a decision, and everything will be alright!"

I could sense that even this was not everything, and the captain probably had some other motivation for his sudden decision. But what he had already said was plenty for me, and I didn't try to tease out the rest. I didn't even try to dig around in Uraz Tukhsh's brain, although I did have some opportunities. After all, it was not for nothing that the captain had brought in his enforcers and flattered me. He must have watched the end of the training in the cargo hold, so he probably knew about my psionic abilities and decided to take some precautions.

"Don't worry, captain, I will finish this voyage and take my band of gypsies with me at the first opportunity so the other captains stop looking down on you. I don't know how I'll get to my home planet, but

I've gotten out of a similar jam before."

"Gnat, don't think me so obstinate and harsh. I'm not going to throw you to the hands of fate on the first asteroid we reach," the Aristocrat said with clear relief, now just trying to smooth over the sharp edges.

The Captain demanded the Navigator turn on the big screen and pointed me to the star map:

"Look, Gnat. Our Third Strike Fleet is going to capture the planetoid Ursa-II-II. It is the only satellite of the densely populated Meleyephatian planet Ursa II, and it houses the planet's shield generators. Most likely, the satellite has already been taken, because it cannot have put up serious resistance. The Meleyephatians have removed all their combat ships from the system to fight the Miyelonians and suppressing terrestrial batteries doesn't take long. Right after taking down the shield, there will be a traditional ultimatum to the inhabitants, and they will surrender without a fight to avoid orbital bombardment and total destruction. I think it will all be over within one ummi. Anyway, both on the planet itself and its satellites, there are quite a few small but heavily trafficked space ports. I'm sure we'll find many ship owners happy to leave the war zone and I am willing to hire a small shuttle with my own money to send you back home."

That was very noble on the captain's part, which I immediately told him. Uraz Tukhsh replied with a slight bow and started to answer, but he was interrupted by the old Navigator:

"My Captain, we're arriving to the Ursa system. The computers have already begun the countdown until we come out of hyperspace. Forty-seven, forty-six, forty-five..."

"Excellent news," the captain turned rakishly in his hoverchair and floated over to the instrument panel. "I would bet anything that the Waideh-Tukhsh landing troops were first to set down on the enemy planetoid! My great relative Waid Shishish probably would not have missed the excellent chance to bring honor to our clan!"

A thought flickered by in my mind that I should take him up on this bet. To my eye, he was looking at this bloody space war through rose-tinted glasses. Nothing is that easy and, in such grand-scale operations, even the most carefully laid plans can get snagged up. What was more, I felt a stronger and stronger tension in my chest, sensing a growing alarm or even disaster. I was accustomed to trusting my presentiments. But I still kept silent, not wanting to jinx it and be blamed if I was right.

"Five, four, three, two..." Ayukh continued the countdown. But I just couldn't settle down.

Danger Sense skill increased to level forty-one!

"Dmitry, turn sharp left and spiral!!!" I shouted before the countdown was over, then the main screen flickered on.

And the pilot obeyed! Due to the sudden thrust,

I couldn't hold on and fell out of the chair, rolling along the floor as the ship slammed to the left and started spinning on its lengthwise axis. If not for my Listener armor's forcefield, which absorbed most of the damage, I would definitely have broken something. As it was, I slammed my head and right shoulder into a metal wall and it hurt very bad.

My vision faded for a moment in pain, but I still was able to see our little starship as it astonishingly threaded the needle between two huge pieces of twisted metal. How lucky! Then the shuttle dodged a twisted and sparking Greiss Ukhkh-Tor assault robot five feet from us. The assault mech, just like the ones I'd admired earlier, was twice the size of our shuttle and colliding with it at high speed could have had very severe consequences. But we got lucky...

Eagle Eye skill increased to level sixty-three!

Another piece of wreckage flew right past us and was eviscerated by the symbiote. The subsequent series of heavy blows to our energy shield and armor were palpable, but not deadly.

"What is that?!" the captain shouted, coming to his senses and testing his buckled belts with shaking hands in the copilot's chair.

I had already stood to my feet and, holding my hands on the tilted monitor, booted the ship scanner, setting the search to low distance and maximum detail with an emphasis on metal. Our ship shook hard again as a large piece of debris grazed us but was deflected by the energy shield. The scan finally came back and I told everyone in a cracking panicky voice:

"That was a piece of Captain Leng Amothy Yore's *Grokh-Uvachch* battleship of. What's more, based on the scan, lots of other ships from the Third Strike Fleet met their end here..."

Chapter Seven

Mutiny

HOW GLAD I WAS that I had the presence of mind not to bet with the captain about whose clan had been first to land on the planetoid! Apparently, it hadn't been such a walk in the park, and the plan had gone awry with many first-wave starships lain low in a pitched battle with the Meleyephatian fleet. And that included Kung Waid Shishish's biggest guns, like his only battleship and a few heavy cruisers. I saw that with just a cursory review of the data on the ship scanner. There must have been some leaks or treason at play, because the Meleyephatians had spun a thick web of gravity and thermonuclear mines right where the heavy ships of the Third Strike Fleet had come out of warp. In fact, some had not gone off and were still floating in space among the starship carcasses.

The Meleyephatians had also taken severe losses based on the innumerable fragments of their small frigates also strewn about. The remnants of that fleet, no more than two hundred small-class starships, were now huddled in around the planetoid Ursa-II-II, hidden behind the space fortress's energy shield and protected by its many terrestrial batteries. The main part of the Meleyephatian fleet, where I saw a few heavy cruisers, unusual clusters of joined-together ships and some auxiliary-class ships, was currently fighting an intense battle with the united flotillas of the Geckho, trying to keep them away from the planetoid with its deadly cannon batteries.

Scanning skill increased to level nine!

You have reached level sixty-six!

You have received three skill points! (total points accumulated: fifteen)

By the way, about those points... I tried to remember if twenty-four hours had passed since I got the first of them. In other words, did I risk losing some if I died, or was there nothing to be afraid of? I remembered for certain that I had not spent skill points since the end of my class transition to Listener and was saving them up to improve Scanning. I wanted to spend all of them there after I got the easy levelling out of the way. I had been worrying about it for some time, but figured I'd hit it soon enough. But the Shiamiru had just barely evaded thousands of bits of debris, which would have put us all in the grave so the issue had become critically important. So, had a full day passed or not?

I considered it. All my calculations showed that it hadn't been more than twenty hours. My heart immediately settled. Death could only set Gnat's progress bar back to zero. Nevertheless, I didn't want to risk it and placed all my remaining points into Scanning, bringing it to twenty-four. Woah! The result was so obvious so quickly! The picture on the ship scanner screen instantly became more comprehensible and distinct. I could even tell how the space battle for the planetoid was going.

Seemingly, the Geckho were winning. The fleet of large Meleyephatian ships had taken heavy losses from at least three flotillas of Geckho cruisers and had been forced to retreat from the shelter of the planetoid. Innumerable speedy Geckho interceptors then ducked between the enemy starships and jammed the Meleyephatians' electronics and navigation systems, not letting them flee. I also saw that the *Tinakuro* heavy cruiser had survived. So the Third Strike Fleet still had a flagship, and commander Kung Waid Shishish was still in charge.

I told my observations to the Geckho on the bridge. The old Navigator, with huge headphones on his furry head was listening carefully to the chatter on the fleet channel and confirmed my observations:

"That's right! Despite the heavy losses on our side at the very beginning of the battle, we've already practically won. Our main goal now is not to let the Meleyephatians' most valuable ships escape, and the Kung is shouting angry curses, promising to execute all the interceptor pilots if even one Meleyephatian ship escapes."

"But there are rumors the Meleyephatians will get reinforcements soon," Dmitry Zheltov continued, also listening carefully to the fleet channel. "Also, on the group channel, Leng Uravi Tor, commander of flotilla eighteen, demands that we change trajectory and return to formation, because we are too far from the main group."

"So go then!" the captain shot out. "The last thing we need is to be accused of disobeying orders!"

"I can't! Look at that chain of four Meleyephatian frigates." The pilot pointed at the group of red markers on the tactical map. "They took off from the planetoid and are trying to cut us off from the main flotilla. And I can't go to the side because then I'll be flying into a debris cloud and we'll come out in range of the fortress batteries! Our only chance is to do a heavy burn into the distance at full speed, dodge the broken ships and hope the frigates will lose interest in us!"

And that is exactly what happened. A few minutes of fruitless pursuit later, the enemy frigates all turned away and headed back toward the planetoid with its energy shield and defensive batteries. As a result of these maneuvers, our Shiamiru ended up hell knows where, in a field full of debris and very far from the nearest allied ships. Both the enemies and command lost all interest in us, turning their attention to other starships and more important events.

The captain, pilot and Navigator continued to listen to the discussions on the fleet channel and, at a certain point, all gasped and grumbled in shock. After that, interrupting one another and stumbling in worry, they started shouting that Kung Waid Shishish had just issued a very surprising order to leave the uncaptured heavy Meleyephatian ships and prepare for a final assault on the planetoid.

According to the commander, our recon had confirmed that in no less than a quarter ummi the Meleyephatians would be getting reinforcements! There were around forty cruisers and more than three hundred ships of smaller classes *en route*! It wasn't enough to defeat the Geckho fleet in an honest battle, but it was more than enough to hold out next to the planetoid under protection of the heavy fortress batteries and not let a landing team set down.

"Well god damn! Does the Kung understand that it will be a meat-grinder?!" Dmitry Zheltov shouted in alarm, slamming his fist on the instrument panel in annoyance. "The Meleyephatian interceptors and other small ships are still in play. They can immobilize our heavy ships and turn them into easy targets for the terrestrial batteries. An assault on the planetoid will lead to huge losses!"

"The commander simply has no choice," old

Ayukh said with sadness, lowering his head. "It's either land and capture the enemy fortress, even at the cost of huge losses, or turn and run, admitting defeat in his very first battle at the rank 'commander of many divisions.' Knowing Kung Waid Shishish's character, he'd sooner lose all allied ships in a desperate bid to win than retreat."

I was entirely in agreement with the experienced and wise Navigator there. The commander would not hesitate to sacrifice all his subjects if that would give him even a transparently thin chance of achieving this victory, which was of principle importance. And while everyone in the room sat in thoughtful silence, digesting the worrying information, I walked up to the ship scanner.

Bringing up the planetoid, which we were supposed to take at any cost, I started working my magic with the settings. It was about what I did before when Uraz Tukhsh asked me to thin out the worthless asteroids, but now I set the scanner a bit differently. I wanted to know sources of elevated radiation, the density of electromagnetic fields, the structure of celestial objects, and also temperature gradients and density. I had to combine the results of various analyses and run a few more scans on places I found suspicious. Only then could I compile a more or less complete picture of the enemy base.

Scanning skill increased to level twenty-five!
Electronics skill increased to level forty-five!

Electronics skill increased to level forty-six!

So, what did we have here? An object of irregular shape which, could never be described as spherical. It was more like an oblong uneven polygon, twenty-four miles at the longest point, pocked with craters and crevasses. There were also a few elevated outgrowths, towering over the surface by many miles. The Meleyephatian fortress itself was located deep underground, safely sheltered against orbital strikes by many miles of dense crust. On the surface, I counted six huge generators for the planetoid's huge forcefield and around one hundred seventy batteries with huge mobile turrets. It looked very, very intimidating. So, how to crack this tough little nut?

I turned the picture this way and that, looking it over from every angle. I reached a decision after telling the computer to overlay the firing range of each of the one hundred and seventy batteries. And the terrestrial batteries covered one another very well. Their ranges intersected many times, but due to the uneven landscape, the planetoid's defense had a few weak points. For example, those spire-like outgrowths blocked relatively large sections of space for a few batteries. Then I discovered a narrow circular sector, covered only by one battery. And if this one and only defensive battery could somehow be destroyed, there would be nothing stopping the Geckho from landing a force there large enough to suppress any ground-based resistance.

But what could they use to destroy the huge and probably very powerful laser cannon, which was also covered by a forcefield? There were obviously not enough cannons here on the Shiamiru, we needed something more destructive and powerful...

My gaze caught on the remnants of the mines, floating among the debris of the *Grokh-Uvachch* and other ships. A thermonuclear or high-powered gravitation mine like that would probably be enough for this mission. All that remained was to figure out how to deliver it... although... was there any reason this shuttle could not serve that purpose? Grab one of them with a claw or gravity crane, figure out why it hadn't detonated and then blast off full speed toward the planetoid and slam into a cannon tower! The fortress defenders would definitely not be expecting such a thing from a lone cargo ship that fell out of formation, so it might work just due to the element of surprise. Sure, we'd lose our shuttle, but that was a small price to pay for the whole Third Strike Fleet to break through the enemy defenses and capture the Meleyephatian fortress!

Even in real life, when victory was on the line in a highly important battle, there were always heroes prepared to sacrifice themselves to save their comrades at arms and secure a win. But this was just a game so dying would mean we would just be out of the world for fifteen minutes, then come back at our respawn point. The fleet commander would probably appreciate such a sacrifice if it allowed his fleet to secure victory and would reward the shuttle owner for his lost property. So the decision to sacrifice the ship and open the door for the assault troops looked not merely justified, but absolutely correct.

However, when I told everyone my idea, I met unexpected resistance from Captain Uraz Tukhsh bordering on hysteria:

"You've lost your mind, Gnnnat!!! My Shiamiru cost seven million crystals, plus four million in improvements! You simply don't know my cheap relative Waid Shishish the way I do. He would never agree to compensate such losses! I'd be broke! I'd rather see our fleet retreat and have this idiotic war end all the sooner than be left high and dry! So no, no, and no again!!!"

Fame increased to 57.

Authority increased to 32!

Based on the pop-up messages, not every crew member to witness this dispute supported the captain's point of view, and my suicidal idea was to someone's taste. Dmitry Zheltov, after removing his earphones and switching to Russian, suggested that the two of us bump off all the Geckho on the captain's bridge, lock the heavy armored doors from the inside and do it all ourselves without the stubborn Aristocrat and his henchmen.

But I naturally refused. I had too clear a memory of the Dark Faction murdering four Geckho on the cargo ferry and knew that it would end in our real-world execution, plus huge fines to be paid by our faction. And of course I had no desire to die for real, so I asked Dmitry to settle down and not voice such seditious thoughts.

And then, from the corridor, I saw an enraged Uline Tar throwing herself on our captain with fists, reproach and cursing. I had to admit, I hadn't even heard all those curses before and was somewhat taken aback by the vigor of the usually calm and contemplative Trader. The baffled captain also didn't immediately understand why his bride was so outraged. Uline then wailed in hysterics, waving her arms, stomping her feet and shouting that she refused to obey such a cowardly and pitiful captain! It turned out that someone on the bridge had turned on the loudspeakers, and our dispute was overheard by the crew. The Geckho back there disapproved extremely when Uraz Tukhsh said he didn't want to sacrifice his ship for the common victory. In fact, soon not only Uline was now cursing at the captain and calling him to active measures.

I suspected that the captain's already unimpressive Authority took a deep nose-dive, and Uraz Tukhsh was now somewhat further from Gerd status. With difficulty, the captain pushed Uline out as she continued to angrily insist. Then he locked the door from the inside and turned around, for some reason spitting out his hate at me:

"Gnnnat! I know you did that on purpose to make me look stupid!!! You just can't forgive me for not prolonging your contract, is that it?"

What?! What did I have to do with this? I was just choking in righteous indignation and took in a lungful of air, preparing to say my fill. Fortunately, I didn't have to justify myself. The elderly Navigator Ayukh took a step forward, screening me with his body:

"Calm yourself, Uraz. The human Gnat had nothing to do with it, I was the one who did it!"

"What? You?" Our loser Aristocrat stumbled backward, shocked by our respected Navigator's statement. "But why, Ayukh?!"

"I wanted to stop you from making the biggest mistake of your life. You told me so much about your plans to prove yourself, earn glory and respect from society and become the pride of Clan Waideh-Tukhsh. Here, you have the very chance you've been waiting for! And you missed it... and now your fiancé is disenchanted with you... and you've lost the respect of your crew. I for one will be leaving in the nearest space port!"

Uraz Tukhsh bared his fangs fearsomely and spent a long time boring into his rebellious underling with his gaze, then he turned to the locked door, which Uline was still pounding on, shook his furry head and gave a rumble so loud the walls reverberated and echoed it many times over:

"I haven't missed a thing!!! And I didn't miss my chance

to become a hero. I just have a different idea! We'll blow up that Meleyephatian battery, open a path for the assault and distinguish ourselves, but we'll also keep the Shiamiru intact! You see, we'll land on the planetoid and deliver the mine with the cargo loader, then sail off smoothly out of the blast radius! Dmmmitry, turn this ship around!"

Chapter Eight

The Wreck of the Shiamiru

I WASN'T EXPECTING Captain Uraz Tukhsh to apologize, and I also wasn't going to insist on satisfaction and spoil my relationship with the close relative of the commander any further. With an aura of calm, I ran another scan on the planetoid, getting a clearer map of the area around our proposed landing site, after which I turned off the monitor, left the bridge and returned to my bunk. The last thing I noted in the captain's bridge was that the symbiote had stopped following our ship and disappeared, dissolving in the depths of the cosmos. Just once did I see it on my minimap, where it was shown as a "plasma cluster," then it never came into the scanning radius again. None of the ship's instruments other than the cameras had been able to get a read on the satellite, and I obviously did not take out my Prospector Scanner and use a geological analyzer to clear that up.

If, as our Navigator said, the Symbiote was a good sign and a symbol of luck, it was very bad that he decided to leave us before this highly fraught operation. That immediately led me to certain ideas. I had to admit, I had no faith in our ability to land on the planetoid and use the heavy loader to deliver a thermonuclear mine to the laser cannons.

We couldn't let ourselves think our enemy was slow-witted, especially given how experienced and clever the Meleyephatians were known to be. As such, I had a very hard time believing that the fortress defenders wouldn't have their interest piqued by an enemy cargo shuttle landing on their planetoid (if the Shiamiru even would be able to do that while taking fire from the surface). Oh their interest would be piqued. Would it ever! And if they didn't shoot us down in midflight, they'd probably send a mobile division to handle our landing party, and maybe even a few frigates to turn us into dust. With such unhappy thoughts in mind, I reached the residential module and fell back in exhaustion on my cot.

"Gnat, we all heard what Dmitry Zheltov said over the loud speaker," Minn-O said, greeting my arrival in full battle gear and ready for active measures. "Eduard, and Imran too. If you would have agreed to attack the captain with Dmitry, we would all have supported you!"

I raised my gaze at my wayedda in mistrust and saw a look of utterly sincere and boundless loyalty, like a puppy. Minn-O had not been exaggerating one bit and was prepared to attack the Geckho if I asked. Just what I needed! Thanks, of course, to my wife and friends for their readiness to follow me through fire and water, but I hadn't earned such blind trust. I was a living man of flesh and blood, and also made mistakes or missed chances. Quite often, in fact. Like now, I was worried that I had not used mind control on Uraz Tukhsh. Maybe I'd have been able to make the captain think his plan was wrong and doomed to failure, and he would have refused the stupid idea of risking our whole grand operation just to save his cargo ship.

"My husband, you don't look like yourself! You look defeated and apathetic, as if you don't care what is happening! No matter what transpires, don't you worry. You've got me! I'll always be by your side!" Minn-O took a seat next to me on the bench and embraced me, then put her head on my shoulder.

I hugged the Princess back. Just then I heard an unusual mechanical screeching outside the shuttle, and my wayedda shuddered:

"What is that?"

I answered that the captain had ordered the capture crane turned on to grab a space mine and drag it into the cargo hold. I also quickly warned Minn-O, Imran and Eduard that the Shiamiru would soon start making sharp dodging maneuvers, preparing to land on the planetoid while being fired on from the surface. So I recommended my friends quickly check their spacesuits and fill their air reservoirs as much as possible. That was especially relevant to Eduard, whose huge Space Commando exoskeleton suit was jammed into in a niche in the hold and needed time to put on and boot up. I also told my kitten and the Geckho in the neighboring cabins to prepare their spacesuits.

The ship engineer went past us toward the cargo hold accompanied by two of the captain's Bodyguards. Two or three minutes passed, and Uraz Tukhsh's voice rolled down the ship:

"Technicians, ready the heavy loader! Everyone else, prepare for an emergency landing! Immediately after touching down, technicians open the cargo hold. After that adjust the landing struts and get us standing firm!"

Just after finishing the message, the thrusters started wailing in an unusually high-pitched, simply hysteric tone. Despite the functioning gravity compensators, I felt pressure in the back and head cushion of my seat. I hurriedly lowered the soft hand-holds from the walls and buckled up, preparing for a hard landing. Tini and Minn-O on the opposite bench did the same. Our ship started going faster and faster, spinning rapidly on its lengthwise axis, then started making sudden sharp bursts from side to side, clearly in an attempt to dodge shots from the surface.

The G forces quickly went beyond bearable (and that with functioning gravity compensators!!!). Everything was swimming before my eyes, it became hard to think and be patient, my Endurance Points started shooting down. I even had to, despite the dark in my eyes, hurriedly open my inventory and change my rings from the two Intelligence ones to the pair of +1 Constitutions the Morphian left me when we parted ways. I was very worried for Minn-O and would even have given my rings to her, but the Dark Faction Princess was looking surprisingly chipper. Clearly, her Constitution was significantly higher than my own.

The tone of the thrusters unexpectedly went even higher and their sharp whistle approaching ultrasonic. I braced myself for an impact. Touchdown!!! I shook so hard I almost bit my tongue off with my chattering teeth. My total hitpoints fell by a quarter. Yes, it was harsh, and seemingly we had broken one of the landing supports, because the floor of the starship was at an angle, but that was of little importance.

"Dmmmitry, for such a good landing in these difficult conditions, you are beyond all praise!" Uraz Tukhsh wheezed out on the speaker, after which he coughed and commanded, now back in his usual loud voice: "I'll be first to go out onto the planetoid! If someone tries to go before me, they will be shot at once! I will only be bringing crew I fully trust to the battery on the loader with me: the landing group, the Engineer, and my Bodyguards! The rest are to remain on the ship and await our return! The Medic is in charge during my absence. Dmmmitry, do not turn off the thrusters and keep the Shiamiru ready for a sudden take-off!"

The landing troops fussed about, with their commander stamping fearsomely down the hallway toward the cargo hold. The technicians immediately closed the door into the main hallway, then I heard the heavy loader starting up, the external door opening and the whistle of air gushing out.

Perception increased to 27.

Well, well! The short message that shot past my eyes attracted my attention and blasted away the strange stupor I'd been in since talking with the captain. My Perception had gone up for the second time since entering the game! And it happened while I was sitting with my eyes half open, actively using hearing, not vision. Maybe I should try to use other senses to level it up again like smell, for example or touch...

Minn-O, sitting opposite me, suddenly got on guard, unbuttoned her protective handholds and said with panic in her voice that she had a bad feeling about this. I also was getting a clearer and clearer sense that some unknown disaster was imminent. So what was I waiting for?! After all, I knew perfectly well that Uraz Tukhsh wouldn't succeed! I had to act at once!

I looked on the mini-map and saw that the loader with the landing troops had already left the shuttle, so I decisively stood up and headed to the bridge. Accompanied by the surprised and tense gazes of the Starship Pilot and Navigator, I walked up to the control panel and turned on the loudspeaker, telling the whole crew in Geckho:

"Attention, this is Gerd Gnat! You have probably heard an earful about how my intuition and luck have helped me escape a number of dire situations. Well, I have practically no doubt that staying here on the shuttle means certain death, and that the Meleyephatians will soon destroy our starship. So I suggest that anyone who doesn't want to die stupidly and without glory follow my example and get outside as quickly as possible! We'll exit through the cargo hold. The outside door there is already open, so it will be much quicker that way!"

Authority increased to 33!

I had to repeat that message in my native language so that my friends, who were standing stock-still in the corridor and didn't understand what all the commotion was about, would also start packing. Meanwhile, none of the Geckho were bold enough to object or refute the gravity of the threat or the need to leave. I saw both twin brothers Vasha and Basha put on their armor, hurrying to be the first out. The Supercargo, old Ayukh, and even Dmitry Zheltov, were not far behind despite the fact the captain had ordered them to stay and keep the Shiamiru ready for an urgent takeoff. The Starship Pilot reacted to my exclamation of surprise, turned and clapped me on the shoulder with his heavy palm, answering with a smile:

"Gnat, after all we've been through together, do you really think I'd abandon you to stay with this dumbass captain?!"

I thanked my friend for his trust and hurried to the exit, but there I met Uline in the doorway, who was behaving strangely, and in fact was going the opposite direction to Uraz Tukhsh's personal bunk. I started opening my mouth, preparing to ask the Geckho lady what she was doing, but she put her hand to her lips, calling for silence. I froze and watched Uline walk over to the built-in wall safe and skillfully, clearly knowing the code, put in some complex combination and open the heavy armored door.

"You didn't see that!" the Trader warned me severely, quickly taking lots of bags of valuable red crystals and another couple bars of metal. "I mean, it really is my money, actually my family's. After the recent attack of Miyelonian pirates on the Shiamiru, Uraz Tukhsh's pockets were empty. He couldn't even afford to pay the crew. But my Clan Tar-Layneh helped him out, giving him a decent bonus for arranging my marriage. The captain accepted the gift and has already spent some of it to pay the crew and modify the Shiamiru. But there will be no wedding now. I turned down the flighty and foolish Aristocrat when he left you alone to go speak with Fleet Commander Kung Waid Shishish. So the money I'm taking is gone no matter what! At least this way, someone gets to use it. Alright Gnat, I'm done. Let's run, we've spent too long here

123

already!"

By the way... is that why the captain changed his mind about me? I was reminded that Uline was on edge after the announcement of my arrest. She must have told the captain her mind about his passiveness and lack of desire to defend a team member. Seemingly, that argument had ended in their split. So, now I knew why the captain had fired me! And all these "other races," "notable player," and "no need for scanning" excuses were just a pretext...

We were already outside and had doled out spots on the four levitators when the ship Medic unexpectedly left the shuttle, the last to do so. I basically assumed he would stay, because the captain had no doubt in his loyalty and had even put him in charge.

"Uraz Tukhsh died along with all of his soldiers on the loader," the doctor explained, seeing my bafflement. "They got gunned down by automatic defense systems near the laser cannons. I was in a group with them, so I could tell right away based on the dimmed icons. Anyway Gerd Gnat, I see no reason to sit alone in the shuttle and ask you to take me with you!"

I gave a slight bow to the latecomer, accepting the offer, and pointed at the levitator old Ayukh was going to be driving, which had a free spot. In my headphones, I then heard a distinct grinding of teeth and Uline's unhappy voice:

"After all that, he died pointlessly... How predictable! And how stupid! That egotistical idiot's stubborn greed was the downfall of this mission. And it was of the highest importance for the whole Third Strike Fleet! He's the only reason the bomb did not make it to the enemy cannons. We are the last ones who can try and rectify the situation. Gerd Gnat lead the way! Where are we flying?"

Authority increased to 34!

I pointed at a ridge of cliffs. Based on the map I had from scanning, there was a whole web of cracks and deep crevasses beyond it, which I was planning to use to reach the battery unnoticed. Thankfully, one crevasse just so happened to butt right up against the cannons. They wouldn't be able to see us from the ground, but from above... I jerked my head and froze, distracted by the battle raging up above in space. The hundreds and thousands of bright fast dots appeared to be moving chaotically, tangled in a hateful skirmish. Sparks flew, far off explosions flashed. It almost looked like you could see the laser beams. Then, a volley of rockets took off from beyond the nearest cliffs in the dark sky. And some of them found their targets in space.

Upon closer inspection the vortex of dots did have an order to it. In the groups of moving points, I could vaguely tell our flotillas from theirs. If I understood correctly, Kung Waid Shishish's decision to leave the uncaptured fleet of heavy Meleyephatian ships and turn toward the planetoid had backfired. The enemy's heavy ships did not flee when they had the chance, but joined the planetoid defenders, which seriously complicated the Third Strike Fleet's mission...

Eagle Eye skill increased to level sixty-four!

So, enough staring at the sky. Time to act! Our four levitators blasted off and, gathering speed, rushed toward the ridge of dark brownish cliffs. We managed to make it just under nine hundred yards from the shuttle when suddenly Minn-O La-Fin's frightened voice drew everyone's attention:

"Danger!!! Ship to the right!!!"

Tolili-Ukh X. Meleyephatian Modular Frigate. Configuration: near-space/atmospheric.

The huge and at first glance awkward-looking dark triangular starship slowly came up from behind a hill. Was there something back there?! We'd been looking up for enemies, not even considering that they could come from other directions.

On my command, all four flying boards sharply pivoted and took shelter in a very convenient crevasse. I ordered everyone to hide and try to limit their radio communication, unbuckled from my levitator and, after making sure my magnetic soles were sticking to the iron-nickel ground, ran up the slope to a viewpoint of large icy boulders and carefully peeked out.

And I was just in time. A spark flashed, and right where our shuttle had just been, a crimson flower blossomed in a powerful explosion! The dark frigate unhurriedly approached the fire, then hovered one hundred fifty feet over the flaming wreckage and shot another rocket or torpedo, turning the ground into a boiling lake of molten stone.

Chapter Nine

Wrong-Way Raid

N O WAY OF LEAVING the planetoid. No weapons
capable of destroying the enemy battery. No way
of communicating with fleet command and only a
few hours' worth of air for two of us, Minn-O and Tini,
though the rest had much more. Seemingly, it was time
for us to fall into despondency and despair. But our
little squadron of twelve members of three races was in
high spirits and full of vigor. Despite all the challenges
and danger, we were still alive and were not about to
give up without a fight!

So, just after destroying the Shiamiru, the
Meleyephatian frigate took off into the sky like a Roman
candle, joining the defenders of the enemy planetoid.
After that, I held a small meeting where we discussed
the main issue — what to do next? We had no

thermonuclear or any other kind of bomb that could destroy the terrestrial battery and thus clear a path for Geckho landing ships. What was more, I had very serious fears that even if we were able to destroy the laser turret tower by some means, the Third Strike Fleet Commander Kung Waid Shishish and his military advisors simply wouldn't understand the opportunity we had given them, and all our sabotage would come to naught.

Why had we not contacted command and told them about the weak point in the defenses while still on the Shiamiru? Good question. I personally didn't know why Captain Uraz Tukhsh hadn't done it. Maybe he was afraid they would assign the mission to someone else, who would then get all the glory. And maybe he assumed nothing would happen to the ship after landing, and he would have plenty of time to communicate the information? Although... what if we were shot down during landing? It was of course not impossible that I was unfairly demonizing the captain and Uraz Tukhsh, not having much experience in military matters, had just not considered it. Or perhaps it was the other way around, and he had good intentions. For example, maybe he didn't say anything because he was afraid of the important information being intercepted by the Meleyephatians, or that they might take measures and close the gap in their defenses? Who could say...?

One way or another, the problem of transmitting

information to fleet command had become crucial. Ayukh said that he could do it if he could get access to some Meleyephatian comms equipment. The old Navigator didn't know their language, but he had encountered Meleyephatian starships, navigation systems and comms devices before in his long space career. All that remained was a "minor issue." We had to dig up an intact enemy transmitter. But where?

"Alert! Another starship!!!" Imran shouted, forcing us all to scramble up the hill and, after taking cover behind the boulders and uneven points on the surface, hide and stop talking.

It was the same type of frigate, a Tolili-Ukh X, and it was as if it had come out from behind the neighboring hill. Maybe this was the same one we saw before? Maybe, but it was hard to believe. It had taken off from the planetoid and no one had seen it turn around and land again. Copying the course of the first frigate, this Tolili-Ukh X passed over the still smoldering lake of molten rock where the Shiamiru was destroyed and took off vertically into the starry sky.

"Maybe they have a repair base there," Vasha Tushihh suggested, looking in agitation at the quickly shrinking enemy frigate, fluidly joining the whirlpool of the far-off space battle. "So damaged Meleyephatian ships land somewhere beyond the hills, quickly get patched up, fill up on rockets and go back into battle?"

"That seems very likely. And we can help our fleet if we stop these constant reinforcements," the

Supercargo piped up.

The Supercargo went by the name Avan Toi, and he was worth telling about in much greater detail. First off, I had never met such a massive and corpulent member of his race before. The level-eighty Geckho looked almost like a ball in exoskeleton armor. Without any armor he wasn't much different from a furry perfect sphere on reinforced-column legs. Then poking up off that were his small-eared head and two stubby front arms protruding awkwardly. Despite his corpulence, Avan Toi moved with impressive grace and skill and I had never seen the Supercargo seem self-conscious about his appearance in my whole time on the Shiamiru. And no one in the crew gave him a hard time about his weight either. In fact, Avan Toi enjoyed great respect from the team, and now his idea was immediately supported by Uline and the twin brothers.

"If we can't blow up the battery," Uline said, "we can try to damage the Meleyephatians another way by attacking their repair base and, at least for a time, paralyzing it!"

Basically, all the Geckho were unanimous in their preference to change target and attack the repair base. Most likely, I could have leaned on my Authority or even applied my psionic abilities to make the Geckho go back to the initial plan and attack the cannon battery. But I didn't do that. The new target was much closer, which was quite an important factor given our limited time and oxygen. Also the repair workshop and its scurrying technicians and mechanics seemed like a softer target for our meagre force. But the most important thing was that I was on guard after hearing that there were automated defensive structures next to the terrestrial batteries. If Uraz Tukhsh's well trained and prepared group of Space Commandos had been entirely taken down in a matter of seconds, where was the guarantee that we would not meet the same fate?

"Alright, it's decided! We'll change targets!" I pointed at the place where the enemy frigates were coming from. "New mission: paralyze the repair workshop! To the levitators!"

WE WERE WRONG. It was not a repair base as we thought, but a closed armored door about ninety feet in length leading into a subterranean complex. Before our eyes, the barrier slid aside twice, letting a Tolili-Ukh X frigate out from the bowels of the rock both times.

"They're coming out so fast! Are they stamping them from a mold?!" Dmitry Zheltov moaned out in Geckho as he laid next to me, no less stunned by our discovery than me.

"Most likely, they have a module warehouse under the rocks and an automatic assembly plant," explained the wise Ayukh. "The Tolili is a Meleyephatian modular frigate, which can be quickly assembled by robots for various purposes. For example, they can quickly assemble a high-speed interceptor. Or if they need a heavy long-distance fighter or assault plane, they build that. They stick on the stabilizer wings, then it can land on a planet with a dense atmosphere. If they put on other systems, it can be a cloaked recon ship, or even a noncombat ship for extracting minerals."

"Once upon a time, the Geckho were also taken by this idea of a universal situation-dependent ship," Uline Tar spoke up, lying on the slope and placing rocks on top of herself for extra camouflage, "but then my race began to favor narrowly specialized ships. It was just too wasteful and inefficient to produce and store mountains of modules that might never be used."

As I listened to their conversation, I was watching the enemy complex with the rapt attention, trying to find defense systems on the approach. As far as I could tell, there were none. My IR-Lens couldn't see anything distinct either and was actually malfunctioning because the takeoffs raised the temperature of the area too high. Scanning also didn't find anything. It only revealed red-hot and molten stones, solidified glass, swollen and hardened with dark bubbles on its surface. Even from this far away, my radiation gauge started humming in a nasty tone as soon as I pointed it at the molten stone near the entrance to the enemy complex. Something had definitely "made a boom" there not so long ago. Maybe that was what explained the lack of defensive structures — they had been swept away by a powerful explosion.

Turning back to the silent Ayukh, I built on that thought:

"As far as I understand, the Meleyephatians are putting together close-radius ships so they can attach more weaponry, bolster defenses, and quickly join the battle with minimal crew."

"That's exactly right, Gerd Gnat," Ayukh agreed, eagerly breaking into an explanation. "Instead of expensive hyperspace thrusters that eat through energy, they're adding extra shields and weaponry because these ships will never have to leave the bounds of this star system. Although as for the crew, that's disputable. If the Meleyephatians have respawn points on the base, our enemies will have basically unlimited reserves and can throw out another ship every twenty-fourth of an ummi. Look, there's another!"

And in fact, the armored door slid to the left, spitting another identical triangular Tolili-Ukh X frigate out of the underground complex. Our whole group pressed against the stones and froze motionless until it passed. We stood no chance if it saw us. But as soon as the enemy ship hid behind a hill, I jumped out and commanded:

"Forward! Take your places on the levitators! We

need to get into the base before the next ship comes out!"

We crossed the nine hundred feet between our shelter and the base entrance in a matter of seconds. Boldly unclipping from my still moving flying board, I ran up first to a strange intact wall panel in the blackened stone that caught my attention from afar. It was a stone disk one and a half feet in diameter. The surface had a carefully carved shallow spiral with a large number of turns. Uhh... This didn't look much like a control panel for the external doors, although... who knew with these Meleyephatians? At the very least, there was nothing else even distantly reminiscent of a sensor panel or remote control that I could see. I ran my gloved finger over the winding spiral, cleaning the dust and sand out of it, and trying to figure out what to do.

Your character lacks the Break-in skill.

Ah, that's right! What was I doing taking the lead with my mismatched abilities. I should have let a Thief do it. And I had a great specialist who knew how to break all kinds of locks and security systems.

"Tini, open 'er up!" I pointed my kitten to the strange spiral, then walked away.

The Miyelonian teen instantly had his thief tools in hand — a code breaker, a tangled coil of wires and fasteners, and some kind of electronic meter with a screen and arrow. Tini stood, looking at the stone disk in thought, then lowered his head, downcast:

"Master Gnat, I don't have enough skill! I need Break-in level seventy and Electronics over fifty!"

God damn it... Although the Electronics... maybe I could figure it out on my own when I saw all the circuits. I ordered Imran to break the stone panel out of the wall with his blade. A moment later, the Gladiator handed me a flat stone disk. And on the back side there was... nothing! No wires, no computer chips or circuits, just bare stone and traces of cement or some kind of hardened glue. What the crap?

I felt very dumb. I was trying to navigate the wires, but that was clearly the wrong idea. Actually, I should have activated the scanning icon! Uhh... I didn't understand a damn thing... there really were some kind of electronics inside the spiral stone, but there was no way of saying for sure that they had any connection to the massive door blocking the entrance to the subterranean complex. Maybe it was a clock. Or simply an element of decor meant to glow, vibrate or beep in certain conditions. I couldn't figure out a single thing even at maximum zoom on the mini-map. It was possible that this device simply had broken due to the recent nearby explosion. Although... there was another way to open the gates! Inside the cliffs, on the other side of the massive doors, I could see a device on the map:

External gate control system. Interface chance: 7%. Total control chance: 0%.

I could barely hold back an explicit outburst.

Just seven percent chance that I could hack or break the system with my mind, and absolutely zero to open it with my current skills. I realized I was still wearing the Constitution rings, so I opened my inventory and put the Intelligence ones back on. But that didn't change things much, just brought the interface chance up to twelve percent. No, this was not the way forward...

All we could do now was wait for it to open again and let another starship out. And hope that we wouldn't burn to death here on the red-hot stones or die from the extreme radiation. Then we would be able to slip in unnoticed (very low chance, to be honest), or just hope that the space frigate would be limited by the narrowness of the tunnel and could not turn us to ash with its cannons.

Wait! Now that was interesting! On my mini-map I saw a creature the game system identified as an enemy on the other side of the gates. Clearly, our arrival had not gone unnoticed and someone had decided to come up to a viewing window or surveillance system and figure out why there was activity on this side of the door. I couldn't see the creature's name on the map, just race and class:

Meleyephatian. Level-45 Technician.

I allowed the enemy to come up closer and shot my right fist outward. Got it! Hit you, overgrown little spider! And while I've got you under my control, how about you open up the gates for us!

Psionic skill increased to level fifty-one!

Mental Fortitude skill increased to level forty-six!

I warned my friends what was going to happen and ordered them to take out their weapons and prepare for a serious fight. Sparking blades appeared in Tini and Imran's hands. Basha, Vasha and Eduard took out their heavy many-barreled cannons and activated the plasma-grenade-launchers on their exoskeleton armor. The others got their weapons ready as well. Basha Tushihh even extended me a Targeting System, suggesting I mark targets just like at the Relict outpost, but I just shook my head. I was now controlling an enemy player, so I was afraid to lose concentration and mess up the whole operation.

As soon as the thick reinforced and probably very solid door started to move, our squadron burst inside, instantly shooting every enemy we saw in the first room. I followed my friends in and managed to shoot the Dark Faction Pulse Rifle a few times. I even hit once.

Rifles skill increased to level forty-nine!

There were either six or seven Meleyephatians, and they didn't even have time to react to our incursion. And the Technician who opened the gates for us died along with his allies. Almost the whole large ovular room was occupied by yet another Meleyephatian frigate ready for takeoff, but apparently it had no crew yet. And I didn't see any markers on the mini-map. I sent Imran and Tini to check it out and they climbed out of the enemy spaceship almost at once to say that it was empty.

There was a long wide corridor going deep into the cliff, and I could see some flashing lights coming from it. I could also make out some movement and the glow of a forcefield blocking the path. I could even see the silhouette of the next unassembled frigate. Apparently, the automatic starship assembly plant was located there, and was still plugging away. But why did the frigate right next to us still not have a crew? I asked that aloud and got a very believable answer from Minn-O:

"What business does a crew have at a factory? The crew shows up after the ship is ready. There's a hole in the right wall over there and, from what I can see on my map, there's an elevator shaft. Seemingly, the crews come up the elevator from somewhere deep inside the underground base, take their frigate and go into battle."

Exactly! I told the twin Geckho brothers and Eduard not to waste any time and use their heavy weaponry to stop the elevator: break all the panels, power sources, gravity platforms, cabins and cables, then launch a few homing grenades into the very depths of the shafts to break everything they can and ideally collapse the shaft itself.

Authority increased to 35!

"Ayukh, Dmitry, you take the frigate! Check to see if the systems are ready, I would like to know if we can fly out on it. But first turn on the comms and tell command about our raid. Ayukh, I assign this mission to you! You know the frequencies and codes, but most importantly explain to the Third Strike Fleet landing teams how to come in for a landing with minimal risk. Everyone else, after me! We're going to take care of the assembly plant!"

Chapter Ten

Targeting

THE FORCEFIELD I saw in the distant corridor let us through without the slightest resistance. As Uline Tar explained, it was a one-way field, which only stopped air from going out of the inhabitable spaces. And past it there was an air mixture a person, Miyelonian or Geckho could breathe, so I ordered Tini and Minn-O La-Fin to turn on their space suit air pumps at once to increase pressure in the tanks.

I only gave this order to the kitten and Princess; however the Supercargo, Medic and Trader also began pumping air into the reservoirs of their space suits. The Medic took advantage of the brief pause and started handing out a couple antiradiation pills to everyone because, according to his calculations, the dose of radiation we'd all received during our time outside the subterranean complex should have been deadly, although it was also reduced by the antiradiation properties of our spacesuits. I also obediently took and swallowed an antiradiation pill, even though I was not too worried about radiation, nor oxygen reserves. After all, my Listener armor had great defense against radiation and allowed me to store enough air for four and a half hours, so I would be fine.

Uline, also having swallowed an antiradiation pill, walked up closer and drew my attention with a suggestion:

"Gnat, it would be great to film a little clip right now to show that we were the first soldiers from the Third Strike Fleet to enter the enemy underground complex! That would mean both a boost in Fame for all group members, and Authority for you as commander. Then we could sell the clip to news channels!"

"Excellent thought! Go ahead!" I approved the Trader's initiative, then started taking everyone's flashlight to make proper lighting and get good shots.

While the other crew members were monkeying with their space suits, the video clip and medical care, Imran and I walked around the huge factory. There was light but it was so dim that, even with my high Perception, I had to turn on a flashlight. Imran couldn't see anything without an additional light source. There were no enemies here in the assembly plant, just robots flying and wheeling around on set paths, turning gravity cranes, shuffling assembly units, attaching piece after piece to the slowly moving frigate carcasses on the conveyor belt. The starship closest to the exit was almost ready. The robots were attaching its weapons systems. Another three Tolili-Ukh X frigates at various stages of assembly were on the belt already.

We stopped next to the freight elevator. Its raising platforms were hauling up all kinds of modules from the bowels of the planetoid with enviable regularity and they were instantly picked up by the scurrying robots. I had to stop the production line. But how? I immediately got the idea to use my Prospector Scanner to jam all the devices and get quality scans of Meleyephatian frigates and other complicated equipment, which probably also was of interest to humanity.

After warning my friends to turn off their levitators and walk away, I took out one of the geological analyzers and prepared my scanner. In the settings, I put cavity, metal and structure analysis to maximum. Minerals and organic materials were of no interest to me now, so I put those bars down to practically zero. So then, here we go! The tripod gave a familiar click, then I spread out the metal feet and placed the analyzer on the floor.

Scanning skill increased to level twenty-six!
Cartography skill increased to level fifty-three!
Electronics skill increased to level forty-seven!

The lights went out as predicted, as did my flashlight, the assembly apparatuses and the conveyor belt. The flying bots fell to the floor. The airflow from the elevator shaft was so strong that I could barely stay standing. The forcefield had turned off, and the breathable air whooshed out of the subterranean complex. However, two or three seconds later, it all came back online and got back to work like nothing had happened! What the crap?! Everything was supposed to short out, that's what always happened!!!

"This complex is probably powered from somewhere down below, in the depths of the planetoid. It's all being controlled from there too," Imran commented.

Yes, that seemed to be the case. There was just an assembly plant here, and it was all being controlled from someplace else. And also there, they were able to switch all the malfunctioning equipment back on.

"Ugh, I'd like to know how this all works..." I said thoughtfully, looking from side to side and not finding any panels or controls anywhere. "I'd like to get down into the brain center of this whole complex and make the ship of my dreams. Big and spacious, fast, maneuverable and with a great engine for long hyperspace jumps. And I want powerful weapons and to be able to land on planets as well. Imagine the surprise in our faction if such a craft landed in the middle of our capital citadel!"

"Oh yeah!" My friend smiled happily, picturing the scene, but he quickly grew serious. "But your starship would be confiscated immediately for study, and I doubt they'd ever give it back..."

Imran had voiced my own doubts and fears

without even knowing it. Even if I did get a starship, the faction directors probably would find their own plans for it, and they would have little to do with my own. Could I really refuse to give my faction such a valuable trophy? No, of course not. Even my closest friends wouldn't be understanding if I did that. Voluntarily give it to the faction? Well, in that case, they would declare their gratitude to Gnat for an artifact of such unimaginable scientific value. They might even give me some kind of letter of recognition, and pay out compensation of a few thousand crystals (because the faction simply had nothing else), but then they would keep the starship for themselves...

I gave a heavy sigh at the upsetting thoughts but I didn't have time to answer the Dagestani Gladiator. Just then, the ground underfoot gave a palpable shudder and I heard the alarmed and delighted voice of Eduard Boyko in my earphones:

"Commander Gnat, mission complete! We blew the elevator to smithereens and it looks like we took down a group of enemies on their way up. The game rained down so much experience that it hurts. I got three levels at once!"

"Great! Now come join us in the assembly plant. There's an elevator in here, and we need you to pull the same trick... Actually, wait! First cordon off the outside entrance into the underground complex! We've probably attracted the attention of the fortress defenders at this point, so some Meleyephatians will soon be trying to blow us out of here!"

A minute later, I heard the Space Commando's unconfident voice in my headphones, honestly admitting that he didn't understand how to fulfill my order. There was a security station with a bunch of spiraling levers at the exit. It had a big round screen, but the framerate was too high and there were a few pictures overlaid on top of each other when I could see anything. The screen was clearly not intended for the human eye. But which of the instruments closed the door? The Space Commando didn't know that and didn't have the stones to figure it out by trial and error.

"Gerd Gnat, don't have him close the door yet. We still haven't gotten comms online. Ayukh and I will close it later ourselves!" Dmitry Zheltov's voice rang out in my headphones. "We've just about figured out this Meleyephatian frigate. The control systems are of course unusual, but I think we can get it out of the shaft. Ayukh has already activated the communications systems and he's working his magic with the settings. In a few minutes, we'll be able to tell fleet command our message!"

"Gnat, enemies!!!" Minn-O brayed, running up to me and pointing downward. "Lots of Meleyephatian soldiers! They're coming up to us on the cargo platforms!!! They're still pretty far down, but there are a lot of them!!! I can see more than one hundred markers!!!"

I ordered Vasha, Basha and Eduard to come to

me at once, using the levitator to move fast. Twenty seconds passed, and the three huge soldiers jumped down next to me. I pointed them at the still functioning elevator, which I could not stop. There were a lot of boxes on its top platform now, and I barked:

"Enemies are coming up after us, a lot of them! Your mission is to blast the cargo elevator to the hounds of hell, killing the enemies, stopping the delivery of the components and blocking the shaft completely. As soon as you're done, we'll all go to the ship! There won't be any point in sitting here cut off from the rest of the complex in an assembly plant, so Ayukh and Dmitry, as soon as you figure out the frigate controls, come find us. Then we'll wait for orders from command and join up with the Geckho forces!"

That plan of action was met with great enthusiasm by almost everyone. Just Eduard Boyko had his doubts:

"Uhh, Gnat, that all sounds well and good, and launching rockets down the shaft of a cargo elevator is not gonna be hard. But, uh what if it really... f's us up?" Eduard actually used a different word, the real one in fact, but I won't reproduce it here. "It's just that marking," he said pointing at the next shipment of containers being unloaded and the many boxes, "I've seen it before on the ammo boxes for my Space Commando armor. I'm pretty sure it means: 'Caution, explosive!!!'"

I should have listened to my friend, I know. But

time was pressing and the enemies were getting near. I could already see the first of them on my mini-map. I really had no other plan of action, so I tried to reassure him:

"Eduard, that's actually what we want. The bigger it blows the better! Hopefully it will be enough to kill our enemies, block everything down below and do as much damage to the Meleyephatians as possible! Give me the Targeting System! I'll target your homing grenades!"

The Space Commando just shrugged his shoulders and stood obediently in formation with the two Geckho brothers next to the elevator shaft. Basha handed me a Targeting System and, just after the cargo-laden platform slid aside, I leaned over the shaft and started pointing. My Danger Sense skill was shooting through me, and I had already seen why. Son of a bitch! While we were bickering, the first of the enemy assault troops had just about reached the assembly plant!!! They were less than ninety feet away, around ten huge spiders in metal suits. They were stuck onto boxes and preparing their weapons for battle.

"Fire!" I shouted in a voice not my own, just after the frame of the Targeting System focused on a target. And that target was a pile of boxes marked "Caution, explosive!!!"

All three of my soldiers in exoskeleton armor shot a burst of homing grenades. I even saw the rounds leaving a smoke trail behind them and dashing down the shaft.

Targeting skill increased to level twenty!

Danger Sense skill increased to level forty-two!

And then... the world suddenly went dark. Before my eyes I saw a set of messages I had nearly forgotten:

Your character has died. Respawn will be possible in fifteen minutes.

Would you like to review your statistics for this game session?

Chapter Eleven

Dead Division

I REALLY WANTED to read the statistics of my game session, hoping to find an answer for a nagging question: what just happened? It was obvious that our rash actions had led to the explosion of lots of boxes of ammunition, and seemingly blown up in the elevator shaft. I mean, I was killed instantly despite my forcefield and ancient Relict armor. Most likely my nearby friends were also hit by the powerful explosion, so they were probably also going to respawn. But maybe some of them had escaped? Had we managed to stop the incoming Meleyephatians? And what happened to the ship?

Unfortunately, the information provided was very meager and contained no further explanation: 32 hours and 10 minutes in the game, 5 new levels, 92 (!!!)

skill improvements, one player killed... Hm, I wonder who that might have been? Had my one accurate shot from the pulse rifle actually killed one of the defenders of the underground complex? To be honest, it seemed unlikely unless that Meleyephatian was already seriously wounded by my friends. Almost half a million points of experience... but what for, where was it used in the game? Now growth of statistics, like Strength, Constitution and Perception... that, on the other hand, was very important in the game that bends reality. There had been serious progress in Fame and Authority... Also not bad. But in any case, my game ended in disaster:

Your session ended due to: death.

Decisively throwing back the lid of my virt pod and sitting up, I saw two people in the room. I was expecting Imran who'd also died but, much to my surprise, I also discovered Roman Pavlovich of the Second Legion, Gerd Tamara's deputy. In the game, he played a high-level Grenadier. Large and burly, the middle-aged man had a clear gray streak in his short dark hair and was holding a beautiful bouquet of bright crimson roses in his huge calloused hands. He was clearly delighted to see me. I though was somewhat baffled. Was he here to greet me? Anyway, the severe soldier's first words cleared that all up:

"Hurry up, Kirill. The party started an hour ago. SHE has already asked for you three times. Here, assuming you haven't had time for another gift, you can give her these!"

Fortunately, I instantly realized who SHE was, and didn't embarrass myself by asking such a stupid question. But to my great shame, I only then remembered that today was Gerd Tamara's birthday. And I'd promised the famed leader of the Second Legion I'd be at the party. It hadn't turned out great. I hadn't prepared a gift for the unordinary girl, so I obediently took the bouquet.

However... I looked at the taciturn Imran standing to the side. He wasn't too happy. And probably he wasn't my only soldier not in the best state of mind. It was safe to assume my whole squadron was feeling anxious, waiting impatiently until they could reenter the game and have their commander tell them all the details and consequences of what happened. So I returned the beautiful bouquet to the Grenadier:

"Roman Pavlovich, my squadron of twelve with three different races has just died on the planetoid Ursa-II-II in the assault of an underground Meleyephatian base. And we just lost a starship... two actually... and we'll respawn in ten minutes on a comet with an unbreathable ammonium atmosphere. What's more, it isn't yet clear how we'll get off it. I can't just leave my soldiers waiting and go party. What kind of a commander would do something like that?!"

The severe Grenadier considered it and seemingly didn't put much stock in my words, because he unexpectedly turned to my Dagestani friend and asked him to confirm:

"Is that really what happened, just as Gnat says?"

Imran, as if expecting just such a question, gave a happy smile and started expounding:

"I swear on my mother it is! And not only that! Gnat didn't say anything, but there was a real meat grinder in space. Hundreds of Geckho and Meleyephatian ships bit the dust! It's way cooler than *Star Wars*, it honestly gave me goosebumps! And we were the first of the whole Geckho Third Strike Fleet to land on the Meleyephatian asteroid. Dmitry Zheltov is just awesome, he made a masterful landing under fire from the enemy batteries! He's a real *jigit*[2]! Then we flew on flying skateboards! After that, we broke into the enemy base and captured a spaceship assembly factory! But the Meleyephatians got us eventually... We couldn't hold the position..."

"Sounds like you're really kicking ass!" Roman Pavlovich complimented and even whistled. Then he looked unconfidently at the bouquet in his hands and set it on the edge of my virt pod: "I'll tell Tamara that you can't come to her party right now. But still, I implore you Gnat. Try and make it! Don't upset the girl! She's been getting ready all day, getting all gussied up. She redid one hairstyle over four times! She spent at

---

[2] Translator's note: something of a brave knight in the cultures of the Northern Caucasus.

least an hour practicing her smile in front of a mirror and even tried laughing for the first time I can remember. She won't say it, of course, but the whole Second Legion knows who she's really trying for. I have three grown daughters myself, so I've seen that glimmer in a girl's eye when they've grown up. Tamara is like my fourth, I love her like my own. So don't hurt my daughter's feelings, try and make it to her party!"

SO, RESPAWN TIME had come. Loading! The first thing I saw was that I hadn't gotten a boost to either Fame or Authority. That was bad. It meant command must not have known about our heroic raid on the enemy underground complex, and we had died there in vain.

I appeared at the Geckho military base on the Un-Tesh comet indoors and protected from the corrosive atmosphere, which is where I'd put my respawn point earlier with all the rest of the Shiamiru crew. First of all, I checked my equipment. My Listener suit was still in perfect condition and on my body. That was the most important. I also had all my weapons. But I couldn't find the Targeting System. It must have dropped as loot where I died. Hopefully that wouldn't damage my relationship with Basha Tushihh. After all, it did belong to him...

Ah, and there he was. Both Basha and his twin brother Vasha appeared a few feet away and started looking around, batting their lashes and getting used to the bright light. Uline Tar showed up next to them, and another two right after her: Minn-O and Tini. The kitten ran right up to me and pressed up to my body, demanding I embrace and calm him. Seemingly, the underage Miyelonian was very worried he'd died alone and would respawn very far from every player he knew.

"I also wouldn't say no to some reassurance and affection," the Dark Faction Princess said, watching with a strange jealousy as I warmly embraced my ward and whispered words of encouragement. "I lost my spacesuit, too... so, am I the only loser in the squadron?"

Minn-O La-Fin was standing in slippers and a track suit, over which she had a bandoleer for weaponry. All that was left of the spacesuit now was a helmet on her head. Mhm, tough break... Now we'd have to figure out how to get Minn-O out of this underground base onto the surface of the toxic comet.

We had to wait twenty seconds for the Medic and Supercargo. For some reason, they were in no rush to enter the game. Then Imran came, clearly having spoken with Roman Pavlovich from the Second Legion. And last of all was Eduard Boyko. The Space Commander was in high spirits and, right after finding me with his eyes, shouted out in joy:

"I got a hundred seventy-four frags! Gnat just

imagine, one hundred seventy-four!!! Before this, I played for almost seven months and only killed one enemy when I strangled a Dark Faction Spy next to the Prometheus. And now over a hundred! Sure, most of the experience canceled out because I also died, but..."

The Geckho asked what the man was talking about so enthusiastically, and I translated Eduard's words for them. Basha Tushihh, looking the Space Commando from top to bottom waved his paw scornfully and bared his teeth in satisfaction:

"Snot-nose! I got two hundred and three frags in that session. But I didn't get any experience for the last ones. And my brother Vasha got a whole four hundred kills. By the looks of things, we turned those Meleyephatians to proper dust!"

I quickly added up all the results my companions had told me. Almost eight hundred dead enemies! Woah! We really gave the planetoid's defenders some heat! But where was the rest of my team? Why weren't they entering the game?

We waited another ten minutes, but nothing. Dmitry Zheltov and Ayukh just weren't coming. I couldn't say about the old Navigator. I didn't know him well enough to predict his actions, but my friend Dmitry would definitely have come into the game right after respawn. And that meant...

"That is a very good sign." Basha Tushihh was first to give an opinion on the matter, saying exactly what I was thinking. "I bet those two on the frigate didn't die!"

"And that means the ship probably made it, too!" Uline said, rubbing her hands together just like a person. "By all Geckho laws, that is our shared trophy, and such a frigate must be worth eighteen to twenty million crystals, and that's at minimum!"

"And split equally, that's one and a half million each!" the Supercargo added, quickly doing the math. Everyone around started smiling and rumbling in happiness.

Well, well! I didn't think our trophy was worth that much, but I trusted the experienced Trader's estimate. Hopefully she was right. I needed money badly, and I definitely would not refuse my very own star frigate. Although we shouldn't have been counting our eggs before they hatched. I mean, we were calculating each person's share of the value of the Tolili-Ukh X frigate, which was god knows where and might not even have survived.

Now was not the time to sit with our heads in the clouds and daydream. We had real business that needed to be dealt with now: figure out the situation on the front and our position here on the military base. Where to go, where to register as respawned, and what we should do next. I said as much, and Supercargo Avan Toi promised to figure it out, as he knew the structure of the base. He told us not to go anywhere, then disappeared.

He was gone for a while, twenty minutes at least.

In that time, we managed to walk through the neighboring rooms and even talk with soldiers from other downed starships, most of whom were just milling about and awaiting further orders. As we immediately figured out, very many of them were landing troops. The Meleyephatians were aggressively pursuing the Third Strike Fleet's landing ships. Finally, Avan Toi returned and loudly declared the joyful news:

"We won!!! The enemy surrendered, the shields have been deactivated around the Ursa-II-II satellite and the planet Ursa-II as well. Now we're landing on the planet and capturing strategically important targets. No more reinforcements are needed, so new squadrons are not being formed. They won't be asking for anyone from the base." Then Avan Toi started rumbling, showing his fangs and summarized with dismay: "The fleet leadership has no time for respawned players, either. They have plenty of other problems now. So we are apparently stranded on this comet for the long haul..."

"And what about the captured frigate, did you figure anything out?" Uline couldn't hold back, impatiently interrupting the storyteller.

The fat Supercargo looked downcast and, with a heavy sigh, announced the bad news:

"From what I was told, the Third Strike Fleet took heavy losses. No more than a third of our starships made it. So captured trophies are going to the owners of ships downed in combat as compensation.

Trophies and awards are going to be given out personally by Kung Waid Shishish. And in that there were more losses than command planned on, there isn't enough compensation to go around. Seemingly, luck won't be shining on us today..."

All around a collective sigh of disappointment rang out, to which Avan Toi hurried to announce:

"In any case, we don't know anything for sure yet, too little time has passed. Also, Waid Shishish hasn't gotten around to it yet. Maybe when the commander finds out about our raid, he'll appreciate our contribution and reward us..."

"Mhm, sure. I wouldn't hold my breath! He'd sooner give our frigate to his relative Uraz Tukhsh to compensate his lost ship and as a reward for bravery," Vasha grumbled in dismay. Uline couldn't hold back either and commented acridly:

"More like a reward for stupidity and cowardice! Uraz Tukhsh, you see, was unwilling to part with his ship... You really have to try to die that pointlessly!"

"But no matter how you spin it, it was our captain who first set foot on the enemy planetoid," the Medic intervened. Everyone around suddenly went silent in embarrassment, having remembered that the captain put the Medic in charge, which meant he trusted him fully.

In an effort to smooth over the strained silence, I hurried to speak my mind, saying Waid Shishish probably had a whole list of those requiring compensation for losses, and he certainly wouldn't have the time to worry about us. And really how could the commander find out about our heroic deed? Had Dmitry Zheltov and Ayukh managed to send a message about a breach in the Meleyephatian defenses before the explosion? It seemed unlikely, because they hadn't figured out the communications systems of the alien frigate yet.

And also, Dmitry and Ayukh could hardly have known what we were doing in the subterranean complex anyway, because they were inside the Meleyephatian ship the whole time and didn't see anything. They probably didn't even know what had caused the explosion. Without that information, lining up the big blast in the Meleyephatian complex, which had killed almost eight hundred defenders, with our actions would have been hard. Although... I called Uline aside and quietly asked how much of a video clip she'd managed to film.

The huge Trader cringed in dismay and admitted honestly:

"Gerd Gnat, everything went wrong with that... I wanted to make it nice, but the lighting was worthless, and your scan turned off the camera at the worst possible moment. I had to set up the lights and camera all over again and lost a bunch of time. I only managed to recite the first part of the script, then some of the background fell in scene with all the moving machinery and frigates on the conveyer belt. The material is simply not up to snuff. No news agency will pay for it..."

"Still, make sure to keep the footage!" I demanded. "Being paid by news agencies is entirely secondary here. That video is the only proof of what we accomplished on the planetoid, and at least some counterweight to the entirely feasible accusation that we broke the captain's order and deserted, leaving a combat ship right in the middle of an ongoing battle."

"Do you think they'll accuse us of that?" Uline asked, anxious and even afraid, to which I just shrugged my shoulders indefinitely:

"Who knows? Uraz Tukhsh accused me of turning on the loudspeaker in the Shiamiru to make him look bad. So nothing would surprise me now..."

I had to admit, I was in a very foul mood, and there was plenty of reason. I had been fired by a close relative of the commander and was now sitting penniless on the edge of the Universe, very far from the lands of my native faction. I had a fleeting hope to keep a captured frigate, but it seemingly wouldn't come to fruition. Even if it had survived, there was a high probability it wouldn't be going to me and my friends anyway, which also upset me. I was very depressed by the indefiniteness of the future, as well as the fact that I couldn't expect any news about all those things for the next few hours.

I had to admit that I was having an unlucky streak, and this whole voyage had so far only brought dismay and loss. However... Here I suddenly noticed that everyone around was silent and watching me, clearly expecting some commentary or even orders. I could not allow myself to look despondent! My friends wanted to see an expression of calm confidence on my face and to know that their leader had a clear plan of action for every eventuality.

Like it or not, I had to live up to these expectations and the role I'd taken on as squad commander:

"Uline, try and sell the footage to the news channels anyway, maybe they'll take a shine to it. If they don't want to pay, give it out for free. We could all use a boost in Fame. But first consult with the local military leadership to make sure we aren't accidentally revealing military secrets so they don't come after us for that. Avan Toi, you have the best understanding of this matter, so go help Uline!"

Psionic skill increased to level fifty-two!

Authority increased to 36!

I turned next to the Medic and asked him to track down our former captain. I was reminded that Uraz Tukhsh had promised that after the end of the battle with the Meleyephatians he would hire a shuttle to bring me and my friends wherever we wanted. This was the very time to remind the Aristocrat of his promise, because we needed to get off this toxic comet.

I gave Basha and Vasha the mission to leave into the real world and try to get in touch with the old Navigator Ayukh if he also left the game. He was from a famous clan. His name was known too, so it would probably be possible to find a way to get in touch with him. I asked the brothers to figure out where Ayukh was in the game, and also to figure out the situation with the Meleyephatian frigate.

And finally, Tini... I called my ward over and, looking him right in the eyes, said in Miyelonian, which the others didn't understand:

"You'll have the most important mission of all. I want you to get in touch with Leng Amiru U-Mayaoo in the real world..."

"Who?!" the kitten pressed his ears back in fear and crouched down, covering his head with his paws. At least he didn't piss himself.

"You heard right, Tini. The Great Priestess of your race. If you cannot reach her directly, get in touch with any member of the First Pride and tell them you have a message from a human by the name of Gerd Gnat for the incarnation of the Great First Female, which must be given in person. I'm sure that Leng Amiru will hear you out or read the information in your thoughts, which would also be fine. So then, listen. I have a very rare and dangerous item and I want to try and sell it to her. It's the Great Priestess's tail! I'm sure she won't want to see it fall into the hands of her opponents and spoil her reputation. Tell her that my price is one million crypto."

The kitten's eyes went wide, but he didn't have the gall to refute my order. Great! After telling my friends to meet back up here in exactly one ummi, I was intending to leave the game, asking Eduard and Imran to accompany me. But then the Princess suddenly stopped me:

"And what about me? Gnat, you gave everyone a mission but forgot about me! What am I supposed to do?"

"You..." I wanted to give Minn-O something that looked like a serious task, and at the same time would not cause the Dark Faction to accuse my wayedda of espionage. "You... Ah, that's right! I've heard from you and your ruling grandpa Leng Thumor-Anhu La-Fin, that a player can be transferred between factions and even brought into a parallel world. Well then, I need you to figure out the details of that process! I cannot have my beautiful wayedda only available to me in the virtual world! I want you with me in real life, too!"

Minn-O looked at me in deep thought, then her eyes lit up. The Princess smiled in satisfaction and said in the Dark Faction language:

"Very (unknown) move, my husband. I approve! That (unknown) goes both ways, and you (unknown) could be in my world with me! I'll be sure to figure it out for you!"

Astrolinguistics skill increased to level seventy-nine!

Chapter Twelve

A Classical Raymonda

THE AROMA OF MEAT and vegetables on the grill wafted into my nostrils as soon as I left the corncob, so I just followed my nose. The leader of the Second Legion's birthday party was being held in a large clearing in a park under the Dome, past the volleyball and tennis courts. Today there were canopies out and even a stage surrounded by tables. Not far away, portable grills were smoking and hissing away.

Imran and Eduard accompanied me to a ribbon stretched around the perimeter and, after handing me off to Second Legion soldiers, said goodbye for the next five and a half hours and went to do their business. I stepped over the ribbon with a huge bouquet of bright red roses and headed into the center of the clearing.

Music was thundering and celebration permeated the atmosphere.

"Gnat, wait!" an unfamiliar dark-haired soldier of Asian descent grabbed me by the shoulder and handed me an orange t-shirt with the emblem of his legion — an ancient Greek helmet with a high ridge inside a white circle, surrounded with the words "Second Legion." "Today, every guest is supposed to wear a t-shirt with our symbols. It was the commander's idea."

Ah, a party for the inner circle. Clearly, Tamara had done that to once again emphasize the uniqueness of her soldiers and inflate their ego and prestige under the Dome. I didn't argue and, after quickly pulling the number 1470 polo off, changed into the orange t-shirt. They didn't keep me any longer, especially as Roman Pavlovich was already hurrying out to meet me.

"He's here? Great! Have him come quick to the striped tent. Tamara is in there with her friends trying on different outfits before they go on stage. We have a little show coming up. We wanted to shake things up around here. Every Second Legion soldier was supposed to play a role in this famous theater production."

I imagined the scene if I walked into a tent full of girls changing without knocking. Most likely, they would shout in fear, then I would take this bouquet of thorny roses to the face. So, I didn't really want to.

"Roman Pavlovich, if your daughter is changing

and getting ready, maybe I'd better go see her after the performance. And I can give her the bouquet then, too!"

"No, let's do it now. Take pity on the poor girl. She's all worked up!" the severe deputy insisted, leading me by the hand through the crowd of soldiers before the stage. "Tamara has been waiting for you a long time and is very anxious. She has been asking about you practically once a minute. She should be going on stage any time now, but you just wouldn't show!"

I had to submit to the respected veteran's requests and go straight into the tent. And thankfully I was wrong about what I'd find inside. There was no shouting or half-naked girls. Also, most of the actresses' costumes consisted of just a cardboard crown, a cape made of curtains and a paper skirt over track pants or jeans. Well everyone except one girl. Tamara was wearing a pure white ballet dress with a bodice and layered fluffy skirt, thin white leggings and real ballet shoes to top it all off! And on her head was a small elegant tiara inlaid with glimmering gems. It looked very much like it was made of real gold and silver! Some amateur performance this would be. Seemingly, the Second Legion hadn't spared any expenses on this single-use outfit their vaunted leader.

"Tamara, forgive me for being late. Happy birthday!" I handed the dressed-up birthday girl a bouquet of roses and decisively kissed her, which made her start smiling and blush red.

"Thank you, Gnat. But this is not only my celebration, it is for everyone in our Legion!" Tamara said with a sweeping gesture, pointing at her friends and all the people outside the tent. "Today we finally finished the fortress in the Karelia node, and our faction was able to add another eighty-seven players! Lozovsky has already handed the curators a list of what kind of people the faction needs."

It was very interesting and informative, but our conversation was cut short by Journalist Lydia Vertyachikh coming into the tent. She was both a guest of the party and the MC. After a short nod to me the tall lady, also wearing an orange Second Legion t-shirt, asked the actresses to get ready to go on stage.

"Three minutes until your number begins! And you Kirill, go quick to table one," Lydia said, pointing me to a long large table right in front of the stage. "They reserved a spot specially for you there where you'll have a great view."

I left the tent and hurried to the table. The serious muscular men, many of whom I had seen in Tamara's company before, but none of whom I knew well, greeted me warmly, shook my hand, slapped my shoulders and let me past them and nearer the stage. I could hear quiet whispering behind me like: "He came," "That's nice," "Gnat made it," "Little Tamara will be happy," and with surprise I realized that such a seemingly small thing as whether one guest showed up to a party had captivated the minds of many of Gerd

Tamara's underlings. The soldiers sincerely loved their dainty little commander and were just as worried as she was.

Finally, I elbowed through to a free spot and just barely managed to sit down before a faceted shot-glass filled to the brim appeared before me.

"Penalty shot! For being late!" I heard demanding shouts from all directions and gave a heavy sigh.

I had never been one to indulge, especially because alcohol had a very strong effect on me. I just instantly got wasted. Since my student days, when I got swinishly drunk at a few parties, I had firmly made up my mind that strong alcoholic drinks were not for me. In good company, I could allow myself to drink wine or beer, or like in the interview with Lydia Vertyachikh, vermouth and juice, but two hundred milliliters of vodka... I swallowed the spit that came up my throat. Sure, I might not fall under the table right away, but I would definitely start slurring.

Still, it was too late to turn back. Hundreds of eyes were boring into me. Roman Pavlovich was loudly giving a toast: "To the Second Legion and to its leader Gerd Tamara!!!" So I had to raise the glass. Ugh... do or die! I decisively took the first sip and had a hard time not showing surprise. There was water in the glass, mixed with just a tiny bit of vodka for smell. Roman Pavlovich, Gerd Tamara's first deputy, gave me a barely noticeable wink, showing who was behind this. I quickly settled down, finishing the "vodka" unhurriedly and with dignity. Then I turned in various directions and demonstrated the upturned glass, having received cries of stormy elation and even applause from the Second Legion troops.

At first, I was afraid because I didn't see the logical jump in my Authority. But soon I realized I was not in the game, but the real world. Damn, no surprise I was so confused really! Seemingly, I was now more used to the virtual world than the real one. And that really shook me because from there it was a short trip to the madhouse. Was I losing my grip on reality?

Fortunately, few noticed my confusion and embarrassment, and the ones that did wrote it up to alcohol. The people sitting next to me obligingly passed a plate of pickled vegetables and suggested I chase my shot. And then, just in time, a few skewers of shish-kebab were brought over from the grills and the impatient soldiers all turned to the meat. I also came away with a skewer of aromatic lamb, but I didn't manage to get to eating before everyone around came at me with muted shouts of: "Quiet! Tamara is coming on stage!"

All voices went down, the music started, and I even found it dimly familiar. But I understood less of ballet than an old Aleut hunter knew about modern helicopter engines, so I was not ashamed to read minds in the audience. That told me this was the classic ballet *Raymonda,* set to the music of composer Alexander

Glazunov. The people sitting around me were sincerely touched and happy, watching the spinning dancers, and I also watched the dancing girls. You may call me a hard-hearted blockhead, who with no understanding of true beauty, but ballet was clearly not for me because I couldn't see why this work was so venerated. I simply watched the girls move about the stage to the music, spinning, jumping, sometimes making mistakes and falling out of synch, worrying, and trying to please the audience.

Nevertheless, my obduracy and absolute lack of understanding did not hinder me from jumping up with the other viewers and applauding loudly, showing the appropriate level of admiration for the mastery and boldness of the dancers. After handing the flowers thrown on stage to her friends and sending the audience air kisses, Gerd Tamara hurried back into the striped tent, wanting to quickly change out of her white ballet dress into something more befitting a feast.

I then, taking advantage of the pause and the fact that everyone in the party was near, estimated the number of guests and came to the conclusion that the Second Legion was here in full.

"If all the soldiers are here, who is guarding Karelia?" I asked my table, above all Roman Pavlovich.

"Guarding from who?" Gerd Tamara's deputy asked, sincerely surprised. "Your father in law promised five more days of ceasefire, and the Geckho confirmed that understanding, so the Dark Faction wouldn't dare break it. And other than the darksiders, Karelia only has NPC animals who won't be attacking the citadel. The Harpies live in the neighboring node, too, but they have become greedy. They not only won't attack for free, they won't even flap a wing these days. But of course, there is always some garrison in the Karelia fortress. Right now there are fifteen First Legion guys, and plenty of common players. Plus, Phylira's Centaurs took a contract to build a road from the Capital node into Karelia, so they can help out if anything happens."

It was strange to hear Dark Faction Leng Thumor-Anhu La-Fin referred to as my father-in-law. At any rate, the great mage was Princess Minn-O's grandfather, not father. But still, I didn't poke holes. What Roman Pavlovich said was true overall. The ceasefire with the Dark Faction had allowed us to finally finish building the fortress in Karelia and send the most capable squadrons to do other business. And where did they get sent, if it was no secret? I was not ashamed to ask that question.

"No, it's no secret. Tomorrow in the early morning, the full Second Legion and half of the First are being sent far to the south, to the New Bavaria node. It's our duty to help our new German allies. By the way, Gnat, have you seen the news on TV today?"

I had to admit that, before coming under the Dome, I hadn't watched TV for a long time, and here at the military base I figured the regime of secrecy made any contact with the outside world strictly limited. But my answer made Roman Pavlovich and the other soldiers laugh:

"Come on, Gnat! This isn't a prison, we can even leave the building if we get it agreed to by the leadership. Just so you know, we were initially thinking of holding this party not under the Dome but in a restaurant in Sergiev Posad or Dmitrov. But the feds didn't approve of so many players leaving the dome at the same time. Still, no one is stopping us from getting news from the outside world! Anyway, today our minister of foreign affairs unexpectedly flew to Germany for emergency negotiations. Officially, they say that they'll be discussing bilateral projects and an unfinished underwater gas pipeline. But you and I understand why he really went out there!"

"The alliance between our factions in the game that bends reality?" I suggested, and I was not wrong.

I knew already after talking with the Germans that the Human-6 Faction was in dire straits. Their starting node was on an island, which was very favorable for initial development, but it was not large and was separated from the continent by four miles of salty sea water. They had sailed to and occupied two nodes on the coast of the gulf two months ago, and that was when their problems started. The NPC Naiads considered the shore theirs, and after the newcomers arrived, they started sinking all their boats, dragging fishermen and pearl divers to the bottom of the sea and harrying the humans in hundreds of other ways.

Using modern technology from the real world, above all echolocation equipment and underwater video drones, the H6 Faction figured out the position of the Naiads' underwater cities and wiped them off the sea floor with powerful depth charges. But that only served to further enrage them. Other species started coming to help the small three- to five-foot long Naiads. Black deep-water creatures up to nine feet long, and white giants up to twenty-one, but the main thing was that the ghastly sea monsters they controlled. All connection with the capital island was cut off, and the only way of moving between it and the shore were two single-engine aircraft, which had been brought in piece by piece from the real world.

"But how are three hundred of our soldiers, even the most experienced and well-armed, going to help? Or are you going to go to the depths of the sea with aqualungs?"

"We do have aqualungs, but not many," answered another soldier, who I guessed was Rupor in the game. "But first we'll try to solve things peacefully. The Naiads no longer speak with the Germans, but maybe they'll negotiate with us. Our Diplomat Ivan Lozovsky is now accompanying a large caravan of Peresvets with cargo for the Geckho space port, but right from there, he promised to take the ferry to New Bavaria. And if the negotiations don't work out... well, our troops need to do something in the five days of cease-fire and improving skills and leveling up never hurt!"

"What's more, we'll have a bit more than three hundred," added the other player, a joker with curly red hair. "The second half of the First Legion will also go to New Bavaria but later, after the big hunt. It's just that in the forest nearest the Citadel, where there has never been anything more dangerous than a wolf before, we've been seeing some leviathan. It has eaten four players. We do not even know what kind of creature it is. No one managed to see it before they got killed. But the lumberjacks are afraid and refuse to go into the woods until the problem is handled. So the First Legion wants to spend tomorrow and the day after combing through the forest and exterminating everything even remotely dangerous."

Everyone around me went silent instantly and stood up. I didn't understand why at first. As it turned out, Gerd Tamara had slipped through to a free place at the large table. And that seat just so happened to be opposite me. The Leader of the Second Legion had changed her pure white dancing outfit into an unremarkable track suit and was at least a head and a half shorter than all the huge muscle-bound dudes around her. But still some unseen power could be sensed in the miniature girl. Even a totally new faction member, knowing nothing about Tamara and seeing her for the first time in this group of cutthroats would have instantly been able to tell that the fragile doll-faced girl was in charge and the others would follow her to hell and back.

"Well, how was it?" She asked me.

The information I'd read about the opera came in handy. I answered totally sincerely that this was my first time seeing *Raymonda* and the main actress was sincere and delightful, conveying all the feelings of a beautiful girl on a long journey after a gallant knight.

I guessed right. Seemingly, I'd never have thought up a better answer. The tension and worry instantly fell off Tamara's face and she started looking satisfied and even happy. Roman Pavlovich, sitting next to his adopted daughter, gave me a surreptitious thumbs up, as if to say, good job, keep it up! With Tamara's arrival, all conversations about business, Naiads, the Germans and Dark Faction went quiet. Now, everyone was wishing Tamara happy birthday and giving toasts in her honor. And this time I wasn't able to twist out of it. A shot glass was filled with surprising speed as soon as I set it on the table. Tamara then demanded she also be poured some alcohol and none of her soldiers were brave enough to contradict their leader.

"Say, Gnat, what held you up?" she asked at a certain point. And I raised my eyes to her and... turned to stone like a rabbit in front of a constrictor.

Tamara had asked quietly and politely, but I saw the cold challenging gaze of an inquisitor and could sense that a truthful answer was very important to her and she was applying all her abilities and skills to get it. The merriment and conversations instantly went quiet. Dozens of eyes were staring at me and I felt like I was being interrogated. I was not sure I could lie now, even though I didn't need to.

I honestly told her about the Geckho military base and the crushing might I had seen there. I told her about the Meleyephatian fortress and the grand space battle. In comparison with the forces that met there, all our sectarian struggles for resources, disputes about who owned what node and all our conflicts looked like nothing more than children's' squabbles in a sand box over mud-pies and shovels. Humanity in its current form had no chance of stopping such might if it wanted to destroy our planet. Just one tong of safety was very little, and we stood very little chance of developing enough to repel an invasion of any of the great space races.

"Do you mean to say that we are doing nothing down here by fighting the Dark Faction and saving our world from destruction?" Tamara had still not raised her voice, but I could sense how the others at the table had started to perceive me. A minute earlier, they considered me one of their own, but now they looked at me with cold tense gazes, seeing in me a potential enemy. Despite the strain, I was simply in awe of Tamara's abilities. It was true wizardry on the part of the delicate little girl to manipulate a crowd so skillfully.

"No, you're doing exactly what you must. The Dark Faction is a clear enemy, trying to destroy us at any cost. Leng Thumor-Anhu La-Fin will spare no human or material resources and has even invited the legendary General Ui-Taka to advise him. In their world, he is considered the greatest strategist of his time. So a conflict with the darksiders is inevitable, and here we either win or die. Coruler Thumor-Anhu finds the concepts of humanism, mercy and sympathy utterly foreign. In the last year, he was not troubled by murdering six million people just to bring down the number of mouths to feed during a famine. So we cannot expect mercy from him if we lose."

I saw the soldiers listening intently, simply hanging on every word. Seemingly, the details Princess Minn-O had told me from her grandfather's biography had not been heard by our faction before. But they fit very neatly into the picture they already had of a ghastly and murderous enemy. But to me, it seemed the time had come to tell them my own impression of the situation:

"Beyond the objective of winning the ongoing war with our unpeaceable Dark Faction neighbors, there is another no less important goal: in less than one tong, we must be able to withstand a possible and even expected attack from outer space. We have to reinforce very seriously, implementing advanced technologies from the great spacefaring races, and also obtaining friends and allies. First of all and most importantly, we need our Geckho suzerains to think of humanity as a valuable ally, something worth defending after the tong of safety is over. Second, there are other humans in deep space. To my eye, they are our most obvious allies. Third, the galaxy is not limited to just people and Geckho. There are also other spacefaring races. Cultivating friendly and mercantile relations with them would mean crossing them off the list of potential aggressors, and maybe even making allies. Those have been my three main objectives, and I consider my work no less important than yours!"

Gerd Tamara spent a long time looking at me, as if she couldn't find the words to answer. And the soldiers of the Second Legion were in silence together with their leader for so long it made me uncomfortable. Finally, the miniature girl's gaze came to life and the corners of her lips stretched up. At that, Tamara was clearly afraid. I could see her top lip quaking and her left cheek twitching.

"Gnat, my head really hurts from all this loud music, sound and smoke from the fires. I need to go somewhere quieter. Why don't you come with me? We have something to discuss, and I have everything to continue the feast in my room."

Chapter Thirteen

Sad Celebration

I SUSPECT THAT the delicate dark-haired girl's head was aching not so much because of the loud music and smoke as from the alcohol. I had to admit that, during the celebration, I was surprised that none of the experienced adults had warned their young commander to stop when she tried to keep up with the soldiers of her squadron, pouring herself glass after glass. On the way to the residential area, I even had to hold Tamara up, because her legs stopped obeying and were bending into bizarre sine-waves as we went up the park path.

"Everything is a-alright, Kirill. I'm f-fine!" the little headstrong Tamara was stubborn when I suggested she go take a rest on the bench.

Despite her vain attempts at resistance and threats to "shoot me in the game again if I didn't let her go right now," I picked her up and carried her into her building. Yana, who was at reception, hurried to get out the electronic key to Tamara's room and ran ahead to open it for us. And I carried the her into the room and carefully set her down on a large couch after quickly removing her shoes and placing a plush pillow embroidered with a cartoon Mermaid under her head.

"Don't leave, Gnat!" she asked when I was turning to go. "Sit here with me for a second. I admit, I overdid it, but the weakness will pass soon. I have very high Constitution in the game that bends reality, and that gives me good regeneration here in the real world, and high resistance to toxins. Ten minutes, a half hour maximum and I'll be back to full strength."

I looked at the fragile girl and had a hard time believing in her high Constitution. Nevertheless, I didn't go anywhere and sat on the edge of the couch, giving a kind-hearted chuckle:

"Constitution, you say? I couldn't even feel your weight when I was carrying you. All you're 'constituted' of is skin and bones."

I was actually bending the truth, and Tamara had a very harmonious body-shape for her small height. Of course, you couldn't say she had "mile-long legs" or a double-D breasts but she was pretty cute.

Tamara first smiled at my joke, but then decided

to comment with notes of pity:

"You shouldn't be laughing. I actually have high Constitution, best in our faction. My Constitution was fifteen at first, but I put all five from the Labyrinth in it, then raised it two more with practice. And when I became a Gerd, I put six of my eight stat points into Constitution as well, giving a total of thirty-two. When you add the bonus points and rings, I have a whopping thirty-four. For a Paladin, it is the most important statistic, which defines the number of hitpoints, endurance and resistance to all kinds of damage. If I didn't have such high Constitution, I wouldn't be able to wear my exoskeleton armor or use high-caliber machine guns."

Constitution thirty-four?! That inspired respect, no way around it. As did the speed with which Tamara recovered from the alcohol. Five minutes before, her tongue was slurring and she could barely stand, but now she was singing like a nightingale and looked utterly normal. I suspected that her ability to quickly recover from wounds and poisons was well known to the Second Legion, which explained their lack of concern about her alcohol abuse. But a different part of Tamara's tale had caught my interest:

"So you passed the Labyrinth? I heard that they waited almost a day for you and were very worried."

"That is true. But I spent almost all that time in the character generation room. I was too afraid to leave..." it looked like a shadow ran across her face. The smile instantly crawled off her face and her eyes went dim. "Kirill, do you have any idea what it's like to suddenly wake up in a healthy body after four years being blind, deaf, paralyzed and talking to yourself at the edge of madness?! I saw myself in a mirror, I COULD SEE myself, move my arms and legs, and... I couldn't stop bawling! I didn't know where I was or why I suddenly got better, but I was horribly afraid that moment of joy would end as soon as I left the tiny little room."

Tamara extended her little hand and carefully placed it in mine. Her fingers were unnaturally cold, and I squeezed her hand to warm it up.

"Then I spent a lot of time in thought, choosing between a Paladin and a Matriarch, and reading all the information. I had no one to ask for advice, so I had to figure it all out and think for myself. But I didn't have any problems with the Labyrinth itself, because I had walked through it many times in my sleep. Yes, it came to me in my dreams as I lied there blind and paralyzed. And so did you, and this room, and really this whole day, even my dance. Imagine, I started practicing it four years ago!"

"You saw me in your visions?" I hooked into the girl's words, and Tamara gave a distinct nod:

"Yes! Many, many times. I saw your face, your glowing blue eyes... And I recognized you the first time we met in the game. Or to be more accurate... not right away, but when I saw your dead body. Back then, I thought you were pitiful and weak, and I was very disappointed. But now you've changed. Now you're a reputable and intriguing man like in my visions... By the way Kirill, could you bring me some water? I'm just dying of thirst. The cooler is next to the fridge. There's a clean glass right there."

When I came back a minute later with a cup of water, Tamara had already managed to get a dark soft plaid and wrap herself in it up to her chin. Clearly, she was freezing. Although... I noticed her track suit, hurriedly thrown on a far-away chair. And her crumpled up leggings and lacy black underwear were on the floor behind the chair. It was not hard to imagine how Tamara now looked under the plaid.

She instantly realized I had figured it out, and a mischievous twinkle glimmered in her eyes:

"What, it's my room, I can do what I want! Legally, I'm of age, and our staff psychologist Irina Chusovkina is in shock after every time we talk. In her words, my emotional and psychological age is double my biological one, and all her tests put me around thirty-five."

I don't know, I don't know... Too many ghastly tests had fallen on this little girl's shoulders, which could have turned her character harsher, warped it and made it rough. But personally I saw her as a silly little teenage girl, barely out of childhood and striving to become an adult. Tamara, beyond all doubt, was my type physically. Basically dead on. But there was something wrong in all this. Both that she was drunk and young, not in control of her actions and that I now had a travelling wife Minn-O La-Fin, even though it wasn't in this world and my relationship with the Princess was still quite far from intimate.

As if having read my thoughts, or guessing them surprisingly accurately, Tamara went on:

"I know what you're thinking, Kirill, but a wayedda is merely a favorite, a lover who does not stand in the way of you having other girls. I am not trying to make a play to be your wife either. I saw my future in my visions and I know that it is not fated for me to marry, and that I will die very young. But like any other lady, I want to be desired! Just tell me, am I not good enough? Do you not find me attractive?"

I answered that, beyond all doubt she was attractive. Tamara was clearly encouraged by that answer and, holding the plaid in embarrassment with two hands at neck level, she sat up in bed.

"Kirill, if you'd be so kind please go out to the fridge. On the upper shelf I have some vermouth and juice, just what you like! Make us a couple of cocktails. I'm already back to my senses, so I suggest we keep celebrating my birthday!"

To be honest, I thought the cocktails were too much. She had only just sobered up, so this was just making things worse. I didn't go anywhere and just kept sitting and looking at the domestic and red-cheeked Tamara covered in the plaid. She didn't look one bit like the fearsome war chieftain I was used to.

"What?" she asked, looking even more embarrassed, although it seemed impossible. "And what do you... want from me? Say it out loud! Or at least mentally send it!"

The birthday girl had gathered her courage and raised her big dark eyes to me, which now had none of their usual severe coldness, just timid hope. Our eyes met, and the girl didn't turn her gaze, inviting me to mental connection.

"Sleep!" I gave a mental command, repeating it out loud.

Tamara's eyes closed obediently. Without letting the plaid out of her tightly clenched fingers, her last defense and barrier, the girl's head fell on the pillow. I then gave a heavy and pitiful sigh. It was very hard to get through the Paladin's mental defense both in the game and the real world unless she wanted it and was open. Yes, I had taken advantage of her trust and good opinion, and that was low. But it still seemed to me that I had done the right thing, not taking advantage of the inexperienced girl's temporary weakness.

I adjusted the mermaid pillow under Tamara's head, brushed the disheveled dark hair off her face, gave her a tender kiss right on her lips and headed to leave. In the hallway next to the door, Roman Pavlovich was sitting on a folding stool with glasses on his nose and a book in his hands. When I came out, the gray-haired man shuddered, closed his book, removed his glasses and raised his head in surprise:

"Did you two have an argument?! Or do you not like my daughter for some reason?"

I could hear offense in the gray veteran's voice, and I hurried to reassure him:

"Quite the opposite. I like Tamara a lot. But your daughter is too unique and pure a creature to simply sleep with a man spontaneously when drunk, or simply because she saw something in her dreams. So I didn't ruin her life, instead I just used my magical abilities and made her fall asleep."

Roman Pavlovich's thick brows shot up in surprise. The veteran went silent and answered thoughtfully:

"Oh, Little Tamara is going to be so mad... but actually it's for the best. She'll have more fury for the war with the Naiads. And you're a good guy, Gnat. You did the right thing. Thanks for treating my daughter so tactfully! And now where are you going, your room? Anna is waiting for you there. I just saw her walk past."

I was actually planning to go get some sleep in my room which was on this floor, but Roman Pavlovich's words stopped me. Anna? A great girl, but now was not the time... If I went to go see her now, Tamara would not only get mad, she would want to kill me. I had left her naked in bed to go have fun with another girl. No woman could ever forgive such a thing!

"No, I guess I'll go into the game," I sharply changed my plans, which made the deputy leader of the Second Legion nod approvingly. He took his book back out. *The Way of the Shaman. Book One,* is what I managed to read on the vibrant cover. I wonder what kind of book that is? Some kind of "DIY for dummies" book? I wasn't expecting the Grenadier to feel inclined to the occult, although people had been surprising me a lot lately so it could be.

And then, as if the heavens were rewarding me for good behavior, Roman Pavlovich's radio turned on, and an unknown hoarse smoky voice said:

"Pavlovich, this is Artyomov. You wouldn't happen to be in residential building five, would you? Dmitry Zheltov just climbed out of his virt pod. He says he needs Gnat at once. Also, no one is answering the phone in Gnat's room."

"Tell Zheltov to wait outside corncob fifteen," I said to Tamara's adoptive father and hurried to meet the Starship Pilot, who I hadn't seen for quite a while.

Chapter Fourteen

Not Just a Dream

I COULD TELL FROM AFAR that Dmitry was upset. I couldn't sense any joy in his demeanor when he saw me accompanied by my now ever-present bodyguards. Dmitry just lowered his head and sat on the lowest step of the corncob's spiral staircase, waiting for me and not even trying to come say hi. Up close, it became clear that my friend was fearfully tired. His eyes were sunken, his gaze was absent and the fingers on both of his hands were shaking slightly. I walked up and sat down in silence next to him on the step, letting him start the conversation.

"It's all gone wrong, Gnat..." Dmitry started, but waved a hand in vexation, lowered his head and went silent.

"What went wrong? Was the frigate destroyed?" I asked, voicing the first thought that came to mind. That only made him more despondent:

"It's total shit with the frigate too... No, it wasn't totally destroyed, but after the explosion of the planetoid, it can hardly be told apart from useless wreckage. The explosion threw us out into space, turned us over and slammed us into the nearest cliff, breaking and tearing everything that could be broken or torn. There are no engines left at all. The main thruster was torn out 'with the meat,' along with the maneuver drives, and there never was a hyperspace one. You might as well say there is also no power unit, because it's all shot to shit and the repair will cost more than buying one new. All that remains is one forcefield generator of three. All the electronics need replacing, there are no cannons, guidance or navigation systems, the climate unit was destroyed... It would be easier to just tell you what we do have! Even the hull was pierced and dinged up. Only two sections can still hold pressure. Basically, in this form it is no longer a frigate, but a piece of composite flecked with glass and metal scrap."

Hrm... Zheltov was painting this joyless picture with too much verve and detail, so I was also upset imagining an uncontrollable heap of trash drifting around in space. Seemingly, the dream of owning my own starship would have to be set aside...

"We got lucky and Ayukh managed to set up and turn on the friend-foe system, so we weren't turned to ash by our very own fleet. Around an hour after the battle, our frigate was caught by a gravity crane and brought into a huge mothership of the sixteenth auxiliary flotilla along with a bunch of other broken ships, both Meleyephatian and Geckho. Ayukh spent a long time arguing with the repair-guys, but still insisted that our ship be classified as repairable. And now the navigator is trying to draw up ownership documents for himself. I don't know if he'll manage or not. They say it's hard to do that now and such questions are decided only by the fleet commander."

Dmitry was repeating what I'd already heard from the Supercargo. Captured trophies would be handed out at Kung Waid Shishish's personal discretion and only he could decide who this or that captured ship would belong to.

"So, what else went wrong?" I asked the Starship Pilot. "I mean, you started out saying everything had gone wrong including the frigate."

"Yes, Gnat. But the destroyed frigate is not the main thing that has me upset," Dmitry continued hitting me with bad news. "It's good that you're sitting down. Here's the news: our former Captain Uraz Tukhsh has become a Gerd and was officially recognized as a war hero. He even got a purple ribbon of honor to wear on his shoulder from the ruler of the Geckho race Krong Daveyesh-Pir. It is kind of like the

Gold Star medal in Russia. Just imagine! Just so you appreciate the scale and rarity of the honorable trophy, after the grand battle there was only one other person who earned such a ribbon: Commander of the Third Strike Fleet himself, Kung Waid Shishish!"

I was sitting with my mouth gaping in surprise, unable to believe my ears. How was that even possible?! Uraz Tukhsh was not known for his bravery. In fact, it was more the opposite. Also, he had died due to his own stubbornness and poor foresight long before the battle ended! Or had the young ambitious Aristocrat gone all out and put his life on the line not only in the game but also in the real world by moving his respawn point to the deadly enemy planetoid, then finished his mission to deliver the mine. If so, there was no disputing it. It was a truly foolhardy and heroic feat, which merited the very highest award.

I asked Dmitry Zheltov to tell me in greater detail about what our former captain had done, given all his close companions thought he was a cowardly loser. My friend was eager to explain, trying to convey the tone and pathos of what he'd heard in the news as much as possible:

"According to the official story on the galaxy's news channels, Uraz Tukhsh was in the reserve flotilla on a noncombat auxiliary Shiamiru shuttle but saw the Third Strike Fleet's difficult position and decided to sacrifice his own ship to secure a victory for the Geckho. To that end, Uraz Tukhsh ordered his crew to grab a thermonuclear mine with the gravity crane and personally stood at the shuttle's helm, preparing to pass through the planetoid's forcefield and blow the mine, destroying a terrestrial battery and clearing a path for a landing team. He told the commander of the Third Strike Fleet his plan and the wise Kung Waid Shishish immediately approved it and even ordered his fleet to push back the Meleyephatian interceptors to the opposite side of the planetoid to cover for the lone forgotten cargo ship. Using his amazing piloting abilities, Uraz Tukhsh gracefully dodged dense fire from many Meleyephatian batteries and sent the starship right into an enemy cannon. The mine blew and destroyed not only that turret but the neighboring ones as well, and detonated the ammunition warehouses in the underground base. Inside the planetoid there was a series of high-powered blasts, after which the field generator switched off and the shield dissipated both from the planet and its satellite. The Meleyephatians were thus forced to surrender and it was all because of the courageous young captain Gerd Uraz Tukhsh and the wise fleet commander Kung Waid Shishish."

When Dmitry finished his story, I was still sitting with my mouth open, not knowing what to say. What kind of crap was that?! Where had this tall tale even come from? It had nothing in common with reality! I was simply choking in panic and indignation, not able to digest the fact that our little squadron's accomplishments had been swooped up by the cowardly Aristocrat! Full of righteous indignation, I asked who had come up with this nonsense, to which the Starship Pilot answered cautiously:

"I don't know, Gnat. But it doesn't seem like Uraz Tukhsh did it alone. Our former captain is not high enough caliber to do something like that without the agreement of more influential Geckho. What's more, they'd never just take him at his word. If I understand correctly, this story was first given by Fleet Commander Waid Shishish, who used it to explain the abrupt end of the battle to his subordinates. After that, the news about Uraz Tukhsh's heroic self-sacrifice was trumpeted around the whole galaxy, and now any story other than the official one is quashed by influential Geckho."

I also understood that perfectly. The severe and quick-to-anger fleet commander Kung Waid Shishish had told his version, naming himself and his relative war heroes. That got picked up by news channels and thus gained official status. And now the great ruler of the Geckho race Krong Daveyesh-Pir had confirmed it by giving awards to the two much-vaunted heroes. And now, after it was all over, if I or some other member of Team Gnat started saying it was not true, and that two glorified war heroes had merely ascribed others' actions to themselves... It would hardly be taken positively, especially by the two "heroes."

On the other hand, my squadron had twelve

soldiers of three different races. How could Kung Waid Shishish be so sure that none of us would talk, and that the truth behind the Meleyephatian fortress's explosion wouldn't leak? Did he just think no one would believe us? I mean, after all, we had a video from the underground base and the Meleyephatian trophy frigate, and those were iron-clad proof that the official version didn't add up. And without this material proof, the unanimous voices of twelve players backed up by Truth Seeker testing were also a serious argument.

Or was Kung Waid Shishish hoping that we would be afraid to contradict him? Maybe that was so. As vassals of the Geckho it would, to put it lightly, not be smart for anyone from Earth to call our Kung a liar. But after all, there were members other Geckho clans with me, and Tini the Miyelonian, who didn't depend on the fierce Kung one bit, so it would be hard to keep all the witnesses quiet.

Or did the commander of the Third Strike Fleet think he could censor us, so we wouldn't be able to tell anyone? In the game, sure, it was totally possible because all twelve of us were now located in space under the Kung's control at a Geckho military base or on an immobilized frigate inside a huge mothership. But in the real world, how could he get to all of us? Especially, once again, my ward Tini who lived in Miyelonian space. Or the Geckho lady Uline Tar, who came from the influential and rich Clan Tar-Layneh, which did not depend on Waideh-Tukhsh in the slightest and was not subordinate to them.

There was, truthfully, a radical option to force us all to keep quiet in the real world. A series of instant deaths in the game that bends reality would cause level and skills to fall, then stats as well. And every subsequent death was punished more and more. While Fox was giving athletic training, she told us that it was enough to kill a player with an empty progress bar five to seven times in a row. Then their level would fall to zero and their skills and even statistics would be blanked. That meant death, and a final one. After that, a player would never again leave their virt pod. And the Morphian assassin for hire was an authoritative source in this matter, so I didn't doubt what it told me.

But even such a harsh method was not a one-hundred percent guarantee of silence. In the breaks between respawns and deaths, the victim would be in the real world sometimes and could talk with their friends there, so the information would spread a bit no matter what. Also, I didn't believe in the slightest that the famed "leader of many divisions" Waid Shishish despite his quick temper and harsh ways, would commit cold-blooded murder. In one way or another, our squadron had brought him victory, and he would have to be a real psycho freak to repay that with calculated murder.

So what did that mean? If neither threats nor force were enough to keep us from talking, the only remaining option was to buy our silence. And that meant very soon someone would be getting in touch with me or my squadron. Either the Kung himself or a trusted individual, maybe even our former captain, the now vaunted war hero.

I glanced up at the rings of the spiral staircase. Seemingly, like it or not, I would have to go up to the fourteenth floor of the corncob and enter the game so a potential envoy would have someone to talk to. Standing from the stair, I shook the dirt off my track suit and patted my comrade on the shoulder as he sat in silence picking his nose:

"Dmitry, go get some rest. You can barely stand. But I'm going into the game. I bet that very soon some very important people are going to try and get ahold of me with an offer I can't refuse."

The graduate of the space military academy gave a short nod, stood heavily and started heading for the residential buildings when he suddenly stopped, turned and asked with renewed interest whether I had seen his girlfriend Lydia Vertyachikh. I answered no even though I had seen the Journalist at the Second Legion ball. But Dmitry wouldn't be let into that closed-circle shindig. What was more, when I had left the party hand in hand with Gerd Tamara, Lydia Vertyachikh was red from wine and dancing, sitting in embrace with one of the young athletically-built handsome lads of the Second Legion and whispering something. So there was a great probability that my friend would no longer be finding his debauched girlfriend at the party.

MY CONCLUSIONS were not wrong. Just after I appeared on the Geckho military base, Gerd Ost Rekh walked up to me. This was the same Shocktroop who had flown in with a boarding crew to "arrest" me before.

"Gerd Gnat, we've been waiting a long time. Please follow me into the sound-proof meeting room," the Shocktroop pointed down a long corridor.

Authority increased to 37!

Despite the respectful address and totally peaceable sound of what he said, the envoy was on guard and holding his hand on his belt holster. And I had no doubt that the Geckho had been ordered to bring me to that room, regardless of any possible resistance. I of course would never have dreamed of resisting and was impatiently awaiting the upcoming conversation myself.

After just three minutes walking the bewildering corridors of the underground base and passing two posts of armed guards, we entered a small round room with mirror walls. The Geckho who accompanied me ordered me to go into the middle and wait, then hurriedly left and closed the door behind them. Five to seven minutes passed, and I even managed to get bored. That was plenty of time to look at my endlessly elongated or many times condensed reflection in the carnival-style mirrors. But suddenly the light went out and, a second later, a glowing projection appeared in front of me. It was Kung Waid Shishish sitting back splendiferously in his throne.

I instantly got down on one knee and gave a deep bow, expressing the proper respect to the all-powerful master of Earth. And at that my soul was exultant. The great Kung had deigned to speak personally with me, which must have meant the honorable Geckho was going to reward me for the victory. What was more, I always found it easier to negotiate directly with authorities than their puppets and underlings. They were too bound by instructions they simply didn't have the power to break.

However, the beginning of the conversation was unexpected and he was not talking about the Meleyephatian planetoid at all:

"Gnnnat, I heard your wife said insulting words about me. I admit, I am very upset that you did not slap her and punish her immediately, so I await your explanation."

Oops... Honestly, I had already forgotten that unpleasant incident. But apparently the local spooks recorded everything faithfully, managed to get it translated and had even reported to their boss about the human woman's insults. I needed to answer immediately, so I improvised:

"My lord, I am sure that my foolish young female is not to blame here. She has no filter on her speech, and a big mouth. Sometimes I think her tongue works all on its own without consulting the brain. So blame it on her tongue. And blame the leaders of her faction, who never explained the political order of the Galaxy to her, and never showed her the great ruler of our large planet. I think those loose ends and clearly insufficient respect to the suzerains merit the most serious censure and punishment. My opinion: you should take one random node away from the Dark Faction. That punishment would be equal to her violation and would force them to show the Geckho proper respect in the future. And I have already spoken with my junior wife. I didn't kill her, I didn't even raise a hand, but she is trembling with worry and, I assure you, will never make that error again."

Psionic skill increased to level fifty-three!

Mental Fortitude skill increased to level forty-seven!

Mental Fortitude skill increased to level forty-eight!

"You think so? But you didn't recognize me on our first meeting either. Don't you think that punishment is too severe?" The most powerful Geckho had his doubts.

"No, not at all. My Kung, you need to be harsh sometimes, to nip disrespect in the bud and avoid problems in the future," I said in the tone of a wise and experienced advisor, meanwhile feeling exuberant. Would it really work?!

And really, why not? Only then I realized that

the great "leader of many divisions" had neither time or reason to sort through all the confusing and complicated interrelations between his many vassal factions on some far-off little planet. So he would have no idea that the Dark Faction was hostile to mine, and might even think the opposite, given Minn-O was my wife. And that was exactly why Kung Waid Shishish was surprised at the severity of the punishment I was proposing, but it didn't make him reject it.

"Well, Gerd Gnat, you know human psychology better than me, so I agree to your suggestion. Let it be so! The level of one randomly chosen node of the faction of your junior wife shall be reset to zero. My advisors will give the orders to the Geckho diplomat on your planet."

Psionic skill increased to level fifty-four!
Mysticism skill increased to level six!
You have reached level sixty-seven!
You have received three skill points!

It worked!!! I was glad at the new level, but much more at the gift I had just managed to arrange for my "father in law." Leng Thumor-Anhu La-Fin would be very surprised when the official representative of the Geckho demanded the Dark Faction drop a claim and abandon one node. It would be ideal if the blind lot pointed at the enemy capital node, which was level four. Amazing, even. Minus two thousand three hundred forty-nine players. Our enemies would take a good long time to recover from that!

I was distracted from my rainbow dreams by the voice of the Geckho Third Strike Fleet commander:

"Alright, let's finish this formality and get to more important matters. Gnat, I wanted to hear directly from you what happened on the enemy planetoid."

I didn't spend a long time slavering and delving into details (because I didn't doubt that my influential sovereign had probably already heard everything). I just said I had been carrying out an order the Kung gave me at our last meeting to prove my value as a good luck charm, bringing victory to the Third Strike Fleet.

"You don't think that's a bit too much pomp?" The commander was even somewhat taken aback by my impudence and showed me the purple ribbon he had just been awarded.

I had to reign in my vigor and demonstrate loyalty and readiness for dialog:

"My Kung, I already know the official version of events and I have no qualms with it. Whether Captain Uraz Tukhsh did it, or some Precursor artifact blew up elsewhere, or the light of the nearby star simply refracted through swamp-gas and started a fire... I do not care and will tell whatever story is most beneficial to my lord."

He clearly grew calmer and even rumbled in satisfaction. I then got to the trickiest part:

"And yet we both know that even a quarter ummi after the destruction of the Shiamiru and death of its captain Uraz Tukhsh the battle was still underway which is a weak point in the official story. Also, my squadron of twelve players was still alive and fighting the Meleyephatians in the bowels of their underground base. We killed around eight hundred fortress defenders and caused a series of underground explosions which led to the shields falling and the capitulation of the Meleyephatians. Our evidence is a captured frigate and a video clip."

"I have already bought the rights to all your footage," Kung Waid Shishish sharply threw out. "And I hope you understand Gnnnat, that those scenes will never be viewed on a single news channel in the galaxy."

I nodded in silence, trying not to show the Kung my dismay and annoyance. God damn it... The Kung was resourceful. We had been deprived of our very strongest card. And meanwhile, the fleet commander stood up to his gigantic height. I was still kneeling, so I now felt absolutely tiny.

"Yes, Gnnnat. The footage will be destroyed and your fame will not be growing. But I value your squadron's contribution to the common victory and will not be ungrateful. As compensation, all the soldiers who entered the enemy complex will be given fifty thousand crystals. What else do you want? The captured frigate? I'm prepared to let your team keep it on the condition that you keep your mouths shut. And I will come to you specifically as commander if the silence is broken. Do you understand that responsibility Gerd Gnat? Yes? Great! The frigate and other trophies will soon be brought to the Un-Tesh comet so and go get your ship!"

I understood that he was preparing to end the conversation and hurried to say one last thing:

"I'm sure that my Kung would like to demonstrate his generosity and good will by letting us keep the Meleyephatian frigate but, with the way it is now, I'm afraid the starship will not be so much a gift as a burden. Lots of parts were destroyed in the blast: the power unit, the thrusters and a plethora of other critically necessary systems. Without those, the frigate is nothing but an immobile hunk of scrap. I don't know what we could even do with it."

Psionic skill increased to level fifty-five!

"Yeah?" Seemingly the commander didn't know the true state of the trophy, and my words came as a surprise. "Well alright. I'll order minimally necessary repair and service so your starship can take off from the Un-Tesh comet and reach a nearby station. But from there it's none of my concern, and you'll have to get the money to improve it further on your own. By the way, it's actually good that the captured ship has been damaged and will not be useable for some time. Until all this hubbub settles down, I don't want you and your friends hanging around the Third Strike Fleet. You'd sow discord with your chatter. If I ever need a good luck charm again, I'll find you."

Authority increased to 38!

And at that, the call ended. The hologram of the Kung disappeared, and I found myself back in the round hall of mirrors. I was falling over in exhaustion. My mana was long since depleted, and the last few minutes of speaking with the great Kung had eaten up all my Endurance. After a few deep breaths, I allowed my long held-in emotions to burst forth, shouting in full-throated joy and nearly going deaf from the three-hundred-sixty-degree echo that thundered back.

In this game, I had long had a dream. It was weak and only on the edge of my consciousness. It was technically impossible in fact. I was afraid and embarrassed to admit it even to my closest friends. It had come during my very first space flight on the Shiamiru and, since that time, that dream had been badgering me day in and day out, nourished by new emotions, knowledge and facts. The dream was to get my own starship and cross the endless cosmos to find new mysteries, adventures and undiscovered stars. To have total freedom and no longer depend on mad aristocrats or faction directors or anyone else for that matter. It was a beautiful dream. And now I had a starship, so it was not just a dream. What next? Why, go out to find new dreams of course!

Chapter Fifteen

The Team Reassembles

THERE WERE ANOTHER TWO or so hours until Team Gnat was supposed to return, and none of them had shown up yet. So I decided to spend that time intelligently. First I found Gerd Ost Rekh, who knew his way around the military base and went to the local bursar's office to pick up twelve identical bags of red crystals. After that we had a quick bite in the local canteen and, after again making sure none of my squadron was yet in the game, I sat down to study the Relict language.

It was getting easier and easier to understand new symbols. Some easy sentences I could now translate basically on the fly, but the more complex ones were still beyond me. And at that, I couldn't shake the sensation that there would be a qualitative jump soon when hundreds of the individual glyphs would come together into a complete picture, allowing me to understand the basic rules of phrase construction.

"Listener, awaiting command."

I looked through pages of partially translated but basically incomprehensible text. I randomly hit upon an unfamiliar blinking symbol and activating it, expanded a line that brought me to the settings page. So this was where the link to the drone and machine control page was. I had once accidentally closed it without really knowing what it was and I was never able to find it again!

It was right when I got the suit, and any time the red blinking text came on the helmet screen, I simply dismissed it. It blocked my view so I just got rid of it indiscriminately. Somehow, I'd even deleted a page from the settings. After that, I spent a bunch of time digging around trying to find the information about my missing small Relict guard drone. I had even started to worry I had lost that information once and for all and my unique trophy along with it. But now I'd tracked it down.

I stuck the machine control window into the quick-access panel so I wouldn't close it and lose it again, then began to study the opportunities it provided. So what could be done here? In the whole list of machinery under my control there was only one active line:

Small Relict guard drone. Location unknown. Condition unknown.

Not a lot. My drone was god knows where, but it could apparently take commands. Hmm, I really wish I could figure out how to give one...

"Fly to me!" I commanded mentally, and unexpectedly received an answer. It was weak and took a bit but it was unmistakable! First, a request to confirm came into my mind, then the same message was written in red symbols before my eyes on my face shield.

The small guard drone thinks there is a high chance (over 99.78%) that your previous command was in error. Confirmation requested. Listener, should your drone fly to its master? (Yes/No)

What a stubborn hunk of metal! It spent so many thousands of years doing nothing, and when I asked it to switch on, it threw a fit! I chose "Yes" almost mechanically, but still wanted additional information. I wanted to know what the drone didn't like about my seemingly simple and easily comprehensible command?

Estimated time in flight: 257,143 years, 215 days, 6 hours, 11 minutes.

Chance of being detected and destroyed by automatic Precursor defense systems: 84.1%.

Chance of biological death of Listener master during flight: 100%.

Critically low batteries. Insufficient energy for

complete functioning of all systems. Chance of premature end of flight due to technical issues: 61.2%.

Oh, fu... It turned out that hunk of metal was much smarter than its master, which is why it didn't want to fulfill my stupid and suicidal order. I hurriedly canceled the command and ordered the drone to stay hunkered down and wait for me.

Machine Control skill increased to level forty-two!

Psionic skill increased to level fifty-six!

Electronics skill increased to level forty-eight!

Just then, Minn-O appeared a step away. And the Princess looked so out of breath and simultaneously frightened that it was like she had just run away from a pack of rabid dogs and only slipped away at the last second by climbing up a tree. And my wayedda's first words confirmed that I was not so far from the truth:

"Gnat, you should see the horror in my homeworld! Grandpa is all in a huff, he turned a servant girl to ash just for dodging his hand. On the video phone, he yelled at me so much I thought he'd kill me!"

"Did he find out about Kung Waid Shishish's order?" I immediately guessed, and my companion's eyes went wide in surprise:

"How'd you know?!"

I explained that I had recently had a difficult conversation with the Geckho military leader, who was upset to have heard my junior wife insulted him. And so I knew that Minn-O's faction had been penalized, and the level of a random node was reset to zero.

"That's exactly right, Gnat. I was talking to Coruler Thumor-Anhu about moving physical bodies between factions when a mage attendant suddenly entered. He simply had no face on, so I immediately guessed an envoy was bringing bad news and was afraid of my grandfather's legendary outbursts. The messenger said that Geckho Diplomat Kosta Dykhsh had come to our lands in the game and demanded we immediately abandon the Citadel hexagon, which you call the Graveyard node. My grandfather was surprised and thought it must have been a mistake. But the mage attendant fell at Thumor-Anhu's feet and said it was not and he could not dispute the suzerains' decision, because the Geckho Diplomat had come on an order from Kung Waid Shishish himself! Gnat, this is all because of me!"

Minn-O started sobbing and pressed herself to me, seeking support and consolation. The Princess was quaking like an aspen leaf in the worry and fear. Tears flowed down her face like a river, so I embraced my travelling wife firmly, calming her and saying words of encouragement. Two minutes passed before Minn-O was at all settled. Then she dried her tears and continued:

"I got very lucky because grandpa was too shocked by the news to figure out who's fault it was. I realized soon enough what caused it though, quietly left the room and hurried to my virt pod. I managed to slip out of the palace and get to my pod, but I didn't have time to enter the game... I had to answer a call and hear everything Thumor-Anhu thinks about my mental capacity. It was very hurtful and even more frightening. Thankfully, grandpa cannot control minds via videophone otherwise he would never have let me enter the game. At a certain point, I simply couldn't bear the string of accusations and cursing, turned off the video phone, got into my virt pod and hurried to close the lid. And now I'm not even sure I should leave the game to receive all the ghastly insults Coruler Thumor-Anhu poured out in his rage..."

I could sense that the girl had begun to quiver slightly again. There could be no doubt that Minn-O was panicking in fear of her ghastly grandpa, and was afraid not of some abstract bad, but real physical pain.

"Do you think the old man would ever hurt you?" I asked untrustingly. Minn-O answered with a sad smirk:

"Do I think?! I still haven't gotten over the 'little dose of pain' Thumor-Anhu prescribed me as punishment for what happened on the ferry! And here I'm afraid I won't get by with just a little dose this time! Judge for yourself, the Citadel is a well-developed level-two hexagon! But more importantly it has huge munitions storehouses, impressive defensive lines and many-level underground passages. There's so much work poured in, tens of thousands of man-hours! And all that will be lost because of me!"

Lost? The node would just be reset to zero. Then the Dark Faction could move right back in. The worst they have to do is wait two or three days to level one, then ten more to two. But that wasn't such a harsh punishment. Sure, their maximum number of players would go down temporarily, and maybe some of the weaponry from the Graveyard node wouldn't work, but that was all temporary and not that bad. Or was I not getting something? I was not ashamed to admit that I did not know all the rules here.

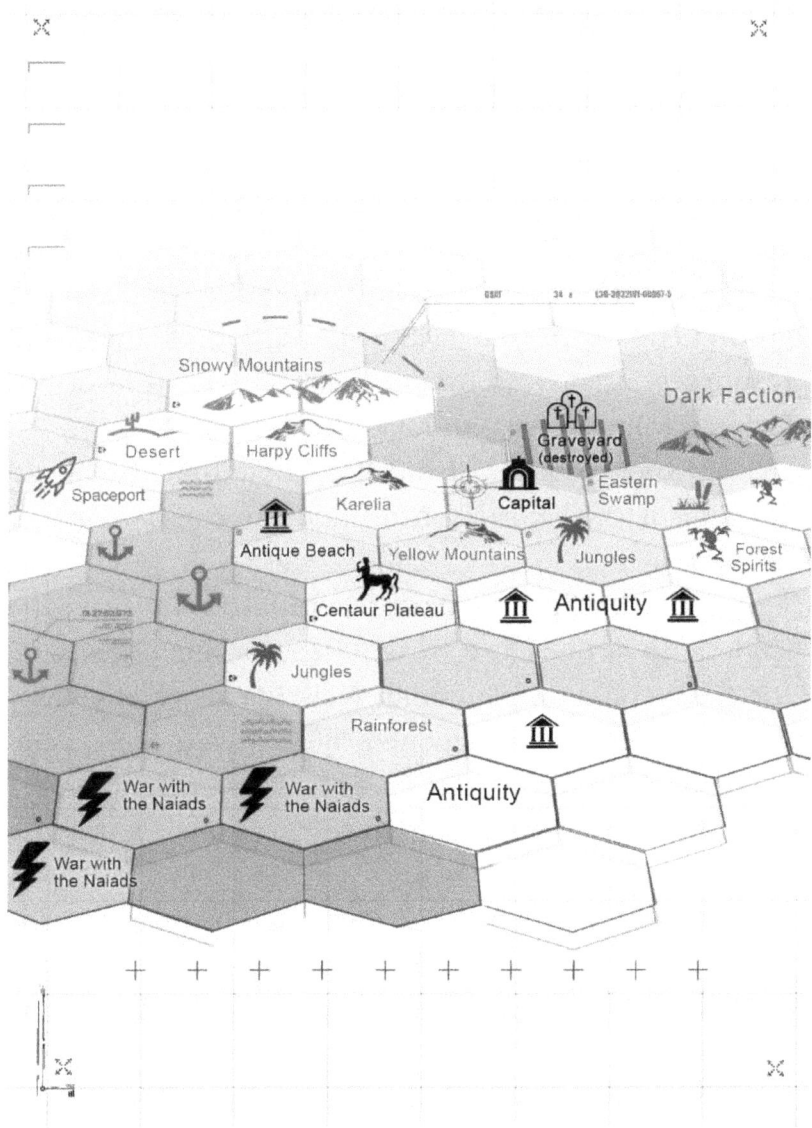

Minn-O didn't believe me at first and thought I was mocking her. Then she explained anyway:

"Gnat, some of the buildings and defensive structures cannot exist without a high enough hexagon level! As soon as it drops below, they self-destruct. Didn't you know? And the central hexagon fortress will also be destroyed. We'll have to build it again from the ground up and that will take a lot of time and resources. Just the building materials for a level-two fortress will cost forty thousand crystals!"

I had to admit, I did not know that. But I did consider it the right time to hand my companion her bag of crystals:

"I've got fifty thousand here, a reward from the leadership of the Third Strike Fleet for our bravery on the Meleyephatian planetoid. Well, it's also a payoff for silence about what happened there. If you want, send it to Leng Thumor-Anhu La-Fin as compensation for the lost node. But I'd say you should buy yourself a space suit and decent gun."

Minn-O didn't think for long and declared she would choose the latter option, buying a good armored suit and weaponry so she could be to the level of my team.

"Great!" I said, approving of the Princess's choice. "There's a trading terminal nearby. I'll show you how to use it."

But Minn-O stopped me, saying that wasn't all the news. As it turned out, she had carried out my mission and more or less figured out the algorithm for changing faction. The Princess was even prepared to serve as a test subject to enter the Human-3 Faction and my home world.

"I am your wayedda and must go with you everywhere, not only in the game! Grandpa told me the technology for transferring bodies between worlds hasn't yet been fully tested and might be dangerous. The first tester was supposed to be Tyulenev, but the process was stopped because you demanded him back. But I'm prepared to risk it, because I cannot imagine going back to my faction now!"

It was interesting and promising news, but I asked Minn-O not to rush changing faction. First, it wouldn't hurt to consult with wiser members of the great spacefaring races and check the algorithm to avoid risking Minn-O's life. What was more, I needed to get the transfer agreed on with my faction's leadership. And I also needed a guarantee she would be treated humanely, because the last thing I wanted was for the Princess to basically be made a hostage and instrument of pressure on her grandpa.

"So don't rush it, Minn-O. And don't be afraid of your grandpa. As soon as you get the chance, tell him what I said. Coruler Thumor-Anhu La-Fin has clearly forgotten that the situation has changed fundamentally and you are now my wayedda. From now on, only I can decide how to treat you, certainly not him. And insulting my wife means insulting me.

Any attack on you is an attack on me, too. And so if even a hair falls off your head, your faction won't get by with just one destroyed node! Make sure to tell your grandfather that I'm the only reason he's still alive, because Kung Waid Shishish was extremely mad and was seriously considering execution in the real world, either of you or the leader of your faction. It took me a lot of effort to talk the great war leader down to a softer punishment and never let Thumor-Anhu La-Fin forget that!"

Psionic skill increased to level fifty-seven!
Mysticism skill increased to level seven!
Authority increased to 39!

Yes, I had seriously exaggerated my part in the conversation with the Kung, because I figured the Princess would never be able to check if I was lying, and I thought she would like this story better than reality. But Minn-O squirmed out of my embrace and walked a few steps away. Did she sense the falseness? Or had my last words hurt her in some way? As it turned out, it was the exact opposite. Much to my surprise, the Princess bowed to me at the waist and said with unconcealed triumph:

"I have been waiting to hear such a thing since my first memory! I have been hoping all that time I would find a hero capable of challenging the great and terrible Coruler of humanity Thumor-Anhu La-Fin! All these years, I imagined myself locked up in a tower, a Princess guarded by a ghastly monster and I was waiting for my knight in shining armor. And now he has come! My husband, if only you knew how much joy you've just brought me! Why for you I'd..."

Authority increased to 40!

I don't know what else Minn-O was going to tell me, because my kitten entered the game, so she got embarrassed and fell silent. Tini then, after seeing me, shouted out with unhidden joy:

"Master Gnat, I pulled it off!!! The great Priestess Amiru U-Mayaoo spoke with me and agreed to buy her tail for one million crypto! She ordered the trophy brought as quickly as possible to any Miyelonian station to a representative of the First Pride or the station owner. Also, the great Amiru blessed me and ordered me to accompany you everywhere! And she asked me to say that she found only partial data about the Relict classes in the Star City archives, but it seems the Listener is just an intermediate stage in class evolution, after which comes either Thinker, Devourer, or Administrator. And those are their three highest classes, which were generally reserved for Relict rulers."

Astrolinguistics skill increased to level eighty!

So then, it turned out that unfamiliar glyph in the description meant "Devourer!" Most likely, depending on preferences and skill leveling, a Listener could choose the path of an intellectual, administrator or war leader. But how did I make my choice? What skills needed to be leveled and to what points? I wanted badly to get more detailed information on that account, but Tini couldn't add anything. Most likely, even the wise Amiru U-Mayaoo didn't know more.

And then practically at once Vasha, Eduard Boyko and Imran appeared nearby. And just a second later Basha and Avan Toi also showed. Was it meeting time already? I looked at the countdown timer. Yes, right on the dot. The last seconds were just ticking by. Exactly as the timer rang, Uline Tar popped into the game. Almost everyone was here. We were now missing only the Medic.

"He's not coming," the Supercargo told me, not hiding his bitterness. "I recently spoke with our former Captain Gerd Uraz Tukhsh and found out the medic returned to him, vaunted war hero and all that..."

"All the worse for him," I said with a calm and confident tone, trying not to show that one of my squadron deserting had hurt me. "Then the Medic's share of the reward will be spent on repairs for our Tolili-Ukh X. I ask the rest to come one by one and collect their first salary from their new captain, Gerd Gnat!"

Authority increased to 41!

Psionic skill increased to level fifty-eight!

"Did Kung Waid Shishish really let us keep the starship?" Supercargo Avan Toi shuddered, and the rest of the group also lit up.

I answered that I had a personal talk with the fleet commander and had received assurances from him that our right to the ship would not be disputed, and the frigate would soon be brought to Un-Tesh. I also told them honestly that the ship was in a very bad state and would need lots of money for repair. But I already had a few ideas on that account and was hoping to quickly make the frigate good enough for interstellar flight.

Chapter Sixteen

Free Captain

"IS *THAT THING* really gonna fly?" I asked Zheltov with unhidden doubt. When the gates of the repair hangar slid aside, I saw a twisted and crumpled hunk of metal which was only vaguely reminiscent of a frigate.

"Come on, Gnat! It's already looking more or less okay. You should have seen what a state the frigate was in right after the explosion!" the pilot reassured me. Then patched up pointed with pride to some rectangular patches on the lower part of the body. "Ayukh and I already repaired the biggest holes down there. We got the seal back up in every residential sector, and they all hold air now. The Geckho military repairmen even gave us a jump drive during our flight on the mothership! It's a bit crappy, to be honest, from some totaled shuttle and a bit weak for a frigate. A power unit and both kinds of thrusters wouldn't hurt, though. Then we could theoretically fly."

"Theoretically?" I hooked into the pilot's word, and Dmitry Zheltov gave a crooked smile:

"What did you think, Gnat? This thing can fly in space, but where? We won't be able to tell where we're going or be able to control it... We don't have decent locators, our forcefield barely turns on, the instrument panels are not adapted for human eyes, it has no landing supports or stabilizers, it doesn't even have an artificial gravity generator..."

I reassured the pilot that the Third Strike Fleet Commander had promised basic repair for our frigate, after which the starship could be brought to a neighboring station. And I said I would demand that the repairmen carry out that promise. My friend was encouraged by these words, and he was back in high spirits after getting the sack of red crystals.

Here I suddenly noticed a tear in the body of the ship. There was a gigantic flat millipede crawling out of it gracefully clacking its innumerable legs over the uneven surface! And apparently this overgrown insect was made entirely of metal! What the heck?! I just got a ship, and now it's infested with parasites? I read the name of the creature:

Kirsan. Autonomous Mechanoid repair bot.

Uhh... Repair bot? So it's helping us? Meanwhile, the metal millipede crawled to one of the dents in the hull and stopped right above it. Under its flat belly, a bright bluish flame appeared like an electric welder. I hurried to turn away as not to hurt my eyes. Dmitry followed my example.

"There were plenty of those things on the Geckho mothership. They're some kind of automatic repair bot." Ayukh confirmed that they were kind of like living creatures despite their appearance. They were apparently quite intelligent even. But in my opinion, they were just robots. The remnants of Mechanoid technology, having outlived their masters. The Geckho didn't pay them any mind. They crawled all around and helped out, fixing everything they could find. There were three of them on our frigate already and Ayukh said not to have them leave. And there, as a matter of fact, was our Navigator now. He could tell us!

Ayukh walked up to us rumbling happily and not hiding his joy. Greeting me warmly, he extended some kind of electronic tablet in a rubber coated case:

"Gerd Gnat, here is the documentation! The commander finally transferred the title! I wrote you in as captain so you can decide what to do with the remaining vacancies."

I opened the case and, beyond a tablet computer, discovered a flat dark-blue crystal in a special recess, inside of which I could see some complex electronic chips, and little colored bulbs blinking intermittently and faintly.

Identification card. Gerd Gnat. Free Captain.

"This is the captain's key," the Navigator explained to me enthusiastically. "For now, it doesn't have a particular purpose, just show it in spaceports when you go through checks. But later, after we change out the electronics on the Tolili-Ukh X frigate, we'll need to use it to link the ship to you and set access level to various sectors for the crew. The second small key I kept for myself as the most senior officer, and a second copy goes to the main pilot. That way, only three crew members can turn on the ship's engines and give the command to take off."

Fame increased to 59.

Electronics skill increased to level forty-nine!

Machine Control skill increased to level forty-three!

You have reached level sixty-eight!

You have received three skill points! (total points accumulated: six)

This was it! I was officially recognized as a Free Captain with my own ship, I'd even received documentation! I set the crystal key into my inventory and picked up the tablet. Its screen immediately lit up.

Tolili-Ukh X Frigate. Standard Meleyephatian Module Frigate. Configuration: (undetermined).

Status: critically damaged, needs repair.

Energy shield: 100% (2,300,000 of 2,300,000 units).

Hull strength: 2.2% (176,450 of 8,000,000 units).

Maximum speed: undetermined, no main thruster.

Maneuverability: undetermined, no maneuver thrusters.

Maximum hyperjump distance: 0.831.

Attention! You are the first owner of this frigate and may give it a name.

The last line intrigued me. Given there was a purpose to giving my firearm a name, what would it do for a starship? I asked the Navigator.

"A small bonus to maneuverability and speed," the all-knowing Ayukh immediately replied. "But not all captains do so, because there are also plenty of downsides. The most obvious is that a named ship is easier to track because any automated scanning system will see it not as some abstract Tolili-Ukh-class frigate, but under a specific name. For traders or smugglers, not wanting to advertise their comings and goings, that is a clear minus. Pirates, fighters and headhunters also don't always want the enemy to see exactly what ship killed them. That keeps them from figuring out who was captain and harboring a vendetta. But others use it to raise their Fame. Overall, naming a starship isn't always good."

I started to see that there was no reason to rush this very serious question, and to start I needed to figure out how to use my ship. No, I was not planning to become a pirate, headhunter or smuggler. I was more interested in searching for valuable minerals and anomalies approximately like I did for Uraz Tukhsh, but now as my own boss.

"Gerd Gnat, turn to the next page. It's much more informative," the Navigator advised me, and I did.

A colored diagram of the Tolili-Ukh X Frigate appeared, showing the present state of the ship's equipment. I looked at the guide, which said what each color signified. Gray meant "not installed," red was "critically damaged, inactive," orange was "working, but with issues," yellow meant "needs attention, minor issues," and green just stood for "everything's fine." Most of the frigate's systems were colored gray for inactive some in red, and just the forcefield and hyperspace thruster were colored orange. It was about what I had guessed based on the appearance of the badly damaged starship, this was just a formal confirmation.

I turned to the third and last page and discovered a crew list which was practically unfilled. For now, there was just the green captain field with my name Gerd Gnat, and some text below saying that my skills could give a few positive bonuses, but they were inactive.

I first of all checked what would happen if I set Dmitry Zheltov in the main pilot slot. He was a Starship Pilot by class, so this was the position he should have had. The slot lit up green, showing that this player was totally compatible with the assignment. Below that, I saw the words:

Player ability bonus: Maximum speed +7%, Maneuverability +14%.

Great! Awesome as a matter of fact! And most likely these bonuses would grow more with time as the pilot leveled his skills. Now the next thing I needed to do was move the old Ayukh into the empty Navigator field and voila!

Player ability bonus: Hyperspace jump time reduced by 25%.

All hyperspace jumps would be a quarter faster! Say what you will but that was a significant bonus! I already knew I got very lucky with the experienced Navigator, but only now could I appreciate just how fortunate I was. And that reduced time would be especially obvious during long trips. For example, when we went out to get my Small Relict Guard Drone, which had to happen sooner or later.

Everything was also clear with Supercargo Avan Toi, and the bonus that showed up after that was great: loading and unloading time was reduced by a third. The two twin brothers Vasha and Basha fit perfectly in the loader slots, too. However, like in my case, their bonuses were still inactive.

I didn't find an appropriate player for the role of Senior Mechanic. But it was surprisingly easy to drag one of the automatic repair bots into the slot, then set the other two as his assistants. The bonuses from this trio went to structural integrity and repair speed! When I, not hiding my surprise, told Ayukh about it, the experienced Navigator wasn't the least bit surprised:

"That's exactly how it should be, Gnat. Actually, repair bots are little different from players. They can even respawn after death. And the fact that they're not talkative, always keep busy and don't need to be paid is pretty nice. It's good they agreed to join the crew. Now they'll never leave us. And maybe you as a captain could control them or prioritize their tasks? Because that there is cosmetic," Ayukh said, pointing at the metallic millipede smoothing out dents in the starship's hull. "It can wait. Now above all we need to restore the climate unit in order to start recycling air and not have to lug around tanks full of oxygen."

Yes, the idea to send the repair bots to higher-priority missions was correct. But how could I do that? Although... I supposed they were mechanical, so I had the chance to take them under my control and use my Machine Control skill. I activated the Scanning icon and, among the many possible options nearby, I discovered three identical repair bots:

Kirsan-class repair bot (your subordinate). Interface chance: 100%. Total control chance: 100%.

I tried to mentally command to all three of them to leave their present tasks and repair the climate unit. The millipede stopped working on the outside of the chassis and slipped back through the crack into the frigate, so apparently the command was accepted.

Scanning skill increased to level twenty-seven!
Psionic skill increased to level fifty-nine!

Machine Control skill increased to level forty-four!

Alright then, such a complicated order and it worked! I was very proud of myself. Up until that very moment, I had yet to think over the issue. Just how did other captains control their repair bots? After all, they didn't have this modified Scanning skill! I opened the drone and machine control page I had saved earlier and... facepalmed! There they were, all three repair bots! And they were marked as awaiting orders. There was no need to go through all that rigamarole!

Hrm... If a person had inflamed tonsils, you could probably find a way to get them out without going through the mouth... Seemingly that was about what I had just been doing instead of using the function the game provided. Although every cloud had a silver lining. I had both finished my mission and leveled my skills. By the way, if these Mechanoid repair bots were so smart, could they fully replace a ship mechanic?

I chose the Senior Mechanic of the three identical bots, ordered the millipede to come meet me, then went up a ladder (there was not yet a gangway) and came aboard my starship. I immediately noticed that the ship looked much better inside than out. Yes, the floor had bundles of power cables stretched along it and the elevator to the upper deck wasn't working but if I didn't know how warped the ship was, I wouldn't have been able to tell from the corridor and nearby area.

The millipede climbed up skillfully to me and

stopped to receive orders. I then took my Annihilator from my inventory and showed the mechanical repairman the handle and seven grooves for fingers or whatever the Relicts had. Then I showed it my hand, and even removed a glove to make it clear:

"Five fingers. Seven grooves. Not comfortable!" I repeated to Kirsan in Geckho, at the same time mentally repeating myself.

The millipede raised the front part of its body and extended its thin jointed arms to the Annihilator. I internally braced myself, but gave the valuable artifact to the repair bot, hoping greatly that it wouldn't be shooting me and selling the weapon for parts.

Kirsan turned the ancient weapon over in its thin little jointed legs thoughtfully, then returned it and my tablet vibrated. I hurriedly took it out and turned the screen on.

Captain, the Senior Mechanic has sent a list of parts and materials necessary for repair:

- *4 RTH-2356 Resonators.*
- *63 cm of 0.05 mm wolfram thread.*
- *4 6-mm Boron nitride metal drills.*
- *1 Plasma welder.*
- *1 12x12x6 cm carbon fiber bar.*
- *3 PP-56 Quartz lenses.*
- *12 OP-5 Power fire extinguishers.*

...

- *4 bolts of fire-proof abrasion-resistant flooring, 150 ft. x 5.9 ft each.*

> • 3 empty 200-liter high-pressure tanks with KKG/78 valve.

The full list was three hundred eighteen items long. And though the first of them were things I could more or less imagine were for modifying and repairing my Annihilator, the fire-extinguisher and other stuff was definitely not. No, some of this must have been for something else, most likely the ship...

Here I noticed Uline just in time as she entered the repair hangar accompanied by the Supercargo and a whole delegation of Geckho in base-employee uniforms. Apparently, these were the repairmen the Kung had sent to fix up my starship. I called my furry friend over and showed her the materials list.

"Gerd Gnat, I'll look it over and order it later alright? But first, let's get away from this noisy crowd. We have some very sensitive topics to discuss, and I don't want any eavesdropping. For example, who should be the owner of this trophy frigate, how much money are we going to spend on repair, and how will we divvy up the profits."

Chapter Seventeen

Business Partner

I T WAS TOO LOUD in the hangar, so Uline and I decided to go inside the starship, where there was no one other than the three repair bots. The elevator wasn't working, so the only way to the upper deck was via a vertical shaft using chaotically placed metal brackets in the walls. Maybe the eight-legged spider-like Meleyephatians didn't need a proper ladder here, but for me and especially the hefty Geckho lady, it was a strange and uncomfortable way up.

"Woah, it's dark up here," said the Trader, coming up after me. She turned on a flashlight and led the beam along the metal walls and down the corridor to the bridge. "There's your captain's bridge, Gnat! It's so spacious! Ah, there's an emergency light over the entrance so we won't be totally in the dark. Let's talk here, but close the door so we can keep this confidential."

I let Uline walk in front and entered my cabin, covered the thick armored door leading into the dark corridor and squinted when the bright light came on. After that, following Uline's example, I reached for a special handle in the wall and pulled out an unusual rope structure that was a hybrid between a wicker chair and a hammock. After I figured out how to sit in the hanging and rocking structure, it was pretty comfortable. Uline then, confidently sitting on a legged armchair, took out a tablet and showed me a table she'd drawn up.

Honestly, I didn't realize it was a table right away, because this was the first time I was seeing such a thing in Geckho writing. But I followed the lines, and discovered they merely served to contain blocks of digits and texts.

Astrolinguistics skill increased to level eighty-one!

Estimated profit shares for the Tolili-Ukh X:

#	Name					%
1.		1,200,000.00				
2.	Gerd Gnat	200,000.00	100,000.00		300,000.00	6%
3.	**Uline Tar**	**100,000.00**	**50,000.00**	**3,640,000.00**	**3,790,000.00**	**76%**
4.	Ayukh	100,000.00			100,000.00	2%
5.	Avan Toi	100,000.00			100,000.00	2%
6.	Vasha Tushihh	100,000.00			100,000.00	2%
7.	Basha Tushihh	100,000.00			100,000.00	2%
8.	Tini	100,000.00			100,000.00	2%
9.	Dmitry Zheltov	100,000.00			100,000.00	2%
10.	Imran	100,000.00			100,000.00	2%
11.	Eduard Boyko	100,000.00			100,000.00	2%
12.	Minn-O La-Fin	100,000.00			100,000.00	2%
13.					**4,990,000.00**	**100%**

"Alright, Gnat. The frigate is seriously damaged, and I estimate its worth in this state to be no more than one million two hundred thousand crystals. That is what's shown in the first line. Kung Waid Shishish gave the trophy not to one individual, but to everyone who took part in capturing it, so I gave everyone a fair share of that. But as commander, I figured you deserve twice as much. Good thing the Medic left us, because you just got his share."

"I understand the first column, but what about the second?" I asked, pointing to the broken lines of Geckho meaning "one hundred thousand" and "fifty thousand."

Uline was clearly glad that I didn't have any questions about the first part, and explained eagerly:

"Gnat, to repair the starship we need investments, and pretty hefty ones at that. We each got a bag of crystals as a reward for our heroism on the planetoid, so we can use those funds for the repair. I managed to talk with everyone besides Tini and Ayukh and none of them are willing to spend their money for the common cause. I am intending to spend my fifty thousand on the repair, though, which I indicated in the table. Opposite your name, I put one hundred thousand, which is if you agree to add not only the Medic's money but some of your own as well."

"Let's call that good," I said not wanting to dispute it, even though I wasn't happy with all the Trader's judgements. Then I asked to go to the next column.

The Trader gave a rumble of satisfaction and made sure the door was closed and no one was listening then set six heavy bags on a shelf.

"These are the crystals I took off the Shiamiru before it was destroyed. Of course this is probably more Clan Tar-Layneh's money than mine... But no one is going to find out except you. There are three million four hundred thousand crystals here. Beyond that, I have another two hundred forty thousand in a bank account. And I am prepared to invest all this cash in repairing the frigate. Thus, my total investment in the ship came to three million seven-hundred ninety thousand crystals, and that is no more and no less than seventy-six percent of the total. And thus, that is the share of the future profits I lay claim to. As I do to the dominating portion of votes. Your percentage of the profits comes to six percent. That's three times more than any other team member! To my eye, it's all fair. What do you say, Gerd Gnat?"

Mental Fortitude skill increased to level forty-nine!

No, she wasn't trying to use mind control, although it was close. The Trader was speaking so coherently and confidently it pained me. Uline clearly believed she was acting honestly and considered her offer fair and beneficial to all. Before answering, I took a deep sigh and mentally counted to ten to calm myself and not raise my voice to my great but quirky friend.

"Uline, I won't dispute your estimated value of the frigate. After all, you are a Trader by class not me, so you know better. However, you're forgetting one fairly important detail. The ship will be repaired and will grow in value. And that is my personal contribution because I convinced the Kung to pay for it!"

Psionic skill increased to level sixty!

Mysticism skill increased to level eight!

And here I apparently didn't manage to get by totally without magic as the game algorithms had registered some extrasensory activity. Uline didn't think for long and eventually admitted I was right:

"Okay, Gerd Gnat, that is fair. I cannot accurately evaluate the increase in value from that repair yet, but I'd estimate the worth of the maneuver thrusters taken from totaled starships, cheap main thrusters and other second-hand equipment to be... And the hyper wasn't your doing, so... seven hundred thousand crystals... alright, let's even say seven hundred fifty thousand. Let's write you that in your column. That means that your share goes up from six to eighteen percent, and mine falls to two thirds."

I mentally checked Uline very carefully and discovered that the furry lady was not lying. Her estimate of the second-hand equipment at its cheapest (and we had no reason to expect anything else from the tight-fisted commander) was approximately in line with reality. Alright, I'd accept this and continue the conversation.

"Also Uline, it would be nice to talk with Ayukh. I bet such a respected Navigator has saved up something in his long life and might want a piece of the action. I also need to have a talk with Minn-O. Yes, my wayedda doesn't have much in the way of money now but she is still a Princess, and her grandfather Leng Thumor-Anhu La-Fin is a very influential and wealthy Coruler of humanity. It is possible that the old mage will agree to invest a million or two crystals in his granddaughter's enterprise."

Uline clearly looked sad, but still agreed. Although she also noted that she would really like these additional investments not to bring her share down below half, because then she would lose control. So seemingly, the time had come to play my trump card:

"But Uline, that has to happen! No matter how you'd like to be sovereign ruler on this ship, it won't work because I also have savings. First of all, I have a million crystals worth of Miyelonian crypto in my hands." Here for effect I took out my wallet and brought up the balance on the screen. "I hope you can read Miyelonian numbers. There are one hundred forty-three thousand crypto here, and that is a bit more than a million in Geckho money."

"But Gerd Gnat, where did you get it???" She didn't even try to hide her astonishment, but I placed my hand to my lips. Geckho seemed to like that gesture, which called for silence.

"I'll tell you later. But that isn't all," I assured the Trader and took the trophy tail of the incarnation of the Miyelonian Great First Female out of my inventory. "Uline, I hope greatly for your good sense and discretion, because this is the very item that sparked this galactic war. I have a buyer ready to spend seven million crystals for this tail."

"But it's clearly worth more!" Uline Tar couldn't hold back, staring wide eyed at the extremely rare item.

"Doesn't matter. This trophy is too dangerous for me to keep or to let it go to an unknown or even criminal buyer. I'm going to return the trophy to its owner. I have even spoken already with Leng Amiru U-Mayaoo and said I would turn it in at the first Miyelonian station we reach for one million crypto."

Authority increased to 42!

Uline Tar was clearly in shock and looked at me then at the fluffy pure white tail, then glanced at her tablet and checked something quickly.

"We won't even need that much money for the repair," the Trader said, raising her huge lemon-yellow eyes. "By my calculations, we only need to spend ten million eight hundred thousand crystals to repair the frigate. Now we have potentially more! And it seems to me that isn't all the surprises you have in store and you could easily get by without any investment from me, and especially without Ayukh or Minn-O."

"Yes, that is true. And I have another very interesting and potentially rewarding venture, but who tells all their secrets at the same time?" I smiled happily, then turned serious. "Uline, I might be able to get by without your finances, even though it would be a bit hard. But there are a whole bunch of reasons I would like the starship to partially belong to you. You're a beautiful Geckho lady I fully trust, and we could be business partners."

The Trader rumbled exceptionally loudly, very satisfied at my trust and offer to work together.

"Gerd Gnat, I have known since we first met that you aren't like the others and will achieve a great amount. I believed that I needed hold on to you. Unfortunately, my kind doesn't understand that and will think I lost a business dispute. And if only that was all! I tore up a high-potential engagement with Uraz Tukhsh just a half ummi before my fiancée became a war hero. After that, instead of selling the rights to the video clip from the Meleyephatian base to some news channel, I showed the footage to Geckho military and it was confiscated... My family will think I am making a huge error, abandoning everything to bet on working with you. But the longer I talk with you, the more convinced I become that I am not making the wrong choice! So, I am immensely proud and joyful to accept your offer! Two thirds of the profits to you, one to me. Well roughly, not considering the small shares of the other crew members. Does that work?"

I was totally satisfied with that, and we shook hands just like people, cementing our understanding.

Then I took out my tablet and placed Uline Tar into the captain's assistant slot. But I asked the Trader not to advertise our agreement to the other team members on the frigate. I told her just to limit herself to the basics like Gnat and Uline got together enough money to repair the ship, but the other team members did not need to know the financial details.

I had plenty to worry about. Sooner or later, this talk could reach Imran, Eduard Boyko or Dmitry Zheltov, then the leadership of my faction. I did not want one bit for the Human-3 Faction to find out how much space currency I had at my disposal. That would be an additional cause for envy, anger and extra attention from leadership. I preferred to avoid all that. After all, it was not hard to predict how Lozovsky and the other directors and curators would react: "Ah, you got a lot of space currency, so help the faction out and quick share your money with us!" And it wasn't that I didn't want to help my allies, I just figured an intact starship would bring somewhat more benefit to humanity than extracting a couple million crystals from me by pressure or blackmail.

"Don't you worry about that, Gnat," Uline reassured me when I shared my worries. "Who knows better than a Trader that finances are best kept quiet. If your factionmates think you a modest player without much money, let them stay mistaken on that account. But if your faction needs crystals that bad, I could offer to buy out Eduard, Imran, Dmitry and Minn-O. One hundred thousand is a very respectable sum, and I bet few of them would prefer a mountain of crystals to a hypothetical share in the profits. And for a small percentage, I could even act as middle-man and arrange for that money to be transferred back to your home planet."

It was quite an intriguing offer. I was sure that the several tens or even hundreds of thousands of crystals being transferred from deep space would be a massive boon to the Human-3 Faction. Although in Minn-O's case of course, I would first have to wait for her to transfer to my world so that the money she received would not be going to the enemy. However once again, all these issues would have to be dealt with later. And so I suggested that Uline wait until the frigate was done being remodeled because our priority mission now was getting the ship into working order, so we had to save our funds for that.

Chapter Eighteen

Propaganda and Diplomacy

I T WAS THE MIDDLE of the night under the Dome, and I didn't catch Lozovsky in his office. In theory, that was predictable, even though fairly often there was work underway in the admin building at such an ungodly hour. And it wasn't exactly abandoned now. I ran into Alexander Antipov in the hallway having left his office give a tour to a large group of shadowy outside military men. One of them, a plump middle-aged officer with major patches, unexpectedly walked up to me and extended a hand in greeting:

"Kirill Ignatiev? I've heard so much about you. You turned it around brilliantly with the Graveyard node! You neutralized quite a large threat to the Capital! I recommended your leadership to pay you a bonus for that!"

The major slapped me on the shoulder good-heartedly and rushed to catch up to his colleagues, leaving me to stand in confusion. Who even was that? How did he know me? Unfortunately, there was no one to ask, because Alexander Antipov had left with the rest. Now there was only one light on in the whole gloomy hallway. It was coming from the cracked-open door of our former Leng Radugin's office. I walked up closer and listened to bits of the important meeting going on there, which must have included at least a dozen people:

Grain crops for dry soil... not enough fuel for the combines... we need to plow the virgin soil of the Centaur Plateau... move the third grain elevator further away from the front...

I had always respected farmers and their difficult work, but I was pretty far from understanding it both in the real world and the game. I asked a guardsman, who told me the faction leader had gone to his room just ten or fifteen minutes earlier. I figured Lozovsky wasn't sleeping yet so I hurried to his place. I had a bunch of issues I wanted to discuss, and I needed to take advantage of the opportunity.

Based on the sour face Ivan Lozovsky opened the door with, I immediately guessed that I'd come at a bad time, and he was not too happy at his unexpected midnight visitor. I was especially clued in by the sound of his shower running. Clearly the faction leader was not alone. I did not know who the secretive Diplomat was dating and I suspected that few in our faction were privy to such information.

Not wanting to ruin my boss's date, I was intending to turn and leave, but Ivan Lozovksy pointed me to two chairs inside. There was romantic dim lighting provided by three candles in a pretty candelabra on the newspaper table. Nearby there was champagne cooling in a bucket of ice and two flutes waiting to be filled. All that only reinforced my conviction that I had poked my head in at a very bad time. Wanting to get out quickly, I set out my recent news as briefly as possible: the talk with Kung Waid Shishish, the Graveyard node, Minn-O wanting to join our faction and the trophy frigate.

The faction leader had no reaction to most of the information as if he already knew it all from other sources. He answered the question about Minn-O changing factions extremely curtly: "not opposed," but when I told him about the trophy frigate, he lit up:

"A starship? And you're its captain and even co-owner? I'm both intrigued and surprised! Although... We'll have to tell the Geckho very delicately. First, we have to ask Kosta Dykhsh if a starship that partially belongs to a member of a different race is even allowed to enter the Geckho's exclusive economic space. You see Kirill, most Geckho flew to our newly discovered earth with a clearly defined goal — to get fat trading with us backward outworlders. I have seen how our suzerains underpay for all our stuff and crank up import prices for theirs! Just look how many middle-men every transaction has to go through! And each of these greedy cheats wants a piece for themselves! If us outworlders get our own starship, all these middle-men would be cut out, which would take profit away from the Geckho, so they would give it a hostile reaction."

I had somehow not considered such an obstacle before, so all these legal and other sticking points were a bitter pill to swallow. After all, my starship would immediately lose half its purpose if we could never fly it to Earth! Ivan Lozovsky tried to reassure me:

"I do not think the Geckho forbid vassals from flying to their homeworld. But there's gonna be lots of red tape, and we won't get anywhere without greasing the palms of some civil servants. And that will take money. A good deal of it, in fact..."

The faction leader gave a heavy sigh, stood from his seat and took a sealed bottle of cognac and a two glasses from the cabinet. "Want some?" he offered. I refused.

After a day and a half in the game, I was collapsing in exhaustion and my only wish was to crawl quickly into my room and drop dead in my tracks. Fortunately, I didn't have far to go, just one floor up the stairs, because the Diplomat lived in my same building.

"As you say," Ivan Lozovsky didn't insist and

filled his glass to the rim. "But I'm gonna need some. To calm my nerves. In the last day, I died four times from Naiad tridents and the teeth of the monsters they summoned."

"So the negotiations aren't going smoothly?" I guessed. The faction leader shot his cognac in one go, winced and gave a brief nod. "Yeesh, it's warm. What filth... Not good at all!"

After a short breather, the Diplomat told me in greater detail about the Naiad problem:

"There weren't really any negotiations as such. The Naiads wouldn't even talk and killed me immediately. Then they killed me again when I decided to take that negative experience and tried to arrange a talk a different way. Seemingly, the underwater NPC's cannot tell people of different factions apart and perceive me along with all our other soldiers the same as the hated Germans. I couldn't even get a word out of a captive Naiad in a cage. I had to give our legionnaires the wave to unholster their weapons..."

Lozovsky fell silent and winced. A shadow ran across his face as if he was remembering something bad. Apparently the war with the underwater mobs was not going well. I decided not to rub salt in my boss's wound and changed the topic, turning back to the trophy frigate. But the Diplomat wanted to continue talking about the war with the NPC Naiads, asking me a very unexpected question:

"Kirill, have you seen any *Godzilla* movies?"

What? Yes, I'd seen a couple, but what did the gigantic monster invented by Japanese producers have to do with this? As it turned out, quite a lot:

"Godzillas, as the monsters are called by the Human-6 Faction, are just one type of creature the Naiads have summoned forth from the depths of the sea. They aren't one hundred fifty to three hundred feet tall like in the Japanese movies, and they can't shoot lasers with their eyes, but they're huge, dangerous and extremely strong. And beyond that, there are other monsters like gigantic octopuses, krakens and sea snakes... A whole zoo of mythical beasts! It was just terrifying!"

After seeing the mistrust and skepticism on my face — as if to say monsters couldn't scare me! — Lozovsky immediately corrected himself:

"I was wrong to call them scary. Our soldiers aren't afraid of these creatures at all and have succeeded at killing them despite their size. In fact, that isn't even what I wanted to talk about. Kirill, have you considered where the game takes all these mobs from? Forest spirits, harpies, mermaids, naiads, centaurs... After all, these are not characters from parallel worlds and not extinct animals. But then what? Where did they come from? When I first saw a Godzilla, I recognized it immediately even though this was the first time I had seen one in the game. So, I was visited by a very interesting thought."

"They're all from myths, legends and popular

fiction?" I interrupted him, and Lozovsky clapped his hands a few times for show, applauding my quick thinking.

"Yes, Gnat! Apparently, all the mobs that live in this virtual games are something humanity believes in or once believed in, or something a large number of people fear. And that, if you think about it, is really scary! After all, it means that somewhere in the distant and still unknown nodes of the virtual Earth, there might be dinosaurs, angels and demons, and even immortal beings with divine powers. After all a huge number of people believe in and worship them! By the way, the centaurs have told us vague rumors that some flying lizards live in the nodes past the Southern Mountains. They sound just like dragons!"

Lozovsky filled another glass to the rim, took it in his hand, raised it to his lips, held it there and... set it back on the table. He raised his eyes to me and gave a weary chuckle:

"Stop looking so serious. You're not in class. Don't fill your head with all this nonsense! Can you really believe everything you hear? My day has just been hard, so I'm having delusions."

"So in the end it worked and we helped our allies?" I asked. The Diplomat was delighted to change topics:

"I won't exaggerate, we didn't achieve our overall objectives. But I cannot say that sending our elite troops south was totally senseless either. We got to know our allies better, showed that we keep our word and agreed to continue working together. With a joint attack, we squeezed out the Naiads from the Seashell Spit — it's a long point that goes almost five miles into the sea. It's strategically important for controlling the New Bavaria node's bay. Beyond that the Second Legion cleared a network of seaside caves of Naiads and other dangerous life forms when they were filled with water at high tide. And although it's still too early to say there's been a turnaround in the war against the NPC Naiads, the situation is much more favorable to our allies, and things are now looking up."

The Diplomat was speaking confidently and eloquently. According to him, the whole campaign to give military aid to our allies was going wonderfully. But I had known Ivan for a good amount time, long enough to know there was something false in his bravado. He had not managed to hide his disappointment behind the veneer of his fine words. Clearly, he was expecting a lot more from the campaign. It looked a lot like the Naiads and other sea creatures had stumped my faction leader and he could not think up any effective methods against the dangerous NPC's who quickly restored their losses. Nevertheless, I didn't refute what he said, allowing the garrulous Lozovsky to continue:

"We found out a lot of new things about geography and nature of the virtual world, and the game itself. We nailed down a trade agreement with the

Germans. They have much-needed titanium and in basically unlimited quantities. And that means we'll have an aviation industry up and running very soon, followed by long-distance recon and the end to the Dark Faction's air superiority! We also have something to offer them — steel alloys, grain, alien technology, and rounds of any caliber..."

"You're selling rounds now?" I interrupted, not hiding my surprise. "I remember not that long ago, the faction had a deficit, especially of 12 caliber hunting shells. Also, all our detonator capsules were being brought in from the real world, and fuses too."

The diplomat sat back in his armchair and gave a happy chuckle:

"Kirill, those times are long gone! Our faction is growing, providing for the production of everything we need in our lands. The ammo plant at the Prometheus and the underground chemical laboratories in the Yellow Mountains are now producing powder, casings, shells, bullets, mines, capsules and fuses... Sure, we haven't found the lead to make soft bullets and shot in our lands yet, but our technicians have made an alloy with similar properties out of bismuth, antimony and tin. In the real world, our economists are losing their minds because those bullets cost thirty times more than lead ones, but we have our own priorities here and we need to do what we can with what's at hand. Plus, it's better than hauling heavy lead in from the real world."

I was in complete agreement with this, and the leader's words were very encouraging. It was nice to hear that my native faction was solving its problems. But as for trade... I remembered the ghastly so-called road, or more like trail to the south. Even our Peresvet ATVs couldn't make it through. Could we really bring cargo that way?! Lozovsky reassured me:

"For now, we're trading through middle-men. We have a deal with the Geckho to use their ferry, which the Naiads don't touch. But in the future, after the Centaurs build a decent road along the gulf, all shipments will go through territory under our faction's control. Yes, Kirill, you heard right! Other than Centaur Plateau, which has already become a level one node for us, two seashore nodes will soon be joining our faction. We call them the Rainforest and Tropics nodes. Two Centaur chiefs whose herds lived in these territories recently died of dietary disorders and Elder Mare Phylira was gracious enough to take them under her protection."

I chuckled. What a surprising coincidence! Two hardened war-chiefs of the Antiquity Faction went down almost simultaneously under such strange circumstances... And not long before that, the soldiers of the First and Second Legions had passed through their lands, probably spoken with the Centaurs who lived there and given gifts to the chieftains... Well, it wasn't hard to figure that leadership had taken the secret deal from Phylira to quietly off the other leaders of Antiquity in exchange for their nodes. I raised an eye to Ivan Lozovsky, who fell silent and looked closely at me.

"Kirill, I can see you've figured it out," the faction leader said coldly. "But keep these guesses to yourself. There's no reason for the other players, and especially our NPC neighbors to find out the dirty sides of in-game politics."

I promised to avoid mentioning the Centaur leaders and changed topic to the First Legion combing through the forest near the Capital. Had our soldiers found the dangerous Whangdoodle that was attacking the lumberjacks? Lozovsky again frowned in dismay and shook his head:

"Not yet. Gerd Tarasov's Spies and Sentries have combed through it three times, looking under every bush, checking every cave and cranny. They even shot any living creature bigger than a squirrel. But as soon as our soldiers went south, the attacks started up again! Yesterday two farmers were mauled, and today Mikhalych the Geologist was eaten whole when he tried taking a shortcut back to the Capital. It's a real thorn in our side... But we'll definitely find it! I want to take our Prospector there tomorrow with protection so he can search for the dangerous beast. He can scan the whole area, we'll even give him plenty of analyzers. And if the Prospector cannot do it, then I..."

He went abruptly silent midsentence because the bathroom door flew open, and we were joined in the dusky room by a quickly striding Anya. I froze with my jaw hanging open in surprise, because my now apparently former girlfriend was wearing only a towel on her head and a pair of soft fluffy slippers. And if Anya from First Medical was embarrassed to find me in the room, it was just for a few seconds. After that she went on the attack:

"It's all your fault, Gnat! I waited four long days for you. But in all that time, you didn't even bother asking how I was doing or come into your own room, where I spent almost all my free time! I figured you didn't want me, so I left!"

"Alright, I won't bother you," I said, standing up and heading out. "I'll admit, Anna, you were my main candidate for Medic on my starship. But now I understand that was not the right option. The fur-covered Geckho and Miyelonians would be too shocked to see your total lack of body hair, so I'd better find a Medic of one of their races."

Yes, it sounded dumb, and I should have kept quiet rather than act like some pissed-off teen, but I simply didn't have the self-control. I had already gone into the corridor when I was chased down by a running Lozovsky.

"Kirill, please forgive me! I didn't know. I thought you and Anna had already broken up. Please, forgive me again, I never meant to hurt you."

I gave an unhappy chuckle and, giving the faction leader a friendly pat on the back, wished him a pleasant evening. I turned back around, intending to go to the stairs, but Ivan Lozovsky stopped me again:

"I understand this is not the best time, but I do have a job for you... it's a bit unusual but very important and delicate in nature."

I stopped. I was intrigued and, despite my exhaustion and anger, willing to listen.

"You see Gnat, I haven't been able to get in touch with the leader of the Dark Faction for a few days. I think Leng Thumor-Anhu La-Fin is ignoring me. He's never done that before. He always answered my requests via official diplomatic channels. But now, it seems he is mad about the Graveyard node and is showing it that way."

"The old mage really might be mad," I agreed, remembering my wayedda's state after the conversation with her grandpa over video phone. "The great mage yelled at his granddaughter over the lost node. After all, it was her fault. It got so bad that Minn-O felt the need to run into the game and ask to join our faction!"

"That may be so. But there are just two days until the ceasefire with the Dark Faction is over. I want to talk with Leng Thumor-Anhu about potentially prolonging it. Our faction has just crawled back from the horror of a war of extermination and state of resignation. We have started actively growing, and we have free resources and very promising projects to the south. So we do not want a war with the Dark Faction right now! I suspect that they also have better things to do. Our spies say they're actively expanding into the northern mountainous nodes, for example. Overall... tell him my offer through Minn-O. And please again, forgive me for Anna!"

Chapter Nineteen

Ready for Takeoff

IF ANYONE THOUGHT that Anna leaving would make me so mad I wouldn't be able to sleep right away, they were very wrong. I slept like a baby. Maybe it was because of the many days without sleep, or I had just foreseen my fleeting relationship with the little medic ending that way, but I was not upset for very long. By morning, totally coming to my senses and thinking over what happened, I concluded that Anna had made that decision not yesterday but much earlier when she refused to fly with me into space. So the break-up was inevitable, and it was good it had finally happened.

I walked into the cafeteria and ate a big breakfast with a large number of unfamiliar faction members. Everyone around clearly new me though and whispered amongst themselves quietly, picking at my faults and sharing all kinds of rumors. Finally, Dmitry Zheltov showed up along with Imran and Eduard Boyko.

"Well captain, is today our first flight?" Eduard asked, voicing what the others were probably thinking.

"If we finish the repair..." I answered evasively, afraid of overly optimistic prognoses, to which all three of my companions snickered:

"How are we supposed to go anywhere with you for a captain?! You didn't give us a minute of leave! And the Geckho repairmen aren't used to our rough language. They really kicked it into gear when you decided to 'practice your command voice' and translated all your expressions to their language. Only army sergeants or construction foremen are bold enough to talk like that!"

"I even wrote down a few choice phrases in my game notepad for later," Dmitry Zheltov said, clearly happy. "After I'll finish this two-year contract under the Dome and start building myself a dacha[3], I'll need them to yell at the builders. What did you say to that Geckho electrician again...? Ah! 'Hey big furry monster! If you forget the polarity one more time, you clumsy-handed abortion victim, I'll introduce a red-hot soldering iron

[3] Translator's note: a unique kind of summer cottage popular in Russia.

to your deep inner world.' Exactly what our Diplomat had in mind when he said to treat every Geckho with respect! The Geckho started respecting you so much that the foreman hooked up every device personally after that."

Only Imran wasn't enjoying it and, in fact remained sullen and serious:

"Gnat, are you sure you didn't take too big a risk? I mean, what if the suzerains get mad and zero out one of our nodes?"

I just gave a good-hearted laugh and hurried to reassure my Dagestani friend, because his anxiety was totally unfounded. There were no high-profile players among the Geckho repairmen. Also all of them were technically my underlings until the job was done. So it didn't smell of insubordination or insulting powerful our overlords.

After recalling the previous day a bit longer, I suggested that we go back to our pods and meet again in a few minutes in the virtual world. And in fact, despite their light teasing for my methods of communication, and fears about the potential insult, we got a lot of work done yesterday. I spent my last sixteen hours in game helping the Geckho technicians fix the starship. Together with the electricians, I changed out and hooked up broken instruments on the captain's bridge, then I looked carefully as they tested and calibrated it all. After that, Imran and I welded in a stairwell between the decks. Using a vibrant paint spray and my Scanning ability, I had examined the weld seams for microcracks. There was air leaking from the compartment that contained the frigate's front landing supports. I also accepted the climate unit the three repair drones had fixed. Then I changed out the lighting down the whole corridor of the second deck. I had even hauled out building waste like a common manual laborer.

At first, Uline grumbled that a high-profile player like me, and especially a captain was above getting their hands dirty, saying that was why there were underlings. She said it would surely make my Authority fall, and I would suffer because of it. But not paying any attention to the Trader's groaning, I not only worked without tirelessly, I got the other team members not to sit with their hands folded either. Even the noble Princess Minn-O had laid new floor in the hallways and painted the walls with a spray bottle. Even captain's assistant Uline wasn't able to weenie out of it for long.

It must be noted that the rest of the team and Geckho repairmen reacted totally normally to my methods, and my Authority in fact grew twice. My Scanning, Electronics, Eagle Eye and Machine Control skills were leveled well. At the same time, I increased Psionic and the mana-restoring Mysticism, because I was actively spending Magic Points, conversing mentally with the repair drones and driving on my lazy workers. In the end, just before leaving the game, Gnat reached level sixty-nine. And now, as I walked up the corncob and closed the lid of my virt pod, I was looking over my improved numbers with unhidden pride:

Gerd Gnat. Human. H3 Faction.	
Level-69 Listener	
Statistics:	
Strength	14
Agility	17
Intelligence	23 + 3
Perception	27 + 2
Constitution	16
Luck modifier	+3
Parameters:	
Hitpoints	1516 of 1516
Endurance points	1121 of 1121
Magic points	709 of 709
Carrying capacity	62 lbs.
Fame	59
Skills:	
Electronics	53
Scanning	31
Cartography	55
Astrolinguistics	82
Rifles	49
Mineralogy	49
Medium Armor	52
Eagle Eye	66
Sharpshooter	32

Targeting	20
Danger Sense	42
Psionic	62
Mental Fortitude	50
Mysticism	14
Machine Control	48
Attention!!! You have nine unspent skill points	

Yes, my "classic" combat skills had fallen a bit behind. Rifles, Sharpshooter, Targeting and even Danger Sense were behind Astrolinguistics, but my psychic abilities and Machine Control were growing by leaps and bounds. I could feel a stronger and stronger pull toward a half-mage half-technician, which is basically what the Listener was. That meant I was developing my character properly.

Nine unspent points... Where to put them? On the one hand, I could fill the hole in Scanning, still gaping after it was zeroed out. I still couldn't get used to the low detail on the results of my scanning and their low level of information. On the other hand, there was a way to quickly level Scanning. I just had to buy a hundred geological analyzers (and now I could easily afford such expenses) and search on asteroids or planetoids for minerals and whatnot. In a day or two, I could bring my Scanning skill up to one hundred easily, so why waste the points?

I thought and weighed all the plusses and minuses, then decided against it. I put seven right into Mysticism. I was very impressed by that skill, I was a big fan of having more Magic Points and the faster they came back the better. Even at a low level, Mysticism had a clear effect, and it would be even greater the more I leveled it!

Mysticism skill increased to level twenty-one!

My Magic Points increased instantly from 709 to 759. Not bad, not bad at all! That meant an additional few seconds of mental control over an enemy and the ability to not worry so much that I would run out of mana in my direst moments.

I put the remaining two points into Machine Control. I had only just come to appreciate all the benefits of this new ability, and they were impressive. It could open doors without Break-in or put enemy robots out of commission with a mental command, controlling all kinds of drones and bots, and even... here I took a heavy sigh and crossed my fingers... the ability to control a starship directly with my mind without any Pilots or Navigators!

Yes! Apparently I could mentally command any ship system from thrusters to cannons and control them without the skills necessary to pilot a starship or shoot a heavy turret. I suspected that the quality of this piloting or shooting would be horribly low, an order of magnitude below what a professional was capable of, but it meant I could substitute for a missing player in a critical situation, so why not?!

THE FIRST PERSON I met after entering the game was Avan Toi. The corpulent Supercargo was using a special scanner to read tags on a huge pile of containers, taking that down in a palmtop and marking the boxes for Basha and Vasha. That told them what to bring into the cargo hold, what into the galley and what into the other sectors of the ship. When I showed up, Avan Toi clearly lit up and hurried out to meet me:

"Captain, the goods Uline ordered have arrived, along with the spare parts and equipment. I'll check the list now while it's all here. As you asked, provisions were purchased with an eye to the different races on board. That's the good news. The bad news is that we're having a hell of a time filling the other vacancies. Not a single Geckho has enquired about our openings for Medic, Engineer, or Gunner the whole time. And though it is okay to fly without a Gunner or a Medic, there's no getting by on a ship like this without an Engineer…"

Ayukh then walked up to greet the captain. After hearing the Supercargo's words about difficulties finding crew, the old Navigator said his point of view:

"There is a military base here on the Un-Tesh

comet, so I suppose this is a very bad place to find crew. The ones who survived the battle with the Meleyephatians are now in the Ursa system. The ones who died and respawned, as a rule have been assembled into flight crews and do not want to change that. They're just waiting for a ship. What's more, the mentality of most crew here is different. They're courageous obedient warriors, accustomed to doing everything by command and have no idea what it's like to be a free-thinking fortune-seeker."

If the experienced Navigator was right, searching for new crew here on the military base was an exercise in futility. Most of the soldiers probably felt disgust just thinking about leaving this warm place where everything necessary was provided and joining a crew of adventurers to head out who knows where without firm confidence in the future. But still I asked for the advertisement not to be deleted. I mean what if someone came anyway? Beyond that, I was holding another reason in mind. It was fully possible that the Morphian from before was still here on the Un-Tesh comet, so I wanted to leave it a convenient chance to rejoin me on my new ship.

Of course, where else would the Morphian be than on a Geckho military base where it was so easy to get lost among thousands of players? Fox had run and hid at some point during my talk with the fleet commander. I checked that by scanning. And not just once. That meant she had been on the base for some time, but where had she gone next? Was Fox really going out into battle on one of the Third Strike Fleet's starships? What could that possibly hold for her? She had told me that this was "not her war," after all. But as far as I knew there were practically no flights anywhere. Before the battle, the Geckho were trying to maintain the secrecy of the operation as much as possible, and after that all flights were suspended.

I cast off the thoughts about Fox, activated the captain's tablet and shook my head in satisfaction. Most of the systems were now marked in green, which meant they were working just fine. Yes, there were lots of gray inactive ones, but my ship now had a main thruster and maneuver drives, lidar and gravidar. Plus, the repairers were now finishing installing additional shield generators. The frigate didn't have any weaponry other than jamming equipment, or atmospheric stabilizers. Really it was missing lots of necessary equipment. In fact, the ship was really just boilerplate now. Sure it could be more or less steered through space, but even that was a great accomplishment given where we'd started.

Uline Tar walked up looking so serious and important I was afraid. I first noticed she had a bright new emblem on her matte metal armor suit — a spiral Galaxy with three comets below. A popup told me that this chevron meant: Captain's First Assistant. Clearly my furry friend was very proud of her new status and was trying in every way to emphasize that.

"Gnat, without a decent Engineer, I can't say for sure what modules can be combined together, and whether our power unit is strong enough to activate them. But still I dug up all possible modules for Tolili-Ukh X model frigates. As expected, most of the offers are inside Meleyephatian Horde space. I even found a ship registered in exactly the same configuration as ours is now. We can buy a kit to assemble a modular frigate for just seven and a half million."

"But can we enter the Horde's space? We won't be stopped?" I asked in surprise. Uline hurried to reassure me:

"Why not? You're a Free Captain now and you don't belong to any of the warring nations. We won't be allowed to any secret Meleyephatian sites of course, but there are no other limitations. We can go through customs and fly wherever we want!"

It was great, of course, that the prices for starship modules in Meleyephatian space were not high, but what could we do there without money? First of all, I'd have to get my reward for the trophy tail, and Meleyephatian stations were not exactly the place for that. And again we'd have the problem of how to convert crypto and crystals into... what currency do the Meleyephatians use?

"Me'eli or melki as they're known. They are only in electronic form, and Miyelonian wallets can be used to store and send them. But you're right, captain, there could be serious problems with trying to exchange such a large sum right up to confiscation of your ship..."

Uh, no. I didn't want that kind of entertainment! I was in no mood to risk my starship so stupidly and I asked Uline for other options. The Trader hesitated:

"Well... there is one Miyelonian station where you can get trophy ships and components for cheap. But I'm afraid you aren't going to like it."

"Is it the pirate station Medu-Ro IV or something?" I immediately guessed, and Uline grunted back not anxious, but delighted with my ability to think on my feet. "And why won't I like that? I think it's a very interesting option! Yes, the customs on that station are... unique, to put it lightly, and take some getting used to. But if we behave ourselves, no one will touch us, and the prices there really are attractive. What's more, I actually need to make a courtesy call to a counterfeiter who bit off more than he could chew. Also there is a Translator on the station who I'm sure would love to join our team. And a Trillian Merchant who promised me he'd hold onto a nice ring for me. Overall, let's go... What's wrong, Minn-O?"

My wayedda had no face on. I had never seen the Princess in such a defeated state. Had my threats not worked, and the ghastly old man raised a hand to his granddaughter? I asked her that. Minn-O raised her teary eyes to me and said:

"My husband, the Coruler of Humanity High Mage Thumor-Anhu La-Fin passed away yesterday at the age of one hundred and eighty. A three-day mourning period has been declared on the whole planet. The great mage's burial will be tomorrow at the ancient cemetery of House La-Fin."

Chapter
Twenty

Takeoff!!!

I HAD NO LOST LOVE for Leng Thumor-Anhu La-Fin. The vastly powerful mage was an enemy of my faction and me personally, and he never hid that. If the ghastly old man could have, he would have obliterated not only me but my entire world without the slightest hesitation or compassion. But now, squeezing Minn-O as she sobbed bitterly, I couldn't shake the feeling of heavy personal loss, and I especially was not thinking of gloating at the Dark Faction leader's death. After sending Eduard Boyko under the Dome to tell our allies what happened, I asked the Princess for more details.

"The servants say that grandpa fell ill after speaking to me. He went black in the face, his arms started quaking, and he couldn't even hold the video phone. Thumor-Anhu took his usual magical elixirs to restore his strength and stumbled into his personal chambers. He was discovered there two hours later when one of his servants risked entering the fearsome mage's bedchamber to check up on him. The coruler was lying on the floor next to his bed mumbling incoherently with bulging eyes. That kicked off a big hullabaloo. Grandpa was put in bed, and they looked for his mage doctor for a long time, but he was nowhere to be found. Everyone was at a loss and didn't know what to do. First Councilor Avir-Sin La-Pirez and other relatives were all called in. And by then, rumors about what happened to the Coruler had already reached the other influential magical families, and the palace of the La-Fins became packed with mages and people from ruling families. They brought in a council of the best doctors and healing mages, but they couldn't do anything because Thumor-Anhu was already dead."

Minn-O La-Fin started sobbing again. I then asked a seemingly obvious question:

"And why wasn't the great mage brought into his virt pod to have the game heal him?"

My wayedda raised her teary eyes and shouted with unhidden bitterness:

"Well Gnat, it was because it was calculated murder! Coruler Thumor-Anhu made many enemies in his long life and crossed many people. So all these healers were just pretending to help, and in fact were drawing out time to so my grandfather would die!"

I had to reassure Minn-O again. The rest of the

team, seeing this was not a good time, didn't bother us and dispersed, getting to their own business. Finally, I asked the Princess who would be the new head of the La-Fin family.

"You, of course," my wayedda replied, surprised I was even asking.

"Me???" the news was so shocking I couldn't hold back and started screaming.

The Princess got herself together and began explaining lucidly:

"If I had magical abilities, or if we had a child, maybe there would be other options. But you're the only mage in house La-Fin, so there's no other way. You're the new head of my ancient ruling family!"

This was, to put it lightly, unexpected news. I was the new head of one of the most ancient ruling houses of the magical world?! This had to be some kind of joke. And it wasn't very funny. I mean, what kind of a ruler would I make?! I didn't even exist in that world! By the way... I cautiously asked my wayedda whether I had to personally be present at all the ceremonies.

Minn-O looked at me like I was a stupid little baby:

"Gnat, what are you talking about?! You'd be killed the second you showed your face in my world! You're a claimant to the throne of one of the Corulers of humanity and the heir to a huge fortune. No one there wants you alive except me! The La-Fin family is very rich, and many mages have long desired my family's wealth. But they wouldn't dare bare their teeth at Thumor-Anhu while he was still alive. However, before the great mage's body was even cold, all these vultures had already started demanding a piece of the pie! My house controls huge territories, billions of subjects, corporations and banks... and now there is no one to defend our holdings. I see a huge redistribution of wealth on the horizon. All more or less influential families will want the fattest slice they can get, and there will be such bloody battles that the world will shake! This has happened before, two hundred years ago when the Az-Dur Coruler dynasty collapsed. Those times are now called the 'seven years of madness.' That's how horrible it was. So you mustn't come into my world. In fact, you should get me out of mine as quickly as possible if you value your wayedda's life even one bit!"

Saving my traveling wife's life was a mission of unquestionable importance. But it was not my style to give up without a fight and let someone else take my property by threatening and outright blackmail. Any time punks from higher grades would tell me to turn out my pockets in school, I would kick them in the groin or knuckle-punch them in the bridge of the nose. And it didn't matter if that got me in deeper trouble and beaten harder. All the bad kids at my school learned that painful lesson. I even gained a reputation as a "psycho who's not to be messed with."

And now I could not bring myself to give up my

inheritance to some fly-in vultures. No, it rightfully belonged to me and my wife. What was more, I was now a senior mage and head of house La-Fin, so it was my sacred duty to fight to protect my family riches! And despite all that, I remained realistic and shared Minn-O's fears about the danger of going to her magical world. I would just cause too many problems there and would be immediately killed.

You might wonder how I could fight for my property from a parallel world. On first glance, it seemed impossible. But I didn't see any contradictions. Princess Minn-O told me all the more-or-less significant figures of her world were already in the game that bends reality. And that meant I could easily make contact with them. And holding so many cards, I was sure I could come to an agreement with these important personages. My acquaintance with the master of Earth Kung Waid Shishish was one such card. It forced any opponent to reckon with Gnat. The zero-ed out Graveyard node was a good example of what I could do.

Another even better card was my frigate, which could bomb mercilessly from orbit and wipe any node off the face of the planet. Yes, now my ship was nowhere near in intact, and didn't even have any weaponry. But the Dark Faction didn't know that, so they would take my threats of orbital bombardment with all due seriousness. Anyway, I believed it was possible to come to a peaceful agreement.

"Minn-O, find me the game names of the vultures who are trying to lay claim to our property!"

I tried very hard to make my voice sound confident. It was funny to watch Minn-O, slain by sorrow, suddenly stop bawling with her head buried in my shoulder, and raise her teary face in surprise, then stand up to half a head taller than me.

"W-why do you want that, Gnat? You don't mean to say you're planning to go against the strongest mages of my world, right? With all due respect husband, they'll turn you to dust!"

"In your world, perhaps they are strong. But here in the game they're just mages with strong and weak sides. I need their names and, if you can, figure out the coordinates of the game hexagons they might be found in. No," I jumped out ahead of a possible objection, "this will not be espionage on your part. I simply want to have a serious discussion about the future of our family. Don't you want our children to be safe?"

Such a direct way of posing the question instantly knocked out the support for any potential objections, and the Princess nodded back very quickly.

"Now that's great! So, let's get to the ship. The technicians said the repair is finally over. There's no reason to stick around here anymore, let's take off as soon as possible!"

Psionic skill increased to level sixty-three!

My mana, by the way, had drooped to practically

nil during my talk with my wayedda. I continued smiling tranquilly, kissed Minn-O on the cheek and pointed at the gangway. And only after the princess had left and hidden from view, I wiped the abundant sweat off my temples and forehead. That conversation was unbelievably hard... It was not merely speaking with a pretty girl. It felt like my chest was being crushed by invisible restraints and I had to break taught ropes and disarm a trap. And it looked very much like I had demolished all the blocks and limitations in the Princess's mind, though. Clearly, her grandpa had put them there to control his beloved granddaughter, hoping to steer Minn-O's thoughts.

But even these difficulties were not all that had me worried. It was very hard to explain it in words, but every minute I felt more and more urgently that we had to get off this comet right away. I couldn't find any logical explanation for the strange desire, but it was getting harder and harder to ignore the growing itch. It was probably not just an urge to quickly reenter the vortex of new adventures, but a warning of some still unclear danger. And it threatened not only me but my ship if we went too slow. But my Danger Sense skill was silent, so I was confused and not sure how to reconcile my contradictory feelings.

The last of the Geckho technicians finally left the tin-can frigate, and I got a confirmation from the Starship Pilot that we were ready for takeoff. The Senior Mechanic also confirmed and, a bit later, the Navigator.

We were just waiting for Eduard Boyko to come back from the real world, and the last boxes of equipment and spare parts to be loaded on.

I was watching the frigate systems check as the Supercargo and assistants hurriedly threw the last containers into the cargo hold. Then Dmitry Zheltov's voice rang out in my earphones, sounding upset:

"Captain, there's a significant desynchronization in the maneuver drives. It isn't critical, but I'll have to get used to it and learn to compensate. I suggest after takeoff we go through the tail of the comet so I can practice dodging the ice chunks and set up all the thrusters, shields and lidars."

"I agree, but let's not go far," I immediately warned. "That way, if any problems are more serious, we can come right back to base... Hey Kirsan, where are you going? Get back to the ship right now, we're taking off!"

The repair bot had left the starship for some reason and was loitering around the still unloaded boxes, either searching for a part or wanting to help load. The metal millipede stopped at my exclamation and, drumming its endless little feet, glided nimbly in my direction. Raising the front half of its body and stopping in front of me like a cobra opening its hood, it clearly wanted something. What though? Maybe it had all the parts together and wanted my Annihilator for repair?

I extended the ancient weapon to the bot, but Kirsan didn't take it. It stood next to me for another thirty seconds with its body raised, attracting attention and trying desperately to tell me something by gesturing and blinking its mechanical eyes. But then it seemingly lost faith in my imagination and crawled toward the ship.

Naturally, the repair bot's behavior seemed strange. I even checked the millipede and other bots with my Scanning ability just in case. Was this Fox telling me it had come? But no, my mini-map was showing normal mechanoid repair bots. The other crew members were also just who they appeared to be. Eduard Boyko returned to the game and distracted me, so I threw all this unimportant information out of my head.

I walked into the frigate last of all, stopping on the gangway and casting a long attentive gaze over the repair hangar. I ran a test scan, comparing the number in my crew with my list and gave a heavy sigh. Everyone was there, no extras. Despite all the opportunities I'd given it, the Morphian had decided not to rejoin us...

E HAD ALREADY been spinning around for twenty minutes in the cloudy tail of ice and ammonia crystals that extended far beyond the comet's core, but the Starship Pilot just could not set the thrusters right. In the words of Dmitry Zheltov, two maneuver thrusters were on the fritz, giving an unpredictable delay of between three and twelve seconds. And the main thruster was also giving just seventy-three percent of its predicted power and periodically turned off as well. The pilot was nervous, mad and threatening to rip the hands off the cheap Geckho commissary officers who had stuck us with this poorly refurbished crap.

I sent the repair bots out to fix the problems and help the pilot, but I also needed their help. The gravity locators were going haywire, periodically showing some massive dangerous objects nearby. The radar was also spitting out nonsense, sometimes showing things that weren't there, and other times showing nothing. The lidars hadn't detected any danger, and the external cameras weren't showing anything larger than a fine icy haze. The malfunctioning of the ship locators was a serious reason to return to base, because flying in the endless cosmos with such problems was too great a risk.

I was already morally prepared to give the order to return and fix the malfunction in a calmer setting, when suddenly... the picture on the outside cameras sharply changed. Just two hundred miles from our frigate, hundreds if not thousands of starships appeared! By then, we had managed to get more than five thousand miles away from the comet's core, so the ships that appeared could not be guarding the Geckho military base. What was more, the tactical map was showing that these were primarily Tolili-Ukh X frigates, big clusters of them. There were also plenty of heavy cruisers, though. With every second, more and more new ship markers appeared and each and every one was of Meleyephatian assembly. I had barely realized that when a siren kicked on, announcing a combat alert. Strange of course, that we hadn't seen all these ships earlier, but it looked very much like we had come face to face with the Meleyephatian fleet as it prepared to attack!

Danger Sense skill increased to level forty-three!
Eagle Eye skill increased to level sixty-seven!

I felt a shooting pain in my chest. Before the message came in that my Danger Sense had improved, I already knew that we'd landed in VERY deep trouble. The two hundred miles between us and the enemy was nothing at all in space. At this distance, the Meleyephatians would not miss. Actually, it was strange that they hadn't fired yet...

"Dmitry, fall back!" I shouted, stopping the pilot as he started taking our frigate away from the mass of ships. "No dodging maneuvers. Don't provoke them! Fly calmly and smoothly. Navigator calculate a jump to the Medu-Ro IV station at once! Tell me when the frigate is ready for a hyperspace jump. And Ayukh, prepare a message for the defenders of the military base. We must warn the Geckho!"

Authority increased to 43!

"Yes sir, captain! But that will be all we have time to do," the old Ayukh grumbled, nevertheless completing my command. "The transmission will be immediately intercepted and we will be destroyed. It looks like they haven't made up their minds about us yet. After all, we do have a Meleyephatian ship!"

I was also counting on that when I ordered the pilot not to make any sharp movements in this tense situation, so we wouldn't be revealed. If I were in command of the Meleyephatian fleet, I would have been in no rush to destroy one of my own ships, which seemingly had emerged from hyperjump a bit away from the rest. I would first have tried to figure things out. And as for sending a message to the defenders by other means... there was another way!

"Avan Toi, Basha, Vasha! All of you immediately leave to the real world. I don't know how but I need you to send an urgent message to your race's military: in the game that bends reality, the Geckho base on the Un-Tesh comet will soon be attacked by a Meleyephatian fleet! The enemy already has around two thousand ships in the tail of the comet! Have that relayed to the comet defenders and Kung Waid Shishish! Tini, you exit and give a similar message to Leng Amiru. The Miyelonians are allied to the Geckho in this war, and they just might make it in time to help!"

Authority increased to 44!

Uline Tar ran onto the bridge in a state of alarm and suited up in her combat armor. There really was no reason for the Trader to be there at such a critical moment, and I was going to send her away but I didn't have time. The communication screen flickered on and a message came in from one of the cruisers. It was just crackling, squawking, screeching and rustling. I didn't understand a damn thing, and neither did anyone else. All that was clear was that the Meleyephatians were demanding something. But what was it? I'd like to at least have a vague idea... I turned to the Trader:

"Uline, do you remember when I asked you how Uraz Tukhsh spoke with the Miyelonians on the pirate station Medu-Ro without knowing a word of Miyelonian? You mentioned some kind of device..."

"Yes, Gnat. An automatic translator has long existed for all the main languages of the galaxy." Uline dug in her sack and took a dark plastic disk the size of a saucer from her inventory. "This is a base model. It's a useful and necessary item when there's just no other way. But high-quality translators, as with weapons or other equipment, require high stats to use. Above all they need Intelligence and Perception, but also decent Electronics, Astrolinguistics and a bunch of other stuff. But for such a basic one as this, the quality of the machine translation is dog shit. It only translates individual words, but the emotional and sense weight in Geckho depends on combinations of words, length of pauses, volume and other minor things. So often the machine translation warps the meaning of a phrase so much it means the opposite!"

I stopped Uline from digging further into the explanation. This was not the time. I asked her to prepare the translator, then replayed the message. A mechanical voice in Geckho translated all the creaking and squawking thusly:

Free Captain. Identify. Forbidden. Screen of distortion. Center.

At first glance, it was a totally senseless collection of words. But ordering the rest of the crew members on the bridge to be silent, I tried to decrypt the missive:

"Seemingly, we have been taken for a Meleyephatian Free Captain's ship. Clearly, they think we're going to take part in the attack on the Geckho base. Now they're demanding that we identify ourselves. I didn't understand after that... some kind of screen of distortion and center... totally unclear."

"Well Gerd Gnat, they might be talking about the distortion generator," Ayukh said, marking one of the ships in the enemy armada on the tactical screen. "This ship is creating a distortion screen, which warps the light rays of the visible spectrum and dampens many other kinds of waves. In fact, it has created a screen of invisibility, which is where the Meleyephatian fleet is hiding."

A distortion screen! And it was clearly of colossal dimension, given that a whole fleet was able to hide behind it! So that is why I couldn't see all the ships even though my instruments were showing a large number of massive objects nearby and some kind of distorted signals from them! So... it seems I guessed what the remaining words meant:

"Most likely, they were asking us to come closer to the center of the distortion area, so our frigate won't unmask the remaining fleet! Dmitry start gradually moving the frigate toward that point," I placed a marker for the Starship Pilot at the end of a direct line through the nucleus of the comet and the distortion generator ship, but thirty miles behind it. "And go calmly, with no sharp bursts. Ideally head toward the Medu-Ro system when you do, so we can jump out right after all the calculations are complete. Ayukh, give the pilot our vector."

Cartography skill increased to level fifty-five!

Astrolinguistics skill increased to level eighty-three!

You have reached level seventy!

You have received three skill points!

Our frigate took a wide curve and began approaching the enemy. I wondered how the Meleyephatians would react. My heart was pounding in my chest, the last seconds stretched on for a long time. In the strained silence, Dmitry Zheltov's voice sounded very sharp like a pistol shot:

"Strange that this fleet doesn't have any landing ships," said, the Starship Pilot, drawing our attention to that bizarre fact. "How are they going to capture the Geckho base on the comet?"

"Well, they aren't planning to capture it," our omniscient and experienced Navigator answered. "It is not in the Meleyephatian tradition, and they have no use for one more base in this sector of the galaxy. They will simply blow up the comet together with the base. See that huge destroyer that just showed up on the screen? Those titans with their massive firepower are used to get through forcefields and destroy space stations, planetoids, comets and other celestial bodies."

My chest grew cold. The Meleyephatians were going to destroy the Un-Tesh comet together with the military base! But my respawn point was there!!! If our ship was shot down now, and the comet was destroyed, my character would appear in the vacuum of space, hopefully wearing a sealed spacesuit. Although... perhaps that would be worse because then I'd have to die a long and tortured death after four and a half hours suffocating. And every subsequent death would be instantaneous...

Damn... The situation was coming together not only worryingly, but critically dangerously in a way that cannot be overstated. It threatened me and my friends with a final death both in the virtual game and the real world! A player could not survive the irreversible final death of their game avatar, a fact I had heard many times. After a character's stats all reached zero, which affected the body in the real world, the owner would be as good as dead. Yikes, I really did not want to experience that...

"So Ayukh, what's there? Are we gonna be ready for a hyperjump soon?" I hurried the old Navigator, who was frantically calculating and very quickly moving the star map around on his screen.

"I'm done drafting the message for our military. It can be sent at any time. But the jump parameters are still being calculated. This computer is too weak. It takes a long time to run a calculation... Uline, give the bot what it wants!"

I then also noticed that Kirsan was acting weird. The metal millipede had its claws latched into the automatic translator disk and was clearly trying to take it from the Trader. Uline was resisting desperately, cursing and even kicking the repair bot, but after Ayukh's admonishment, she unclenched her fingers. I didn't hear the millipede say anything, but a message was clearly transmitted somehow, because a metallic voice distinctly said:

"No hyperjump. Bomb on thruster. Three."

"What?! The ship is rigged to blow? Show me right now!" I leapt out of my seat with all possible agility and dashed after the bot who, as it turned out, could move pretty fast when it wanted to.

Machine Control skill increased to level fifty-one!
Psionic skill increased to level sixty-four!

Only after the fact did I notice that I had given the command without any captain's tablets or opening the game menu, just with my voice, doubling the message mentally. But the repair bot understood me perfectly! And I also understood what exactly Kirsan wanted to tell me on the station, and why he wanted to attract my attention.

Following the swift-footed millipede, I went down to the lower deck and ran through the mechanical area. Then throwing back a grate, I squeezed into a utility closet that was quite narrow even for a human, which was to say nothing about a Geckho. Apparently, it served to provide access to the hyperspace drive. But while we were parked on Un-Tesh, the Geckho technicians hadn't ever made it back here, because the engine was already installed, and the huge furballs were simply too large.

Nevertheless, someone had clearly made it in: all three of the corrugated metal cable sleeves leading from the power unit to the hyperdrive were rigged with identical flat round bombs that looked a lot like hockey pucks. They probably weren't too powerful, but they only needed to upset the synchronization of our finicky thruster systems, and the starship would be blasted to atoms by a colossal burst of energy.

Magnetic bomb *(armed!!!)*
Attention! Disarming this bomb requires the

skills: Electronics level-55, Explosives level-55, or Break-in level-55. Character class must be either: Sapper, Geologist or Thief.

Statistic requirements: Agility 15, Intelligence 12.

Attention! Your Electronics skill is too low.

Attention! Your character lacks the Break-in and Explosives skills.

I needed just a tiny bit more Electronics, a mere two points. And I could easily have solved that problem by investing what I had. But that wouldn't help, because Gnat didn't belong to any of the required classes. A Thief could remove these mines, and my ward's main Break-in skill was up to 63. I knew he had Electronics somewhere around 55, too. But I sent Tini into the real world and I had no idea when my kitten would be back.

The Navigator's voice rang out in my headphones.

"Captain, calculation of hyperspace jump parameters complete, the frigate is currently on the correct vector. We can jump at any moment..."

"Stop!!!" I cried in a voice not my own. "Don't activate the hyperdrive!!! There are three bombs on the power cable. If you activate the hyper, we'll be blown to smithereens! I'm trying to figure something out."

"Well hurry up, Gnat," Uline threw out. "The Meleyephatian ship has asked us to identify ourselves again. We have aroused their suspicion somehow."

I already knew that time was pressing, and we

needed to do something urgently. Maybe I could deactivate the bombs with a powerful electromagnetic pulse? After all, they were not simply shells filled with explosive material, but fairly complicated devices that monitored power flow and would detonate only when the hyperdrive was turned on. Hey, speaking of complex electromechanical devices... I activated the scanning icon. There they were! Each of the three had an identical label on my map:

Magnetic bomb. Disarm chance: 72%. Total control chance: 32%.

A seventy-two percent chance of turning each of them off... Hmm... On the one hand, that didn't sound so bad. But on the other, I would have to repeat that trick three times and then the situation won't look quite so puppies and rainbows. What was the chance of not blowing up three times? I remembered a statistics course I'd taken, calculated that and immediately grew sad. Just thirty-seven percent... not great, to put it lightly...

Although, I might increase the chance of escaping by placing my unused points into Machine Control. I did just that, spending all three and bringing it to fifty-four. The chance of disarming each bomb grew from 72% to 77%, which was of course not bad. But the chance of successfully disarming all three was still less than half. Forty-five percent to be exact. So, should I risk it, or wait for Tini?

"Gnat, the Meleyephatians are messaging us

again!" there were now clear notes of panic in Uline Tar's voice. "They're threatening to shoot us down if we do not identify ourselves at once!"

"Friends, prepare for a jump, I'm just about done…" I said confidently into the microphone.

I then wiped the abundantly pouring sweat off my forehead and looked at the repair drone, carefully observing my torment with its dozen mechanical eyes.

"If I survive, I'm drinking myself silly at the first space station we reach!" I promised the bot and chose the menu item "Disarm bomb."

Something inside the puck gave an abrupt click, which made me instinctively cover my head with my hands, although knew it was no use. But there was no explosion. Externally, the bomb did not change, though some important changes took place in the dangerous device's description:

Magnetic bomb *(disarmed)*

Got it! And in the same exact way, before I lost my nerve, I turned off another bomb. And I stopped next to the third. My hands were shaking and I couldn't concentrate one iota.

"Gnat!!!" it was now Dmitry Zheltov. "Two Meleyephatian interceptors are headed toward our frigate! Best of luck down there, but I'm taking off in ten seconds!!!"

We couldn't wait any longer and chose "disarm bomb."

Machine Control skill increased to level fifty-five!

Psionic skill increased to level sixty-five!
You have reached level seventy-one!
You have received three skill points!

"Ayukh, send the message!!! Dmitry blast off!!!" I shouted into the microphone, and the slight burst and even hum of the hyperdrives a second later told me we had escaped.

Completely powerless, I crawled on the metal floor and pulled the long metal millipede toward me like a house pet, slapping it on the back in approval:

"For that, I'm gonna color you white, Kirsan, so I always remember what you did for me! I don't know if you understand me or not, but I am eternally grateful to you!"

The captain's tablet vibrated, I extended a hand and turned on the screen:

Captain, the Senior Mechanic has sent a list of necessary materials for purchase:

- *1 can of AAB-2 white enamel paint*
- *1 paint sprayer*

Chapter Twenty-One

Alien Guest

AFTER WAITING for every crew member who had gone into the real world to return, I called an emergency meeting. I held it in Geckho, which every member of my team spoke on some level. For half the crew, it was native. Gnat and Dmitry Zheltov spoke fluently, and the rest understood reasonably well. The worst speakers of the furball language were Space Commando Eduard and Gladiator Imran, but the others translated the difficult parts. There was no furniture on the starship yet, so I ordered still untouched carpeting rolls thrown around the most spacious area to use as seating. With time, this was going to become the break room. I made everyone attend, even Zheltov because the ship was on autopilot so he was free for the next two ummi.

There were two main topics to discuss: the bombs and the Meleyephatian attack on the Geckho military base. And although I personally was much more worried by the first, I understood that the Geckho were puffing with patriotism and made up half of my crew. To them, the situation on the front of the ongoing space war was of higher priority, so I began with that.

"Captain, I sent your message to a very old friend who serves on the comet immediately after I left the game," Supercargo Avan Toi reported. "I admit, he didn't believe me at first. He thought it was some kind of prank. He called me a clown... But, when he realized the gravity of the situation he promised to immediately get in touch with leadership and signed off. And when I reentered the game, I was awaited by a rise in Fame. Clearly everything is in order and the message got where it needed to go!"

Yes, that seemed to be the case. I got a boost in fame as well. Two even. Clearly the name Gerd Gnat was flittering about in urgent messages between powerful leaders, and I had become a better-known figure. I agreed with the conclusion of the corpulent Supercargo. The Geckho command had clearly been informed of the danger, so I thanked his underling for the job well done.

Basha and Vasha also reported that they'd sent their messages. Neither of the twin brothers had any personal connections with notable military figures of the Third Strike Fleet. For that reason, they sent theirs to the fleet's press service, on an urgent message line and another few to public addresses vaguely linked with the Third Strike Fleet. Basha Tushihh had also gotten in touch with our former captain Uraz Tukhsh in the hopes that Kung Waid Shishish's close relative would tell the commander about the impending danger.

"But instead I came up against a strange anger and hatred from our former employer. It was motivated by nothing and bordered on pure hysteria!" Basha Tushihh was clearly upset and confused. "I had to hear a whole stream of flagrant lies and threats! Gerd Uraz Tukhsh accused me and all of us together, but above all Gerd Gnat of betraying and deserting him. Allegedly, we abandoned him at the most difficult moment, running from his team and taking a trophy ship for ourselves which should have been his to compensate the loss of the Shiamiru! He refused to do anything for me, especially send a message to Kung Waid Shishish, who our former captain is even madder at."

Everyone went silent, clearly shocked. The silence was broken by Uline:

"As deplorable as it may be, we must conclude that we now have a personal enemy."

"You know, we already had a clue," the Supercargo spitefully snorted, pointing a furry hand at the three disarmed bombs, which I had set out for all to see.

In response, Uline grumbled threateningly and

bared her teeth:

"I don't believe it! Yes, my former groom is somewhat cowardly and not always a good guy, but he always acted honorably! Gerd Uraz Tukhsh could not have planned a calculated murder, and he also didn't have the ability to mine our ship in the Ursa system or on the military base! He just wasn't there!"

The Supercargo laughed in offense and assured us that such a glorified war hero with the purple ribbon of honor had no need to do such things personally. He could probably have found someone willing to carry out all the dangerous work for a minor reward, or maybe even for free in expectation of gratitude.

Uline started grumbling again, this time much louder and more frighteningly. I was even afraid that the Geckho lady might throw herself on her opponent. But the conflict of two team members did not continue, so I didn't have to split them up or psychically chill them out.

The last to speak was Tini. The kitten said that he got directly in touch with the Great Priestess of his race with no troubles or extreme bureaucracy, and one of the four incarnations of the Great First Female eagerly heard out the alarmed teen. After that, Leng Amiru U-Mayaoo admitted that she had no connection with the military, because her work was purely of a peaceful nature. But she promised to send the important message to her friend Leng Keessi-Miau without delay. She was commanding one of the Union of Miyelonian Prides' fleets.

"But as for our next stop on the Medu-Ro IV station, Leng Amiru U-Mayaoo was not exactly happy. In her words, that station was only technically Miyelonian property, and the Free Captains were in charge there, so the exchange... you know what, master... there might be problems with the crypto. And also, it's impossible to guarantee the safety of your ship or cargo if we go there. But after enough consideration, the Great Priestess advised us to get in touch with the head of the Pride of the Star Strangler, or the leader of the Pride of the Agile Paw and settle the delicate issue through them."

I didn't tell my ward how upset I was about revealing our frigate's route to an outsider because I understood that punishment would lack all sense. First of all, keeping a secret when talking with a highly experienced Truth Seeker was utterly impossible. Second, to any Miyelonian the Great Priestess was an incarnation of absolute good, the keeper of the history and traditions of their race, and even identified with the mother figure. So they simply could not think of her as a stranger.

I was not familiar with the head of the Pride of the Star Strangler. Tini had also heard very little about them, and most of it was bad. That meant that I had to go to the head of the Pride of the Agile Paw, the friendly casino owner, who had once offered me a job.

Then our conversation was interrupted by the

repair bot. This was probably the same one I had promised to paint white, though I was not certain. All three millipedes were totally identical, both in terms of appearance and on the mini-map.

"Kirsan, what do you need?" I asked, because the repair bot did not just crawl past, but raised the front part of its body and started drumming a semaphore with its jointed feet. It was clearly trying to attract our attention. "I do not understand. Uline, just give him your translator, let him explain."

Ancient enemy. Danger. Yes. No. Maybe. See captain.

Ancient enemy? Who the heck could that be? My Danger Sense was silent, so there was seemingly no direct threat, and Kirsan just wanted to tell me something.

"Take me, show me!" I ordered, getting up from the carpet roll.

This time, everyone ran after Kirsan even though, "see captain" probably meant this pertained to Gnat alone. "Ugh, I guess Kirsan isn't totally intelligent," I thought with pity when the millipede, simply choosing the shortest possible route, ducked into the still empty elevator shaft and gracefully ran up the vertical wall to the upper deck. We had to run to the opposite end of the hallway and use the recently installed spiral staircase. We met back up on the upper deck, and the millipede led us to the captain's bridge.

"Aw, [beep] your mother..." Dmitry Zheltov

couldn't hold back the surprised exclamation. That earned him a weak, but significant crack from our Dagestani guardian of morality. However, the pilot was not mad. He might even have not noticed, too distracted by the image from the external cameras. "How did it find us? We changed ship, and this is pretty far from the Ursa system. Or is that a different one?"

And in fact, spinning endless loops around our frigate, a speedy disk-shaped object was flittering about, which I immediately recognized as a symbiote. Last time, such a satellite was a great help to the Shiamiru, having cleared a path for our shuttle in a debris field. But what did it want from us now?

"I guess Uraz Tukhsh was wrong," old Ayukh mumbled happily. "The symbiote was not prophesying luck for him, but one of us."

"And I know exactly who," Uline answered without missing a beat, staring significantly at me.

Authority increased to 45!

Ignoring my business partner's hints, I turned to the repair bot, extending him the automatic translator:

"Kirsan, do you know what this is?" I pointed at the oval dancing about on the monitor.

Ancient enemy. Mechanoids war. Automatic Precursor defense system. Monitor space. Monitor hyperspace. Search. Intercept. Destroy.

For the usually taciturn Kirsan, this was a more than detailed answer, and we all understood it. By the way, I had heard about these "automatic Precursor systems" before. My Small Relict Guard Drone had given a high probability that it would be intercepted in space and stopped by one. Seemingly, these Precursors were their neighbors in the galaxy, given the Mechanoids and Relicts considered them enemies. So were the Relicts and Mechanoids perhaps allies in that long-ago war? Maybe Kirsan had seen me wearing the Relict Listener suit, which is why he was so open with me?

"And what that satellite doing? Why so close of us? He is basically crawl along our fuselage!" Minn-O asked in Geckho, demonstrating an imperfect but impressive mastery of the language.

I didn't think there would be an answer to that question, which made the Navigator's words sound all the more surprising:

"The Symbiote is repairing our hull. Meleyephatians use materials with shape memory to build starship hulls. In certain conditions, for example when they get hot enough, or are hit with ultrasonic or neutron radiation, damaged pieces revert to their initial shape. Even holes heal over without a trace."

"Yes, I've also heard that," the Trader confirmed. "But as far as I know, it is a very energy-intensive process. The Symbiote needs a bottomless pit of energy! Where can it get that?"

Just then my captain's tablet vibrated, and I read an incoming message:

Captain, you have received a power unit interface request from [unrecognized system]. Allow? (Yes/No)

Here was the answer to Uline's question! I chuckled and gave my permission, limiting its energy use just in case, so we wouldn't end up sucked dry. My manipulation of the frigate systems went unnoticed by the Starship Pilot and Navigator. Dmitry gave a whistle of surprise. Ayukh's massive jaw dropped, his gaze shifting from the power display to the continuing repair by the symbiote.

Machine Control skill increased to level fifty-six!
Electronics skill increased to level fifty-four!
Electronics skill increased to level fifty-five!
Authority increased to 46!

The Symbiote was still shown on the mini-map as just an unidentified "plasma cluster," which the ship's radars could not identify. But I didn't run a higher detail scan to study it, nor did I use the Prospector Scanner, afraid to spook our rare and skittish interstellar guest. As far as I knew, there had never been a recorded case of these satellites behaving aggressively. Also, I didn't sense any danger from it and trusted my intuition, which was whispering that it was not worth risking such a useful bonus simply to satisfy my curiosity, and this satellite might come in handy again sometime in the future.

I made sure everything was working alright and reassured Kirsan, while the other crew members suggested we return to the break room and continue the meeting.

NOW WE WERE DISCUSSING the magnetic bombs. Upon closer examination, we discovered they were of Geckho origin, absolutely identical and part of the standard kit of Sappers and Saboteurs of that race. However, the list of suspects was clearly not limited to these two classes. As it turned out, removing an armed bomb was very complicated, but basically any player with high enough Agility and Intelligence could install them.

But who could have gotten them on our starship and when? It was incredibly important for all of us to find answers to these questions. So I suggested we have a brainstorming session, saying any ideas about what happened even the most unbelievable or potentially hurtful.

First of all, we tried to answer the question of when. The most obvious time was during our prolonged stay at the military base. After all, before that, no one knew for certain who the Tolili-Ukh X Frigate would belong to and no one knew that exact ship would be sent to us. But not all the facts lined up there, either. On the base, only the fleet commander's repairmen had access to our frigate, but I personally found it hard to imagine some huge Geckho technician squeezing into the narrow gap, getting stuck and cursing vibrantly, though in a whisper as to remain undetected.

"I have a full list of technicians who worked on the frigate," Uline pointed to her palmtop, which is where she kept all this information. "We can find and interrogate them later. Although I agree with the captain, that a Geckho could not fit into such a narrow gap. Maybe a child? Although I didn't see any children on the military base. Maybe one of the crew members saw some suspicious activity during the repair."

No, no one saw anything. But Eduard Boyko wanted to say something, and our Space Commando's idea really was new:

"I say we check our quiet little Princess and see if she had something to do with this! Minn-O is always silent, never goes anywhere and tries not to get in anyone's face. And meanwhile, she has the most motivation to destroy our starship, because this vessel is our trump card in the war against her faction! After the death of Leng Thumor-Anhu La-Fin, who protected and sheltered his granddaughter, the Princess would have to prove her loyalty and use to the faction. And destroying a starship fits easily into that logic! What's more, Minn-O may be a bit tall, but she's thin as a matchstick and could easily make it into that narrow space. Try as I might, I for one could never squeeze in there."

Eduard had started speaking in Geckho, but quickly got flustered and switched to Russian.

Nevertheless, Minn-O understood perfectly. So she stood up and, looking Eduard right in the face, answered with a surprising discretion and calm:

"Alright, let's say I really was going to blow up the starship. Where could I get the explosives? The only time I went to buy anything, two people were with me the whole way to the vending machine: Uline and Gnat. They saw my purchase list, what's more they entered it in the machine for me, because I can't even read Geckho. And they can confirm that there were no magnetic bombs on that list."

"That is true," Uline Tar confirmed readily. "The human lady bought a big list of all kinds of crap. It had a new firearm, professional Cartographer gear, and personal items like jewelry and cosmetics. But there were definitely no magnetic bombs!"

Minn-O gave a slight bow to her furry roommate for the support, then continued her speech:

"What's more, Space Commando Eduard will soon be finding out that I am changing factions to be with my legal husband. Your leader Gerd Lozovsky has already agreed, and now, I need to get to Human-3 territory in the game to begin the body transfer procedure. To me it is very important. In fact it is a question of life and death. And how, I ask, would the destruction of this starship — my only way of getting to Earth — help me with that?"

Eduard apologized to my wayedda and admitted that he didn't know all that. However, he then quickly suggested I mentally check Tini. Just in case, because the little Miyelonian would have the easiest time slipping into the narrow access closet, and his skills and class would allow him to easy handle traps and explosives, both removing and installing. To be fair, he was the only one who really fit the profile. Honestly, Eduard couldn't even think up a single motive for the Miyelonian teen to blow up our starship, but Tini didn't object and just told me to read his mind.

That's just what I did. And... I froze. The suspicion that my ward was involved in the planting of the explosives was immediately upended. Tini had nothing whatsoever to do with that. However, my ward was not quite so simple as one might imagine. First of all, I immediately saw that the little thief had rifled through the backpacks of every crew member and even taken a few baubles. He dug through my stuff too, but he didn't risk any pilfering. I decided to discuss that unbecoming information, but not in front of the others. Later, just between us. But that was not the main discovery.

Some of the kitten's memory fragments were blocked! Someone had very skillfully closed a few episodes off, most notably almost half of his recent conversation with Leng Amiru U-Mayaoo! I suspected that the kitten himself couldn't even remember what he'd spoken about with the Great Priestess, beyond what he told me. And there was some strange mental programming, commanding the little thief to take certain actions in certain situations... I wasn't going to untangle all these cobwebs now. It was too hard for me anyway.

But from what I could see, there were plenty of curious incidents. Most of all, Tini's Fame was now all the way to seventeen! Clearly, my ward was quite well known, which was a great surprise and strange for a Thief, whose profession usually meant doing one's best to maintain quiet obscurity. Also, my kitten was getting some payments on the side! For every day he stayed with Gerd Gnat, the teen's electronic wallet got fifty crypto. And that was a ton of money for an underage thief, who very recently had been getting by with pickpocketing. And apparently Tini was spying on me voluntarily. No one had forced or blackmailed him. Well, quite the find...

Psionic skill increased to level sixty-six!

Mysticism skill increased to level twenty-two!

I was out of magic points and forced to stop reading my ward's mind. I looked to my now silent team, clearly surprised at how long I was taking. I hurried to reassure them:

"Tini definitely didn't place the bombs!" After that sentence, I changed to Miyelonian and, while the others were loudly conversing amongst themselves, I added just for the kitten: "But we need to have a very serious chat!"

Chapter
Twenty-Two

Family Matters

I HAD THAT CHAT with Tini in my cabin and it left me with contradictory feelings. On the one hand, my kitten admitted that his digging through our bags was not exactly legal, and definitely not dignified. But the Miyelonian thief didn't feel any guilt for it. He was prepared to return the small things he'd stolen like Uline's fur-bleaching brushes, or Imran's extra underwear. He would even apologize. In Tini's own word's he had taken these things not to sell or keep, just to level his thief's skills.

The kitten had approximately the same carefree opinion of his espionage. The orphan teen was proud and happy beyond words that the great figures of his race had paid him attention and even given him an important mission. He was to remain with the only

Listener in the whole Universe and help him in any way possible. Tini didn't see anything untoward in that and in fact thought he was doing me a huge favor by helping influential Miyelonians have a hand in my fate. The kitten sincerely believed that the attention and protection of the most powerful Miyelonian leaders such as the Great Priestess Leng Amiru U-Mayaoo or the most popular commander in the space fleet Keessi-Miau should not be squandered, and I needed to try and maintain friendly relations. Tini simply deified his protectors and even would have spied on me for free, if they asked. And he was all the prouder to receive fifty crypto per standard day, once unthinkable for a poor orphan like him.

It was a big struggle, but I managed to get the idea through to my kitten that round-the-clock surveillance and the scrupulous attention of prominent Miyelonians were not much to my liking. Free Captains did not always act within the bounds of law, after all. Some were smugglers, some pirates, and the rest were in no hurry to advertise the sources of their income. At the very least, that reduced competition. Our team also had to hide their commercial secrets, and it wasn't even certain that these secrets would have a shade of criminality. I tried very hard to drive the simple thought into my ward's head that the success of our enterprise depended on the ability of all team members to keep a secret. And that was why I really did not want him trumpeting our valuable findings and discoveries to strangers. In the end, I forbade my kitten from sharing information about the state of our frigate, mineral deposits, profitable trade routes or interesting anomalies with anyone outside our crew.

In the end, Tini understood, and even promised not to reveal any secrets. But the Miyelonian teen was not prepared to totally stop sending reports to his highly-placed contacts. The kitten walked away in a state of deep contemplation, and I understood him fully. Two important but distinct interests were at loggerheads — loyalty to his captain Gerd Gnat and a thick stew of awe and desire to serve the powerful Miyelonians. And I was not at all sure that Tini would choose my side. But was it worth judging my ward or limiting him? Hardly. When I was in Uraz Tukhsh's crew, I also kept the interests of my faction and home planet in mind. The alien captain always came second.

But still, as much as possible, I tried to tweak the adolescent's system of values and priorities. Let him think himself chosen, worthy of attention from the powerful. Let him send his reports to the Miyelonians, especially if he was getting money. But these reports could not contain information the captain wanted kept secret, or facts that were damaging to his master or team.

Psionic skill increased to level sixty-seven!
Mysticism skill increased to level twenty-three!

Yikes, how difficult this conversation with my ward had turned out... My mana, which hadn't had time to fully recover since the meeting, was back down to zero. And the door hadn't managed to close behind Tini before my travelling spouse slipped into my room. When I saw the Princess, I tried to stretch out my face into a pleasant and polite smile and not to let out the groan of despair trying to burst out of me. My wayedda had come at such a bad time! Conversations with Minn-O always required serious psychic interaction and a large expenditure of Magic Points. But I was bone dry...

Meanwhile, just after closing the door behind herself, Minn-O La-Fin blurted out that I shouldn't pay any mind to Eduard Boyko's accusation, because it was "all false." The Princess declared that she was not trying to prove herself to her faction after her grandpa died and was especially not planning to blow up our frigate. What was more, Minn-O herself thought that Eduard had only accused her because he liked her. She said he was following her like a creep. For example, while repairing the ship, the Space Commando tried to be in the same brigade as the Princess constantly and if it didn't work out, he still found a way to be near. Minn-O constantly caught attentive gazes from her unwanted admirer. Eduard had tried to speak with the Dark Faction Princess a few times, including on frivolous topics that had nothing to do with ship repair. And a few times while working together, seemingly on accident, he had touched her... here Minn-O went deep red and used a euphemism: "where you can't see without a mirror."

So Minn-O's indignation was not played up. Some unpleasant episodes really had taken place. I was even reminded of a conversation over lunch under the Dome, where the topic of the pretty Dark Faction girl and beautiful NPC Naiads had come up. Eduard had said something like "well they'll never make a proper girlfriend, because they don't exist in our world. They're virtual, not real." And although all that happened before the Princess said she was switching to the Human-3 Faction and our world, which immediately made her fully real, I still promised to speak with my underling and demand that he leave my wayedda alone.

So that issue was solved, but Minn-O was in no rush to leave my cabin. Again checking to make sure the door lock was working, she took a deep sigh, unfolded a hammock chair, hung it up and took a seat opposite me. Apparently, I could look forward to another long conversation about the politics of her magical world, the finer points of the competing magical families and complications with keeping the La-Fin family holdings.

"Gnat..." she faltered and turned deep red in embarrassment. "Say, why don't we play strip poker!"

What?! My brows shot up in surprise. Well, well, that was the last way I expected this to go! I probably looked awkward, because Minn-O was tittering and trying to convince me:

"It's free time now, you let the crew have leave. Uline is asleep, your factionmates have gone into the real world, and the Geckho are playing Na-Tikh-U. But I don't know that game, so I decided to suggest we play a different one. I even took a deck with me. But for us newly-weds, playing for money would be boring and stupid."

The Princess really surprised me. But all in all, why not? Although... I didn't want to win by cheating, so I honestly told my travelling mistress she had no chance:

"I have the highest possible luck modifier, and my Perception is twenty-nine, so I can tell the cards apart by the backs, and I'll always know exactly which cards you have. And it isn't in my nature to give up, so you're going to just lose again and again."

"Well, losing also has its plusses," she said, not upset in the least. "And I'll be able to rouse you a bit. As it is you just sit around all official and beetle-browed. All your thoughts are occupied with fixing the starship, politics, war and other serious things. You never have any time for your wife!"

Her reproaches were totally justified, and I was prepared to admit my error and correct it quickly. I stood up from my seat and sat in the hammock next to my wayedda. Then, decisively embracing Minn-O, I kissed her:

"I really don't think we need any cards now. There isn't enough free time to waste it on that kind of nonsense!"

MINN-O WAS NOTHING like any of my past lovers. First of all, her ashen gray skin was unusual for our world. And next, she was trying to please me, but her inexperience and apparent ignorance of the basics of sexual mechanics truly befuddled me. I had to explain and show her things patiently and carefully as not to spook her. As it was, the highborn Princess was shaking in fear and worry. And naturally, there could be no mention of any "wild passion" here, although everything basically went exactly the way it was meant to. But when I tried to get out a condom (still from old reserves I hadn't sold to Phylira) Minn-O was sincerely insulted and demanded that everything go "as nature intended."

After we had "built on our success" in the ancient art of love a number of times, we simply lay in the hammock, embracing and placidly cooing about anything and everything. And that included "boring politics," and the various visions of Earth's future after the tong of safety passed. At that, Minn-O mentioned one very important thing, which I was intending to tell Ivan Lozovsky as soon as I got the chance.

Seemingly, the node the Geckho had occupied

on the virtual Earth, the Spaceport, had begun appearing in her real world! Satellites over the alternative magical world, had detected a strange weather anomaly on an ice continent. Their pictures showed a small area with a different, much warmer climate. And also, unusual structures had been noted there, which experts quickly recognized as the Geckho space port and surrounding buildings. But the scientists who had been sent to study the anomaly had returned with nothing. For some reason, that part of the ice continent was unavailable, as if it simply didn't exist. Members of the land expedition hadn't seen any anomalies and had just passed through it, immediately finding themselves on the other side of the forbidden zone. But still, all attempts to ask the suzerains what was happening were ignored.

"I heard my grandpa swearing up a storm in a meeting with his advisors. After all, it turned out that the Geckho, without asking permission, just took and occupied part of my home planet! They isolated an area and built something there, and they were in no hurry to inform the human rulers of that world!"

"Well, not exactly rulers anymore," I corrected my wayedda. "As much as it may hurt, Earth already formally belongs to the Geckho, and more accurately its viceroy Kung Waid Shishish. The Geckho just have no inclination to share information with their vassals, making us basically gather crumbs of data about the game that bends reality and its rules. And most people have no other way of figuring that out other than through the Geckho diplomat. But you and I are in a more privileged position. We can speak with members of many alien races, so it is our shared mission to figure out what happens to new planets after the tong of safety."

Just then, a polite knock came at the door of my bunk. I looked at the naked Minn-O and she gave an understanding nod. A moment later, my companion was lying next to me in full gear, even her helmet for some reason. I threw my clothing and armor from my inventory into the proper slots as well, jumped up from the hammock and went to open the door. It was Imran.

"Gnat, sorry if it's a bad time, but I have a message from Ivan Lozovsky. He wanted me to tell you the Dark Faction has a new leader, a level-23 Strategist named Gerd Ui-Taka."

"He's a little green for a faction leader, don't you think...?" I asked dubiously, but then shuddered. "Wait... Ui-Taka? I know that name... Minn-O, isn't that the big General you were telling me about?"

"You have a great memory, husband," my wayedda smiled. "Yes, that is the man. The best strategist of my world according to many authoritative mages. He's a general popular with the armed forces. He seized power over the Second Directory by force. He's the first nonmage to rule in the last eight centuries."

Imran eagerly added to the description of the

new Dark Faction head:

"A real badass, or so they say. He asked to hold negotiations with our faction and came to our Capital on the antigrav that used to belong to Mage Thumor-Anhu. He not only came without weapons or armor, as agreed, he didn't even have bodyguards. But even wearing a simple light toga and surrounded by our soldiers, he looked like he was in charge. All of our guys say he looks brutal, basically like the Terminator. His jaws are square, his body is pure muscle. You could send him straight to a Mister Universe competition! But the most important is his gaze. It's attentive and calm at the same time, like a strong confident lion. His new First Advisor came with him, too. His name is Gerd Mac-Peu Un-Roi, a level-ninety-three Mage Diviner."

"Wait, what about Avir-Syn La-Pirez?" Minn-O shot out, unable to hold back the surprised exclamation. "I mean, he's my grandfather on my father's side and was Thumor-Anhu's First Advisor, right hand and the second highest-level player in our ranks! Avir-Syn was the most obvious candidate for new faction head, or at least deputy! Why not him?"

Imran could only answer all the emotional questions with a shoulder shrug:

"I can't tell you things I don't know. I'm just telling you the news. But as for why those exact players are the new leaders of the Dark Faction, you probably have a clearer picture."

"Strange, of course. Although... Avir-Syn

probably has plenty of concerns in the real world with the La-Fin family inheritance and his respectable age doesn't allow the old mage to overexert himself... But there were other mages much stronger than the young Diviner. Some are even level 100 plus. Very strange that all of my father's trusted individuals got skipped over. Ah, sorry Imran. Keep talking!"

Minn-O had just been thinking out loud, and my Dagestani friend was waiting patiently until the Princess finished. But I was thinking about something else. I was contemplating this genius leader, who enjoyed huge authority among the military. He also had a mage diviner as an advisor who Minn-O had described as very talented and capable of predicting whether an attack would succeed or not... That seemed like a very strong combination, if not to say nearly cheating. They'd be hard to take down if the Dark Faction decided to go on the offensive.

Imran was seemingly somewhat wounded by the mention of the enemy top players, because he couldn't resist a comment:

"By the way, speaking of level-one-hundred players, our faction has one now! Gerd Tarasov, Leader of the First Legion! I heard the announcement myself under the Dome on loudspeaker. And Gerd Tamara isn't too far behind, she's level-98."

Well, well! I guess our "legionnaires" leveled up a good deal on those sea creatures! I was especially impressed by Gerd Tamara's progress, as she'd nearly caught up to our usual record-setter Igor Tarasov, even though she was ten levels behind him before. After all, at level-one hundred, a player could take three new skills, and that meant not only increasing abilities, but also a quick jump to 101, 102 and maybe even 103, because new skills leveled very quickly, which filled the progress bar.

Meanwhile, Imran continued:

"Ivan Lozovsky wanted me to say the negotiations were very hard. We had six people: five of our faction's six Gerds, minus you, and a staff officer, who was transmitting messages to the outside curators. The Dark Faction set the following conditions — cease our expansion to the north and surrender the Karelia node. With that, they were willing to sign a 'treaty of everlasting peace' and they even agreed to have the Geckho serve as guarantors."

"But giving up the Karelia node would mean losing our route to the Geckho spaceport!" I objected. To me this sounded more like a demand for capitulation. "And the spaceport means trade, new technologies and our path to the stars! The alternative by ferry is too unreliable. Sure, it's here today, but that all depends on the furballs' whims. And they might jack up the transport prices, or even totally refuse to take our cargo! Plus, there are lots of things the Geckho won't transport by ferry, and building our own ships is not just one week's work. Also we would need more players with special skills for sea travel. No, giving up the Karelia node is a surefire path to defeat!"

"Lozovsky also thought so. He refused the offer," Imran reassured me. "But not everyone agrees... Some of our faction's negotiators were willing to accept almost any concession to obtain a peace treaty with such a strong enemy. It all led to endless fighting. Our side just never reached a consensus. In the end, the leader of the Dark Faction gave us three days to make a decision. After that, in his words we'd 'talk with cannons instead of diplomats.'"

Chapter Twenty-Three

Second visit to the Pirates

AFTER RELAYING THE MESSAGE from the faction head, Imran asked my traveling mistress to leave the cabin so we could talk alone. And although the Dagestani athlete said it as delicately and politely as possible, the Princess still got offended and turned to me for support. Nevertheless, I was on Imran's side because I knew that, without a good enough reason, my friend would never offend a woman. So I asked Minn-O not to be stubborn and return to her cabin. The Dark Faction Princess gave a snort of dismay and cast a gaze on me that didn't promise anything good. But still she left.

The door had just barely closed behind Minn-O

La-Fin when Imran continued:

"Gerd Lozovsky asked me to tell you alone, without anyone else around, that the war is unavoidable. In his words, not trading with the Geckho is an obvious dead end. It would mean turning down all the grandiose plans we don't have the money or materials to complete. What's more, there are now Naiads in the bay near our shores. They may be the ones the Germans expelled from their traditional homelands. So now there might not be any other way to the space port..."

"The Naiads won't touch the Geckho ferry, so they won't disturb our trade with the suzerains. But our own fleet, if the faction does decide to build one, will surely be sunk. But I interrupted you, continue!"

"That isn't all Lozovsky is worried about. All our neighbors, from the NPC Centaurs and Harpies up to the Germans now see the Human-3 Faction as a force to be reckoned with. And that makes them try to curry our favor. But if we show even one day of weakness, we'll lose all that. And together with our authority and respect, we will quickly lose all our allies, who will then run to a stronger player. And really 'everlasting peace' with one faction does not mean peace with all parties in the 'great game.' It's just a brief respite until our weakened faction is captured by someone else."

I totally shared that fear. Without new technology and complicated equipment, our faction would remain on the periphery of grand-scale politics and would very soon roll back to a mere source of cheap lumber. Eventually we'd just be wiped off the political map. Still, those were all words and thoughts. What did leadership want from me now? I asked that directly. The Dagestani gave an unhappy chuckle:

"Lozovsky wants a miracle out of you. Yes! Those were his exact words! He wants you to use all your political and family connections to repeat the trick with the Graveyard node, or something totally new, but just as compelling and destructive. As he put it, only such unexpected and powerful blows can force the darksiders to reckon with us."

A miracle?! That was quite the tall order! For now, I had no clue how I'd do it. Kung Waid Shishish was far away, and the most powerful master of Earth wouldn't listen to me. The Geckho would not interfere in struggles between their vassals on principle. And as for my family connections, they had seemingly disappeared along with the death of Coruler Thumor-Anhu La-Fin. His granddaughter Princess Minn-O just did not have the political weight in her world, so she wouldn't be much help.

"And our boss also asked if the faction could count on a starship for the war. Wait, Gnat," here Imran interrupted me, not allowing me to voice my doubts and objections, "Gerd Lozovsky already knows the frigate is damaged and doesn't have weapons. He also knows that Uline Tar is co-owner of the ship. But he thinks that you can entice her, especially given her class, with profitable trade routes. Our faction has money now. Not as much as we might want, but we are willing to spend one hundred eighteen thousand crystals on high-impact alien weaponry. And I am willing to add some of my own funds. Eduard and Dmitry too, probably. And you won't just sit on the sidelines I'm sure... We could also try and sell platinum again or something from the real world that might get Uline Tar's interest. In one way or another, we'll definitely find enough to entice the Trader! Lozovsky also said that even without stabilizers and whatnot, a space frigate could be useful as an untouchable observer. It could provide firing coordinates to our cannons, for example. Overall, everyone in the faction is counting on you, Gnat! Make us a miracle!"

With those words, Imran gave me an encouraging slap on the shoulder and walked out of the captain's bunk, leaving me in deep thought. They wanted a miracle... But where was I going to get one?!

"WE'VE REACHED the Medu-Ro system. The station is in viewing distance!"

The Starship Pilot's message tore me out of my hours-long contemplative silence. I was trying to think up a strategy for the next three days that would allow me to achieve all my goals in that limited timeframe. I raised my gaze to the screen and... sharply came to life. Wow! What a pretty sight!!! My oldest dream had come true. I was seeing a space station firsthand. It was something of a twenty-mile-long metal spindle, blurred somewhat by the forcefield surrounding it. And in nearby space were dozens of unbelievable ships, from tiny nimble Miyelonian interceptors to... what even were those giants? Ore freighters and isotope space-ice mining ships based on the game information. And all this space-age wonder had a similarly impressive backdrop — the pitch-black volcanic planet Medu-Ro IV with its crimson fractures, and the huge light-blue local star. An unbelievable, fantastic sight!

> *Eagle Eye skill increased to level sixty-eight!*
> *Cartography skill increased to level fifty-six!*
> *Mineralogy skill increased to level fifty!*
> *Fame increased to 62.*

Woah, woah. So many system messages after a long break! And the last was most likely connected with our ship being examined by the station's automatic systems. My instruments showed that our frigate was now being hit with all kinds of detectors and scanners. And they were probably most interested in the symbiote. Just then, the satellite decided it didn't like all this attention, unclipped from our fuselage and darted off, picking up unbelievable speed and disappearing into the depths of space.

"Captain, we've received a message from the station dispatchers," Ayukh told me, and I asked to have it sent to me.

"Free Captain Gerd Gnat. Human. Purpose of visit: to purchase parts and repair my ship," I replied when the emotionless metallic voice asked me to identify myself in Miyelonian.

Five to seven seconds passed, and the same lifeless voice answered:

"Permission to access spaceport zone granted. Landing bay 16-4. Follow the instructions and illuminated arrows to enter the dock. Welcome to Medu-Ro IV!"

Another forty minutes later, after waiting in a small line and passing into the long shaft that pierced the whole station, our frigate entered the hangar and stopped, held firm by gravity cranes.

"One day's docking fee for a frigate-class ship is four thousand one hundred crypto. I have only crystals," Uline told me somewhat alarmed, but I reassured my partner, saying I had enough Miyelonian currency.

I even payed for two days up front so the station couldn't possibly complain. Then, after lining up my crew before the starship, I led a short information session:

"Some of you have been here before and know the finer points of this station. But I'll explain for the others. Medu-Ro IV does not belong to any of the great space governments, everything here is controlled by the Free Captains. And that means there is no law here as such and might makes right, so to speak. If something can be obtained not by paying, but by force, that is exactly what any local will try to do. So the biggest crime you can commit here on the station is to show weakness, or even worse, lack of confidence or cowardice! After that, you will immediately be made a victim who not only can be insulted and robbed but must be. Do you all understand that?"

A few not-overly-confident responses rang out. Without even falling back on my psionic abilities, I could tell what the vast majority of my crew was now thinking: "why the hell did we even stick our noses in such a wild and dangerous place?" I had to explain:

"However, Medu-Ro IV is the largest trading hub in this part of the Galaxy. The market here has everything, and at fairly reasonable prices. Yes, smugglers trade here and pirates unload stolen goods, but for us, transparent origin of new parts is nowhere near the most important factor. Our biggest priorities now are low price and high quality. As a rule, those are not a problem on Medu-Ro IV because con artists are not well liked here and are killed on sight."

I took a pause and made sure everyone was listening closely. Even Tini, a native of the station, perked up his ears and hung on my every word.

"Now, about the rules for how to behave on the station. There are just three, so it's easy to remember. One: only VERY self-confident high-level players or idiots who will soon be ripped to shreds walk around here alone. Always stay in a group! Two: thieves here are like fleas on a stray dog, especially in the spaceport recreation zone. Geckho who don't know what a flea or dog is, ask any human. The most important rule here is: always keep an eye on your bags!"

I had to take a brief pause, because Minn-O started laughing awkwardly. Clearly, the Earth native found it funny that someone might not know such elementary terms as dog or flea. But Minn-O quickly apologized and put on a serious face.

"The third and most important rule: the common language here is Miyelonian, so you will probably not understand what is expected of you. If you think you might be in trouble (and you're probably in pretty deep by that point) you must never demonstrate fear or even mumble. You must respond confidently in your native language or with gestures, referring them to your captain. I will handle them. And if you happen to hear the sentence 'Ah-sahntee maye-uu-u rezsh shashash-u?' that means they are challenging you to a fight to the death. Do not take out your weapon and, preferably with lots vulgarity and middle fingers, tell that asshole to go... to me again. I'll handle them. And you four-fingered Geckho, use either of your inner fingers... Basha, you can try it out as much as you want later. Now is not the time! Kirsan, this goes for you too!"

Authority increased to 47!
Authority increased to 48!

Well, well. My Authority grew twice after that fairly brief speech! Seemingly, my team now thought me a true space-pirate expert, capable of solving any problems that might crop up. Maybe because of that, when I asked who was willing to follow me to the pirate station, everyone wanted to come including the repair bots.

Chapter Twenty-Four

Familiar Mugs

I OF COURSE DID NOT bring the bots with me. There was too much work for them on the frigate. I also left the Supercargo and Navigator on the ship because I was planning to order some cargo and modules to modify the starship and I needed someone there to accept them. And I chose Eduard Boyko to stay behind as security. I ordered the Space Commando to don his full exoskeleton armor and never let his guard down, because carelessness was too costly a pleasure on the dangerous station and could have the most serious consequences. I planned to also leave Basha and Vasha to help Avan Toi, but then I figured having two big strong Geckho at my back would make me look very fearsome, which would be great on the pirate station.

But before going anywhere, I ordered all crew

members to change their respawn points to Medu-Ro IV. And I recommended that they put it somewhere beyond the walls of this hangar, so they wouldn't end up locked inside like I once had. I made the same changes in my respawn settings, which immediately made me feel at ease. Now, no matter how the Meleyephatian and Geckho battle ended on the Un-Tesh comet, my life was not at risk.

By the way, the situation with the Geckho military base on the comet was still unclear. In the official real-world news, nothing had been said about it yet, and Avan Toi had so far been unable to contact his old friend and get the news first hand. All that remained was to hope that help had come in time, and the Meleyephatian fleet was defeated. I wished the Geckho luck with utter sincerity, because the safety of my native earth depended on the power of their space fleet.

And so, once again reminding my friends to stay together, I led my group down the familiar round corridor, a huge ring that wrapped around the central shaft. By the way, I was on the very same floor, sixteen and I conveniently already had a map of it. Confidently leading my group to the fork toward the elevators, I drew their attention to a sign:

"This says: Document check. Registration service. Last time, I never figured out what documents were meant to be checked here and just killed the guy working there."

"It's normal crewmember cards," Uline responded, walking a step behind me. "Everyone who goes into space has them, or at least they should. Mine doesn't work now, because I changed ships, but they aren't hard to get redone. Also, drawing up a new one for Imran and Minn-O at the checkpoint will be easy enough, and will ward off potential problems. But Ayukh should have given you a captain's card. That is actually checked."

We turned down a side corridor and in just ninety feet I saw the very same Gladiator that gave me such a fierce greeting before:

Aik Ur Miyeau Miyelonian. Pride of the Comet's Tail. Level-66 Gladiator.

The lean five-foot tall gray Miyelonian draped head to toe in weaponry had not changed one bit since our previous encounter... uhh... actually how long ago was that? I did the math and couldn't even believe it: just fourteen days! A mere two weeks! Strangely, I felt as if a whole eternity had passed since then. So much had happened! Then the fur-covered Gladiator had seemed a fearsome and insurmountable obstacle, but now I had significantly outgrown Aik not only in level, but combat ability.

"What, you're still standing here leaning against a wall? Isn't it boring to stay in one place for days on end?" I asked instead of a greeting, at the same time showing him my Free Captain card.

The Miyelonian, mechanically running his

scanner over the blue crystal, stashed his tool in his inventory and raised his surprised whiskered face:

"Free Captain Gerd Gnat... have we ever met before?"

"You can say that again! You sawed off my hand, and I still have your tail in my inventory."

His face brightened. He had finally lined up the pitiful lone Prospector with nothing worth stealing and the high-level Listener standing before him in unique ancient Relict armor and a team of loyal soldiers in tow.

"Woah! You've changed a lot, Gerd Gnat! I'm just killing time here... But which Free Captain would take me as crew? After all, they all want recommendations, a high level and a long list of trophies to prove combat ability. But where can I get that on the station?!"

Authority increased to 49!

I was a bit worried that Aik would then start checking the rest of my team's documents. And they didn't have working ones or in some cases even have them at all. But apparently, the whole check was limited to scanning the captain's card. The Miyelonian Gladiator stepped aside, letting us through to the space station. What, just like that? It was actually a bit boring...

I looked at the bored gray tomcat, who went back to leaning against the wall. Aik didn't look like he was training day and night to raise his combat skills but who could say? Captain's assistant Uline Tar constantly complained our crew wasn't filled out. She said a frigate class ship needed around twenty-five or even thirty crew members, but we had just ten. And just two were of combat classes: Imran the Gladiator and Eduard the Space Commando, which really was not enough and made us vulnerable in case of a conflict. Preferably, to set a Free Captain's mind at ease, there should be at least a dozen strong warriors. But where to get them?

I turned back to the Miyelonian:

"I propose a test: if you can defeat my level-59 Gladiator, I'll take you to space as a fully-fledged crew member. And if you cannot defeat an enemy seven-levels lower then you, don't get any ideas. I don't want anyone like that, keep practicing."

"Agreed!" the Miyelonian instantly came to life, and a pair of glimmering blades appeared in his hands.

Here I changed to my native tongue and called the Dagestani Gladiator:

"Imran, this tomcat wants to join our crew. Put him to the test! It's a simple blade battle without any firearms, and it will be to the death. If you win, you'll at least get his tail, and that means the respect of any Miyelonian. And if you get lucky with the drop, you might get a blade to match your other Miyelonian one. And if you lose, don't stress. We'll wait for you here!"

"Don't you worry, friends. I can do it!" Imran promised us all and after some thought, removed the armor he'd been gifted by Kung Waid Shishish, remaining just in his athletic shorts. Two blades also showed up in our soldier's hands.

I asked the others to walk away and form a circle. The two duelists faced off inside it.

"Ah-sahntee maye-uu-u rezsh shashash-u!" Aik Ur Miyeau said distinctly and gave a deep bow to his opponent.

"And good luck to you, space cat," the Dagestani answered with a mirrored bow.

The battle was over very fast. It lasted at most a second and a half. Aik, using his instant jump ability, darted behind Imran and slashed with both his blades... but Imran was no longer there! And he didn't run away, just stepped aside, turned around and started attacking thin air a second before the overgrown cat got there. It only took one stab, and the Miyelonian's impaled body collapsed on the floor. Well, Aik blew it. He wasn't going to join my team now, and he had no one to blame but himself. He spent lots of time here standing around with nothing to do. He should have been training.

Eagle Eye skill increased to level sixty-nine!

"It was all over so quickly, I didn't even see what happened," Minn-O admitted, utterly struck. Seemingly, the rest of my crew was in a similar boat.

I gave a few distinct claps, congratulating my friend. And it bears noting that Imran leveled up to sixty in that fast-paced battle and probably grew some skills and his self-confidence.

"Good job! Well executed, steady and no

superfluous movements. Did you practice with Tini?"

"Who else?" Imran chuckled happily, wiping a bloody curved blade on the breathless body then stowing both weapons back in their sheaths. "Back when Ayni was training us on the Shiamiru, I realized that a quick jump behind an opponent is too predictable and would only work against the completely inexperienced. Tini caught me once with that trick, but I figured it out. Vai[4], bad luck. He didn't drop any loot. Too bad, I wouldn't mind a second sparkling blade. And for some reason his tail won't come off!"

"You're supposed to take the trophy right away. If you wait too long, you can't do anything with the body. But don't you worry, Imran. I just so happen to have Aik Ur Miyeau's tail in my inventory. You can have mine!" With these words, I gave the Gladiator my trophy and helped him clip the gray tail to his helmet.

Honestly, that one was marked as from a level-64 Aik, who was now 66, but I figured that was trivial. No one from my crew noticed.

---

[4] A common interjection in the Caucasus region

WE WENT UP the elevator with a group of Meleyephatians. The three spider-like merchants were communicating actively and speaking in gestures, not paying us any attention at all. I couldn't sense any aggression from them, and seemingly the eight-armed merchants had no concern for my Geckho or Miyelonian friends. It was a bit weird given their races were at war, but apparently some Free Captains were totally uninvolved in politics or military, and Meleyephatians were just as welcome at Medu-Ro IV as any other race.

As soon as the elevator reached our floor and our paths diverged, I asked Uline Tar her opinion on the matter. The Trader was surprised:

"What's so weird about that? A Free Captain is free, they aren't contingent on any government, army or other political force. A Free Captain is not beholden to any authority but their own, and their starship functions as their own little state. Of course, if a Free Captain does take active part in combat operations, they will eventually make enemies with whoever they choose to fight against, as you might expect. But if they remain neutral, no one will forbid them from entering the space of another race, clan or pride."

"Hold up, are we marked as participants in the war on the Geckho side?" I asked, panicked. "After all, we stormed the underground Meleyephatian base, then warned the Geckho about the attack on their comet!"

Uline gave a happy rumble, as if I'd just said

something very funny, and tried to reassure me:

"Gnat, believe me, a couple battles or secret communiques are nowhere near sufficient grounds to be officially declared the enemy of even a single clan! A great spacefaring race needs much more than that. There are even professional mercenaries, who fight for pay. But once their contract is up, they revert to neutral status. Still of course, if someone notices a Free Captain has fought against them too frequently, they might decide to declare them an enemy. But in that case, you'd find out before anything happened. Whenever you're declared an enemy or a criminal, you get an official system message."

Over that conversation, I didn't even notice but we'd reached the registration desk. And my heart quickly started beating faster, because a familiar face! A short golden-orange Miyelonian was sitting behind the desk greeting visitors. She was now speaking with a transparent round alien that looked like a huge bubble. The system told me it was a Cyanian. Seemingly, this bubble's documents weren't exactly checking out, because he was blowing air and whistling in anger as the lady behind the desk spoke. But I was not so interested in this individual as the orange cat in white shorts on a tall chair:

Gerd Ayni Uri-Miayuu. Miyelonian. Pride [undetermined]. Level-79 Translator.

Gerd? Ayni was now a Gerd? That said, why not? After the footage of her killing the Great Priestess was broadcast to the whole Galaxy, my Translator friend probably had more than enough Fame. We stopped five steps from the desk as not to get in her way. But clearly our little crowd had drawn Ayni's attention. She raised her gaze to us, spent a few seconds batting her lashes in surprise and... tipped over her chair, rushed to me with a joyful cry and buried her fluffy face in my armored shoulder:

"Gnnnnnnaaaaaaaaaat!!! You came for me!"

Miyelonians are not known to be emotionally open, especially when others can see. Their society does not look kindly on such behavior, and so her shameless unrestrained joy was touching. I squeezed Ayni close as she shook in worry. Her body temperature even went up noticeably.

Meanwhile, the bubble took advantage of the opportunity and, with a sharp jerk of a pseudopodium, gathered all the electronic cards from the desk, crammed them into its body and slipped out. Ayni seemingly didn't even notice the illegal entry, she was too busy recounting all her troubles.

She was ejected dishonorably from her pride. Everyone was suspicious and hated her. Her close relatives had turned away from her. And even when it came out that the killer was a Morphian imitating her, it didn't much change things. She knew no peace now either in the game or the real world. Enraged religious fanatics followed her everywhere. Ayni was killed in the game three times a day, and she tried to stay out of the real world as much as possible to avoid a similar but more devastating fate there.

"I see you've become a Gerd," I said, trying to distract her from the difficult memories. But Ayni only became even more upset:

"You can say that again! My Fame rating is now three hundred eleven! Every Miyelonian in the Universe knows my face! But my Authority is minus ninety-six and every Miyelonian from little children to bald old men know me as the evil murderer of the incarnation of the Great First Female! They all think the space war started because of me, and you'll never convince them otherwise!"

Hrm, not fun. And I was sure that Ayni was not exaggerating. Every day, hundreds and thousands of Miyelonians came here to the Medu-Ro IV station, and some of them went through registration at this very desk. Sure, some acted out because their minds were clouded with hate, even though they probably knew she wasn't really the assassin. But most Miyelonians seemingly could restrain themselves, because the Translator was dying at the hands of fanatics only two or three times a day. In my world, I suspect the situation would be somewhat worse.

Alright then, I suggested we leave our past hardships behind and officially took the orange cat into my crew as a translator and experienced personnel manager. Then, I pointed her to the members of my team:

"You've already met my kitten Tini. He's grown a lot professionally and in level and become a proud and capable member of thieving society. I won't introduce the rest. You can read their names yourself, then just get to know them. And just so you know, even though you don't know any of them, they all know you well..."

"Yes, I already am aware that the Morphian was traveling under my identity," Ayni reacted with utter calm, even though I could hear sadness in her voice. "I got a few Authority boosts, which I could not explain otherwise."

"Yes, that is true. I didn't figure it out anywhere near right away either and, once I did, it was too late. We were too far from here. But it's good that you figured everything out and I don't have to explain."

"Indeed you don't..." the orange cat answered, then squeezed me with a renewed force as if afraid to let me go and lose me again. Then, her voice became very similar to the plaintive mew of an abandoned kitten. "But Gnat... I bought a spacesuit... back then and got ready for a long journey... And for a long time, I couldn't believe... that... that you left without me, despite all your promises!"

Miyelonians never cried over grief or grievances. They had tear ducts; however, they were not linked with emotion. But in human terms, Ayni was basically blubbering and sobbing. She was shaking like an aspen leaf and meowing out loud, having forgotten her manners or that strangers could see. Although that probably wasn't really accurate. Ayni clearly did not consider me a stranger, and more likely saw me as someone who she could finally speak her mind to. And she also considered my crew family so, for the first time in the last two weeks, she thought she was among friends, and could finally let out all her sadness.

A few minutes later, Imran came up alarmed. Stringing Geckho words together unconfidently, he asked me and the orange Miyelonian what happened.

"Everything's fine now, strong and nice human, I'm almost back to normal," the Translator assured him, as she calmed down quite quickly. "Captain Gnat, please, I await your orders."

I released my embrace, letting the now calm Miyelonian go, then pointed at the glass desk and tall chair next to it:

"First of all, we need to officially register you as a member of my crew. And the others need proper documents drawn up as well. As far as I know, that is generally done here."

"Yes, that is true. Seven crypto for each set of documents. Foh!" the orange Miyelonian looked embarrassed and put her ears back in a comical way. "It would probably be wrong to take money from members of your own crew, right Gnat? I can try to register them for free, then wipe the evidence from the computer. I hope the higher-ups don't catch wind of this."

"Now, now. No need for the self-sacrifice. Do

everything by the books. I'll pay. Here's my crew list," I opened a tablet to the proper tab, adding Gerd Ayni Uri-Miayuu as personnel resources officer. She immediately gave the whole crew morale bonuses, which was unexpected and very nice.

While Ayni entered information into her terminal, Captain's assistant Uline walked up. After finding out why I was taking so long, the Trader greeted the Translator like an old friend and asked her to advertise our vacancies on the station. The most critical were Engineer, Medic, Copilot and at least one, if not two Gunner positions. And we also needed soldiers of all classes, at least five.

"Yes, I'll make the advertisement now," Ayni agreed obligingly, deftly tapping her fingers on the holographic screen and moving variously colored rectangles across it. "But you'll have to clarify. Which of the Tolili-Ukh X frigates is yours? There are four on the station now. Where should I send the candidates?"

"Docking bay 16-4," I answered quickly and immediately asked the orange cat if she really could see all the starships docked at the station. When she answered in the affirmative, I asked Ayni to figure out if there was a Tiopeo-Myhh II interceptor on the Medu-Ro IV station under the command of Free Captain Rikki Pan-Miis.

"That is not done, Captain Gnat. It's confidential information," the new crew member warned me. But still she looked up the answer in the employee database. "Yes Rikki Pan-Miis's interceptor is here on the station. Hangar 34-11. But if you want to have a talk with the Free Captain, you'd better hurry. He has requested and already received permission to leave the station. His interceptor is taking off in..." here, attentively observing the lady cat, I distinctly saw the game go out of synch. Based on her lips, Ayni said something else, probably using a time unit she was familiar with, but I clearly heard the words: "twenty-five minutes." She then went on to say, "To be honest though, Captain Rikki Pan-Miis has to pay three days' docking fees first."

Psionic skill increased to level sixty-eight!

In the end, I couldn't get by without magic, and the Miyelonian had to be slightly pushed to break the rules. But it didn't matter. In one way or another, I had the information I needed.

"Great! You girls keep drawing up documents for our crew. I'm gonna take the guys to pay a visit to a filthy counterfeiter!" Here I made a predatory grin and moved the Annihilator into my main weapons slot.

"No! Gerd Gnat don't leave me again! I'll go with you!" In the space of a second, Ayni was wearing a silver light-armor suit and space helmet. Two curved blades started glimmering in the Translator's hands an instant later.

I didn't think this was a good time to pressure my underling with my authority and order her to stay. And wasting Magic Points to convince her before an encounter with space pirates was not a good idea. What was more, Ayni Uri-Miayuu was a Gerd, a high-profile player and was thus entitled to say differing opinions. In the end, I let Ayni come with me.

"And what am I, chopped liver?!" Uline Tar objected, also taking out a laser pistol. "I want to go with you too! Sure I'm a peaceful Trader, but I've been itching to punish that Rikki Pan-Miis. He was one of the pirates that captured the Shiamiru, beat us up and robbed us! He was the one who took my Relict artifacts! And Basha, Vasha and Dmmmitry are gonna wanna talk with him about the money he stole as well! Show us the way, Captain!"

Chapter
Twenty-Five

Danger Rating

I T WAS NOT THE SMARTEST decision to take noncombat characters with me to the showdown. Ayni, sure. The Miyelonian lady, as with all members of her race, had natural bonuses for bladed weapons and movement speed. What was more, just the sight of the orange Translator, who had once cut down half the crew of this pirate's interceptor, would probably arouse fear in Captain Rikki and his crew. Sure, this was not the same deadly Ayni, the outrageously high-level Morphian, but the pirates didn't know that! So I could justify Ayni. But Uline?

Once, Uline told me that she had never used weapons before and had no combat skills. Since then, lots had happened. There was even the assault of the

Meleyephatian military base, which Uline Tar took part in on even footing. Also, the once peaceful Trader now had a laser pistol. But still, I thought it was a bit rash to use the furry Geckho lady as a fully-fledged combat unit. I had almost made up my mind to send Uline Tar to the frigate, but without knowing it, my business partner tipped the scales in her favor:

"I'm so happy!" the Trader couldn't hide her elation, walking with the rest of the group toward the elevators. "This is my third time on the Medu-Ro IV station, but it's the first time I'm not shivering in fear at every shadow. I just love walking with my head held high! I'm not some helpless victim! I'm about to go out and face my fear! And no matter how the shootout with the pirates ends, I'll remember this as one of the most important turning points in my life!"

So clearly it would have been very wrong for me to send my business partner back to the frigate at such a psychologically critical moment. It would have shredded my good relationship with Uline and that would have had very negative consequences. What was more, I was hoping there wouldn't be a shootout, and that I could just scare Captain Rikki into compensating my faction the two million crystals. But even if I was wrong about scaring him, the crew of the Tiopeo-Myhh II interceptor had just six players, and only three of them were dangerous. I had seven soldiers, and we had the element of surprise, so I figured our chances of teaching that nasty counterfeiter a lesson were high.

We took the elevator down to the thirty-third floor of the space port, and I led my group to docking bay number eleven. The door was predictably locked, but that obstacle didn't stop me for a second. I already knew these doors could be forced open with an electromagnetic pulse. What was more, I had a professional Thief with me and, in the worst case, I could try to repeat the trick of mind-controlling someone inside. But first I needed to evaluate the situation, so I activated Scanning.

Scanning skill increased to level thirty-two!

My mini-map showed just two players beyond the wall: a level-84 Miyelonian and a level-89 Geckho. They were fairly far away, almost at the very edge of my radius. And the system was stingy with their information. It didn't even show their classes. But I already knew who they were. Based on their races and levels, inside were Captain Rikki and his big strong guardsman. Strange, of course, that there were so few enemies. Still, they had around twenty minutes before takeoff, so maybe the remaining crew members were coming later.

"There's just two of them! We've picked a great moment! Let's not waste time. Tini, open 'er up!"

My kitten obediently crouched down next to the number pad and took out his tools. He brought out his code breaker and, before a minute had passed, the lock gave a quiet click. I praised the self-satisfied Thief and ordered everyone to take out their weapons and get ready:

"The captain's assistant is a huge Geckho warrior. Take him down right away before he figures out what's going on and takes down half our group. But I need the Miyelonian captain alive! Everybody got it? Alright, let's go!"

I REALIZED WE'D MADE a mistake as soon as the door opened. Instead of the pirate captain and his big scary bruiser of a guardsman, we saw two unfamiliar players in the blue and orange jumpsuits of station technicians. They were standing on a tall folding ladder and seemingly changing out or polishing the interceptor's armor plates. And although I realized my error and lowered my Annihilator, I didn't react fast enough to stop my allies. An instant later, the body of the Geckho repairman lay shot full of bullets and laser holes, fallen from the ladder. His Miyelonian partner shrieked in fear and dropped his tools, something like a screw-gun and a bolt-gun, then threw both of his hands up, surrendering to the mercy of his unknown attackers.

"Uhh... where's captain Rikki?" I asked the terrified repairman, who happened to be an Engineer by class. He was also of a decently high level:

Orun Va-Mart. Miyelonian. Pride of the Interstellar Pilgrim. Level-84 Engineer.

As no answer followed. I tried to psychically reassure the terrified Miyelonian, and at the same time show my peaceful intentions, insofar as that was possible:

"Come on now, lower your hands, we won't hurt you! We simply have questions for the captain of this interceptor, Rikki Pan-Miis. Do you know where he is?"

The Engineer glanced at the breathless body of his partner again, but still lowered his hands and answered, now totally at ease:

"Buh... I don't know... The customer is supposed to have returned already. He ordered us to get his ship ready for takeoff. He said he'd pay us when he got back."

I walked up closer and stopped next to the ladder. I picked up the screw gun the dark red repairman had dropped and put it back into his hands:

"Alright then, I have to admit we made a big mistake. We thought you were someone else. Here's compensation for your trouble, and your partner's loss of progress." With these words I took out my wallet and transferred five-hundred crypto to the long-haired Miyelonian. "And this is for you both. Don't even think of keeping the money from that Geckho!"

The Engineer unhurriedly took out his communicator, read the incoming message and his mouth peeked open in satisfaction, revealing a row of small sharp teeth:

"Buh... I'm not mad. Anything can happen here on Medu-Ro. You could always get mistaken for someone you're not!"

"And when you say your customer left to the station, does that mean he went into this hallway? Or did he leave the game into the real world?" I continued to interrogate the no longer stupefied station employee, trying to think up a strategy contingent on his answers.

But Orun didn't have time to answer. A couple steps from me, two Miyelonian figures appeared at once: Captain Rikki Pan-Miis and his ward Avi Wi-Rikki had entered the game. I had to shoot with my Annihilator point blank while rolling to the side, because both enemies had seen me and immediately reached for their weapons.

Agility increased to 18.

Rifles skill increased to level fifty!

Sharpshooter skill increased to level thirty-three!

Psionic skill increased to level sixty-nine!

You have reached level seventy-two!

You have received three skill points! (total points accumulated: six)

I wasn't sure I could ever do that again! Sure, I was already holding the Annihilator and my enemies had just entered the game and were thus at ease, but I beat a Miyelonian's reaction time! Yes! I was faster than two Miyelonians, a race famed for their deadly speed and unparalleled mastery in close combat! And at that,

I detected the threat without Danger Sense even tripping. Or at least, before my body reacted to it. Nevertheless, I correctly identified who to kill and who to mind-control! I mean, just imagine! I was very proud of myself!!!

Showing off for my audience, I stood up with unhurried dignity, then looked to visually confirm. Avi Wi-Rikki was fallen on the metal floor of the hangar, dead of blood loss and shock. It would have been hard to survive having his right arm and shoulder shot off along with a large chunk of torso. Pirate captain Rikki Pan-Miis was frozen like a statue midway through stabbing the thin air where I was standing just a few seconds earlier. And meanwhile, my companions' jaws dropped as they stared and batted their lashes in astonishment.

"Capture him!" I pointed the huge Geckho brothers at the paralyzed enemy. Only after that did the muted scene come to an end. All the players in the hangar flew into motion. I heard shouts of surprise and wonder from all sides:

"Master Gnat, forgive me, I dropped the ball..."

"Captain, are you wounded?" Uline and Ayni asked in two different languages.

"Now I know how you took down my group on the ferry!"

Even the Miyelonian Engineer, who we'd all forgotten about, edged in:

"Guys, your captain is a real badass! He took

down two dangerous pirates by himself! You wouldn't happen to need an Engineer on your ship, would you?"

Authority increased to 50!

An Engineer! An Engineer was asking to join my crew!! I just had to not spook him!!! Trying not to reveal my delight, I raised my eyes to the Miyelonian and asked with an acrid smirk:

"Have you ever even been in space, Engineer? Or have you spent all your time in the game polishing pirate starships on the station?"

"You insult me, Captain!" Orun Va-Mart objected with utter sincerity, and I could sense he was not faking it. "I've spent half my life in the cosmos! First as an Engineer's assistant on a Viiye-class ore freighter, then as senior Engineer on a Shiamiru shuttle. Then, my former captain lost his ship and cargo here in the casino and I found myself stranded on Medu-Ro IV..."

I put on a falsely ambivalent tone and sent Uline and Ayni to interview the jobseeker. Then I returned to the captured pirate captain, who had already been disarmed and was being held firmly by my two powerful Geckho enforcers. First of all, I grabbed the Miyelonian none-too-politely by the chin, turned his face up and met gazes with him.

"How did this human get here? Now I've stepped in it! And the whole Pride of the Bushy Shadow is on a great hunt. Just my luck! And asking them for help... no, it's better to die than give big boss Abi another reason to

think I'm a loser. The Eternally Cursed really pulled me by the tail when I agreed to the counterfeit crystal scheme... I should have just said no. At least then I wouldn't have these problems now... Although, how could I have refused my pride leader?"

My last doubts dissolved, as did any pangs of conscience: Rikki knew he'd slipped my faction counterfeit crystals for our platinum and understood perfectly why I'd come looking for him. Hilariously, despite his bewildered, nearly panicked thoughts, the Free Captain was growling frighteningly through his teeth, trying to throw me off:

"Gnat, you'll pay for that dirty attack! Did you think you'd take down two pirates and that would be it? On the contrary, this is only the beginning! You have no clue who you're messing with! The whole Pride of the Bushy Shadow will come to my defense!!!"

"Is that so? Well, color me unconvinced." I replied mockingly to the young scared captain, trying to make myself out to be a badass veteran. "Did your pride even make a peep when I captured your frigate before? No, they're proud warriors. They have no time for losers like you. What's more, as bad luck would have it, your whole pride is on a great hunt, and won't be coming back any time soon! Also, I am familiar with Miyelonian customs and I know a surefire way to show respect to your pride, no matter what I do with you. I just have to cut off your tail and stick it on my helmet!"

"You wouldn't dare!" the young pilot shrieked,

no longer hiding his fear but losing at least half his bombast.

"Oh I think you'll find I would... But You're right, I'd better have someone else do it! For example, my Gladiator," I said, pointing at the Dagestani athlete, who was playing with the blades he'd taken from Rikki, getting used to his new weapons. "But Imran doesn't really understand your traditions and doesn't know what part to take. So instead of your tail, he might snip off that little thing dangling between your legs..."

That threat was the final straw. Rikki went totally limp and mentally surrendered.

"I don't have enough money to give you back the two million crystals..." he began to whine pitifully.

I could easily check that, though. I nodded to Tini and my little thief unclipped the bags from the Miyelonian's sides, dumping the contents onto the hangar floor. Baubles, rags, some small electronic devices... Ah! A blue electronic crystal key on a chain, just like mine. I raised the captain's key and threw it to Dmitry Zheltov. The Starship Pilot easily caught the trophy and started twirling it around his finger.

"If you can't scare up the equivalent of two million crystals in any currency, I'll just have to take your interceptor!" I threatened.

Rikki twitched in the hands of the Geckho brothers and, much to my surprise, bared his teeth.

"You're lying! You'd never get my ship off the station! None of you have the skills, and no one would let you!"

The pirate captain really believed that I wouldn't be let out of the hangar. Strange. What could possibly stop me? Rikki managed to stump me, but just for a second. I figured it out and laughed:

"Do you think I'm so stupid that I wouldn't know to pay your docking fees before takeoff?! After that, I'd have you pilot the ship out for me..."

"Master Gnat, here's his wallet. And I've got something interesting!" Tini drew my attention and I lowered my gaze.

Oh! An artifact from the Relict base! The flat rune-covered ring-shaped disk was the perfect size for the slot in my Listener armor chest-piece.

Pyramid Signal Booster (Listener armor suit accessory).

+3% armor suit forcefield capacity per level.

+15% Scanning radius.

+70% more data transmitted to Pyramid.

Statistic requirements: Intelligence 26, Perception 26.

Skill requirements: Electronics 70, Mechanism Control 50.

Attention! Your character's Electronics skill is insufficient to equip this item.

Attention! This object is for the Relict race and cannot be used by Humans.

I don't know why I would want to increase the volume of data transmitted to this mysterious

"Pyramid," or what it even was, but just for a threefold increase (for now) in forcefield capacity, I needed to take this "Translator." Sure, my Electronics was not high enough, and the object was again race-locked, but the skill could be leveled, and I already knew it could be made suitable for human use.

The pirate captain's wallet was... not the same model as mine. More advanced, seemingly. I took the thin gray plastic rectangle from Tini's hands and tried to use it. It was no use, just a piece of smooth plastic. Rikki, watching me carefully, started grinning in satisfaction, entertained by my failure. Bad move! I met eyes with the smirking Miyelonian.

"That Human will never manage to activate my wallet. After all, he needs to enter a code right on the inactive surface, and he doesn't know it. I don't even remember it right every time. Good thing grandma sewed a secret hint on the inside of my bandanna. Then, you need to touch it to my left hand. He'll never figure it out... What?! Why is he taking my bandanna?! As long as he doesn't think to shine my flashlight at it."

Mental Fortitude skill increased to level fifty-one!
Mysticism skill increased to level twenty-four!

I took the bandanna off the Miyelonian, which was more like a little cap with ear holes. I looked it over carefully from all sides. A complex geometrical design was sewn in and some elements were in fact distantly reminiscent of Miyelonian numbers, but only that. Nothing concrete. I didn't find any hints.

"Tini, did he happen to have a flashlight?" I asked, and my kitten dug through the junk on the floor with his foot until he discovered a tiny flashlight the size of a AA-battery.

"But it doesn't work, piece of crap..." Tini said, smashing all the buttons. No light came out.

"Give it here!" It looked like a broken flashlight, but I nevertheless pointed it at the headband, thinking it might have an invisible beam.

Amazing! Some of the threads on the inside lit up, completing the geometric patterns and making a sensible construction of many inlaid and intersecting rectangles. Ugh, fu, an eleven-digit number! No wonder the captain couldn't memorize it. I traced the shape with my finger on the inactive wallet screen, but nothing changed. Then, I used the left hand of the immobilized Miyelonian and finally unlocked the tricky little device.

Electronics skill increased to level fifty-six!

It worked! So, what did I have here? A balance of thirty thousand two hundred four crypto... Hrm, a bit light for my taste. Still, not exactly nothing. It was ninety-two thousand in Geckho crystals, after all, which was a huge amount for my home faction. But it was also barely enough to pay the interceptor's docking fee. The pirate really did have cat shit for money. But maybe I could take what he owed some other way?

"Where are the remaining Relict artifacts you took from the Shiamiru? Answer!"

The broken pirate didn't hide it and replied that he had sold everything of value long ago to someone named Mava, a famous fence here on the Medu-Ro IV station.

"But only the Relict skull was of value, I got fifty thousand crypto for it. The rest was useless crap: bronze rings and weird disks, generally useless debris... Basically trash. Mava didn't even want to take it and paid scrap metal prices. And I kept that scratched-up stone ring for myself. Mava wasn't even offering a dime for it. I figured maybe I'd find a smart person who could read its properties one day."

"Well, today's your lucky day," I chuckled amiably, stashing the ancient artifact in my inventory. "But that ring is useful only for Listeners. It has no value for anyone else. Now tell me, where can I find this Mava?"

Tini jumped into our conversation and told me he knew, because he had unloaded stolen items there before. Alright, one less problem. I sighed and returned to the most important topic. How was this counterfeiting pirate going to get me back my two million crystals?

"I already told you I don't have the money!" Rikki snapped again.

Alright, he wasn't understanding the easy way. Well, I'd have to try the hard way.

"Dmitry, why don't you try and take his interceptor!" I turned to the Starship Pilot. "If it's on and you've got enough skills to pilot it out of the hangar, we can always unload it for a million and a half crypto..."

"Wait! Don't!" the pirate captain began to squeal in fear. "Alright, I'll pay. Give me back my communicator. I need to make a call..."

I set the multifunctional wallet back in his clawed hand. It was apparently both a communication device and a wallet. I told Basha and Vasha to let Rikki make the call. The huge Geckho brothers released their powerful grip and took a step back. But as soon as that rascally long-haired tomcat was able to move freely, he broke all of our understandings and tried to run!!!

Booonnnnnggg! Rikki wanted to use his fast jump skill to make a quick escape, but the heavy metal hangar door slammed shut right in his face! The Miyelonian was brought to a screeching halt and gained a deep impression from the sudden obstacle. Yikes... I winced in pain, because even from fifty feet I could clearly hear the snap of his breaking bones. Rikki now resembled a pedigreed Persian cat with his flat face.

Machine Control skill increased to level fifty-seven!

Electronics skill increased to level fifty-seven!

Psionic skill increased to level seventy!

Authority increased to 51!

The door really made an impact. A great one, even. Again, no one from my team managed to react, but I read the escape plan in Rikki's thoughts and had planned a countermeasure. And now, I saw unhidden delight in my crew's eyes. They all admired their captain and were proud to serve under me!

"Drag him here before he comes to!" I lifted the bolt gun from the floor and walked toward the runaway pirate, held tight in the arms of the Geckho brothers. "Alright, put him against the wall! Hold his head more evenly, otherwise the piercing is gonna come out sloppy!"

I looked the bolt gun over carefully and examined its various "ammo" options. In the end, I chose a clip of the bolts with the widest heads and stuck the rascally Miyelonian to the wall with four shots in his ears — two bolts per ear just to be safe.

"Vasha, Basha, let him go! Now he won't run anywhere." I turned around and tossed the bolt gun to Orun Va-Mart, who has watching the whole thing. The Engineer gracefully caught the tool and stuck it right into his inventory.

Rikki Pan-Miis gradually came to his senses, which I realized when I heard curses start pouring from his lips. And when the pirate had more or less focused on my silhouette, I turned to the injured long-haired loser:

"Hey, can you hear me? I see you can. Takeoff time is soon. So, it's up to you: either you pay me what I'm owed, or I'll take your interceptor and fly away!"

The Miyelonian tried to move his head and

winced in pain. After that, he took out his communicator, activated the screen and chose a contact. But before calling, he raised his bloodied face to me and demanded I walk ten steps away so I wouldn't overhear his very personal conversation.

"And why would I do that?" I asked, surprised at the pirate's gall. "I gave you a chance and you squandered it. No, you'll call like this!"

"Curse you, Gnat!" the pirate captain squeezed through his teeth, seething. But his brusque voice quickly changed to a high-pitched and friendly one. "Hi, grandma! It's Rikki. I'm glad you're in the game. I need money again. Can you give me a little loan? It won't be for long. Two hundred eighty-six thousand. Yes. I know. Come on, I'm doing fine. I just have to make some payments to my Pride. Oh, thanks! Love you, grandma! Alright, later!"

The captive pirate raised his eyes to me, and I could read fearsome simply burning rage mixed with extreme embarrassment. This bloodthirsty criminal, terror of the interstellar trade routes, was horribly ashamed that his dear old doting grandma was bailing him out. Seemingly, if not for his ears being stuck to the wall, Rikki would have fallen through the floor in disgrace.

An instant later, his communicator gave a peep, and another few seconds later, my wallet vibrated. Right on the nose. It was two hundred eighty-six thousand crypto, equivalent to two million Geckho crystals. My total balance now was four hundred twenty-nine thousand one hundred eleven crypto.

ATTENTION!!! Captain Rikki Pan-Miis's danger rating has fallen to zero.

Captain Rikki Pan-Miis is no longer a wanted pirate!

"You happy now, Gnat?" the Miyelonian asked me, exhausted and resigned.

"Yes, everything has been made right. Give him back the captain's key," I ordered Dmitry, and he placed the blue crystal in one of the pirate's pockets. "We got what we wanted, and now we're leaving."

We didn't unbolt him from the wall, though. First off, Rikki had made me mad with his pompous and audacious talk, so he hadn't earned any courtesy. Second, the starship was supposed to take off in a few minutes, so his crew would be arriving soon. I wanted them to free their captain from this sticky situation.

Funnily, we met two of them on our way to the elevator. It was the captain's girlfriend and that same nasty Supercargo, who spent so long hemming and hawing over my bag overage. They stared my group down, clearly having recognized me Tini and Ayni, but they didn't say anything. We didn't want to talk to them either, so we just went straight to the elevators. The long-haired tomcat in the blue and orange jumpsuit was walking with us and, seemingly, our new Engineer was very glad at the change in his fate.

We were standing next to a full-wall panoramic

window, waiting for the elevator when a portion of system messages jumped in:

ATTENTION!!! The Pride of the Bushy Shadow has declared you a personal enemy and set a bounty of three thousand crypto for the destruction of your starship.

ATTENTION!!! Captain Gerd Gnat is now a wanted space pirate!!! Danger rating: 1.

Fame increased to 63.

Chapter
Twenty-Six

Progress
Vector

MY CREW MEMBERS all sharply stopped and looked at me in surprise. They also must have gotten the system message about my change in status. After a prolonged pause, Princess Minn-O La-Fin spoke up:

"My husband, we are pirates now, yes? Did it go that poorly?"

Authority reduced to 50!
Authority reduced to 49!
Authority reduced to 48!

I could hear plain disappointment in my travelling wife's voice. And that was the least of it! For her, a Princess of an ancient ruling house, falling to the status of a criminal on a pirate ship was probably very unpleasant. Based on the drop in my reputation as a captain, the other crew members were also upset by the change. I had no way to object. I didn't even know what this meant for the near-term and especially distant future. Would traders talk to me outside of pirate stations now? What about prominent players like Kung Waid Shishish or Leng Amiru U-Mayaoo? Was I an outcast and a criminal?

Uline was more knowledgeable here, so she commented, not hiding her dismay:

"Not good... Now everyone will see the status of our captain and his starship. Our frigate might not be allowed to some stations and planets now. But that isn't our main concern. We need to figure out where to go from here, because it is too dangerous to stay on Medu-Ro IV! I already saw what happens to an enemy of a pride. Uraz Tukhsh found himself in a similar kerfuffle once and nothing good came of that!"

"Wait, wait! Drop the panic!" I ordered my business partner, who tended to overdramatize. At the same time, I tried to raise the spirits of my now downtrodden crew. "Based on the tiny bounty, this was purely Captain Rikki's doing. As far as I remember, he would have had around three thousand crypto after paying his docking fees. Seemingly, he spent all that money to cause problems for us. From what I could tell, the Pride of the Bushy Shadow's main forces are now on a big hunt very far from this station."

"How far?" Uline Tar immediately clarified, and I was forced to admit I did not know.

"I was not able to read a precise time of return in Rikki's thoughts, but he was not expecting them back any time soon. I think we must have at least two days in local reckoning. I suggest we spend that time intelligently, get the money we came here for, purchase everything we need, do a quick repair and slip off Medu-Ro IV before the Pride of the Bushy Shadow gets back home."

"A day and a half and not half an ummi more! Then we fly as far away as possible!" my business partner made a counteroffer.

I didn't argue about such minor issues and agreed. I set a timer right away, so I could always see how long I had left. Now I needed to think through what to do next, given the severe time-crunch. After all, a day and a half was a miniscule amount of time. We had to get money, make purchases, then complete a full repair, and even modernization of our frigate, and that was just not going to happen. We would have to sacrifice something and put it off for later. Now, we would only have time for the bare minimum.

The elevator had arrived, but I didn't go inside. I asked Imran to hold the door

Maybe I was not the most righteous man, but it was not in my nature to present the left cheek after being struck on the right. To be more honest, it was not in my nature to even begin trading blows. I always tried to get the jump on an opponent, hit first and do as much damage as possible. I would even throw sucker punches to make sure they would never want to tangle with me again. And I felt the same now. I was in no mood to forgive the Pride of the Bushy Shadow for their aggression or pretend that nothing happened.

"Minn-O, you're a Cartographer by class. You have the largest draw distance on your mini-map. Can you see how many pirates there are in the hangar? Given their pride is now hostile to us, maybe we should pay them another courtesy call to explain their mistake. If we can steal their interceptor, let's take it. If not, let's blow it to smithereens!"

The suggestion was accepted with great enthusiasm by the team. I could see Vasha and Basha bearing their teeth in satisfaction, while Imran and Tini exchanged glances and drew their blades. Minn-O froze for a few seconds just staring into nothingness, seemingly moving her mini-map around and adjusting the scale, trying to find the right area. Then she said we were too late:

"They already left. The pirate interceptor just left the docking bay."

Everyone sighed in disappointment. Too bad... Although maybe it was for the best. Breaking in and starting a fire-fight with a heavily armed pirate crew would be "trading blows," and that was exactly what I wanted to avoid. There would be losses on both sides, and it was nowhere near guaranteed that my team would come out on top. I needed to try something else, not so crude and straightforward. I dwelt on it for a moment, and my soldiers had already restored their self-confidence and were now waiting patiently for their commander's decision.

"Alright, let's split up!" I started telling them my new plan, trying to be as clear and confident as possible. "Ayni and Uline, go to the registration desk and finish drawing up documents for our crew. Imran go with them as a guard. Ayni, I want you to do two other things as well. One: figure out if there are other starships belonging to the Pride of the Bushy Shadow at the station. Two: change our docking bay in the database. Instead of hangar 16-4, put in something else, maybe an empty one. Wait... I just got a great idea!!! There are probably starships of rich space merchants at the station or even army ships with serious protection. So pick one in the database, rename its owner to Gnat and change the ship to a Tolili-Ukh X-class frigate. Now that'll be a surprise for the Pride of the Bushy Shadow if they decide to try and break into our hangar!"

Seemingly, the fluffy orange lady cat wanted to object but, in the end, Ayni said she would do as I ordered. Now, it was Uline's turn. I was reminded that the Trader once said I could send money to my home planet. And seemingly, the time had come to perform the miracle my faction had asked for. If a million crystals suddenly fell from space unexpected and undreamt of, that would count as a miracle. Well maybe a bit less than that because of transfer fees but, in any case, it would be a colossal and very timely cash injection!

Sure, I understood that we could buy much more at Medu-Ro IV than my allies could in the space port on the wild outskirts of the known galaxy, where all prices for imports were jacked up at least three times. But first of all, as in the Russian saying, a spoon is dear when lunchtime is near. What was the use of a deadly arsenal if my frigate was late to the war with the Dark Faction? After all, that was what everything was leading to. We would never make it to the beginning of the conflict and risked arriving to smoking ruins if the battle went unfavorably. Second, they didn't only need money to buy weapons. They had to pay hundreds of NPC Centaurs and Minotaurs, and they could trade with the H6 Faction for goods and services or just rent the Geckho ferry... all that took money, and quite a bit of it. And well, third, I was going to send only one of the two million. I would be using the second to buy things here where prices were far lower, and much more was available.

I explained the mission to Uline and asked her to work out all the details of the transfer — specific timeframes, transfer fees and all the rest. The Trader immediately turned serious and asked me where I wanted all this money to go. The trade terminal in the Geckho space port? It was possible the terminal wouldn't have enough crystals, but it was the easiest and most confidential option. Or did they need to be handed off to someone in particular? In that case of course, it would end up costing more.

Here I considered it. As far as I knew, we hadn't figured out how our secret information was leaking to the Dark Faction yet. And so, it would be very annoying if we had a repeat of last time, and the crystals from the spaceport vending machine got stolen by one of them. It was of course a shame to pay extra but, in this situation, reliability and fast delivery were the most important factors. The Human-3 Faction needed to receive the money, which would still be a lot, and it needed to be as fast as possible. And most importantly, it had to be before the end of the ceasefire with the Dark Faction so they could use it to buy weaponry and defensive reinforcements.

So I chose the person-to-person option. I even suggested my companion try and make the transfer through the official Geckho diplomat Kosta Dykhsh. Of course, the furball would not refuse a little side hustle. Sure, some of the million might get lost to his sticky fingers, but it was the most reliable method I could think up. Uline promised to find that information for me and tell me when I could make the transfer.

"Great! All three of you wait for me right next to the registration desk. I'll show the Engineer to the starship, ask his professional opinion about upgrading the ship, draw up a purchase list and come see you."

I COULD HEAR frustration and even offense in Eduard Boyko's voice:

"How could you go fight pirates without me?! I'm practically the only combat character in the whole crew, and you left me on the back line. I didn't even get to shoot! That just isn't right!"

I fully understood Eduard's disappointment. He'd missed out on something interesting. But I was not going to explain myself to an underling, and I was especially not going to justify myself. I acted the way I thought was most expedient given our time limit. And entertaining my crew was my very lowest priority. Now I also had more important business than reassuring a frustrated soldier. I needed to determine what I wanted to do with my modular frigate as soon as possible so the Engineer could calculate its dimensions and mass. From there he could determine how big a power unit we would need, and parameters for all thrusters. He could only provide a full purchase list after that.

"We also need a spacious cargo hold, big enough to fit an automated mineral extraction plant and at least one automatic loader, better two. Beyond that, the starship must be able to land not only on asteroids with practically zero gravity but also on fairly massive planets with dense atmosphere. And naturally, it must be able to take off from such planets as well..."

Orun Va-Mart stopped jotting in his palmtop and clarified the mass of the planets I had in mind and how dense I was expecting the atmosphere to be.

"1 G gravitation, and a surface air pressure of approximately one hundred thousand Pascals, air density of twenty-nine on the hydrogen scale," I said, giving the parameters of my native Earth, hoping very much that the game would translate all the units into something the Miyelonian could understand.

And the Engineer didn't have any questions. He next asked what I had in mind in terms of configuration and purpose.

"The frigate must have some kind of weaponry, so we can scare off the odd pirate interceptor. Beyond that, it would be desirable to be able to fire from orbit at terrestrial targets on planets like I just described."

The Engineer took that down, gave a doubtful frown, made some calculations and asked if I needed to be able to jam electronics and thrusters on other starships.

"For what?" I didn't understand, and Orun Va-Mart patiently explained that I was describing a typical pirate frigate-raider, made for attacking colonies of mineral miners on asteroids and poorly defended settlements of outworlders on inhabitable planets. All that remained was an expanded hold for a boarding-landing team, a turret homing system, and a unit for jamming electronics and thrusters.

"All common pirate configurations of the Tolili-Ukh X modular frigate are well established," the Engineer continued to harangue me, showing me his tablet screen. "Here's the 'Pack Hunter' configuration for working in a team. Here's the 'Lone Raider' with increased armor and reinforced weaponry. Here's the 'Cloaked Pirate,' which stays hidden with an invisibility shield."

As he said that, Orun Va-Mart had no doubt what his captain was intending to use the frigate for. I was even somewhat embarrassed, because I didn't have anything criminal in mind. But without serious mind control, I would seemingly not be able to convince my new crew member otherwise. I didn't try and prove anything, just familiarized myself with the options. After closely studying the most balanced configurations, I decided to take the "Lone Raider" as a basis, but make a few changes:

"I really need good scanning equipment, because my plan is to search for valuable minerals. As for an electronic jamming system and improved weaponry, I'm not sure... but let's keep it. I'm not planning to hunt trading ships, but we might have dangerous encounters with enemies in space. In that case, we need to be able to hold our own then stop any wounded birds from getting away. But as for the expanded boarding party module, I don't see any need. Better to increase the volume of the cargo hold and put on extra weaponry."

"Understood, Gerd Captain," said the Engineer very quickly and professionally, clearly having great experience with such matters. He made the adjustments to the design and started a program to calculate whether it was all compatible. "Buh... Gerd Captain, we can assemble such a ship, but it will all hinge on a good power unit. At the very least we need it to be able to generate two thousand one hundred units, and better two and a half thousand. And now," here the Miyelonian winced and bared his tiny little teeth, showing disapproval of the low-quality crap on my frigate, "we've got just seven hundred and eleven units. I don't even know what scrapheap you managed to find this old shit on."

"First of all, we need a good power unit," I noted to myself, and the Engineer readily confirmed:

"Exactly! That is the very first step. Without that we can't change the thrusters or install energy-hungry combat turrets or even stabilizer cowling for atmospheric flight. Gerd Captain, two thousand one hundred units is the bare minimum. Without that, the frigate simply will not turn on. And it would be nice to take a bit more power so we have some room to play with more weight. I'd like two and a half or even three thousand units, but then the price starts growing exponentially... Overall, Gerd Captain, look over the financial data yourself."

I told him I understood. At the same time I asked the Miyelonian Engineer what could be ordered right now and installed relatively quickly, because we would need to leave the station in a day and a half.

"Buh... We can order everything on my list right now. We can get it delivered to a more peaceable station. But as for what we can do fast... turrets will be the quickest. But before that, we need stabilizers... maybe the hyper?"

I immediately suggested the Engineer look up a new hyperdrive, because the one we had now was utter trash. The repairmen on the Geckho base never tired of telling me so.

"That is true," the fuzzy Engineer confirmed, spitting in disgust. "I was just too embarrassed to tell you, Gerd Captain. But zero point eight three hyperjump distance is basically nothing. Basically no one has used ones lower than one point five for a hundred tongs. The stations are arranged based on that as the base hyperjump distance. If you order a new hyperdrive, better look for one of Meleyephatian assembly so we don't have to waste time with converters and transformers. But that isn't such a big deal. Overall, order a new power unit and hyper, I'll take these ones off and get all the inputs ready. When they give me the new equipment, I'll need half an ummi to install them, then we can finally get off this station. I'm so sick of it!"

Chapter Twenty-Seven

Enemy of an Enemy

"**N**EXT WE'LL WALK into a huge hall of statues, fountains with pink water and other fantastic sights. This is the pickpockets' favorite place. They love to prey on gaping tourists," I said, pointing to Tini and my ward confirmed with a satisfied toothy smirk. "So don't go flapping your jaws in there. Watch your bags and make sure you don't fall behind! We'll walk straight through without stopping, turn right down a hallway and, without wasting time, go straight into the casino."

"The casino?!" Eduard couldn't hold back a surprised exclamation. "But Gnat, I thought we were here on business..."

I just gritted my teeth, hiding my annoyance. For the tenth time in this short journey, I was regretting trading out the taciturn Imran for Eduard Boyko. Our Space Commando couldn't hide his astonishment and elation when seeing the wonders of the space station, and just commented on everything he saw like a Central Asian aqyn singer. But worse than that, he was constantly making remarks and giving advice. Still, I had to answer:

"Well, we are going to the casino on business. I'm meeting with the owner, the head of the Pride of the Agile Paw. Actually, that's what brought us to the pirate station in the first place."

Then I fell silent because the doors slid aside, revealing the wonder I had just described. The far walls of the huge bright room were washed out and lost in the light fog and smoke. There were colorful bright lamps, innumerable statues and musical fountains. And among all that walked hordes of interplanetary beings of the most unbelievable shape and coloring. There was plenty here to make a visitor gape and drop their guard.

Eagle Eye skill increased to level seventy!

Tini, seeing two Miyelonians walk up to us who were seemingly having a peaceful conversation, hissed like a cat and his hair stood on end, making him look twice as big. After all, it was an odd couple if I considered it. There were no names nor professions over them, and they didn't much look like space voyagers or tourists. The Miyelonians, without saying a word, walked away from us and moved toward a Trillian merchant crawling along unhurriedly and taking pictures.

"Former pridemates," the kitten commented. "I used to be in the same pickpocketing group. Gerd Gnat, I just realized... might it not be worth calling your protectors? I'm sure that one word from Leng Amiru U-Mayaoo would be enough for the Pride of the Bushy Shadow to apologize to you and call off the bounty!"

I gave my kitten an affectionate scratch on his furry head and answered that I was grateful for his advice and would definitely use it eventually, but I didn't yet see a good reason to bother such an influential Miyelonian. To myself, I thought that I really didn't want to end up owing the Great Priestess or any other similarly influential Miyelonians and that asking for help would imply that, one day, they could ask me to perform a favor in return.

We passed through the great hall without incident and soon found ourselves standing before the casino. As usual, there was a group of sharps standing near the entrance. I pointed them out to my friends:

"I won't tell you not to do any gambling. You're not little, and I'm not your nanny. But let me warn you right away: it's nearly guaranteed that you'll lose to those guys if you sit at a gaming table."

Psionic skill increased to level seventy-one!

Mental Fortitude skill increased to level fifty-two!

"I didn't want to that bad anyway…" Eduard muttered, looking cautiously over the local swindlers.

The other crew members said similar things. They'd only come to the casino to accompany their captain, and they weren't going to risk their money. Now that was great! Just what I wanted. I had enough concerns without having to drag an immiserated crew member out of the casino.

"Let's go inside!" I ordered and, in a dense group, we walked through the doors as they slid welcomingly aside.

As with all my past visits, my nose was immediately struck with a tenacious intoxicating aroma of incense. My eyes rippled with the flickering colorful bulbs, and my ears were overwhelmed by the constant racket. Probably, the greatest designers, psychologists and gambling specialists in the Galaxy had come together to create the atmosphere in this cosmic casino. After all, slight disorientation, a sense of recklessness, relaxation and foolish happiness were inspired in visitors of every race. I could see the Geckho bearing their teeth and rumbling in my squadron. Ayni's eyes went narrow, and stupid blissful smiles came over Minn-O and Eduard's faces.

Mental Fortitude skill increased to level fifty-three!

Was that right? Was this some kind of hypnosis or mind control? Or was it my psionic defenses reacting to the atmosphere in the casino? In any case, I tried to shake it off and concentrate. But I didn't manage to even come to my senses before a group of heavily armed security pointed me to a free Na-Tikh-U table:

"Gerd Gnat, please come with us. Our boss has been expecting you for some time."

Well, well! Although, if I considered it, what was so surprising? The owner of the local casino had probably been alerted by the Great Priestess and was expecting me. It was hard to imagine better cover for exchanging a valuable trophy for cash than an opaque gaming dome. Alright then, why not? More with gestures than voice, I pointed my companions at a free table on the second floor of the stands, then to the bar and swarm of Miyelonian bartenders:

"You're adults, you can decide for yourselves. Ayni, translate if anyone has any questions. I just want to warn you, Tini. Last time, you made a pig of yourself, drinking yourself unconscious. Try and keep it a little more under control this time!"

My crew knew what I wanted of them, so I followed the guards and took a seat right on the floor next to a small round table. Opposite me, there were already a few tall stacks of chips for my opponent. I tried to estimate how much was riding on this... uhh... those four black ones were a thousand, those were three, those were five hundred... Sixty thousand crypto?! A bit steep... I mean, that was four hundred twenty thousand Geckho crystals! And I had no doubt that these chips were not some mere window-dressing for a business meeting. This was a wager I was expected to match. Seemingly nettled by her earlier vexing loss, the casino owner had decided to have a rematch for the same amount as we played for before.

And here she was now, the head of the Pride of the Agile Paw! Accompanied by a group of attentive security, the short Miyelonian lady came down to the gaming floor draped head to toe in a free-flowing white gown. This time, the emerald green eyes of the pride leader were hidden behind a mirrored mask. She had learned her lesson last time. She was afraid of me...

The lady cat waved her hand demandingly, and her high-level soldiers hurried to leave us alone. A second later, an opalescent forcefield appeared over us, scrambling the beams of light and trapping in all sound.

"Well, Gerd Gnat, let's pick up where we left off. This time you go first," my opponent said, sitting on the floor opposite me and starting up the random board generator as if our last round had just finished and the week and a half since then had simply not happened.

Taking advantage of the opportunity, I activated Scanning to learn more about my gaming partner.

Miyelonian Female. Level-178 Swindler.

One hundred seventy-eight! That inspired a certain respect. I also immediately realized why the pregnant Miyelonian was hiding her class. Anyone sitting down to play her would instantly be put on guard by her profession. And my opponent's tummy had grown noticeably over the last week and a half. If I wanted, I could probably have told the sex of her two future children. But I of course did not do that, remembering the Miyelonian superstition that knowing would invite tragedy.

"I know perfectly well why you are here..." the pride leader broke the silence, at the same time arranging her pieces on the three-dimensional holographic field.

I breathed a sigh of relief. All the better! I had already started forming the impression that a revenge match was my opponent's only goal here. What could I say? As the Miyelonian knew, I didn't pussyfoot around so I set the pure white fluffy tail on the table before me. However, she sharply jerked up and started shrieking in fear, so I quickly concluded the casino owner was caught completely off guard by the dangerous and rare trophy:

"Where'd you get THAT???"

Danger Sense skill increased to level forty-five!

My heart was pierced with a presentiment of disaster. I noticed her right hand slowly but surely crawling under her clothes, most likely reaching for a weapon. I had to explain double time before this turned into a big misunderstanding:

"I managed to get my hands on the Great Priestess's tail, which the Morphian killer removed. I got right in touch with Leng Amiru U-Mayaoo and she suggested I return it to her for a reward of a million crypto. But she asked me to be secretive and to go through a trusted broker. Among them she named you, the head of the Pride of the Agile Paw. Actually, that was the main reason I came to the Medu-Ro IV station."

The sense of danger immediately dissipated. She took her hand away from her bosom and spent a long time looking at the white fur shimmering in the light of the forcefield. Finally, the head of the Pride of the Agile Paw broke the silence and commented:

"Yes, I do know the incarnation of the Great First Female. Leng Amiru U-Mayaoo blessed my future children when she visited Medu-Ro IV. But to me, it is the greatest possible surprise that she considers me, the leader of a pride of swindlers and cheats, a 'trusted broker.' I have to admit, I am very flattered and will try to live up to the trust she put in me. Gerd Gnat, I of course will carry out the Great Priestess's request and compensate your labor."

Authority increased to 49!

The pure white tail disappeared from the table, and it was so instantaneous that even with my high Perception, I could only see a fleeting movement of the Miyelonian's paw, barely detectable by the naked eye. My wallet vibrated, and I looked at the incoming message. A deposit of one million crypto!!! Finally! How long I had been waiting for this moment! I was ready to jump and laugh for joy, but my opponent's cold and rational voice jerked me back to reality:

"Gerd Gnat, your turn. I'll admit, I didn't know

why you came to visit me. I figured you had come for protection and the tokens I had on the table were my price. Now I know that isn't so but, once a match has begun, it must be finished. Those are the rules. You'll have our protection in any case, but if you can beat me, it will be free of charge."

I gave a showy laugh, revealing my feelings:

"You think I can defeat a professional gambler who is one hundred and six levels higher than me and whose fingers are laden with Intelligence rings? You're either trying to flatter me or lying! By the way, I recognize that ring! Intelligence +3. The Trillian merchant Ussh-Veesh promised to hold onto it for me. I guess he didn't keep his word..."

The Miyelonian ignored what I said about her level and furrowed her brow unhappily:

"Gerd Gnat, don't make false accusations of an honorable Trader! I never could have bought this rare ring no matter how I tried to convince Gerd Ussh-Veesh. I had to beg him to use it for just one game."

So, my opponent was that seriously prepared for this? I guess her loss really stung! I quickly realized how senseless it was to keep arguing with the casino owner and started the game, making a roll and beginning to move my starships along the three-dimensional board. Now while playing, I asked her who she thought I needed protection from. The pirates of the Pride of the Bushy Shadow?

"Who else?" the Miyelonian snorted in surprise.

"Just about every interested party here on Medu-Ro IV knows about your conflict now."

"Come on, what conflict?" I waved it off, as if it was pure nonsense. "It's just that young Captain Rikki slipped me some counterfeit crystals instead of paying fairly. And I flew here to demand he make me whole. And that is basically it..."

"Come now, Gerd Gnat. There's no sense in trying to play clever!" she reproached, shaking her head as she skillfully cut off my front row of ships, dooming them to quick destruction. "The status of 'dangerous pirate' doesn't just fall on your head. It's pretty hard to come by. As far as I know, you've got to capture and rob at least two starships, then players the pirate has wronged can set a bounty on them. What, Gerd Gnat, are you saying you haven't done that?"

Capture two starships? When had I done that??? Unless the game algorithms considered that space battle when I had the Morphian's help and sort of hijacked Rikki's interceptor. It may have been counting when we took the Meleyephatian frigate off the planetoid, too. It also may have taken into account the fact that the same interceptor was initially going to Uraz Tukhsh after the battle, but then I pinched it. Could that really be? Or was it considering the recent high-speed spat in the hangar, when I took the starship keys from the pirate captain and technically very briefly captured his ship? There were plenty of options that somehow fit the bill. You might say it wasn't just two,

383

but three or maybe even four instances of "piracy." But nevertheless, it wasn't fair to make an honest person a wanted criminal for such minor incidents!

Nevertheless, I had to admit that I had captured at least two starships and maybe even more. Although in any case, they had all been coincidental. I never wanted to become a pirate! The Miyelonian found my answer funny:

"So you accidentally stole a starship... and two times... or even three... and maybe four. It isn't every day you hear of such things! Although, strange as it sounds, I believe you, human! Do you think I dreamed of becoming a swindler and professional gambler my whole life? You won't believe it, but I used to be a law-abiding citizen! I dreamed of building open-work skyscrapers, unimaginable arches and bridges, which would simply hover over an abyss! But one day I had to smack down some jerk, then I had to teach a jackass a lesson... I didn't even notice when I became a swindler... it was also an accident."

I managed to pull off a great tactical combo in the game, driving her heavy fleet into a minefield and seriously damaging it. The owner of the space casino even spoke approvingly of my abilities:

"You're doing great, Gerd Gnat! You're already doing incomparably better than last time. With twenty-five or thirty years of constant training, you might even be able to beat me once and a while. But not today!"

In just two moves, my defenses were broken. My

success with the mine field was just a distraction, which allowed my opponent to draw my forces away from the real breakthrough point and win. Hrm... Being able to play even half that well would take lots of work.

"You owe me sixty-thousand crypto," the pride leader reminded me, stretching out her sore back and arms. "By the way, Gerd Gnat, I'd like to give you the chance to earn that back, maybe even more. Interested?"

Losing sixty thousand crypto had me very upset, although I was trying not to show it. However, I was very interested in getting my money back. The Miyelonian first checked to see I had given her all the money, then continued:

"Owning a space station casino is of course nice. It gives a stable income. But it isn't enough. Me and my Pride of the Agile Paw need to grow. Gerd Gnat, you must already know that I have a certain interest in the rare metal business. I already have fast ships and experienced captains. But unfortunately that sphere is already occupied by the Pride of the Bushy Shadow, and it will be very difficult to edge them out. I do not desire a direct conflict with hardened pirates, but I see an easy chance to weaken a competitor. I just couldn't figure out how to take it! And then, you came along, a Free Captain with the same enemy. And an enemy of an enemy is basically a friend, don't you think?"

I also found the alliance beneficial but asked the leader of the pride to tell me what she wanted directly.

"You probably already know, Gerd Gnat, that the main forces of the Pride of the Bushy Shadow are not on Medu-Ro IV right now. They aren't even in this system. I do not have all the information, but my informants have told me they're on a 'great hunt' for a cargo ship transporting ore from a gold mine. The Pride of the Bushy Shadow has no more than fifteen soldiers on the station, and they're all busy guarding their valuable bullion stores. My pride has the forces to deal with them, but the problem is that the guardsmen are locked inside the vault and will not open the door. And that's where you come in!"

"You want me to open the armored door? But couldn't any high-level Thief handle that better than me?" I didn't understand.

"They'd notice and kill a thief, but you could make them open the door!" the high-level Swindler continued. "Just walk openly into their defended corridor and say you want to have a talk with 'someone important.' Tell them you want to make peace with the Pride of the Bushy Shadow and that you are willing to compensate them to be removed from their enemy list. Every member of the Pride of the Bushy Shadow probably already knows about your conflict, so they won't be surprised."

Hmm... For now, it all looked plausible. In the guards' place, I would not be surprised to see Gnat. After all, no one wants to be enemy of a whole pirate pride, so it would seem natural that I wanted to just pay them off and be done with it. The Miyelonian continued:

"The guards do not actually have the authority to add or remove someone from the pride enemy list, but they will probably figure you're some naïve rich guy they can rob, so they'll try that. They'll start suggesting you send them various amounts of crypto 'as compensation.' But you refuse and insist you only have Geckho crystals. That is how you get the guards to open the door. The guards will be convinced you aren't a threat, and greed will probably win the day. As soon as the doors open, your job is over. From there, my cloaked soldiers will sneak in and block the armored door, then my assault troops will storm the vault and do all the dirty work."

Danger Sense skill increased to level forty-six!

I thoughtfully led my gaze over the system message. Even without that, I already knew perfectly well that I was being offered the role of scapegoat, and all the anger of the enraged pirate pride would be coming down on my head. Most likely, after all, every Pride of the Agile Paw soldier would try not to identify themselves. The only reliably identifiable figure would be me, so they'd be coming after me to get their money back. Not good...

However, I wasn't one to turn down a profitable venture just because of a little danger. First of all, I asked her to tell me what I stood to gain for becoming target number one of a dangerous pirate pride.

"One hundred thousand crypto now as a down payment, then you can take everything you can carry from the vault! Well, and my pride will defend you from the Pride of the Bushy Shadow on Medu-Ro IV for let's say... three days. My guys will look like simple mercenaries, who you paid with the money you took from the vault, so the Pride of the Agile Paw's participation will go unnoticed."

Wow, she actually thought I was that big of an idiot. Who would accept such an offer? What was one hundred thousand cryptos to me, compared to the million and change I already had in my wallet? A practically unnoticeable blip. But it would cause so many troubles my life would turn to hell. And really how much could I carry? Gnat's maximum carrying capacity before movement speed penalties set in was sixty-two pounds, of which twenty-two were already occupied by armor and weapons. But even if I came naked, sixty-two pounds of platinum... I took out a calculator... was sixty thousand crypto, exactly how much the Pride leader had just taken from me for "protection." Come on, she could not be serious!

But as always there was a kernel of rationality. Serious adjustments would have to be made to the conditions, though. For example, the valuable loot from the vault would have to be taken by one of the twin Geckho brothers Vasha or Basha, maybe even both of them. In exoskeleton armor, each of the loaders could carry six hundred sixty pounds, and that was a different story. That would be enough money to justify the risk. And then, in a day and a half, I was going to leave the station in my improved starship, so they'd be going on a wild goose-chase!

Yes, there was a certain risk. Captain Rikki Pan-Miis from the Pride of the Bushy Shadow knew where my faction was located. But I somehow doubted that the pirates would risk sneaking into the Geckho's exclusive economic zone to demand my faction return stolen metal. Heavy ships could not get in unnoticed, and cloakers or nimble interceptors... I imagined Ivan Lozovsky or any of the Legion leaders reacting to the pirates' demands and smiled. I'd like to see them try! In that case, my faction would get its own cloakers or interceptors.

"A million crypto advance," I forwarded a counteroffer. "Don't worry, I won't just fly off with your money, because my starship currently has its thrusters and power unit removed, you can check. Beyond that, I will not go into the vault alone. It would look too suspicious to see a wanted captain wandering around this dangerous station without even a couple bodyguards. I wouldn't believe it. So I'll bring three soldiers and we take from the vault as much as the four of us can carry. And finally, three days of protection, but not only from the Pride of the Bushy Shadow. You will protect me against any potential enemies on Medu-Ro IV. Otherwise, what's to stop the Pride of the Bushy Shadow from paying some mercenaries to take me out?"

Now it was her turn to think. The leader of the Pride of the Agile Paw then, tired of sitting, gave an ailing meow and laid face up on the floor. Clearly, the pregnant Miyelonian lady's back was aching. I patiently waited in silence, trying not to break the casino owner's train of thought. And my patience was rewarded. The lady cat braced herself with her paws, sat up heavily and suddenly removed her mask. At the same time, a name lit up above her head:

Gerd Myaur-Za Vka. Miyelonian Female. Pride of the Agile Paw. Level-178 Swindler.

"Alright, Gerd Gnat, I agree to your conditions! In fact, I am impressed by your offer. It shows that you are aware of danger, account for risks and approach business with a cool head. I am very glad I found such a qualified man for the task and I hope we can work together for a long time. I reveal my name to very few, but you have certainly earned the honor!"

Authority increased to 50!

You have reached level seventy-three!

You have received three skill points! (total points accumulated: nine)

"Now wait. My soldiers need to get ready. The operation will begin in half an ummi. And, if you'd be so kind, please take this ancient signet back to the merchant Ussh-Veesh on the third floor of the visitor stands. It's hard for me to walk up the steep stairs with this big belly."

Chapter
Twenty-Eight

Possible
Earnings

ITHOUT a professional Engineer, I could not navigate the innumerable models of thrusters and power units offered in the catalogue. So I sent Tini to go get our new crew member and bring him to the casino. And I spent over an hour in an isolated VIP box alone with Orun Va-Mart looking at screen after screen of parts.

Uline Tar first insisted she be personally present at every purchase given the extreme amounts of money. But she quickly realized it made no sense because she didn't understand a word of Miyelonian, so she had no basis to judge other than the picture. At first I tried to translate for her, but I didn't know enough of the outlines or phonics of the narrowly specialized technical terms in either Geckho or Miyelonian. And Uline refused to bring in our professional Translator, not wanting to reveal financial secrets to Ayni. So she just opted to leave the VIP box and join the other crew members relaxing in the casino.

"This power unit is not a bad option," Orun Va-Mart poked a claw into one of the items. "The manufacturer is a Cleopian company that makes quality off-brand ship parts. It has Meleyephatian inputs, and it gives two thousand seven hundred units of power. It isn't new, to be fair, and doesn't come with a guarantee. The serial number has also been wiped. Most likely some pirates took it off a broken ship. But at just two hundred forty-five thousand crypto, it's a real bargain. Suspiciously cheap even..."

"If it makes you suspicious, we better not risk it," I said, not wanting to buy some pig in a poke with no guarantee. "I'm okay with a slightly more expensive power unit, if we can count on it. How much would the same one cost new and with a guarantee?"

The Engineer flipped through another few pages and pointed at the screen:

"Here's a new one, fresh off a Meleyephatian production line. It comes with a five-tong guarantee. And it's in stock here on Medu-Ro IV. But the price stings: eight hundred eighty-eight thousand crypto."

I couldn't hold back an explicit outburst. Almost

nine hundred thousand crypto! That was six and a quarter million Geckho crystals! Those prices were some hot bullshit! That would nearly clean me out, especially after buying a good hyperdrive for a million crypto. To be honest, Uline had managed to finagle a seven-percent discount, but the purchase still ate up a good chunk of our overall budget.

The starship of my dreams would have cost an extreme amount, and I was not mentally prepared to spend that much. We'd nearly blown through our whole budget and the million crypto advance, and that was before we got aerodynamic stabilizer wings, maneuver thrusters or an expanded cargo hold, which was to say nothing of weaponry!

"But this is two hundred units of output higher than the models we were looking at before. And two hundred units means two more laser turrets, and a good combat tracking computer, plus the quality near-space scanners as you wanted. It'll be expensive, yes. But just imagine how your Authority will grow among the local pirates when the Free Captains find out that Gerd Gnat's ship is top of the line!"

A dubious argument, to put it lightly. I would have preferred the local pirates not to know such intimate details about my frigate. Ideally, no one would even notice my ship. I looked at the time. Damn! The secret operation to break into the enemy pride's vault was near, and the Engineer and I were still just fussing around, unable to choose a power unit. Then we'd need to wait for it to be delivered, and next we'd have to install and calibrate the thing, which would take a whole bunch of time... With a heavy sigh, I made up my mind:

"Alright, let's go with that one. Then I'll call Uline here. Have her talk with the seller and try to work out a discount with her trading skills."

I stood from the bench and skillfully tossed an empty disposable glass of light alcoholic cocktail into the incinerator, then I turned off the forcefield dividing this small box from the stands. I wanted to go find my business partner, but I didn't have to go far. Uline Tar was standing a couple steps away, and she was not alone. In fact, she was talking to two Humans I'd met before and immediately recognized:

Denni Marko. Human. Gilvar Syndicate Faction. Level-90 Bodyguard.

Valeri-Urla. Human. Tailax Faction. Level-97 Beast Master.

Here she was, the mysterious alien girl with eyes too big for a normal human! I'd only ever seen such disproportionally big peepers before in Japanese anime. In person, her eyes looked very unusual, though I won't hide that I found her attractive. And next to her was her burly muscular companion who I had a little brush with last time.

On my previous visit to Medu-Ro IV, I was not able to have a normal conversation with these mysterious people. But they intrigued me, because they were clearly not from my Earth, but also not members of the Dark Faction. I just bandied a couple sentences back and forth with them, then a First Pride convoy took me to the Truth Seekers for an interrogation. Back then, I was being charged with murdering the Great Priestess of the Miyelonians, and the situation was not favorable for conversation.

"Here, Gerd Gnat," Uline pointed at the two Humans with a wide wave of her furry paw. "These people saw our vacancy advertisements and would like to join our crew! And I actually know them somewhat. They took a few voyages on the Shiamiru with Captain Uraz Tukhsh. Denni Marko is a pretty good shot with ship cannons and wants to be our Gunner. And he asks his companion be given some other role. He says he won't go without her. They say they've already been to the docks, but the address in the ad led to an empty hangar... well you remember, Captain Gnat. You asked for me to do that..."

Authority reduced to 49!

"No. No want now. Not to know pirate is captain. We not be pirate," the Bodyguard interrupted my companion with his clumsy but comprehensible Geckho, then decisively turned and prepared to leave.

"Wait, Denni!" the dark-haired big-eyed girl stopped her companion. "I don't want to join a pirate crew any more than you. But we can't just hang around here on the station! How much longer can we wait? With my profession of taming little animals, it's very hard to get a contract. But at least you'll have decent work!"

Denni Marko stopped, considered it for a second, but then shook his head with determination:

"No! Am no pirate! Period!" with these words, the muscular Bodyguard rudely pushed aside Eduard Boyko, who was carrying two glasses. When a bit of the Space Commando's drink spilled, Denni muttered something indecipherable but gruff then headed to the stairs down from the stands. He didn't appear even slightly concerned with whether Valeri-Urla was with him.

Valeri then turned to me and we met eyes in passing. After that, she lowered her gaze to the floor, nervously drumming her fingers on a carved green pendant around her neck. And she said with a slightly embarrassed smile, as if apologizing for her companion's brash manner:

"Denni is just stubborn. And very jealous. I need to have a talk with him. Gerd Gnat, we'll find you later! I hope I can convince him."

Successful Intelligence check!

Successful Perception check!

Danger Sense skill increased to level forty-seven!

Mental Fortitude skill increased to level fifty-four!

Holy crap! A psionic attack was just made on me, and there couldn't be the slightest doubt! Seemingly, Valeri had tried to read my thoughts or had even tried to make a psychic command, but whether she had achieved that or not, I had no idea. Some Beast Master! And by the way, speaking of beasts, where was Valeri-Urla's invisible predator? I quickly ran a scan and found a marker near her on the mini-map:

Little Sister. Shadow Panther (animal). Valeri-Urla's pet. Level 82.

There she was, the deadly invisible beast was always at its master's side. Dangerous little thing! And that could apply both to the predatory panther, and Valeri-Urla. I always kept one ear cocked around people like that!

As soon as she was out of earshot, not hiding his surprise, Eduard commented:

"Woah, Gnat. Did you see that?! Different people! The rude guy and that... hot chick. Where are they from?!"

I just shrugged my shoulders indefinitely, because I didn't really know. Tailax, the Gilvar Syndicate... Those names meant nothing to me. I asked Uline, but the Trader didn't know anything about their factions either.

"That's the downside of the pirate status," the Geckho woman added grouchily. "These two people were eager to join our team, but they immediately reconsidered when the found out, even though they've been stranded on Medu-Ro IV for quite a while. They're looking for work but they won't work for a pirate."

"They'll be back, I don't doubt it," I assured Uline. "Just so you know, I'm no less interested in getting the Beast Master than the gunman. Seemingly, I've found a way to help my faction take down the sea monsters."

"Take down who?" the Geckho lady didn't understand, but Eduard instantly knew.

"Captain, the Germans and both of our Legions have been 'bust their teeth over the Naiad problem. If you can solve that, you're guaranteed the respect of our whole faction! You might even be made a Leng and take Lozovsky's job, becoming the big boss yourself!"

I didn't answer the provocative comment. I just chuckled ambiguously and took one of the two glasses from the tall Space Commando, which he was still holding in his huge armored gloves. It was a wonder he wasn't breaking the fragile glass. I took a sip, then sniffed the drink and raised a surprised gaze:

"But this is nonalcoholic!"

An ear-to-ear smile of satisfaction appeared on the face of the ginger hulk, who towered over me by three heads:

"Well Captain, did you think that just because I'm a Space Commando, I drink the strongest booze I can get my hands on? Just so you know, in real life I only drink on Airborne Forces Day with my old military buddies, and then only a little. Even on my own birthday I don't have a single drop. Plus you ordered me and the Geckho brutes to be ready for action and unload all our inventory except a few backup clips."

That was true. I had only informed Uline Tar of

the true nature of the upcoming operation. The other crewmembers remained in blissful ignorance. Minn-O La-Fin had even asked to go into the real world to attend Coruler Thumor-Anhu La-Fin's funeral ceremony. And Ayni and Tini had left to watch gladiator battles somewhere on this huge space station. I had only asked the three other people who would take part in this operation not to go anywhere and, after checking their exoskeleton armor, unload everything they didn't need.

"Uline, there's more work for you," I said, pointing my partner to the trade terminal in the VIP box and the Engineer waiting there. "Orun Va-Mart has found a power unit that will work for us, but the price is exorbitant. Try to negotiate with the seller and work out a discount otherwise we might end up stuck here with a half-assembled starship that can't take off. Every thousand we can save is important!"

"If that's true, Gerd Gnat, I can sell all the old junk we took off the frigate. We can free up seven hundred thousand crystals that way," my partner suggested, but I refused categorically.

"I'd rather invest seven hundred thousand of my personal funds. I have a use for the old stuff. Sure, maybe to you old Geckho technology is just cheap junk. But to my faction, it's unique space artifacts and working alien technology. Both the hyperspace drive and quark-gravity power unit. In my homeworld, science isn't even close to understanding the physics behind them. I'm sure that when our scientists hear they get to study that 'junk,' they'll be so happy they piss boiling water! And by the way, how did transferring the crystals to my faction go?"

"The money is *en route*," Uline assured me. "Your faction will receive it in small-denomination monetary crystals in a quarter ummi. The total commission from all the middlemen came to sixteen percent, seven of which went to the obscenely greedy Kosta Dykhsh."

Wow, the Diplomat really was selfish! Although sixteen percent for an urgent transfer from deep space with delivery in cash and in person was still pretty reasonable to my eye. I was worried I might get a somewhat more "draconian" rate. Alright then, in one hour my H3 Faction would be getting eight hundred forty thousand crystals. To them, that was an unimaginably huge amount of space currency. It would allow them to do lots of things they could only dream of before. That meant purchasing interesting tech, studying new weapons for our immediate goals, and buying raw materials. Considering the million crystals of weaponry and equipment I'd ordered here, things were turning out quite nice for my faction.

The countdown timer from earlier beeped, indicating the head of the Pride of the Agile Paw was expecting me. Alright, time to go!

I told Eduard to finish his nonalcoholic cocktail, put his helmet and weapons on his armor and prepare to leave the casino. Then I waved my hand to Vasha and Basha as well, calling them to stand from the soft armchairs and join us. I handed each of them a +1 Strength ring I'd bought today from the "magic" jewelry dealer Gerd Ussh-Veesh.

You see, I was a man of practicality. The Strength parameter governed maximum carrying capacity, which would define the number of trophies my companions could carry out of the vault. Then I opened the equipment window and looked tenderly at my newest acquisition:

Ruthenium signet ring of the Main Engineer. Intelligence +3 (ancient Precursor artifact).

As a friend and repeat customer, Gerd Ussh-Veesh had cut me a deal on the ancient ring, and let it go for fifty-seven thousand crypto. Sure it was expensive, but I had been planning to buy it for a while, so I didn't feel too bad. And although the name of the item referred to some Main Engineer, I was of course not about to give this artifact to Orun Va-Mart. The Listener class needed Intelligence no less than an Engineer, perhaps even more. With this signet and the other new plus-two ring, my Intelligence was now up to twenty-eight, bringing my Magic Points from 823 to 887. My magic had grown by eight percent and for a "mana addict" like me, that was a very, very significant boost!

I set the Annihilator into my main weapons slot, and my Dark Faction Pulse Rifle into the alternative one, put my helmet on and was ready to go. My companions were also equipped and ready. I was about to give them the command to leave, but then I remembered something very important and turned to Uline:

"I almost forgot! Buy a bucket of white paint and a paint sprayer for Kirsan. I promised him. The specific items are in our purchase list, look there."

"You promised something to a metal repair bot? You didn't make any promises to the vacuum or fridge, did you? Sometimes, Gerd Gnat, you scare me with your extravagance." The Geckho lady shook her furry head in reproach, but still said she'd buy the items.

I remembered the second promise I'd made to the metal millipede as well: to drink myself silly at the nearest space station. And I wasn't going to break it. I was not in the habit of idly throwing my words around. But I decided to do that after robbing the pirate pride's vault, ideally doing a bit of laundering at the same time.

Chapter
Twenty-Nine

Pirate Vault

THE RASPY VOICE of the aged Miyelonian orchestrating the operation rang out in my earphones:

"There, in that corridor with the warning symbol to the right. They have cameras watching everything, and it's full of security systems. Turn down it and walk slowly. Don't make any sudden movements. Have your companions stay a bit behind, so the big group doesn't tip them off. We need you in front so the guards recognize you."

I didn't know the name of the man, where he was or how he was tracking me but, so far, all his instructions were correct. I stopped and pointed out a sign to Eduard, Vasha and Basha: "Private property. No entry." Then I asked my companions to let me go ahead and stay five steps behind.

"Alright. Now go in. Walk slowly and tell me about any cameras or data readers you detect."

So, I guess I'd need Perception. I stopped and changed my Intelligence rings for two +1 Perception ones. The dark long corridor became a bit more contrasting, and I could see a chain of blinking dark-red lights in the distance. They seemed to be data readers or infrared detectors. I ran a scan to make sure.

Scanning skill increased to level thirty-three!
Cartography skill increased to level fifty-seven!

I saw new markers on the mini-map, and reported back in Miyelonian:

"Two cameras. The first is next to the warning sign, the second is ten steps from the entrance. There are motion detectors at floor level in the walls, approximately one every five to seven steps. There is a web of lasers that are invisible to the naked eye. Two actually. The first is twenty steps from the corridor entrance, and the second is fifty. The beams can be seen with Perception level thirty. There are two high-speed turrets in ceiling niches right next to the door. And... I don't quite understand... Ah! A few tiles in the floor can detect when they're stepped on."

"Tiles? What kind exactly?" the director immediately asked. "Gerd Gnat, I'm gonna put you into a group quick. Mark all the traps so everyone can see."

A second later, I got a group request and

immediately accepted. That gave me bonuses to hitpoints, stealth and reaction speed. Nice, of course, but I that wasn't what I did it for. Woah-oh! The group had more than one hundred sixty members. I wasn't even close to appreciating the scale of this operation. And I could see all their names and levels. Among them was the leader of the Pride of the Agile Paw, keeping watch over the operation. There were high-level mercenaries from the Prides of the Star Strangler and Hidden Killer in the combat group as well. And there was the leader of the operation:

Leng Mai-Ti Ur-Miiyaoo. Miyelonian. Pride of the Hidden Killer. Level-188 Strategist.

Quite the hardcore tomcat! I didn't know how much the leader of the Pride of the Agile Paw had paid for such high-level mercenaries, but it was probably at least seven figures in crypto. I marked all the objects I had detected, shared it with the whole group and my Targeting skill leveled twice:

Targeting skill increased to level twenty-one!

Targeting skill increased to level twenty-two!

"Great!" the Leng praised me for the information. "What do you say, Big-Belly?"

"What is there to say, Grumpy...?" came the head of the Pride of the Agile Paw. "Let's block the cameras and motion detectors. Then just stand on the tiles."

Big-Belly? That was an awfully familiar way to call the head of the pride, who hid her identity and even her pregnancy. And she called him Grumpy back? Clearly these two knew each other well, and it looked very much like their relationship was not limited to business. I concluded that this severe Leng was most likely the father of her future kittens! Meanwhile, a new order came in from Leng Mai-Ti:

"Gerd Gnat, you go first and have your bodyguards pretend to accidentally step on the pressure plates nearest the closed doors. First group keep going on the ceiling tiles until you reach the first set of lasers. Second group take the video cameras! Myaur-Za, have your spies walk into the hal..."

Then I was simply thrown out of the group and their channel, so I didn't hear any more details. But I was already deeply impressed. Most likely these were not simple hired mercenaries as I thought, and this was a joint operation of related prides.

I slowly walked forward, demonstrating a lack of confidence to the vault guards who were probably watching me. I ordered my companions to stop and marked where they should stand. Then I stood right under the two dangerous turrets and tried to draw the pirates' attention by loudly asking:

"Is this the Pride of the Bushy Shadow's place? Am I in the right hallway?"

"What do you want, Gerd Gnat?" a voice answered practically instantly from a loudspeaker over the armored door, confirming my guess that they were watching.

"I'm looking for somebody from your pride who's worth my time, preferably the leader. I want to discuss how much needs to be paid to get rid of the bounty on my ship."

The response was a long silence, then another voice said:

"Gerd Abi stays out of little things like that, so you're not gonna get him. You could pay a fine right here and now, though. Two hundred thousand crypto and you're clean."

"Uhh... That seems a bit steep..." I pretended to be unsure and thinking. "The bounty is just three thousand. Where'd this two hundred thousand come from all of a sudden???"

"It's supposed to be a hundred times higher than the bounty. We're already doing you a big favor," the now insolent Miyelonian flagrantly lied, and then...

Listener, a data packet has been compiled for transmission to the Pyramid. Send data? (Yes/No)

I shuddered in surprise when I suddenly saw the two bright red columns of Relict logograms. An intriguing and very rare occurrence, but this was the worst possible time! I needed to think this over well, know what I was doing and first just see what kind of "data packet" it was. But the circumstances, to put it lightly, were not right for detailed consideration. I couldn't just tell the pirates and one hundred sixty attackers to wait an hour or two while I dug around in the settings and read the potentially huge files.

But it also seemed wrong to say no. What if I was missing a unique chance, and bungling something that would never happen again? I could be missing out on a whole chain of new discoveries! What if this was a highly important step into studying the ancient Relict race? With those thoughts in mind, I chose to send. And I got another portion of messages:

Listener, critical error: no response from the Pyramid.

Attempting to use backup channel.

Listener, critical error: no response from the Pyramid on backup channel.

Further course of action undefined. The Pyramid is unavailable!

Transmission cancelled.

Oh well, I guess I'd set my sights too high, hoping for an interesting event connected with the ancient race. This was seemingly just my electronic-packed armored suit waking up after a thousand years of inaction to discover there were no more Listeners or other members of the Relict race to exchange data with.

"Gnat, what's with the silence? Are you gonna pay or not?" the pirate's voice became more annoyed. I answered that I was thinking of how to get out of the situation, because I simply didn't have the money.

"I thought it would be three thousand crypto. That's how much I have left. I exchanged all the rest of my money for Geckho crystals, because I'm about to fly into their space."

Psionic skill increased to level seventy-two!

Yes, a bit of mental suggestion to settle their doubts. I could sense clearly that it would work and my words were finding a lively response in the minds of the pirates on the other side of the locked door. Greed had overtaken caution.

Listener, in case of military action, all public communication channels would be blocked. Thus the algorithms have determined that the most probable reason the Pyramid cannot be reached is WAR! Given the extraordinary situation, we suggest using an emergency channel to contact the Pyramid. (Yes/No)

What was this?! Did I really have to make such important choices, which probably had long-running consequences on the fly? I had no idea what the emergency communication system was or what it might entail, nevertheless I chose "Yes."

And I nearly fell to my knees, because my Listener suit's atomic batteries instantly dropped to zero. I had a hard time keeping my balance when the weight of the armor suddenly fell on my shoulders, pushing me backwards and making me career. The screen went dark. I had to remove my helmet to see anything. Was there a spare atomic battery? Ah, right. I bought an extra for my armor suit and Annihilator. There it was! I opened my equipment window and urgently put the new battery in place, replacing the spent one.

Electronics skill increased to level fifty-eight!

Medium Armor skill increased to level fifty-four!

"Apologies, my spacesuit is on the fritz," I honestly told the observers and immediately returned to the negotiations. "I have the money, but it's all in crystals. One million four hundred thousand Geckho crystals. Does that work for you?"

"Perfect! Get out the money!" the first pirate's voice rang out, not even trying to hide his impatience. "Order your bodyguards to go ten steps back and put away their weapons! After that, we'll open the door and you can come in. And you'll come in alone, without your soldiers."

I ordered my companions to take seven steps back, then put on my helmet because my armor suit had turned back on. In my earphones, Leng Mai-Ti Ur-Miiyaoo's voice rang out at once:

"Gerd Gnat, everything is going well so far! But there's one bit of bad news. We've discovered an emergency communications system from inside the vault that we can't deactivate. The door into the vault cannot remain open for long, otherwise a signal will be sent to the Pride of the Bushy Shadow guard post, and from there it will be sent on to allied prides."

"I see. The door will close behind me. And how long do I have to stay inside?" I asked, to which the operation leader answered that I didn't need to go in at all.

"We cannot allow the armored door to close. Otherwise the pirates will just kill or rob you in there, and all our preparations will have been in vain. Our soldiers are already in position, and the attack will come as soon as the door opens. I'm afraid we will not be able to avoid an alarm, and the area will soon be flooded with enemies. So we're gonna run in, snatch everything of value from the vault and run right out. And it would be better to load up to the max, kill ourselves and respawn somewhere safe with the loot."

THREE MIYELONIANS from the Pride of the Bushy Shadow were standing before me baring their teeth and playing with glimmering deadly blades, not hiding their aggressive intentions:

"Well, where's the cash, Gerd Gnat? Hand it over!"

There were seven other pirates a bit farther away in the depths of the great gloomy hangar, and three of them had their laser rifles trained at my head. And, based on the mini-map, somewhere further in the darkness, there were another six enemies hidden behind container stacks. Miyelonians weren't bothered one bit by darkness. I'd figured that out before, when capturing the pirate interceptor in space. But I couldn't see a thing, because there was a spotlight shining right in my face.

Pretending I was digging in my inventory, I drew out time as long as I could. I demanded proof of receipt, asked how long it would take them to get rid of my bounty, and told them to hurry up because I had to leave soon. At the same time, I did not understand what was taking the attackers so long! And even stranger I was standing right in the wide-open vault doors, but for some reason the pirates were in no rush to close them, as if they weren't afraid to trip the alarm.

And then I realized... Why would the Pride of the Agile Paw want to share trophies with my soldiers? The firefight would begin soon and "accidentally" my guards would get shot in the back, if of course the pirates didn't kill them first. Then after respawn there would be no reason to come back. In any case, the vault would already be empty. Maybe there was an alarm system that couldn't be turned off as they said and maybe not, but I had already been given an explanation that assumed no one in my group would survive.

Danger Sense skill increased to level forty-eight!

The pirates were getting angrier and angrier and they were less and less keen to answer my stupid questions. There was no way to draw out time any further. So I turned my radio to my team's channel, and said what the operation leader hadn't deigned to tell us:

"Guys, the mayhem starts now. Try to survive! It won't be easy, because neither the attackers or defenders want us alive. Accept my invitation to a group and prepare for battle!"

What to do first? Shoot the Annihilator and kill the nearest pirate? Knowing how fast Miyelonians could be, it might not work. Pit some enemies against each other? Yes, it was a good idea to attack the pirates mentally, but there were plenty more who could kill me very quickly. Also, after dying, the mind control would pass and the scuffling pirates would come to. I didn't want my life to come so cheaply... I looked at the mini-map and bared my teeth in satisfaction. The turrets, how could I forget?!

Automatic laser turret. Interface chance: 24%. Total control chance: 3%.

For some reason, my chances were a bit low... Ah, what a jackass I was! I was still wearing the +1 Perception rings! I quickly changed them back, raising my Intelligence by 5 whole points. Now that was better. And it would get even better if I threw all my skill points into Machine Control, raising it to 66. So I did.

Automatic laser turret. Interface chance: 57%. Total control chance: 38%.

I figured I could get lucky with at least one of them! Otherwise, what was the use of having maximum possible Luck? Got it! The right turret was subordinated to my mental command. So, here's for my enemies. I placed markers on all the nearest pirates. Meanwhile, I ordered a disheveled pirate shifting from foot to foot to make a quick jump and attack his comrade from behind with both blades. Then I reached for my Annihilator and, sharply moving from place, shot my fearsome weapon, but not at one of the scattering pirates, at the locking mechanism for the massive doors. Let the fun begin!

Rifles skill increased to level fifty-one!
Sharpshooter skill increased to level thirty-four!
Targeting skill increased to level twenty-three!
You have reached level seventy-four!
You have received three skill points!

I saw the door start to lean. One of the hinges was torn out at the root together with the locking motor. Then I was knocked off my feet by a fierce blow to the left shoulder. One of the pirates took down my energy shield with his blade, and a second got through my armor and stuck his scimitar to the hilt in my chest. Ouch! My life bar fell by a third, and the game warned me I was bleeding critically and had shell shock. I couldn't see anything through a reddish pall. Another blow. How unbearably painful! My life fell even further.

This was seemingly death... And it all came together so badly: I leveled up at such a risky time! My progress bar was empty now, much to my dismay. And that was very, very bad!

I was hit with another stab, or more likely a shot. Mere crumbs were left in my life bar... I needed to do something quick so I wouldn't lose a level or skills with my now inevitable death! And that thought gave me strength. I couldn't see anything, but I could open my inventory. I quickly threw my Annihilator in there so I wouldn't somehow lose the invaluable weapon in case of a bad drop. Then I took out a Geological Analyzer and, losing consciousness, unfolded the metal tripod.

The last thing I heard before dying was a sharp metallic clink through the explosions and gunfire. After that, I saw two system messages on the quickly darkening screen:

Scanning skill increased to level thirty-four!

Your character has died. Respawn will be possible in fifteen minutes.

Would you like to review your statistics for this game session?

Chapter
Thirty

After the
Assault

MY SCANNING SKILL grew? Surprising. I was actually using the Geological Analyzer to disable both laser turrets, which should have counted as activity and thus have filled my progress bar a hair. Yes, it wasn't how I wanted things to go but after my death the turret I was controlling would open fire on my comrades, so I had to turn it off somehow.

But clearly the Prospector Scanner had detected something, I just didn't see it due to the pall clouding my vision. Maybe the mini-map had shown something I hadn't seen before, and maybe the strong EMP had revealed the attacking invisible soldiers by turning off their advanced light-splitting suits. In one way or another though, I had achieved my goal and now, despite my death, I wasn't feeling the least bit upset. In fact, I was serene and content.

After the statistics question timed out, the virt-pod opened. I had no desire to get up from the soft springy bed, because I was planning to go right back into the game in fifteen minutes. But I was not allowed to simply relax. A few minutes later, I heard rapid footsteps from the spiral staircase and an unfamiliar woman's voice called out to me:

"Kirill, do you need help?"

I sat up in the open virt pod and turned. A stylish middle-aged lady with short dark hair was looking at me in panic. She was wearing the blue uniform issued to Dome residents, but I didn't see any numbering on it. That must have meant she was not a player, but some employee. Maybe she was even the guard of this corncob. Although this woman didn't exactly look like a guard. She didn't have the type or build.

"No, I don't need help. I just died and am waiting to respawn."

I considered the conversation over, but the woman was in no rush to leave. In fact, she walked up closer:

"I got an alert that Gerd Gnat left the game but didn't leave his capsule. So I decided to check if everything was alright. I'm sure it wasn't this, but sometimes newbies get so tired after their first session that they cannot crawl out of their pod. Irina Chusovkina, faction psychologist," she finally introduced herself and casually sat on the edge of my pod, looking talkative.

In theory, I was not against it. I had a few free minutes before respawn anyway. After spending so long speaking Geckho or Miyelonian, the sound of my native tongue brought me an unwitting joy. What was more, I had heard a lot about this lady from my friends. They said she was a very authoritative and qualified psychologist specialized in gaming addiction. I didn't think I needed help with that exactly, but I was still a bit alarmed by the time at Gerd Tamara's birthday when I momentarily confused the real and virtual world.

"I've heard a lot about you, Kirill, and I've been watching your success with interest. I've wanted to talk for some time, but you're impossible to pin down. It's very hard to find you under the Dome. You spend a lot of time in the virtual world, sometimes even to the detriment of your real life. Is it really so interesting in the game that it can eclipse the real world?"

Her question had a little trick in it. If I said I did find the game intriguing, I would be confirming that my virtual life was more important to me. I chuckled, imagining that logically I should be seeing a message about my Mental Fortitude increasing. After that, the smile crawled off my face. After all, this psychologist was right. Even in real life I thought in terms of skills, levels and other game elements.

"Irina, the issue isn't my interest in the game, even though unusual worlds and their residents are of course alluring. Why hide it? But no, I would spend a bunch of time in the game that bends reality even if it didn't have realistic graphics, sound effects, or an unpredictable plot. It's just that I'm constantly reminded why I'm here under the Dome. It is not to make friends with the other residents, practice sports, eat for free or live in a comfortable apartment. I am here to save Earth from destruction by the Dark Faction and enslavement by alien invaders. And I'm doing everything in my power to achieve that!"

The psychologist gave a tortured smile and asked whether I thought that lofty goal was taking me too far from real life. I had been living under the Dome a whole month, but I didn't have any real friends other than the few people on my team. I wasn't speaking to anyone, and I had even grown distant from the people I'd spent my first few days with. I was not interested in the mass events held under the Dome. I wasn't even interested in girls. Here the psychologist lowered her voice to a whisper and said that she knew what had happened with Anya and Tamara. Both were angered by my lack of attention.

"Please, don't interfere in my personal life," I asked the psychologist though she'd earned thrice that. "I haven't been fighting with Tamara. I don't know where she got that from. And Anna... no comment.

Direct all your questions to Ivan Lozovsky. Also, I have a legal wife Minn-O La-Fin. That's plenty for me!"

"The Dark Faction Princess, some junior wife, travelling mistress and all that?" I could now hear poorly hidden mockery in her voice. "Kirill, I'm talking about real girls, not virtual characters and fantasies."

I had to admit, that shook me. Who was she to be telling me about life?!

"What do you even know about the game that bends reality and its mechanics?!" I objected sincerely. "Let's see what all your moralizing is worth when this 'virtual character' comes into our world under the Dome!"

"Come on, Gnat. I know more about the game mechanics than you think," Irina Chusovkina reacted calmly to my accusation of incompetence. And I barely noticed, but she had smoothly slipped into using my nickname. "What is your Fame stat now? Forty?"

"Forty?" I couldn't conceal a mocking smirk. "How 'bout sixty-three?! Or maybe even more, because the news about the firefight in the pirate vault has probably already spread to every pride on Medu-Ro IV by now!"

"Sure, let's say sixty-three," she agreed easily. "I'm sure your Authority is sky high too. But Gerd Gnat, have you considered why you still aren't a Leng? Radugin became a Leng with Fame forty-three or something, and his Authority was just like thirty."

Huh... So why wasn't I a Leng? After all, my fame

and authority hit those levels a while ago… That threw
me for a loop, and I honestly admitted I didn't know.
The psychologist was eager to explain:

"Because a Leng is a faction leader. And not
some director formally appointed from above, nor
merely elected to the position. A Leng is a true leader,
who the faction wants to follow. But you aren't really in
any faction! You left yours behind, and their collective
interest is no concern to you! You fly around deep
space, go to war with pirates and probably
successfully. But you do not know the problems your
brethren face. Their plans and desires are also beyond
your grasp. You don't even speak with any of them! And
it's the same here under the Dome. I mean, every
faction member would be glad to speak with you, but
you don't give them the chance!"

"Well, what can I do?" I cast off my pride and
asked the professional psychologist for advice.

"What can you do? It may sound obvious, but
talk more, make personal contact with your faction. Or
there is another option…" here she again lowered her
voice to a whisper, "change faction."

What? She was suggesting I leave my faction?! I
couldn't believe my ears. Irina though, totally
understanding my outrage, continued:

"I have studied your psychological profile in
great depth, and I have no doubt that you would
support your native land regardless of formal
allegiance. But in the meantime no one else, not Gerd

Ivan Lozovsky, nor Gerd Tamara, nor Gerd Tarasov nor any of the others can become a Leng because there is a player with higher Fame and Authority in the faction. And we need a fully-fledged leader for many reasons. Think it over and decide for yourself."

With these words, Irina Chusovkina stood from the side of my virt pod and, wishing me a happy game, walked toward the stairs. I then sat thoughtfully in my virt pod and stared at the wall until a signal beeped out telling me the fifteen minutes were up and I could go back into the game.

ABOVE ALL, I was interested in Gnat's stats. What if I was wrong and my death had happened with an empty progress bar, giving all those negative consequences? But no, everything was as I hoped. I was still level seventy-four:

Gerd Gnat. Human. H3 Faction.	
Level-74 Listener	
Statistics:	
Strength	14
Agility	18
Intelligence	23 + 5
Perception	27 + 2

Constitution	16
Luck modifier	+3
Parameters:	
Hitpoints	1612 of 1612
Endurance points	1209 of 1209
Magic points	899 of 899
Carrying capacity	62 lbs.
Fame	65
Skills:	
Electronics	58
Scanning	34
Cartography	57
Astrolinguistics	83
Rifles	51
Mineralogy	50
Medium Armor	54
Eagle Eye	70
Sharpshooter	34
Targeting	23
Danger Sense	48
Psionic	72
Mental Fortitude	54
Mysticism	24
Machine Control	66

Attention!!! You have three unspent skill points.

And hey, my fame had gone up by two points as

I guessed. I was involuntarily reminded of what she said about my faction and the need to make this key decision. Seemingly, this could be a serious problem in the future. It was preventing me from growing higher than Gerd, and keeping the faction from having a decent leader. And that required very serious consideration, but not now. Now, I was interested in the results of the battle in the pirate vault.

Before I closed the stat table, I used my three free skill points for Electronics, raising it to sixty-one. My goal there was obvious: I wanted to know if I could use the Pyramid Signal Booster, the strange rune-covered ring-shaped disk I'd taken from Rikki Pan-Miis. With Gnat now at level 74, the artifact would give a boost of +220% to my Listener armor suit's forcefield capacity, raising it from 3500 to 11270. That might not have made me quite as resilient as Fox, who could easily survive several blaster shots, but still I would be pretty hard to kill. If I'd had that disk active and locked into my armor, perhaps I could have survived the recent battle. But unfortunately, it required Electronics 70 and I wasn't there yet. Also its racial limitation was still in place...

Anyhow, I respawned in the hallway on the sixteenth floor of the Medu-Ro IV docks, three steps from the doors into my landing bay. Unfortunately, I immediately discovered the Dark Faction Pulse Laser Rifle missing from my alternate weapon slot. It must have dropped when I died... I'd have to pick up something else. For now I filled that slot with the Paralyzer.

I used my electric captain's key and went inside. The area around the ship was a font of activity. The Engineer, Trader, Navigator, Starship Pilot and Supercargo were engaged in a heated discussion, poking their hands into detached sheets of armor and gaping holes in the fuselage. Fifty feet from the dispute, there was a huge hyperdrive the size of a truck hovering in midair. And it was half-dissembled. Some pieces were lying right on the hangar floor.

At the other end of the hangar Imran, Vasha and Basha were unloading containers from a conveyer belt that crawled out from deep inside the station. Based on the markings on the packaging, this was the weaponry I had ordered for my faction, and the rare equipment from Kirsan's list. Predominantly, it was parts to modify my Annihilator. When the captain showed up, the Geckho brothers stopped working, paused the conveyer belt and came to meet me, lowering their heads more with every step:

"Gerd Gnat, we failed you. We just couldn't survive..."

Based on the dents and holes in both of their exoskeleton armor, they had really taken a beating. Basha was even missing part of his chest-piece, clearly blown off in an explosion or severed with a powerful laser.

"It happens... I didn't survive either," I tried to

reassure my soldiers. "Hand your armor over to our millipede mechanics, they'll fix it. I'll mark it priority and they'll get it done right away. And where is Eduard Boyko? Is he not in the game yet? Or did he not die?"

I couldn't see the Space Commando anywhere, and a scan showed that he was also not inside the frigate either. Unfortunately, I hadn't checked whether Eduard had exited his virt pod while under the Dome. And the brothers also didn't know what happened:

"The fighting broke out and us three started working our grenade launcher systems with the targets you supplied. Then the lights went out and Eduard shouted something I didn't understand: 'Urazavedeve!!!'[5] Then, firing constantly, he charged the enemy. After that we can't say, because we were both already dead."

"Gerd Gnat, what does 'urazavedeve' mean?" Basha Tushihh asked curiously.

"It..." how to give a decent explanation without delving into the details. "He was entering a state of combat madness. The fury makes him immune to pain and fear. It's a unique ability of my faction's airborne infantry."

Apparently, that explanation was more than enough for the furballs, and no questions followed.

---

[5] "Ура за ВДВ!" (Ura za VDV!) This cheer pays homage to Eduard's roots as a paratrooper in the Russian Airborne Troops, known by the abbreviation "VDV." Roughly equivalent to a US Marine shouting "Oorah!"

Uline walked up and, not hiding her anger, pointed at the huge hyper:

"The power unit hasn't come yet, and Orun Va-Mart won't install the hyperdrive without it. So now we're just wasting time. And the longer that takes, the more time we'll need before takeoff. Honestly this whole situation scares me. The pirates who died in the assault will respawn and tell their allies what happened. Soon everyone will know about your attack on the vault. We'll make many powerful enemies here!"

Fame increased to 66.

ATTENTION!!! The Pride of the Bushy Shadow has increased the bounty for destroying your starship. Present bounty: one hundred seventy-three thousand crypto.

ATTENTION!!! The Danger Rating of Free Captain Gerd Gnat has risen to two.

"See, that's just what I'm saying!" Apparently my partner could see the changes. "We need to fly away from Medu-Ro IV as soon as possible! Gerd Gnat talk with the Engineer, pressure him, use magic if you have to! He has to install the hyperdrive before other units get here!"

I reminded Uline that the Pride of the Agile Paw had promised us protection for the next three days in local reckoning. But that was paltry consolation for my alarmed and terrified business partner. And then... the doors opened and, to the creaking of springs and rattling of shredded exoskeleton armor, Eduard Boyko entered the hangar. He had really taken a beating... His armor suit had simply no working components left. Compared to that, the Geckho brothers' dented-up armor could have been called "practically new!" With a nasty scraping sound, the soldier raised his right mechanical arm, gave a military salute and reported:

"Captain, mission accomplished! I survived and I brought some loot!"

With these words, he shook a pile of identical gold bars from his inventory right onto the hangar floor. And they weren't just gold in color, they were made of pure gold.

"That's five hundred and ten pounds," the Space Commando told me, not hiding his pride. "There were all kinds of bars on the racks in the vault, and also some coils of wire. And it might have all been worth much more than gold. But I had no idea what they were worth, nor could I identify anywhere near all of them. So I was afraid to mess up and chose good old-fashioned gold. And this is for you, captain. I know you're into this kind of stuff."

This time, Eduard didn't throw the trophy but fairly carefully, insofar as his broken robotized armor suit allowed, set it at my feet. I didn't realize what he had right away. All I saw was scraps of something wrapped in a polymer bubble pack, maybe twisted bits of metal... But then I tried to focus not on the individual fragments, but the whole set and immediately recognized it:

Wreckage of Small Relict Guard Drone.

Uh... My first reaction was fear. Had something happened to my guard drone?! I hurriedly opened my drone management window and breathed a sigh of relief. No, mine was still in working order somewhere and awaiting commands. And by the way... I mentally asked the drone approximately how long it would take to reach me.

Estimated time in flight: 287,506 years, 14 days, 6 hours, 58 minutes.

I compared it with the number I had recorded in my notepad. It would take the drone thirty thousand years longer to reach Medu-Ro IV than Un-Tesh. That meant we were going the wrong direction. Oh well, another request or two from various points in the galaxy and the Navigator and I could sit down at a star map and figure out where the secret object was located.

"Well captain, do you like it? Or was it stupid to bring it?" Eduard Boyko interrupted.

"No matter what, it wasn't stupid. It's an interesting and valuable piece," I reassured my worrying soldier. "But whether I can use it or not, I do not know..."

I sat down next to the transparent package and tried to get a closer look at the painstakingly collected wreckage of the ancient drone. It looked like someone had tried very hard and get each and every tiny bit in the sealed bag. Could I put it back together and get it working? I called Kirsan off the frigate and even shuddered in surprise when I saw the new white paintjob as it popped up right under my hand.

"Say, can this be repaired?" I asked and the bot froze up for a bit, staring into the packaging with its many mechanical eyes.

Uline Tar had the universal translator ready to go and waited patiently for Kirsan to demand the device by shaking his many arms.

Hard. Long. Dangerous. Possible. Need to see better on the frigate. Make list of parts for repair.

I see. I figured such a rare discovery didn't belong on the floor of a docking bay and had to be quickly brought into the starship. I tried to pick up the bag... damn this crap was heavy! I could only slightly raise it off the floor but had to immediately set it back down.

"It's one hundred and sixty pounds no matter how you slice it," the beefy Space Commando chuckled, easily lifting the trophy with one hand. "I don't think the Miyelonians who captured the vault were very happy that I took it for myself. They shouted something at me, waving their hands around, but I didn't understand a damn thing. Then, one step after the next, I made my way through the station thinking 'I hope I'm not carrying this heavy shit for no reason. Maybe instead of this ancient wreckage I should have taken another one hundred sixty pounds of gold.' By the way, Gnat. I saw your laser rifle. The Pride of the Agile Paw put it in the most obvious place, right next to the security console. That was probably so even the most dimwitted vault defenders wouldn't miss it after respawning and would know exactly who to point the finger at."

"I see..." that news didn't upset me one bit. The Pride of the Bushy Shadow would know perfectly well who paid them a visit even without the Dark Faction Pulse Rifle. "Eduard, why did you go all that way on foot? You could have just killed yourself and respawned here."

"Captain, don't you think I thought of that? Especially when I was standing awkwardly next to the elevators and had no real idea of how to tell the sensor panel to go to deck sixteen? But think for yourself: how could I do that from a technical standpoint. I was wearing an impenetrable exoskeleton suit, and I was out of rounds. So I had to push myself forward regardless. And a Trillian space crocodile helped me with the elevators. It was the same guy you talked with in the casino. He recognized me and asked me in Geckho which floor, then traced the figure on the panel."

I asked my crew members not to crowd around the trophies and let Eduard through to the frigate. I ordered the Space Commando to take off his battered armor and, like the twin brothers, give it to our mechanic bots. My Listener armor was also shot through in two places, but it hadn't lost its shield, so I decided to wait. The metal millipedes had enough work as it was.

"So Avan Toi, take this gold and lock it in the safe," I said, pointing the Supercargo to the pile of gold bars. "Uline, I need an estimation of the value of this haul. Just the bars, don't worry about the drone pieces," I corrected, looking at the unconfident expression on the Geckho lady's furry face.

"Why sit here and calculate?" the Trader asked in surprise, looking at her palmtop. "It's an in-demand good. All the bars are certified. Two hundred fifty-six thousand three hundred crypto is how much you could sell it for on Medu-Ro IV. That's one million seven-hundred and nine thousand Geckho crystals. And, by the way, it says the Pride of the Agile Paw is willing to buy."

Seemingly, the Pride of the Agile Paw decided to take advantage of their competitor's temporary weakness and stake their claim. Or maybe the pride needed a formal explanation for where they suddenly got valuable metals in large quantity. This way they could just say 'look for yourselves, we bought it on the open market.' Well, that only played into our hand.

"Uline, let's pay a visit to the casino owner and figure out this gold. We can also remind her that our starship needs protection. And yes, friends, half of that will be paid out to my crew! In crypto, crystals or gold, your choice!"

Authority increased to 50!

My last words were drowned out in stormy

shouts of joy. Team Gnat was exuberant. I heard them praising their captain's name in three different languages. All their resentment over my official designation as a pirate and the bounty on our ship were instantly forgotten.

Chapter
Thirty-One

Big Meeting

T HIS TIME, despite the late hour, there was a light
on in the Dome administration building and it
was packed. All prominent players were required
to attend some big meeting scheduled by faction head
Ivan Lozovsky. Thankfully, Dmitry Zheltov went into
the real world after it had been announced, so I wasn't
even late. I greeted my colleagues and tried to take the
chair closest the door, but Tamara was sitting next to
it. She stood up defiantly and moved to the other side
of the office. And of course everyone noticed her little
walk-out. But they kept tactfully silent and continued
talking as if nothing had happened. Her seat was taken
by Gerd Ustinov. Our head scientist was clearly afraid
to be late and was panting as he came in.

Finally, Lozovsky walked last into the office

accompanied by the fed Alexander Antipov and the same chubby major who had congratulated me on destroying the Graveyard node earlier.

"Colleagues, first of all I want to introduce you to Vasily Filippov, a new player in our faction and my new deputy." With these words, Ivan Lozovsky pointed at the military man, who was now no longer wearing an army uniform, but a dark blue track suit with the number 2018. "Most of you have not made his acquaintance yet, but Vasily Andreyevich helped launch the Dome project and has been one of the external curators of our faction for the last six months. I'll let our new colleague tell you about the tasks ahead of us."

It was strange, but I was less interested in the man's face or body than his player number: two thousand eighteen?! Not bad. The faction was now over two-thousand strong! Good news! And the new player, ever so slightly embarrassed, introduced himself again for some reason and said he had been sent under the Dome and into the game with the mission of standing up to our enemies' new Strategist, General Ui-Taka.

"We cannot react fast enough to events in the game from the real world. So leadership sent me on a two-year assignment under the Dome. I've already studied your copy of the Labyrinth and, as soon as this meeting is over, I intend to enter the game and join the faction. I am very hopeful that with my previous line of work, I will be able to choose the Strategist class or something else connected with military organization. I already have a plan to quickly level my character, and I have a ton of enthusiasm, so I look forward to working together with all of you!"

They all started applauding, and I clapped along with them, greeting our new faction member. But deep down, cats were scratching. The faction was again not taking a risk and consciously sacrificing three potential stat points, choosing one in the hand rather than two in the bush. And meanwhile three stat points would be very significant for any player, especially one in such an important role. It was hard for me to imagine legendary enemy general Ui-Taka making the same choice. Two guaranteed points instead of five potential ones. No, he would clearly choose to put his abilities to the ultimate test!

"Now on to other news," Ivan Lozovsky cut in. "First of all I must tell you that, from here on out, the Dark Faction aren't the only ones who can carry out grand-scale espionage. We now have confirmation from a few independent sources that the group 'Emancipation from Mage Tyranny' has agreed to work with us and proven their seriousness by bombing a large gathering of mages in the Dark Faction homeworld."

Everyone started chattering and, as far as I could hear, mostly disapproved of our using terrorism as an instrument of warfare. Ustinov even called it "flagrant inhumanity" and "letting the genie out of the bottle," implying the possibility of terrorism in Russian cities being used in response. Lozovsky called for silence and continued:

"Let me say one thing right away, so there won't be any malicious gossip. We did not order an act of terrorism. These brave warriors are ideologically opposed to mage rule and decided to fill a plane with explosives and blow it up all on their own. It happened at the funeral of the late Coruler Thumor-Anhu La-Fin, where all the most prominent mages of the parallel world were present. In fact, many of them also play very strong characters in the game that bends reality. We do not yet have an exact number of victims, but there were very many, which means our enemy took significant losses and is now much weaker."

What??? My heart just stopped when I heard the ghastly news. Minn-O La-Fin was at that funeral ceremony! That may have been why the Princess was still not back to Medu-Ro IV, even though my wayedda should have returned ages ago.

As if having guessed my thoughts, Ivan Lozovsky turned to me and added:

"Gnat, I can say for certain that Minn-O La-Fin survived. It was reported in the news in that world. And let me remind you that we would still be glad to see the Princess in our ranks. Her joining our side would have a very serious propaganda effect and would shred the Dark Faction's faith that they could possibly defeat us. As for our agents from the Group for Liberation from

Magical Tyranny... yes, their methods may seem radical, but we do not have other allies in the magical world, so we don't have much of a choice. Alright, on that note we'll end the topic of the terrorism in the magical world and I ask you all not to share what you've heard with other players. Now I ask the leaders of both Legions to report on their readiness for the end of the ceasefire."

Gerd Tarasov spoke first, telling us about a decision to increase the size of the First Legion from two to three hundred soldiers. There were also intensive training sessions, additional enlistment decided via a competition with five candidates per opening. New weaponry was being introduced and implemented. Soldiers and armor were being moved along the road from New Bavaria to the Antique Beach, but the Centaurs building the road hadn't finished and it really only existed on paper...

I was only half listening, still worried about Minn-O's presence at the scene of the terror attack. The faction leader's assurances were a meagre comfort, because saying she was still alive was different than saying she was not injured. And also, I was seriously worried by Lozovsky talking about the plan to bring my wayedda to our world. As far as I knew, the deep-cover and surprisingly well-informed Dark Faction spy in our ranks had not yet been discovered, which meant anyone in the office could potentially be an enemy. And so it followed that our plans were no longer a secret to her allies, which meant she was potentially in danger from that as well. Had the experienced Diplomat just misspoken? Or was it calculated, with secret intentions I didn't understand?

At a certain point, I raised my eyes and saw Tamara sitting opposite me and boring into me with her eyes. We met gazes and... much to my surprise, the dark-haired girl didn't turn away. The leader of the Second Legion wanted to tell me something!

"Gnat, you are of course a real scoundrel, and I am not going to forgive you any time soon, if ever. But there's something you should know. In the game, a Dark Faction player got in touch with the Second Legion. I won't say his name, but he was offering services. He said that in the real world he represented a large group of rebels. And they were not merely 'ideologically motivated' as Lozovsky would have you believe. Well to be fair ideology could be a factor, but their services did not come cheap. They asked for half a million crystals to kill a big group of mages at Thumor-Anhu La-Fin's funeral. Our Diplomat gave his agreement, and I provided mental protection, so our agent wouldn't be uncovered by psionic mages. Then after the attack, Lozovsky paid with the funds he got from Geckho diplomat Kosta Dykhsh. I was there with a group of trusted soldiers at the crystal hand-off providing mental cover, so I know what I'm talking about."

Tamara broke the mental connection, because it was now her turn to give a report on the Second

Legion's preparations for renewed military action. She spoke about reinforcing defensive structures in the Karelia node, the road they'd built with Centaur help from the Capital node all the way to the Harpy Cliffs, the intensive training sessions and her reaching level one hundred.

And in that time, I was in a state of deep contemplation. There could be no doubt that Tamara had told me the truth. I will not relay the puzzled thoughts my brain birthed after that. They were not all decent, and the least offensive of them was a desire to slap my faction head in the face then and there, accusing him of flagrant lying and knowingly putting my wife in danger. But I restrained myself. The time for tearing down my faction head had not yet come. Also, that wouldn't change a thing, it would just put me in a negative light before key players of the Human-3 Faction, damaging my Authority both here and in the game.

But by Gerd Radugin's speech, I had come back around. The former faction head was now in charge of supplying the nodes and players, and he told us about leveling the Eastern Swamp node to two. So that was what increased the number of players in our faction! And meanwhile, Radugin talked about creating underground reserve storage facilities far from the front to hold crude oil and petroleum products in case of a prolonged war. He even gave a concrete timeframe: the faction could last eight days given present reserves, even if the whole oil-production complex in the Eastern Swamp got destroyed again. Overall, it was very interesting and informative.

But when Gerd Ustinov started speaking, I grew bored. Laboratory capacity, reducing design research time, a new requirement of at least two testers per chemistry specialist, the need for some specific condensers and inductor coils from the real world, expanding the size of the Prometheus complex... I wasn't the only one yawning, but everyone was doing their level best to pretend they were listening and understanding everything the scientist said.

Finally, it was my turn. Before this meeting, I was in an elevated and inspired state. I was planning to tell my colleagues everything and hide nothing. But I changed my mind and didn't reveal any secrets, telling them only what they already knew or could easily find out. Yes, I had a Tolili-Ukh X spaceship of Meleyephatian assembly. I was the captain and co-owner, sharing the ship with a Geckho Trader named Uline Tar from a rich and influential clan of space merchants called Tar-Layneh.

How was the ship? Well, how to put it... It was of course no longer just scrap, like when we'd been awarded it by the "generous" Kung Waid Shishish, but it was still pretty dang far from good. The basic repair was done, and the ship could fly. We had recently traded out our old power unit for a higher-capacity one, and we had a new hyperdrive being installed. We purposely didn't sell the old parts though, and at the first opportunity would be bringing them to Earth for our scientists.

When I reached that part, head geek Gerd Ustinov predictably stood at attention. His hands were shaking with excitement as he asked:

"Did I hear you right? Gerd Gnat, do you have a working gravity-quark power unit in your possession?! And it comes with a hyperspace drive, also in working order? Colleagues, do you have any idea what this means for terrestrial science? It will be a massive boon. Understanding how they work that will give humanity a gigantic boost in the field of quantum physics and multivariate analysis! Just those artifacts are more than enough to justify all our expenses on the Dome project! They must be brought to our territory as soon as possible!"

Everyone began buzzing, loudly discussing the news. I was congratulated, praised and promised rewards. Alexander Antipov even said I might get an official medal, although it was with great caution. Clearly, that decision was not up to the federal agent. I basked in the stream of glory, satisfied with the effect. I waited for the enthusiastic exclamations to end and continued my report, trying purposely not to emphasize our problems.

I said the frigate had new electronics, most importantly good near-space scanners, which had run us a pretty penny. Repairing the inside had also taken lots of effort and resources, particularly installing a cargo elevator. At present we were finishing modernization and, in one day's time, we could leave Medu-Ro IV with our small frigate. But where to take it?

"What do you mean?" Alexander Antipov was sincerely surprised at my question. "To Earth, of course! We're on the brink of war, and we desperately need a combat frigate!"

I shook my head, expressing doubt:

"Our ship wouldn't be worth much against the Dark Faction in its present form. It cannot land on a planet, nor fire from orbit. It lacks the stabilizers needed to enter a dense atmosphere and has no weaponry. What's more, you need gravity compensators to land on such a massive astronomical body. We could get all that with time but our main issue now is a serious lack of crew and funds. We should have thirty in our team, but we now have just eleven. And to modify and arm the starship, we need at least another four million Geckho crystals, preferably nine."

The room started buzzing again. Everyone was shaken by the colossal sum. I could see the smiles on their faces go dim one after the next. They all knew that the destitute H3 Faction had no way of improving that, which meant they wouldn't have help from orbit. I even tried to build on that sentiment:

"Uline Tar doesn't have a ton of money. And as

you understand, I don't either. We are working to solve that issue by carrying out various missions for Miyelonian prides. My crew can tell you about a recent successful operations on the Medu-Ro IV station, which helped us get the money for the bare minimum. What's more, we have ideas for profitable trade routes. We can also search for valuable minerals on asteroids. If we really need it, Uline Tar can get a loan from her relatives but we'd prefer to get the money on our own. But no matter what it takes, we will arm the ship, and take on new crew. All that is going to take some time though. For now, flying god knows how many billions of miles and throwing our money into a bottomless pit for fuel just so we can mark targets for howitzers from the Yellow Mountains, and only if the weather is good..." I cringed and shook my head. "It hardly makes sense. And the ship's other owner would never agree. What's more, any quadcopter with a camera from the real world could do the job just as well..."

"No it couldn't," the future Strategist interrupted me. "We've tried that before, a few times. The Dark Faction has electronic drone jamming systems and they instantly destroy or crash anything we send over. Incidentally, we are not behind in that regard, and we do the same to their drones. But I agree with Gnat. It is better to wait and get the ship into fighting shape than reveal our trump card, only to have it prove useless in combat."

"I expect to solve our financial issues in five to

seven days. It should be enough," I said, giving a cautious timeframe and attentively watching my colleagues.

No, no one in the room could squeeze out a happy smile when they heard the news that the Human-3 frigate would have to keep waiting for the significant reinforcement of a space frigate. "Plus, another day or two to install the modules we bought, then a day and a half in flight... That means somewhere around eight to ten days from now we'll have delivered our scientifically-valuable cargo, and a combat starship will be orbiting the Earth, ready to fight our enemies! For now though, you'll have to resist the Dark Faction without us. But I sent a million crystals to buy whatever you need and reinforce our defenses before the inevitable war with the alternate world."

"A million crystals? I heard we got a lot less than that. Like three times less," Alexander Antipov turned to the faction head for an explanation. Vasily Filippov couldn't hide his incomprehension either, clearly hearing about this million for the first time.

For just a second, annoyance and dismay flickered on Lozovsky's face, after which his usual confidence returned. But I managed to detect those emotions and even came to certain conclusions. Seemingly, spending half a million crystals on the rebels in the magical world was the faction head's personal project, not agreed upon by the other directors, nor the outside curators.

"Well, we didn't really get that much," the faction leader admitted. "We got eight hundred forty thousand crystals to be exact. I have a document from Kosta Dykhsh with that exact figure. But friends, you're forgetting our suzerains' thirty-percent tax on vassal income. What's more, some of that money went to pay the almost one thousand NPC Centaurs we hired. Obviously they are not building our roads, defenses and other structures for free. And they'll be fighting on our side as well. We also owed the Human-6 Faction some money. A division of German allies three-hundred-strong will arrive to port in the Antique Beach tomorrow to help us fight the Dark Faction. And they were equipped using that very money. A detailed expense report will be provided to the curators right after this meeting."

The director spoke confidently and eloquently, and everyone clearly believed him. What was more, I had no doubt that such an experienced politician could provide that proof if need be, including witnesses and even hoof-prints from Centaur mare Phylira. But I was sure Ivan Lozovsky was lying. The thirty-percent vassal tax was pure bunkum. That key aspect had been discussed with Uline, and the transfer was intentionally made between private individuals as not to incur any taxes.

But what would I achieve if I placed the faction leader's words into doubt? All the more so without any proof! The most the Diplomat would say was that he didn't have the right to disclose financing the anti-mage rebels because the project was top-secret and not everyone at the meeting had clearance. Sure, he'd get chewed out for hiding the truth, maybe even for misuse of power, but it would end there.

The meeting continued, but I didn't hear any more interesting news. In fact, they were primarily discussing real-world issues. First there was the construction of corncobs number twenty-three and twenty-four. Then the need for a second soccer field and another two tennis courts. We would also be getting a separate building for faction members with families. Next they discussed the night lighting schedule. Some found it too dark, while others were unable to sleep because the spotlights were too bright... It was all circumstantial and minor technical aspects, so I had no idea why we all had to be here to discuss it.

All that interested me was a question from the new Strategist about why I was gathering a team of barely familiar and untested Miyelonians and Geckho. Why did I not want to wait a few days and make a crew with people of my faction? Vasily Andreyevich Filippov assured me that the Human-3 Faction would listen carefully to all my requests and would find or prepare a sufficient number of people of the proper professions. Our mission was, after all, critical for all humanity.

I answered that I was now hiring only the most crucial crew. The bare minimum to finish repairing the starship and fly it. I promised to seriously consider the Strategist's suggestion and soon give a list to the faction of professions with level and skill requirements. And with that, the meeting was over. I hurried to the exit, trying not to show my excitement and happy smile. Everything went exactly the way I hoped!

Chapter Thirty-Two

Faction Power-Broker

I HURRIED TO LEAVE the administration building but, near the doors, I was stopped by Gerd Tamara shouting:

"Kirill, don't run off, wait for me!"

Like it or not, I had to stop, especially because the exit was being blocked by Roman Pavlovich and another beefy Second Legion soldier with crossed arms. Was I in trouble? Seemingly not. Neither of Gerd Tamara's minions had shown any aggression, and the bodyguards who accompanied me under the Dome would not allow this conflict to heat up. Tamara then caught up to me and asked me politely to walk her to her room. So we went into the dimly lit Dome and slowly strolled toward our separate residential building. Both of our bodyguards delicately gave us space, as not to interrupt our conversation.

"You don't look like yourself today, Kirill," she told me, wrapping herself tightly in a track jacket thrown over her shoulders. "You're normally so active, full of ideas and energy. But today I could feel apathy in you and a total indifference. I also could sense you weren't telling the whole story, and in places you were telling obvious lies. Has something serious happened? Are you worried for Minn-O La-Fin?"

"Remember that note you gave me inside the radio?" I answered with a question. Tamara gave a distinct nod. "Well, even though the traitor Tyulenev is no longer among our faction leaders, I cannot shake the feeling that your warning is still relevant. The Dark Faction knows a suspicious amount about us, and our leaders sometimes do strange things that are hard to explain. And that is why I am still following your advice and didn't reveal my true plans even our leaders."

Tamara spent some time walking in silence, digesting the information, then commented:

"If you're talking about Ivan Lozovsky, you must remember that I was the only one who didn't vote for him as faction leader, right? And I still think you should be in his place. But Lozovsky is not an enemy. He's just an unprincipled careerist, willing to step on the heads of his underlings to reach the heights of power. He clearly has no lost love for you, but he's patient while you're useful. Still, if you make one serious misstep, Kirill, our boss will trample you in the mud!"

"Maybe so. I'm not sure about that. But Lozovsky gave half a million crystals to terrorists and hid that from everyone..." I started. Tamara quickly interrupted:

"Our Diplomat is clean. I told him the Dark Faction player's offer, and I convinced him to agree. Lozovsky just handed over the cash after the Geckho confirmed there was a blast at the funeral."

"But... why?!" I couldn't hold back the shout of surprise, and the miniature girl stopped sharply, looked at me and answered with extreme seriousness:

"Because we had to do it, Kirill! Sometimes you have to make harsh choices. A surgeon cannot afford to worry about the pieces of flesh they cut off, if that means saving the whole body. And we must win the war with the Dark Faction at any cost, even terrorism and assassinating the most powerful mages! If that is what it takes to weaken our deadly enemy, I have no regrets. I would do it again in a heartbeat!"

Tamara and I spent some time staring at one another tensely, and I was surprised to realize that I could not read her thoughts no matter how I tried. So, when the Paladin wanted she could simply make an impenetrable psychic block. Finally, I gave in and was first to avert my gaze. After that, we quickly calmed down and continued walking down the shadowy park paths. A little while later, I asked a question that had long been tormenting me:

"Tamara, did you ever think about why that Dark Faction player would want such a colossal amount of virtual currency? I mean, could he ever spend it without arousing suspicion?"

"I did consider that," she said, admitting I was being fair. "And no, of course he couldn't. Unless he's unaccountable to anyone, or very rich both in the game that bends reality and his own magical world. And let me say one more thing. Most likely, this was not some lowly player's idea, but that of someone very high up, possibly even one of the highest leaders of a magical world faction. Whoever it was simply saw an opportunity to get rid of competitors and took it. But you know, Kirill... I don't care one bit who is behind it! Let those ravenous spiders devour one another!"

Over the serious and frank conversation, we imperceptibly reached the doors of the residential building. Here Tamara and I parted ways. I was not going inside, instead planning to go back to the corncobs because I had business waiting in the game. Seemingly, Tamara was upset by my decision, but she didn't try and talk me out of it or ask me to go with her. She stood on her tiptoes and gave me a very quick peck on the cheek and, instantly blushing, asked:

"Kirill, back... on my birthday... you know what I'm talking about... did you consider it? Or did you just leave right away?"

I smiled and tried to joke it off, but it didn't work. It was as if she had latched into me like a tick, holding my jacket with two hands and not letting go. For some reason, this odd girl badly needed me to give her a direct answer.

"Yes, I admit I thought about it," I lied, because I thought that was what she wanted to hear. "Who in my place could resist such a pretty girl?!"

Tamara blushed even more, let me go and said I was totally forgiven. She wished me pleasant gaming, bid me farewell and went inside the building. After that entertaining episode, my mood was sharply improved. What was there to hide? The dark-haired girl was serious beyond her years and I liked her. I was sincerely happy that we had left our misunderstandings and anger in the past.

WHAT A BEAUT?! In a slow gait, I walked around my ship, which was finally ready for takeoff. I couldn't hide my veneration. There was not a trace remaining of the dents and holes in the fuselage, nor of the awkwardly installed armor. The silvery chassis was polished to a shine and glowed like a spotlight. I heard the thrusters warming up for takeoff, and it was like music to my ears. I saw the short arrow-like wings for ultrasonic atmospheric flight, and five suspension brackets for rocket and bomb systems that could be unfolded if the situation called for it. And the weaponry had all been purchased and installed.

We had two laser turrets at the nose. Although they were not the newest or most powerful, they could cut through atmosphere and turn a tank or flying antigrav to ashes. We also had a combat computer that allowed the turrets to aim and fire at moving targets, even ones actively trying to dodge. We also had advanced scanning systems capable of discovering targets even deep underground. Yes, I had to scrimp and pinch pennies the whole way, and didn't always use the best equipment, but the ship was rigged out and ready to fight.

If there was a Dark Faction spy at the recent meeting, their leadership had probably already been informed that my starship would not be usable for at least ten days. Just in case (what if I was wrong, and there was no spy in our top ranks) I was planning to repeat this disinformation to Minn-O, when I met my wayedda here on the station. Yes, the enemies had soothsaying mages, but even they were not omniscient. If they were working from incorrect initial data, they would give inaccurate prognoses to their Strategist, which would make their general make a mistake. And that was exactly what I was hoping for.

Old Ayukh had already calculated how long it would take us to fly to Earth: seven ummi.

Unfortunately, that was slower than last time on the speedy interceptor, despite all the bonuses from our experienced Navigator. It was thirty-nine hours in Earth time. On the one hand, that was quite a lot. But on the other, my H3 Faction could hold out some forty hours even if the upcoming battle went all wrong. Once I heard the war had begun, I was planning to take off and intercede in the conflict as soon as I arrived. The coming of a deadly frigate, which the enemy could not touch would seriously change the balance of forces. I was counting on that.

The Navigator suggested we establish a new base on a different station, the Miyelonian trading hub Kasti-Utsh III, which would make our flight to earth three times faster. I'd heard of this station before. During my very first voyage on the Shiamiru, the Geckho crew had described it as conveniently-located and calm. So I was not opposed to making our base there. There was another reason to fly to Kasti-Utsh III, too. I had already figured out that a local trader called Mava had sold all the Relict artifacts he bought from Free Captain Rikki and other pirates to a partner who dwelt in that very station. I was curious what I might find there. Very few appreciated the true value of those artifacts, and even fewer could actually use them.

So now, everything was just about ready for takeoff from Medu-Ro IV. We were just waiting for Minn-O La-Fin to come back into the game. I naturally was not going to leave without my wife, and the

Princess had just up and disappeared.

The thrusters gave an unexpected piercing whine, then quickly quieted down. Dmitry Zheltov's happy voice rang out in my headphones:

"Awesome ship! I've tested out all the systems, it all checks out. It's got great responsiveness and I can feel the power! It's night and day compared to what it was! And yes captain, Denni Marko is here at firing position asking to tell you he's already checked and calibrated the cannons. Now he can't wait to test them out on something or someone!"

And I was also proud of that acquisition. The two deep-space humans had joined my crew in the end, and I was hoping to find out lots of new and interesting facts about their mysterious human civilizations. Denni Marko and his companion Valeri-Urla had come back, just as she promised and after two rounds of negotiations, they signed contracts for five voyages without any grimacing.

I now had an experienced gunner and a girl with strong psionic abilities and the unique ability to talk to animals. And Valeri's pet had also come aboard, so I could now see Little Sister with my own eyes. The huge panther was a pure white color, could go invisible in the blink of an eye and could move through my frigate in utter silence. The Beast Master assured me that Little Sister was intelligent and never hurt her friends, so she wouldn't cause any problems.

I caught a movement with the corner of my eye

and turned. At last! Five steps away, I saw Minn-O La-Fin, finally back in the game. I wanted to lambast my "travelling wife" for her long absence, but I stopped as soon as I saw her. The Princess looked like a ghost and she could barely stand on her shaky legs. Seemingly, she was about to collapse! I quickly ran up and tried to hold her up in the literal and figurative sense.

Minn-O spent some time darting her mad unseeing eyes all around, then her gaze became more sensible, and focused on me.

"Gnat, my husband! If only you knew what happened!" my wayedda blurted out, hanging off my shoulders. Her pupils were wide in fear and pain. "There was a huge explosion at Thumor-Anhu's funeral! I lost both legs!!! Lots of people died, all I could see were dead bodies and blood."

Minn-O started weeping, recounting the horrible events. I then turned Lozovsky's words over in my head about this "Emancipation from Mage Tyranny" group, the explosion as proof of their seriousness and the half a million crystals we paid for this. So then, now we had our proof... I asked my wayedda to concentrate and tell me what happened next, and how she managed to get back into the game. The Princess wiped her pouring tears and tried to answer, but constantly fell back into sobbing and lost her place:

"I came back around in a hospital... Instead of legs I had bandaged stumps... It didn't hurt at all. I was probably on drugs or being treated with healing magic... Alongside the healers, there was a huge soldier in the tent, the ruler of the Second Directory General Ui-Taka... I recognized him... He said it was his order to have me woken up... Ui-Taka swore he was not involved in the explosion, but many mages accused him of it... Four Directories declared war on his Second Directory... But other mages think otherwise. They blame other mages... The Eighth and Fourth directories traded rocket strikes on their largest cities... The Fifth and Sixth declared war on the Third... There's a great war underway... There have even been some pogroms and anti-mage uprisings... But then, Ui-Taka said I needed to go into my virt capsule so the game would heal me, and I could grow new legs... But at the very end, when I was being carried out of the hospital on a stretcher... the General stopped and asked me to tell my husband Gerd Gnat, that he wants to meet on neutral territory... for example the Geckho spaceport... as soon as possible... I am not totally sure, Gerd Gnat... I was on anesthetics and didn't really understand... but I think he said he wants to offer you leadership of the Dark Faction."

END OF BOOK THREE

Want to be the first to know about our latest LitRPG,
sci fi and fantasy titles from your favorite authors?

Subscribe to our **New Releases** newsletter:
http://eepurl.com/b7niIL

Thank you for reading *Game Changer!*
If you like what you've read, check out other sci-fi, fantasy
and LitRPG novels published by Magic Dome Books:

Reality Benders LitRPG series by Michael Atamanov:
Countdown
External Threat
Game Changer
Web of Worlds
A Jump into the Unknown
Aces High

**The Dark Herbalist LitRPG series
by Michael Atamanov:**
Video Game Plotline Tester
Stay on the Wing
A Trap for the Potentate
Finding a Body

Perimeter Defense LitRPG series by Michael Atamanov:
Sector Eight
Beyond Death
New Contract
A Game with No Rules

**League of Losers LitRPG Series
by Michael Atamanov:**
A Cat and his Human

**The Way of the Shaman LitRPG series
by Vasily Mahanenko:**
Survival Quest
The Kartoss Gambit
The Secret of the Dark Forest
The Phantom Castle
The Karmadont Chess Set
Shaman's Revenge
Clans War

The Alchemist LitRPG series by Vasily Mahanenko:
City of the Dead
Forest of Desire
Tears of Alron

In order to have new books of the series translated faster, we need your help and support! Please consider leaving a review or spread the word by recommending *Game Changer* to your friends and posting the link on social media. The more people buy the book, the sooner we'll be able to make new translations available.

Thank you!

Till next time!

www.ingramcontent.com/pod-product-compliance
Lightning Source LLC
Chambersburg PA
CBHW060758030726
47503CB00002B/305